THE
INCARNATE

G. L. Keady

First published by G.L. Keady
As DREAMRAIDERS
© 2018 Gary Keady

2nd edition THE INCARNATE
Published in Australia in 2023
by Big Island Publishing
Copyright © Gary Keady 2018

Big Island Publishing
PO Box 3027, Tuross Head, 2537, NSW, Australia.
www.bigislandpublishing.au

ISBN:
Print: 978-0-6459739-3-8
Digital: 978-0-6459739-4-5

Edited by: Canon Doyle
Cover design and art: Brandon Evans-Keady

TABLE OF CONTENTS

CHAPTER 1

And within the circle
there dwells a place of birth,
where flesh conjoins
with song and mirth
to seed the egg of earth.
Under waxing moon
the horned one shines
parting precious petals
a virgin blooded shrine
come ye circle serpent, dine.

gk

Western Sydney, May 2007 - Samhain - The witching hour. A circle had been cleared of trees in the forest of a suburban park. At the centre of the circle, an improbable and incongruous sight: a sacrificial altar, six feet high, carved from sandstone with channels around the perimeter. Seven figures stood silently, forming a ring around the edifice—members of a witches' coven dressed in white caftans, evenly spaced around the circle—a Sabbat—a black mass—had been initiated.

In the eerie silence, one of the witches waved her hand in an arcane and intricate gesture. A moment later, the entire coven simultaneously took a step forward, leaving their robes on the ground behind them. Seven females now stood naked: sky-clad, in the ghostly blue luminescence of the full moon.

Two of them, with long grey hair reaching raggedly past their withered, drooping breasts, grasped the arms of a young girl, no older than sixteen. She had silky waist-length blonde hair, doe-slender legs, and budding new breasts. They led her, without protest, to the stone altar. A chant began immediately.

"Spirit, do not fear me; show yourself to me in a form that my eyes can perceive. I invite you to stay with me. Spirit, do not fear me; show yourself to me in a form that my eyes can perceive. I invite you to stay with me."

From out of the darkness stepped a naked man with the horned head of a goat, a He-goat, the horned god with an erect phallus.

His presence caused the chant to grow more frenzied:

"Spirit, do not fear me; show yourself to me in a form that my eyes can perceive. I invite you to stay with me."

The muscular He-goat, his body glistening from the essential oils with which it was anointed, walked through the gap in the circle left by the young girl and positioned himself at the foot of the altar in between the young girl's pale, thin, legs.

From the coven came a new chant, voiced over and over with rising excitement:

"Great Lillith, we seek your blessing, we ask a favour of you if it pleases you! Great Lillith, we seek your blessing, we ask a favour of you if it pleases you!"

The He-goat gripped the young girl by the thighs and then slowly but deliberately dragged her onto his powerful erection. Led by the girl, the coven chanted a new invocation, "Baby, baby come to me, let your spirit roam free, baby, baby come to me!"

The witches moaned and groaned, as one by one collapsed on the ground writhing and convulsing with ecstasy.

The He-goat lifted his head sharply and howled like a wolf at the full moon, as he discharged his demon seed.

Western Sydney, August 2013 – Imbolc.

The circle had been closed, and it was well past the witching hour. In the same cleared circle, in the same forest, under a full moon, but six years later, a naked woman stood next to the same altar. With the pentagram ring still on her finger, now in her early twenties, her long blonde hair reached to the middle of her back. At her side stood a boy of about six years old. This time, there were no other witches present. This time, when the He-goat walked from the shadows, he was dressed in a hooded red caftan. He took the boy from the woman and left her there.

Later that year in the Eastern Suburbs of Sydney.

The morning sun had a bite to it, even though it was only early spring. 2013 in Sydney had been a year of distinctive seasons, so it was expected that spring would be hot, and it was certainly heating up. The Weather Bureau had forecast severe heatwave conditions ahead.

Niki Blake glanced over the top of her Ray-Ban sunglasses at her hubby, Steve, floating aimlessly in the swimming pool. She pondered for a moment. "I love Steve... But right now, he's being difficult! Too much like Dad. Ha! My mother used to tell me that Dad was Mr Perfect, but I remember countless times when he came home so drunk, she'd call him every name under the sun... Ha! I should take Vera's advice and see a therapist." Her thoughts returned to real-time when she heard Steve's voice from the pool.

"Hey Ralph!"

The Bull Terrier sleeping on his back beside the pool raised one sleepy eyelid to peer at Steve.

"Do you understand women, Ralph?" Steve asked, his question targeted at Niki. The dog's tail obediently sprang to life and he contorted to give his penis a serious lick with a long pink tongue, as only dogs can.

"Yes, all us blokes would be heaps better off if we could understand them, Ralph."

Niki ignored Steve's sarcasm and returned to observing the morning sky.

The backyard of their modest two-storey split-level bungalow was equipped to entertain. A red brick paved patio skirted a medium-sized, kidney-shaped saltwater swimming pool with an attached whirlpool spa. The eastern side of the patio area was dedicated to sun worship and eating, with the appropriate furnishings. The easterly aspect combined with the north-south alignment of the house provided maximum exposure to the sun's radiance, all year round. Large tropical plants concealed the two-metre high brick perimeter walls that framed the oblong shaped yard. The landscaping achieved the illusion of a tropical oasis comfortably nestled in Clovelly, a suburb on the coastal fringe of Sydney.

Steve dragged himself out of the pool, grabbed a beach towel to dry himself, and addressed the dog.

"Buggered if I know makes her tick, mate. If you ask me, I reckon she should be the subject of a neurological study at the University of Sydney. Think of it, the first reported case of a twenty-seven-year-old with Alzheimer's disease. Maybe she marks the beginning of the regression of the female species? Something to do with diet, drugs, the pill or even worse, stress! Maybe, she should take Vera's advice and see a shrink."

Ralph looked up and wagged his stumpy tail.

That did it. Niki couldn't take any more of his sarcasm and drew herself up from her comfortable deck-chair with the countenance of a lioness stalking its prey. Ralph's tail stopped wagging.

Niki manoeuvred into Steve's face and snarled, "What would Vera or a therapist know about trying to discuss an important issue with an opinionated, chauvinist, hypocritical know-it-all like you?"

Steve froze in the process of drying his hair, shocked by the intensity of her rebuttal. With a snap, she irreverently prized the gusset of her one-piece bathing suit from the cleft in her bottom, collected her towel and magazine from the desk chair, and stormed toward the sliding glass patio doors. She wrenched the door open as Steve counted to ten. At the same time, he took in her shapely figure. Short but perfectly proportioned-firm breasts, hard, round, full behind, trim muscular legs, long blonde hair and a classically beautiful face with full lips and those stunning to-die-for blue eyes.

"Everything a man could ever want except she's a bitch! Just like her bloody mother!" he grumbled to Ralph, while towelling his hair with a flurry. "After all," he continued snidely but loud enough for more than Ralph to hear, "it wasn't me who made the solemn pledge on our wedding night. Then again, I guess she wouldn't remember promising that we wouldn't even consider starting a family until I'd secured a publishing contract!"

His gibing comment stopped her dead in her tracks just inside the open patio doors, she turned slowly and glared at him.

"I said I'd wait Steven. Sure," then like a boxer's fast jab while on the turn, "I said I'd support us, that's true... but I didn't say I'd wait until I was bloody forty years old with Spaniel's ears for tits and labia like Mick Jagger's lips before we had a kid! No reflection on your writing prowess of course, and not wishing to rustle the delicate creative writer's sensitivity you're always on about! But buddy, you don't have to be Norman Vincent Peale to realise that publishers don't do random door knocks in an effort to uncover the next Steven bloody King."

She softened her tone, knowing she'd hurt him.

"At least you could get a side job that wouldn't interfere with your writing. Then..."

He finished the statement for her, right down to imitating her voice.

"With our combined wages we could easily afford a family... I know... I know the drill! You've performed the pantomime so many times now I've got it committed to memory. It's etched in stone! Right?" He was losing his rag, and he knew it.

"You should be a politician, promise the world and deliver a peanut."

"A peanut, fuck you."

"That's it! You've started with the obscenities... End of discussion!" she snarled.

Steve looked down at Ralph again. "Who the hell's Norman

Vincent Peale anyway? She spends too much time Googling." He looked up sharply, alerted by the sound of footsteps on the staircase inside the house, and realised Ralph was his only audience.

Ralph sat on his haunches; tongue extended panting a smile, totally sympathetic to the cause.

Overcome by self-pity and desperate for some male support, Steve said, "Mate, what is it about women that makes them want to get their own way all the time?"

Niki was in the en-suite bathroom, taking a steaming hot shower. The soothing effect of the water on her body calmed her. However, she fully expected at any moment for Steve to enter the bathroom and continue the argument. The scenario was all too familiar to her after three years of marriage. It felt like they were in constant rehearsal for the big show; divorce. The thought gave her Goosebumps.

"Men are so predictable," she thought, "this has been going on too long... this... is... it! When he comes in here ranting and raving, thinking the shower has relaxed me and I'm ready to endure one of his tongue-lashings, I'm going to give it to him. An ultimatum, yeah, that's it: Steven! Yeah, he hates being called that, reminds him of his mother. Steven, I've had enough! If you refuse to see things my way, then I want a divorce... No, no, too radical... I'll move out! ... No, he'd probably like that, besides, I own half of everything. Got it! Steven, if you refuse to see things my..."

Steve flopped irritably onto the neatly made King-size bed and looked through the open door into the en-suite bathroom. The vision of Niki's utterly beautiful naked body magically distorted by the glass shower partition subdued his anger. He slipped his suddenly uncomfortable bathing suit off but kept the towel around his hips. He called out playfully, "Niki... Niki."

Alerted by his arrival, she readied herself for an attack. However, his playful tone unsettled her.

"Steven," she said with an air of urgency in her tone. "If you... If you—" she couldn't bring herself to spit it out. "If you could... get me a fresh towel?" She clenched her fists at her sides and silently cursed herself. "You wimp! Why didn't you say it?"

The shower door slid open, and Steve handed her a towel, then he returned to the bed where he flopped. Like a boy watching a naked lady for the first time, he feasted his eyes on his wife drying herself in the bathroom. From the bed, Steve could see himself in the wall mirror: his shoulder-length brown hair, thin unshaven face with a pointy nose and chin—his well-defined physique.

But for Niki, modesty had prevailed and she turned her back on him, aware of where his scrutiny was headed. Their constant bickering had led to a total cessation of sex.

Niki walked into the bedroom ignoring his intentions standing out like the lone tree in a desert.

He sprang like a Puma, wrapped his strong arms around her and dragged her onto the bed.

Unfortunately, he had totally underestimated the intensity of her anger. Incensed by his mauling attempt to pin her down and make love, she heaved him off her. He immediately capitulated, aware that if he were to proceed, it could turn ugly. He sat back on the bed filled to the brim with rejection and an overdose of sexual frustration.

"Come on Nik, Mr Happy needs a ride," he pleaded with sad puppy dog eyes.

She ignored him, grabbed a pale blue summer frock from the wardrobe, and dressed hurriedly to get out of the bedroom and distance herself from the torment.

He watched in remorseful silence while she posed at the vanity table and attempted nervously to make up her face. He was waiting for the inevitable explosion, hoping his look of rejection might provoke a little sympathy but knowing instinctively that she was an emotional time bomb, ticking... threatening to blow at any minute. He thought to himself, "First she'll burst into tears... any second now, nine, eight... best to say nothing... six, five."

Her mascara was traversing her cheeks in rivulets of black tears. She glared hard at herself in the mirror, then...

"Two, one..."

The explosion.

The tube of lipstick smashed into the mirror. The bottle of Chanel perfume Steve had bought for her last birthday sailed through the air and smashed against the wardrobe door.

"Great, there goes two hundred bucks!" he calculated out loud.

In her haste to collect her things and leave the house before she emotionally embarrassed herself any further, she snatched her shoulder bag from the bedside table and accidentally pulled the lampshade onto the floor along with the table. The lamp smashed into a thousand jigsaw-sized bits, as did the glass in the framed wedding photo on the table.

"Four fifty." Steve calculated cynically.

The accident only infuriated her further, symbolic as it was. She snatched her shoes from the floor and raced out of the bedroom crying, dragging what was left of the lampshade still tangled in the strap of her shoulder bag.

Steve sat on the edge of the bed bemused by the chaos, still calculating the cost. "Hmm, by the time she scratches the car backing out of the driveway it'll be a two grand freak out. Not bad, not bad at all... could have been worse, last one was three grand." Suddenly his eyes enlarged to the size of dinner plates and he erupted,

"No, the car!" He jumped up and raced down the stairs out the front door towards the BMW parked in the narrow driveway.

Niki nervously hit the ignition button, but the car wouldn't start. Just like in the movies, cars never start when you're in a hurry—it simply turned over and over the way it does when you're having your first driving lesson with your Dad. She looked up at Steve striding toward her, his face pale and mean.

"Start, you stupid thing! Start! If you pound on that window, Steven Blake, I'll wind it down and, and I swear, I'll punch you in the nose!" she sniffled and aggressively pumped the accelerator while continuously pushing the ignition button.

Steve stood resolutely at the driver's side door.

"Niki, you'll flood it. Come on, calm down, let's talk this over. You know we can sort it out. You can't go to work like this."

He tried the door but it was locked.

"Don't patronise me," she growled loud enough for him to hear.

Yelling madly, he pounded his fists on the driver's side window, "Niki, for Christ's sake!"

The engine finally started. With a roar and a blast of exhaust smoke, a menacing scowl broke on her otherwise distraught face.

Suddenly, as though he'd entered an altered state, Steve stepped back from the car, fell silent, and folded his arms—angrily resigned to her departure in his precious car.

"All right, go! See if I bloody care. But I warn you, if you go, don't come back!" he growled defiantly.

The wheels of the blue BMW Cabriolet smoked as Niki backed out of the driveway at breakneck speed onto the street. She spun the steering wheel hard, and the car, tyres still smoking, veered wildly along the footpath in front of the next-door neighbour's property. She slammed on the brakes, and the car shuddered to a halt, one of the rear wheels up on the footpath.

"Wait, Niki! Niki! I didn't mean it! Forget what happened, I honestly didn't mean it!" Steve stopped yelling and then called out even louder in a different tone, "Hey, I own half that car! Leave my half here! You better come back. If you don't, I'll never talk to you again!"

Niki slammed the car into gear and floored the accelerator, tyres smoking. The car fishtailed wildly, first left, into the street then more quickly to the right, and, as if scripted, the left rear fender slammed into the neighbour's rubbish bin, which rose spinning into the air straight towards Steve standing naked in his driveway. The spinning rubbish bin fell away but hurled a shower of garbage into the air that, as if in slow motion, descended upon and around Steve. Cursing to himself, he discarded lettuce leaves, eggshells, and what seemed to be used kitty litter, and ran out onto the road to plead with Niki.

The old lady from the next-door house came out, disturbed by the sound of her rubbish bin being clobbered and the general ruckus. When she sighted Steve, she immediately realised it was just another in the long series of 'Blake's domestic arguments.'

When Niki finally crunched the car into first gear and sped off down the street, she had unknowingly left her husband standing in the middle of the road, stark naked, waving his fists in the air like a lunatic.

The old lady turned the hose on Steve. The cold water instantly alerted him to his naked disposition. In spite of the humiliation, he simply retreated to the safety of his front doorstep and presented the old lady with a well-executed moon in defiance.

CHAPTER 2

Release thy will to the pagan fire
where love regains ancient desire.
And to remain under the spell
of life on earth of heaven and hell.
When life's last breath is a sigh
Let there be no tears in your eyes.

gk

Lunchtime, midweek, a pretty Asian girl in her early twenties found a suitable spot on the grass under the shade of a big Port Jackson Fig tree in Centennial Park to eat her lunch. Being only a few kilometres from busy Sydney meant she could hear the rattle and hum of the city's heartbeat in the distance. The sound was suddenly overridden by the warble of a magpie perched on a branch overhead. She kicked her shoes off and wiggled her bare toes in the long, cool, green grass.

It felt good to rest her tired feet after a stressful morning at work. For a trainee receptionist, Real Estate was a demanding job, and that translated to a hectic time, but now she could enjoy nature, for an hour at least. She opened a plastic lunchbox prepared for a surprise. Her mother made a habit of packing a lunchtime surprise for her at least once a week, and she had an inkling it was today. But there was no surprise in the lunchbox; however, when she flattened her left leg on the grass, she felt something underneath her upper thigh and reached under for it. Thinking it was a stone or a twig, a quizzical expression broke on her pretty face, and her nose wrinkled up at the feel of something unexpected. It was firm but squishy. Withdrawing her hand from under her bare thigh, her expression changed immediately when she recognised what she had. Pinched between her fingers was a human penis. That was her surprise for the day. She screamed.

Being a lone figure, the last man seated at the empty main bar of the Bat and Ball Pub in Redfern at closing was customary for William Thackeray. His addiction to alcohol as a means to cope with life was not only chronic but among his peers, legendary. His short fuse when inebriated was well worth steering clear of. Bill Thackeray was a bad drunk.

He peered at his reflection in the mirror at the back of the bar and found it difficult to recognise the man in his late-fifties, a man with handsome, rugged looks, a face bearing lines of wisdom derived mostly from ill-time spent in the pool halls of life. He waved his hand bitterly to brush away the ravages of time.

Thackeray, or Thacka as he was known by those very few close to him, carried more mental baggage than the cargo hold of an Airbus A380. With his inebriated belligerence curtailed by the lack of opponents or an audience, it was time to leave. As he downed the dregs of a single malt scotch and was about to slide off the barstool, he heard the sound of one of the staff out back whistling a tune that he recognised. It had been made a worldwide hit in 1973 by Aussie singer Helen Reddy, and 'I am Woman' had become the signature song of the female liberation movement. The melody cast him back to those heady days when he was young and impressionable.

He was from a generation that made things to last—where quality determined the value of a product—when 'sorry' was an adequate apology because the word was attached to a self-respecting code of honour. When having a gold fountain pen was a privilege and was worn with pride in the top pocket of your shirt or coat as a symbol of success. When being tipsy meant you'd had a few too many, and when telephone etiquette and good manners were a mark of distinction. Kids were spanked without a class-action suit, and teachers taught manners as a normal part of schooling. When a gentleman would open the car door for a lady and she appreciated it, a courtesy that central locking later eliminated. He had travelled from a time when the feminist movement elbowed women from the pedestal they have since struggled to regain, an era when a single was a record and professional sportsmen competed for honour and pride, not money, which made tickets to sporting events affordable for everyone. When only ex-cons and sailors were tattooed, and there were fewer civil liberties because campaigning for them wasn't a profession. He recalled when song lyrics had a lot more to say than they do today, when the truth in them had borne and galvanized a generation. Of times when battles were fought in the streets for good reason, against battles fought in foreign lands for none.

He lamented in his whiskey-laced mind that growing up in a much different world with different values had put him out of step with his younger workplace peers. Sitting at an empty bar at closing time alone with his alcohol-enriched thoughts dulling his personal hang-ups, Bill Thackeray felt like a curio from a bygone era, as distinct from feeling old. The whistling had stopped, and 'I am Woman' and the memories connected to it faded into the ether. He took a moment to steady himself before attempting the most direct route to the exit, and he was off. Once he got rolling, nothing was going to stop him. Fortunately, he didn't have to navigate past anyone; all he needed to do was conquer the obstacle course of chairs and tables to make it out the door, and then, to negotiate the footpath on Cleveland Street to a nearby cab rank. But tonight, this almost mechanical machination repeated ritually was going to be put to the test. Call it bad luck, but as Thacka careered along the footpath towards the vacant taxi rank, he inadvertently walked directly into an in-progress, violent domestic argument.

Taking up much of the pavement, standing glaring up at a ramshackle old Cleveland Street terrace house, was an ogre of a man dressed only in a white singlet and shorts. He was raining a torrent of verbal abuse upon a woman standing in the doorway of the terrace.

With arms like tree trunks and a hairy back that could have put a Silverback Gorilla to shame, the bald-headed ogre took exception to Thackeray glancing at him as he was staggering past.

"Hey, you? What are you freaking looking at?" the ogre croaked venomously.

Thackeray really wasn't interested in a domestic; he only had getting home on his mind. But the statement and the ferocity of it stopped him in his tracks—and sobered him a little. Not known for backing down, Thacka fronted the giant of a man and, eyeballing him, fired a return serve.

"You talking to me? Because if you are, you'd better get a civil tongue in your head."

The ogre was already at breaking point with his argument, and it served his purposes to take out his frustration on a stranger.

"You! You piece of crap!" he growled and lumbered towards Thacka like a bull at a gate and set himself to throw a haymaker.

Even in his inebriated state, Thacka had read it well; he'd seen it all before: the bigger they are, the harder they fall was the adage. One king hit right on the button from an almighty left that had fooled the ogre who was expecting a right was all it took for the ogre to drop onto the sidewalk like a rock.

Thacka stood over him swaying and growled, "Got anything else to say, boofhead?"

With blood streaming from his shattered nose and top lip, the ogre shook his head. But that wasn't the end of it. The woman, dressed in a scanty nightdress, came running at Thackeray screaming like a banshee.

"You leave him alone, you bastard! I'll call the bloody cops; you king hit him, I saw ya! You animal!"

Thackeray realised then she was no girl; he deduced was mutton dressed up as lamb; in her fifties, no teeth, scrawny with the temperament of a feral cat, she certainly wasn't the sort of person he wanted to tackle at that juncture. He glanced at the road in time to see a cab and quickly hailed it.

As he headed for the cab, the banshee screamed after him, "Who's gonna pay for the hospital, you bastard! Come back here!"

Ignoring her, he climbed into the cab nursing the aching knuckles of his left hand and grumbled, "Paddington, thanks, driver."

Home was only ten minutes away, and even though there would be no-one there to greet him, no-one there to discuss the day, and no-one there to say goodnight, at least it was home, and he'd achieved his goal; for the time being, he'd vanquished his demons.

Wayne Dixon and his wife Sarah were seated at the kitchen table finishing breakfast. Sarah studied her husband's face across the table from her. He was a plain, dour man with hardly any sense of humour, often acting older than his thirty-four years. But she loved him all the same. On the other hand, she was the opposite of him, in fact, most would consider them a total mismatch—but then again it was often said that opposites attract. Sarah had always been a happy, bright, ready to please kind of gal. A vibrant and attractive thirty-three-year-old young mother, she wore her red hair long, had a thin pretty, freckly face with deep mysterious green eyes and her model figure betrayed no physical signs of motherhood.

They had been married five years and then moved to Sydney from Perth for Wayne to take up a post at the prestigious accounting firm of Wallace and Freeman in the city. The job came with a modern bungalow in the fashionable suburb of Randwick, close to the beaches, a car and a reasonable pay packet with the promise of a secure future. Sydney was life in fast lane for them compared to suburban Perth. But the fast lane was nothing more than a traffic jam for Sarah. With all her relatives and friends back in Perth, after a year she still had made no friends in Sydney. The neighbours had kept to themselves and the young mum's she had come across when she dropped six-year-old Russell to school, were always too busy to stop for a chat. So, Sarah decided to take an online course on Clinical and Spiritual Hypnotherapy and Metaphysics at the International

Metaphysical University. The subject of metaphysics interested her because her mother, now deceased, was psychic and Sarah had inherited the ability, and so wanted to learn more about it. But she had to keep her studies a secret from Wayne, because his strict Catholic upbringing meant he regarded anything to do with the paranormal as blasphemous and evil. But keeping it secret didn't bother Sarah, she had an intellectual hunger that needed feeding and besides, she believed she had the right to study whatever she pleased.

It was Friday and she was really looking forward to resuming her studies once Wayne had left for work and she'd dropped Russell at school.

Wayne looked up over his horn-rimmed glasses and his coffee cup and said, "Get Russell up and dressed, we're going to visit uncle Charlie today."

Sarah looked dispirited: it was always the same after she'd had a premonition. Sarah's father had castigated her mother for her insight, consequently, over time, Sarah had learnt to file her visions in a mental junk drawer along with a collection of 'I told you so's' from previous visions.

"Wayne, I've had a vision. It turns out bad. We shouldn't visit Charlie today."

Short on tolerance and big on dominance, he stood up from the table and stared up at the ceiling as though looking for God's assistance. "No Sarah. We've been through this before..."

"I know what you're going to say Wayne, but believe me... it was a strong vision. Please trust me."

He glared at her with contempt in his eyes and barked, "I've made my decision Sarah we're going to Charlie's, now get the boy ready."

Later, with young Russell in tow, Sarah ambled along the driveway to their late-model Corolla. Wayne was unlocking the driver-side door.

"I can't help it if I get visions, Wayne... but there's a reason for it and it shouldn't be ignored." She stopped and picked up Russell, hoping Wayne would change his mind.

She tried one last time. "It's telling us not to go. What harm is there in putting the trip off until tomorrow?"

Wayne slammed his hands angrily on the car roof, and the loud bang caused Russell to cry.

"Because I told the only living relative I have that I would be bringing my family to visit him today, not bloody tomorrow, today. You got that, Sarah?"

Sarah reacted. "So, what's more important, your only living relative or the safety of your family? Shush, Russell, don't cry, love."

Wayne opened the car door, but before getting in, he fired one last volley at his wife.

"You and your stupid premonitions. I'll tell you what's most important... doing what I bloody-well say, that's what!" He slid inside the car and slammed the door shut.

Sarah opened the rear door and helped Russell into his safety chair.

"Oh, fine. His lordship has spoken. Just what gives you the right to determine our fate?"

Wayne sat behind the steering wheel, stiff and resolute.

"End of argument, Sarah!" he growled.

Sydney's Surry Hills Police Headquarters, homicide division, was an open-plan expanse of cubicles. In one of them, Senior DI Thackeray was seated behind a small gunmetal-grey, Government-issue desk, suffering the overkill of banks of overhead fluorescent lighting flickering away at fifty cycles per second and unduly illuminating the stark white walls of his cubicle. He felt as if he was in a Chinese restaurant. With his feet up on the desk, chewing on a toothpick and fidgeting, he nervously finger-weaved a rubber band in his left hand. Bored to the teeth with work or the lack thereof, his mood wasn't helped by the rip-roaring hangover he'd inherited from the night before, a night that included his confrontation with the Cleveland Street ogre, which would be better left forgotten, if it wasn't for his bruised knuckles.

DI Miller, skinny with a rat-like face and a cheeky glint in his eye, stopped at Thackeray's cubicle and peered in at him with eyes like a fox. To Thackeray, Miller looked selfish, judgmental—even a little bitter. He could see how he'd gained his position: with ambition as cold and biting as a winter's day and with as little remorse.

"Keeping you busy, eh Thacka? No phantom Corn Flake killer to chase?" he mocked.

Thackeray was a loner—and due to his propensity for hitting the bottle, he was treated as an outcast. His peers had so much trouble with his belligerence that he'd found it less stressful to work alone.

Thackeray glared up at him, his nose wrinkled, he couldn't stand the man, had him pegged as a first-rate arsehole. For Thackeray, rank integrity was essential, something he felt had been wasted on Miller. Thackeray aimed the elastic band stretched between two fingers and his thumb and fired it at him. It hit Miller flush on the nose.

"You've never really grown up, Miller, you've only learnt how to act in public."

Holding the end of his nose and choking back anger, Miller grumbled, "You talk in riddles, Thackeray."

"Not riddles, Miller, paraprosdokians, and you watch too many cop shows on Netflix!" Thacka said with a gravel voice as he nonchalantly flicked a Berocca vitamin tablet into the air deftly enough to judge it to land in a glass of water on his desk with a plonk.

The sight of the Berocca caused Miller to draw a conclusion.

"At least I don't have to contend with working with a hangover, buddy."

"I feel sorry for people who don't drink, Miller, when they wake up in the morning, that's as good as they're going to feel all day!" Thacka enjoyed the opportunity to deliver his favourite Frank Sinatra quote.

As Miller moved off grumpily, Thackeray downed his Berocca, burped, and then mumbled to himself.

"Well, having a hangover is a damn sight better than having to work with you, buddy."

The phone rang, and he answered it.

"Thackeray. Who? Parker... what? Missing persons? Oh, what happened to what's-his-face? Yeah, Wilson. Oh, bad luck. Okay, I'll be down in a jiffy."

Steve was at his computer in the spare room while Ralph the dog watched him suffer.

Steve said to himself, "I've been suffering from writer's block since I got married." Chewing the end of a HB pencil, the thought crossed his mind as to whether Niki had really left him or not. He was suddenly struck by the realisation that Niki was the household's sole income earner, and that life might be a little difficult without her. He quickly Googled the words 'submit stories Sydney,' and the search produced a list of potential customers for his writing skills. He clicked on the name that attracted him the most. It read: send your true-crime story to us and get paid for it. The website opened, he read the requirements, picked up the phone, and spoke to the editorial desk. After a lengthy discussion, he had a gig—with only one minor stipulation, payment to be made upon acceptance. He sat back proudly in his swivel chair and visualised himself at work.

"Steven Blake - crime reporter," he broadcast to Ralph like a 60 minutes anchor. It had a good ring to it; now all he needed to do was map out how to dig up a story worthy enough for his new editor to buy. Ralph approved, if his tail was anything to go by.

A deathly silence had descended between Sarah and Wayne in the car on the highway heading for Wollongong, fifty kilometres south of Sydney. A storm was brewing outside the car. The sky was growing darker in the south and more threatening by the minute— and south was exactly where they were heading.

Sarah peered at the storm through the windscreen and then broke the ice.

"I don't like this at all, Wayne," her tone topped up with angst.

"It'll be fine, Sarah. Stop worrying; it's only a storm. They get them all the time in Sydney. They call them southerly busters."

A huge fork of lightning struck the bushland just up ahead of them and was followed almost immediately by a deafening crash of thunder. Nature had underscored Sarah's concerns and woke Russell from his slumber to boot.

A little way up ahead of them, a second bolt of lightning struck a big old gum tree and all but severed a large bough. It was left hanging perilously over the highway.

Another clap of thunder shook the car and was followed by the skies opening up with a torrential downpour.

Sarah consoled Russell, "Shush, darling, it's just rain."

Thackeray stepped out of the elevator into the basement of Surry Hill Police HQ and then made his way along a gloomy corridor to a door marked Missing Persons. He'd been through that door plenty of times over the last six years, each time for a terrible purpose and each time he'd departed frustrated. The door and the sign on it reminded him of his two failed marriages, a terrible juxtaposition to the frustration of not being able to solve matters of contention. He opened the door and stepped through his anxiety, prepared to confront a fresh conundrum.

There was no air-conditioning in the basement office. It was so stiflingly hot his armpits immediately sprang a leak. Inside the small room behind a grey Government-issue metal desk, busy cooling herself in the airstream of a cheap electric desktop fan, sat Detective Sergeant Jess Parker.

"Inspector Thackeray, I presume?" she queried.

The attractive woman immediately impressed Bill; she wasn't what he was expecting at all. He pulled up a chair and hogged off as much of the fan as he could get away with.

"DS Parker. Didn't expect to find a good-looking bird in Missing Persons."

"I'm not missing, detective," she jested with a cute smile.

"The southerly will arrive soon. It's been a genuine stinker of a day."

"You're not kidding, especially down here in the dungeon where the budget never seems to reach."

"Yeah, they say you can't get much lower in the force than down here."

"I suppose so," she said. "But from you, I'll take that as a compliment."

The banter was good, made him forget his hangover.

Parker wondered, "He seems physically and mentally strong despite his forty-five years."

"So, Parker, what's so important you would interrupt my day of doing nothing to bring me down to the crypt?"

She swivelled in her chair to a bar-fridge behind her and opened it.

"So, that's what they call down here from upstairs, eh? The crypt? Huh?" she said, swivelling back and handing over a plastic bag she'd taken from the refrigerator. "And I suppose they call me the ghoul or something equally flattering?"

Thackeray held the plastic bag up to the fluorescent light to better view the contents.

"How did you know that? It was supposed to be a secret."

"What, like the corn flake killer?"

"Ah, cops are serial offenders at bad gags, Parker," he quipped, still studying the contents up to the light.

"Aha, do I detect a sense of humour? Now that is refreshing! I thought having no sense of humour was mandatory around here."

"Has this been processed by forensics?"

"Sez so on the tag... sir," she scorned, tongue in cheek.

He checked the tag then said light-heartedly, "So it does, detective, so it does. I'll give you that," he handed the bag back to her. "So, did they get a match or anything to go on?"

Putting the bag back in the refrigerator, she replied, "No, only that it's..."

"The penis from a young boy aged between six and ten. Yes, been there—done that." He lounged back in the chair and folded his arms defensively across his chest.

"Right. Any ideas then?" she queried.

"Nope. Only that it's the MO of my serial killer."

He waited for a quip from her about the corn flake killer, and when none came, she went up a level in his estimation.

"That's why I asked you to my crypt, sir. Being new here, I've heard rumours about—"

"My six-year obsession with my serial corn flake killer or was it my ability to drink the world under the table?"

"Both, sir, but the former takes precedence."

"Parker, I'm a walking rumour at this branch, and they—I refer to all others than myself—are unified in their belief that I'm off my bloody rocker, hence the corn flake for serial gag. It might appear very funny, but to me, it's just damn childish. So, Miss Ghoul Parker, it is, miss isn't it?"

"Oh yes."

"I won't be offended if you choose to join in concert with the tenor because I'm totally bloody-well used to it!"

"It's Jess, by the way, and well, I—"

He wasn't about to wait for an explanation—he was well over trying to talk through the mockery. He stood ready to leave but decided, because he liked her, to leave her with a parting gesture.

"Parker, correction, Jess, in their wisdom, others see no relevance between the six little boys' penises that have turned up in Missing Persons over the last six years and six missing boys who haven't turned up at all. Somehow I remain alone in daring to propose a connection with the bloody obvious!"

He glared at her, prepared for an argument, and was shocked when it failed to eventuate.

"It wouldn't take Sigmund Freud to account for your reasoning, sir. But I'm not sure that's the problem."

His expression softened, but he remained standing for an awkward moment—he wasn't used to having a colleague agree with him on the issue—so he sat back down.

"All of the penises have been found in Sydney parks with no real rationale, except, six years, six penises, seemingly all from little fellows roughly the same age," he said resolutely.

"And no bodies," she added.

"That's right, no bodies," he ran his hand through his unkempt shortish brown hair, making a mental note to get a haircut.

To Parker, his body language exemplified his frustration.

"Poor kids, why mutilate them, leave a bit behind, then dispose of the bodies?" she glared at him for an answer.

"I don't have an answer for that, Parker, but I suspect it has something to do with witchcraft or satanic sacrifice. Something that you'd expect to find in Europe, not here."

He produced a toothpick from his pocket, stood up, and then paced about, chewing it. It was a sign he was relaxing into a comfortable state of mind—deep thought.

Parker sensed that and made a move to bring him out of his shell to share his thoughts with her.

"But you suspect the corn flake killer, right?"

The fist of his mind clenched. He removed the toothpick from between his teeth and leaned on the desk with his knuckled fists.

"Can I trust you, Jess?"

She nodded curtly, pleased at the sudden bond between them.

He lowered his eyes and whispered, "I think I know who it is... Wolfen Moloch—a self-acclaimed warlock and without a doubt, the most evil human being I've encountered in twenty years on the force."

Moloch was Thackeray's Moriarty: a suspect he had banked his career on being the serial killer he was after. But he had never been able to get a shred of evidence on him. He felt that his gut instinct no longer had a place in modern detective analysis, he required more dope on a perp than his experience afforded him—proof beyond reasonable doubt before he could make an arrest. "Your sixth sense won't stand up in court," Wilks, his superior officer, had scolded him countless times. An informant of Thackeray's had fingered Moloch just after the first penis was found, that's how he found out Moloch had been a practicing Warlock: the informant was a former member of Moloch's coven. But before he could get a statement from the informant, he disappeared, all he had left to go on was what he'd been told over the phone, and that wasn't strong enough to make an arrest.

"Why do you suspect this Moloch?" Parker questioned.

"It's a long story."

She sat back in her chair and with a smile said, "I don't know if you've noticed but the phone isn't ringing off the hook. I've got time. Go on."

Six years ago, I took a random call at homicide. The guy at the other end sounded like a nutter, told me there was going to be a ritual sacrifice of a kid, a boy. I thought he was just trying to grass someone up, the way a nutter does—took his number and thought nothing more of it. A year later, around the same time of the year, I get a call from the same bloke, this time he asked for me. First, he gives me an ear full for not following up on his last warning and then tells me there has been a second sacrifice, and proof could be found at Trumper Oval in Paddington. This time I took him seriously enough to go and check it out but found nothing. Again, I was convinced it had been a crank call. Then, later-on that day, I get a call from your predecessor, he's got something he wants me to see. I come down here to the dungeon and he shows me a severed penis from a little boy found, you'll never guess where."

"Trumper Oval."

"Exactly. So now I'm beating myself up for not listening to this guy. Wilks approves pulling out all the stops to find a body. I try to get a meeting with the informant but he's scared shitless of something and goes to ground. I chase up on the number he'd left me but it's from a public phone at South's Juniors in Maroubra. He only ever gave me his first name, Richard; he's a dead end. No body is found, and the case just fizzles out. I hear nothing from this guy for two years then I get a call out of the blue. This time he's freaked out. Tells me the 5th sacrifice will take place and that I can stop it. I drag the name Wolfen Moloch out of him, it was like pulling teeth—and then he hangs up. I realise that by giving me the name he's put himself in danger but I can't do anything about that. So I track down Moloch and so begins this insane game of trying to catch him out."

"What happened to Richard?"

"Just before the latest penis turns up in Centennial Park and then in your fridge, I got a call from Richard to say there was going to be another sacrifice. This time it was different. This time he told me his surname, Riley, and gave me his address, said that he was going away and this would be the last time I hear from him. He confirmed that again Moloch was the perp. Before I could say any more he was gone. I went to his house in Matraville, but there was no one there. The rest you know... But let me tell you about this bastard Moloch—"

She cut him off, "I tell you what...."

He straightened up, taken aback, "What's that?"

"Two heads are better than one. Let's see if we can nail this bastard Wolfen Moloch. But first, let's get rid of the corn flake bit, right?"

"But why join me, Parker?"

"Because you are a man I can trust to fight for justice, for what's true and right."

"Terrific, that sounds like a line from an American soap opera, but you'll get no argument from me," he said happily, as he jammed the toothpick back between his teeth.

"You get me what you have on Moloch and we'll get to work. But first, some fieldwork."

Thackeray cocked an eyebrow at her as she reached her hand across the desk to shake. He wasn't used to having a believer on his side and so took her hand with a suspicious look on his craggy dial.

CHAPTER 3

You take me higher
Under your spell
Higher and higher
Christabel
I'm hot with desire
I'm burning in hell
Each time you come alive.

gk

Wayne undid his seatbelt, leaned across the centre console of the car, and gave Sarah a peck on the cheek to make up for the argument. He didn't get the reaction he expected when Sarah screamed out.

"Wayne! Look out!"

The huge branch of the big old gum tree that had been struck by lightning moments earlier was blocking the road directly in front of them.

Traveling at 110 kilometres per hour, Wayne immediately went into panic mode and hit the brakes. Wrong—the road was wet and greasy—it caused the brakes to lock up and the car to fishtail out of control. With the windscreen wipers struggling to clear the torrential rain, he couldn't see clearly and veered onto the wrong side of the road. Almost immediately, the glaring headlights of an oncoming vehicle blinded him.

"Swerve, Wayne, swerve! Swerve!" Sarah screamed.

Her hysteria made Wayne panic more; he pulled hard on the steering wheel to miss a head-on collision and crashed through a kerbside barrier over an embankment. The car sailed through the air and landed with an almighty thump in a paddock—they were thrown around inside the car like ragdolls. But the fall to earth hadn't slowed the car; they were still travelling at speed and totally out of control. Being wildly buffeted about inside the car from it bouncing violently over the uneven terrain, Wayne had no control—And then it came into view—Sarah was the first to see it: a gargantuan high-tension tower, and they were aimed directly for it.

For Wayne, time had slowed down—the windscreen wipers seemed to be moving in slow motion—drops of heavy rain splashed on the windscreen, exploding into tiny droplets—With a vague look, he slowly turned his eyes from the oncoming metal legs of the high-tension tower to glance at his wife beside him. He noticed that her face was contorted—she was screaming, but he heard nothing. He peered over his shoulder at his son, Russell, and saw that he too was screaming, yet he heard nothing. The only sound he could hear was a strange hum. With their fate sealed, Wayne took a moment to acknowledge his wife with a look of love that she, knowingly, returned.

Right then, the business end of the event returned at normal speed for Wayne—the cacophony of screaming, engine noise, rain battering the car, and the relentless pounding over the rugged ground exploded in his ears. When he looked back through the windscreen, it was just in time to see the nose of the car crumble as it collided with the metal legs of the high-tension tower, and there followed a thunderous crash! It was the discordant sound of metal on metal, bending, twisting, and breaking. With his seatbelt unfastened, the force of the impact catapulted Wayne through the windscreen, across the mangled bonnet, and forcefully into the tower. An avalanche of glass accompanied him from the shattered windscreen.

Sarah's face and arms were blasted with shards of the windscreen.

Her seatbelt was fastened, and the airbag inflated to save her from hitting the dashboard. Just when it seemed the mayhem was over, nature had one last card to play: a bolt of lightning cracked from above and struck the tower. Wayne's mangled, entangled, bloody body, strung up like a puppet on the metal legs, convulsed unnaturally, as though he was performing a macabre death dance. Then suddenly, it ceased—he fell limp—all life had been expelled— the mayhem ended. The rain stopped, thunder rumbled in the distance to underscore the chilling moment, and Sarah, in a semi-conscious stupor, smelt the unmistakable stench of gasoline. A new threat had materialised. With steam rising from the mangled engine, the car could burst into flames at any second. Somehow, in her delirium, Sarah reasoned they were trapped in a time bomb set to explode, and that she needed to do something about it, quickly. The only sound she could hear was a constant high-pitched whistle, like the sound you hear after a loud rock concert. Looking like a post-test crash test dummy, still strapped in her seat, stuck behind an airbag and surrounded by a tangle of twisted metal, her face oozing blood, Sarah miraculously began to move. Battling to remain conscious, there was something bigger than her predicament driving her. Sensing the preternatural eeriness of the situation, having to overcome the pain of her injuries, trying to ignore the threatening stench of gasoline, she managed to reach a blood-drenched shaky hand in between the seats and unbuckle the safety harness that restrained her unconscious son.

Thackeray and Parker were busy observing a dozen uniformed policemen combing the bushland around a small lake in Sydney's Centennial Park. The location was close to where the young Asian girl had found the severed penis only days before. Inside the blue and white checked crime scene tape where the girl had sat on her lunch break, several police were combing the grass and bush looking for further evidence along the verge of the lake in the area underneath the big Port Jackson Fig Tree. Three divers in scuba gear were working the lake. The locale was a hive of activity.

A diver popped out of the water, removed his mouthpiece, lifted his goggles, and called to Thackeray.

"Nothing, sir."

Chewing on a toothpick, Thackeray got down on his haunches at the water's edge.

"Thanks, Dan, call it a day then."

Diver Dan offered a thumbs-up, then swam over to tell the other divers.

Thackeray stood and despondently flicked his toothpick into the lake.

"They've dragged the crap out of it and searched every millimetre of surrounding bush, it's the same bloody story as always—no body."

Parker shook her head. "So frustrating."

Thackeray called out to a young uniformed cop standing nearby. "Richards! PC Richards!"

The tall skinny officer in a police uniform that needed a few more kilos inside it to fill it out had a prominent eagle-like beak of a nose, thin lips but a friendly smile. When he heard Thackeray's call, he left the search party to join his superior officer. "Yes, sir?"

"Your team can quit now. We're done here," thunder sounded, and Thackeray looked up at the sky. "The southerly is close; someone's copping heavy rain down south. Check the size of those bloody thunderheads."

Parker looked up. "Might put out some of the bushfires."

Richards said, "Sir, we haven't checked the stage they've set up in the park for the play about Druids."

Thackeray was still staring at the foreboding clouds, disinterested.

"No, that'll do it, Richards. I know when we're done."

"Besides," Parker added. "It's going to bucket down any minute now."

Richards nodded, and just as he did, it began to spit rain.

Parker and Thackeray made a run for her car. They only just

made it inside when the skies opened up, and rain pelted down. Puffing out of breath, Thackeray said invitingly, "Drink?"

Parker smiled affirmatively, and they drove off for the nearest pub.

Late afternoon on weekdays meant it was too early for the public bar of the Centennial Pub in Woollahra to be crowded. An upmarket pub, it catered to trendy blue-collar office workers seeking to beat the peak-hour traffic on their way home by stopping there for a drink. It would be a welcome retreat for Parker and Thackeray after a frustrating day.

Parker was lucky to find a parking spot right outside the front door of the pub, so they made it inside without taking a bath.

A seat by a big window offered a fine view of the traffic, headlights ablaze, crawling along Oxford Street in the pouring rain. Though it was only 4 pm, the storm had darkened the sky to night.

Thackeray was on his way back to Parker from the bar with two drinks when a guy passing, carrying a tray of drinks, bumped him. The guy lost the lot, but Thackeray managed to juggle his glasses without spilling a drop.

A loud cheer went up from the few patrons at the bar. Thackeray put his drinks on the table and sat down.

"We're a bloody weird mob, you know. Where else in the world would blokes applaud and cheer when some poor bum spills his drink or falls arse over tit?"

"You're not wrong." Parker added. "I lived in London for a couple of years, and they do it a bit, but not like here. But hey, I've got to commend you on your juggling act; it was pretty impressive."

"Plenty of experience," he joked.

Thackeray was beginning to like Parker; it felt good to finally have someone to discuss the case over a drink. He'd been a loner since his first ugly divorce that had left him a cantankerous soak, but maybe, he thought, just like the storm outside, the bad days were passing and clear skies were ahead.

"Practice makes perfect!" He smiled as they toasted.

"To the case, you know we need to find a new name for it other than, you know what," Parker grinned.

"Oh, it'll find its own name eventually," he said, taking a sip of his single malt scotch on the rocks.

"Hmm, hey, how come you're a DI and haven't got a car, while me, a mere sergeant, has?"

"I've been requesting one for the last six years, but it falls on deaf ears. Tell me Parker, do you think a fly..." he motioned with his hand, "turns upside down to land on the ceiling or..." he motioned with his hand again, "does a loop the loop, like that?"

His statement was such a distraction to the theme of the conversation that it left her befuddled. She wasn't expecting such an obscure question.

"I... I," she was lost for words and so just shrugged her shoulders.

"Yeah, it's a bit like the glass half empty or half full routine, isn't it?"

"No, nothing like that at all," she said with a frown.

He downed his scotch.

She hadn't even made a dent in hers.

He stood and pointed at her glass. "Ditto?"

"Wait. Sit back down, Thacka," she said, confused by the tone of his question. "You asked me if I'd like a drink?"

"Yeah, so?" his nose wrinkled.

"A drink, Thacka, we're on duty. I'm not here to get pissed or to watch you bury your demons."

She was about to witness Thacka's infamous short fuse.

Fuming, he stood, leaned on the table with his knuckles, and barked at her, "Give me a bloody break! You're not my wife for Christ's sake! I really don't see how having a couple of drinks will affect my ability to function as a cop, and certainly won't kick-start me crying on your fucking shoulder about my divorces or how I think my peers reckon I've lost my friggin' marbles. I'm not suffering from depression or ADHD, and I'm sure as hell no bloody alcoholic... so, do you want another fucking drink or not?"

He glared at her, waiting for a reply, and when he got a sharp negative shake of her head, he turned on his heels and strode for the bar grumbling to himself loudly on the way.

"That's precisely why I fucking prefer to work alone!"

"So be it!" she muttered to herself, turned off by the tirade. She snatched her car keys from the table and left.

Leaning on the bar, Thackeray watched her leave the pub.

The bartender handed him a scotch.

He skulled it, wiped his mouth with the back of his hand, and ordered another. Thacka was on a bender.

Steve Blake entered Surry Hills Police Station, eager to unearth a crime story worth writing about. He was determined to prove to his wife Niki that he was good enough to earn a living as a crime writer. He found his way to the homicide division and approached the Desk Sergeant, a portly man with a gruff voice.

"Can I help you?" the Sergeant inquired.

"Hi, Sergeant. I'm a crime writer looking for a story about a current homicide investigation."

"Is there any particular crime I can assist you with, sir?" he replied facetiously, with a strong Irish accent.

"I'm looking for something gritty, something that will captivate my readers," Steve said, unaware that the Sergeant was teasing him.

The Sergeant casually typed on his keyboard, saying, "Well, let's see here. You mentioned captivating, didn't you, sir?"

Steve grinned and nodded, "Yes."

"To be sure, to be sure," the Sergeant mumbled.

Detective Miller, the rat-faced detective Thackeray had flicked an elastic band at earlier, overheard the conversation as he passed by and, always eager for a laugh, chimed in.

"I'm DI Miller. What's your name, sir?"

"Steve Blake, crime writer."

"Crime writer, eh? I heard you mention captivating. If you're looking for a scoop, then you've definitely come to the right place," Miller said with a sly smile.

Steve quickly produced his iPhone to record Miller's words.

"Sorry, could you repeat that?" he asked.

Miller faked a surreptitious look around to ensure no-one was within earshot, cupped his mouth with his hand for added effect, and whispered into the recorder, "Sydney's most notorious serial offender, the Corn Flake killer, is on the loose!"

He maintained a chilling stare at Steve, who was left dumbfounded. Miller then casually walked away, leaving Steve bewildered.

"But, Detective, I need to know more!" Steve called after him.

Miller stopped abruptly and looked back at Steve as though taking pity on him, then said sternly, "Sergeant, put Mr Blake in touch with DI Kellogg so he can get the low-down on the case. Sorry, correction, that should be DI Thackeray. He's in charge now, isn't he?"

The Desk Sergeant's face turned bright red as he struggled to hold back his laughter. He managed to nod in agreement.

"Thanks, Detective," Steve said with a grateful smile.

"Here," the Desk Sergeant said, handing Steve a calling card. "This is the main number. Call and ask for DI Thackeray; he's not in right now."

Just as Steve was about to leave, Detective Sergeant Parker entered and overheard her partner's name mentioned.

"Hi, I'm DS Parker. I work with DI Thackeray. What can I do for you?" she asked.

The Desk Sergeant tried to discreetly signal to Parker not to get involved, but she ignored him.

"I'm Steve Blake, crime writer, and I'm chasing the story of the Corn Flake killer," Steve replied, extending his hand for a shake.

"Oh, I see. Someone's been telling you some tall tales, haven't they?" she shot the Desk Sergeant a disapproving look. "Come with me, and I'll fill you in on the facts."

She led Steve to the elevator, and they stepped inside. As they rode down, Steve couldn't help but check Parker out. He found her quite attractive, with her short bobbed black hair, piercing blue eyes, pale skin, and ruby-red lips. She didn't fit the stereotypical cop image in his mind. Checking from the ground up, he noted her shapely legs and nice body shape. He manoeuvred a little closer to take in her odour and was pleasantly surprised to detect the aromatic tang of Armani Code.

The elevator door opened at the basement and he followed her to her office. 'Nice butt', he thought to himself, checking her well-rounded bottom inside her knee length grey skirt.

She perceived he was checking her out but it didn't rattle her, at thirty-two, still single, blessed with looks that often rewarded her alluring glances, she wasn't offended.

She led him inside her small office and gestured for him to sit.

"What newspaper do you represent? We have a special division for—"

Steve interrupted, "I'm freelance." He showed her his iPhone and asked, "Do you mind if I record our discussion?"

"Yes, I do. The protocol here is for you to go through the correct channels for an interview. Give me some ID," Parker replied.

Steve fumbled for his wallet, handed over his driver's license, and said, "This do?"

She took it, jotted down the details, and handed it back.

"Thanks. So, look, you seem like a nice enough guy. Is this your first story?"

"Yes," Steve admitted, blushing.

"Thought so. I'll give you a little off-the-record advice, okay?"

"Thanks."

"First, there is no such thing as the Corn Flake killer."

"But—"

She held up a warning finger, "Miller was just having some fun with you. The Corn Flake killer is a bit of an in-joke with homicide. But DI Thackeray and I are on a case that could use a little help to flush out a lead if you're interested."

"Sounds good."

"Okay. Over the past six years, six penises have been recovered from Sydney Parks."

"Penises? You've got to be kidding me?"

"No. I'm deadly serious. The penises belonged to little boys aged between six and twelve."

"So why haven't I heard about this on the news?"

"Because nothing has been reported by the parents of the boys and no bodies of young boys missing a penis have ever turned up."

"How weird. Surely they would have been reported as missing persons."

"Yeah well, I get a hundred reports of missing kids aged between six and twelve every month. Most of them eventually turn up."

"But if they were missing a penis…"

"Exactly, we would have heard about it but we haven't. Which tells us…"

"There's a serial killer on the loose."

"You've got it, a serial killer."

"Now I get it—serial as in breakfast cereal—that's why Miller called it the Corn Flake killer!" He felt stupid.

"Let's say there are those who find it difficult to accept the serial killer scenario."

"Why? Because of the lack of evidence."

"Correct," she said.

"So, let me get this straight. You and…?"

"DI Thackeray."

"You and Thackeray believe some demented individual has abducted six young boys, one per year over six years, cut off their willies, left the willies behind in parks, and then disposed of the bodies without anyone ever reporting the boys missing?"

"Yes."

"Well, the first two questions are, why hasn't someone reported the boys missing, and why would someone be cutting off little boy's willies in the first place?"

"Exactly. Thackeray has a theory that it's related to some sort of occult ritual or sect, something akin to what you might find in England, involving witchcraft or Satanic worship," Parker explained matter-of-factly.

"So, can I have the story?"

"I'll tell you what I'll do. We need to understand what occurs at occult ceremonies here, if they even happen at all. It would only be through conversations with members of such a cult that we might get a lead. We can't do that, but you could."

"You mean go undercover?"

"Um, not exactly. I can't authorize that. Let's call it journalistic research. You can look for cults on the internet, visit pagan, witchcraft, or occult websites and chat rooms, make connections, attend a meeting, and then report to us what you discover. In return, we'll provide you with the exclusive on the story. Of course, this would require DI Thackeray's approval."

"Okay. Sounds like a deal."

"But you'll have to keep what I've told you about the mutilations and the suspected murders confidential, because possessing that kind of knowledge could get you into serious trouble."

"Understood. So, do I report to you?"

"Yes, but remember this is totally unofficial. If it gets iffy or becomes questionable or unsafe in any way, withdraw immediately. You got that?"

"Absolutely."

She handed Steve her business card.

CHAPTER 4

You with your infatuation
So obsessed with incantation
Demons from your devils hell
I had to bid your sorcery farewell.

gk

'Listen to Your Heart' by Roxette played on the pub audio system as Niki returned to the main bar after attempting to call Steve. The song plunged her into an even deeper melancholy than the message she had left him. Her friend Jacqui emerged from the restroom and noticed Niki with a sombre expression. Without hesitation, she hurried over to rescue her, understanding the reason for Niki's despondency. Jacqui gently took her arm and guided her to a table.

Niki, dressed in her work attire—a knee-length navy blue skirt, a white dress shirt, and a matching navy jacket—displayed a gracefully elongated neck with her hair elegantly tied up. In contrast, Jacqui was dressed to impress, in a black mini, a plunging red blouse, and shoulder-length black hair. She exuded an enticing charm and vivacious personality, making her excellent company for Niki. Although they had been workmates for a couple of years, they rarely ventured out for post-work drinks. However, with Niki's personal issues with hubby Steve weighing on her, Jacqui had insisted on a drink and a heart-to-heart chat to lift her spirits.

"You chose the most inopportune time to call him, Nik. Look at yourself," Jacqui empathetically remarked, placing a comforting arm around her friend's shoulders.

"Even though he didn't answer, it's not easy, Jack. It's hard to just up and leave him. I love that dull, boring, piece of crap," Niki admitted, her voice filled with anguish. "But he's all I can think about... I can't stand it... I even considered going home today."

They settled at a table where their drinks awaited them, and Niki's eyes welled up with tears. To uplift Niki's spirits, Jacqui peered out from beneath her Veronica Lake-like fringe, sporting a mischievous grin. "You know, Nik, men are like frogs, I reckon."

"Frogs?" Niki quizzed.

"Yeah, I watched a documentary on the Discovery Channel the other night about them. All they do is eat and mate. But when they mate, it's insane; they get stuck on top of each other for days. It's called amplexus."

Niki was surprised to find an above-average intelligence lurking within her quirky, dizzy friend. "You never cease to amaze me, Jack."

Inspired by Jacqui's comment, Niki scanned the bar for potential 'frogs' and spotted a few people engrossed in conversations. Nowadays, most workers vacated the city immediately after their workday ended. Gone were the days of happy hour when the local city pub was the social hotspot.

Niki noticed a dwarf struggling to climb onto a barstool to place an order. "Look at him, Jack. How does he reach a payphone? Stand on a stack of phonebooks?"

"You'd be hard-pressed to find a phone book in a phone booth these days. And even if there was one, it'd probably be chained up!" Jacqui quipped.

Niki gazed at the garish blood-red carpet and couldn't help but recall how her high heels had nearly become ensnared in it. "Too many spilled drinks," she thought. "It looks more like something you'd expect to find in a brothel." The notion triggered a revelation. "The single men and women eyeing each other like it's a meat market, it's a kind of brothel... that's exactly what it is. They're all on the make." She swiftly dismissed the thought as something that someone unaccustomed to going out might think, someone like her.

A sudden wave of Jacqui's hand lifted her fringe, revealing the seldom-seen other eye. With the precision of a homing pigeon, Jacqui zeroed in on a couple of available men at the far end of the bar.

Niki caught Jacqui and the guys exchanging flirtatious glances and immediately recognised the game. She grew cautious, mindful of the trouble that Steve had consistently warned her about when it came to Jacqui Dean. He didn't trust their close friendship. She studied Jacqui's attractive form and wondered, "Perhaps Steve is attracted to her, even though he denies it... maybe he'd like to screw her, most men do. She's such a sexy thing."

Breaking free from her reverie, Niki noticed that the two men Jacqui had signalled were circling the bar, drawing nearer to them. "What have you done, Jack?" Niki protested in a hushed voice.

"You only live once, Nik!" Jacqui replied with a playful grin.

"That's not right, Jack. You live every day; you only die once."

"Ooo, look at mine. He looks just like Elvis Pugsley!"

"That's Presley, Jack. Pugsley was in the Addams family."

"Exactly," she grinned knowingly.

"What about Steve? And what if someone sees me talking to..."

"Panic, panic, panic, Steve's not here love and besides, the guy's not going to rape you, just talk. Get real Nik, you're a big girl now." She said, adjusting her mini up a little higher for added impact.

Niki couldn't help but giggle at her. "You're a devil, Jack."

Jacqui responded with a wink and then, with pursed lips, looked up at the two men now standing over them. "Hi, Elvis, do you wear a condom?" Jacqui blurted out, much to Niki's embarrassment.

"Only when I have sex," he cracked.

Jacqui burst into laughter while Niki blushed with mortification. After regaining her composure, Niki thought, "Alright, say as little as possible. Don't let him think you're available. Immediately mention that you're married, and you'll salvage your reputation."

The tall, slender, and friendly-looking guy smiled at her and inquired, "Hi, are you married?"

Jacqui interjected and responded on Niki's behalf, "Nuh! Why, are you a female impersonator or something?"

He kept his gaze fixed on Niki, seemingly captivated. She felt as though he was mentally undressing her, and she didn't appreciate it. "Are you?" she replied, immediately mentally chastising herself for the remark. "Shit, why did you say that, you idiot?"

"I'm a cloud spotter for the meteorological department," he replied straight-faced.

That rocked her. "A cloud spotter?" she repeated, holding back a giggle.

"Yeah, I count them and watch out for big bad ones."

"You're having me on?" she tested.

"No, not at all. I've been doing it for six months now."

Suddenly, Niki felt nervous and uncomfortable; he was moving in on her, and it seemed he would soon be all over her like a cheap suit. There was something deep down inside telling her that it wasn't right. She checked her watch and announced, "Time to go, Jack."

Jacqui gave her a surprised glance.

"We agreed, Jack," Niki said sternly.

"Hey, don't go yet, we only just got here," Elvis complained.

But Jacqui had gotten the message and would honour the agreement upon which Niki had come out for a drink. She got up and announced, "Good night, fellas."

"Wait, can I get your number?" Elvis said, disgruntled.

"Not this time," Jacqui grinned and took Niki's arm. They walked out of the pub, giggling, without looking back.

"Sorry, Jack, but it'll take a little while before I can play those games again," Niki confessed.

"Don't apologise, love. There are plenty more frogs in the pond. While you're my houseguest, I'm looking after you. Now, let's catch a cab home."

Thackeray careened out of the Centennial Pub well after the

peak hour traffic had subsided and hailed a cab. It pulled up in a puddle and splashed his shoes. He looked down at his wet feet wavering and cursed his bad luck.

The cab pulled up outside Parker's inner-city apartment block. He stepped out of the cab into a puddle but didn't care at all since his feet were already too soaked for it to make any difference. Ten feet from the intercom, he had his finger pointed and aimed at pressing the appropriate button. He staggered comically toward it, missed, and hit the wrong button. It rang a few times, then a gruff male voice answered.

"Yeah, who's there?"

"It's me, Parker, Thackeray. What happened to your voice?"

"Wrong apartment, buddy."

"Oops, must've missed."

He studied the intercom again and realised what he'd done. "Silly twit, should've been 27A, not 17A!"

He tried again.

"Hello."

"Is that DS Parker?"

"Yes."

"Look, I apologise, it's me, Thacka, can I come in?"

The doors buzzed and clicked open. He sidestepped through the glass sliding door and staggered across the marble lobby floor to the elevator.

When he exited the elevator on the 27th floor, he found Parker garbed in a royal blue robe waiting at her open apartment door, with her arms defiantly folded in front of her. In cold silence, she ushered him inside, then motioned him to sit in an armchair. A steaming mug of brewed coffee awaited him on the coffee table.

"Drink that, Bill," she ordered resolutely, as she sat on the sofa and pulled up her bare feet.

"You're a good cop, Parker. You're even wearing a blue robe."

"Why, Thacka?"

"Why what, Parker?" he countered with a drunken slur.

"Why wipe yourself out?"

"It wasn't me, Parker; it was the scotch."

"Then you better change your drinks. But I suspect it wasn't the scotch but the quantity of them."

"Good observation... obser... ob-serv-ation. Geez, that's tough to say... Parker, see, I said you were a good defective... correction, detective. Hey, did I ever tell you my mushroom theory?"

She decided to humour him.

"No, Thacka, what is your mushroom theory?"

"A caveman ate a magic mushroom and when he hallucinated looking at a round rock, he en... envisioned the wheel."

"That sounds as reasonable a theory as Darwin's. Tell me, Thacka, did your father drink?"

He glared at her through one eye.

"My father was a very unique person, Barker."

"Parker," she corrected.

"Sorry. I burped as I said it... my father was an opal miner. He used to disappear for months on end, opaling, and then just turn up out of the blue. Drove my mum nuts, and yes, he drank like a bloody fish. You know when he was a young bloke, before I was born, he was working at an abattoir in Bourke. One day he was there on his own and was carrying a sheep carcass over his shoulder when he lost balance and fell onto a meat hook. It lodged in the middle of his back, and no matter how much he tried, he couldn't reach to pull it out. There was no vehicle, and he was losing blood, so he decided to hoof it a mile and a half in the blistering midday heat along the dirt driveway to the highway. He waited there a while until he sighted a car and flagged it down. The driver wound down his window and said, "Yer need a lift?" When my dad turned around and showed him the 'S' hook hanging out of his back, the man fainted. Dad pushed him aside, climbed into the car, sat forward right up on the wheel to stop the hook from pushing against the seat, and drove the twenty kilometres to the hospital in town. After they'd removed the hook and patched him up, he woke in a hospital bed and looked at the bed beside him; there was the driver recovering from shock. That was the sort of bloke my old man was, tough as bloody goat's knees."

"Is that why you drink?"

"I'll tell you why I drink, Parker. I drink because my first wife killed my son. She ran over him in the driveway of our house and blamed me. That led to divorce, which led to guilt, which led to the next marriage, which lasted three months and led to divorce, because I was on the piss and that makes me drink more... so that's why I was on the drink... life is a vicious circle," he slurred.

Parker was struck by his admission. Tears welled up in her eyes at the thought of the demons that must be eating away at him.

"I, I thought, since you're my partner, you needed to know that," he said, battling to keep his vision focused on her.

"Why did she blame you?"

He took a sip of coffee and tried to steady himself in the chair, but his head was spinning, and he teetered.

"That day was my turn to look after the boy, you know, get him off to school, because she was going to work. I got a call from an informant... Ricky, that's his name, ran outside while I was distracted, and she backed over him in the car. He'd only just turned six." Tears were streaming down his cheeks.

Parker put her face in her hands, trying to imagine how he must have felt.

"I'm just shit outa luck, Parker, that's me fuckin' unlucky, and I don't even believe in luck. Look, watch this..."

He struggled to find something in his hip pocket, came up with a two-dollar coin, and then handed it to her. She took it with a bemused look on her face.

"Right, flip it, and I'll call," he said.

"Okay," she flipped the coin.

"Tails!" he called.

Parker caught it.

"It's heads."

"See? Again."

Parker flipped it.

"Heads!" he called.

Parker caught it.

"Tails."

"Told ya."

"One more time... three times lucky," she said and flipped.

"Tails."

She checked the coin in her palm.

"It's tails, you got it."

"No, I didn't. I wanted to say heads, but chose the opposite. Hand me your keys."

She picked up her keys from the coffee table and handed them to him. He held them up.

"There are three keys, watch this." He leaned forward enough to almost fall out of the chair, then staggered over to the front door. He stopped there, wavering, selected a key, inserted it in the lock, and said, "See, it's the wrong key!" He staggered back and flopped in the lounge. "It's been like that since the day my son died, which was right after I began saying that I suspected Moloch of murder."

"You're not seriously saying you believe Moloch has anything to do with you having bad luck?"

"Sure am. The prick cursed me. They say he's a bloody warlock, king of the black arts. He's the sort of bastard who will do anything to avert a threat to himself or his game... anything."

"You could hardly call it a game," Parker said a little perplexed.

"Oh yes, oh yes... a game is exactly what it is! That's what makes the bastard such a tough adversary... he's cunning, intelligent, but more so, he treats it like a game... it's all a bloody game to him."

"I think it might just be a coincidence; bad luck is more your own doing than some mystical external force. I'm sure you can reverse that, don't you think?" She looked at him for an answer, but he was sitting up in the chair, sound asleep. She got up, removed the cup from his hand, grabbed a blanket from the sofa, covered him up, and then ambled off to her bedroom to get some sleep, knowing full well that her discussion with Thackeray meant her dreams were destined to be a collage of frightening imagery.

Sarah woke in a hospital bed, startled to find tubes hanging from her every orifice, connected to an array of machines emitting annoying digital blips and whirs. Her vision cleared from its foggy state to reveal a lumpy but jolly nurse standing at the foot of her bed, reading a chart.

"Where am I?" she tried to say, but the tube in her mouth distorted her words.

However, Nurse Peters, an experienced professional, understood. She peered over her small oblong reading glasses, offering Sarah a warm smile, and spoke with a thick Irish accent.

"Welcome back to planet Earth, Mrs Dixon. You're in Wollongong Hospital, and you'll be just fine."

The burly, big-breasted woman in her late thirties waddled around the bedside, taking Sarah's hand not only to check her pulse but also to provide comfort.

"You have been in an accident that has had you in a coma for a day or so, but you're just fine now. You had a bad bang on the head but otherwise only a couple of scratches and bruises, you're on the mend dear. Now, before you go asking me questions and to be sure you've got a few, I'll be letting your Doctor Bishop know you're back with us and he'll be paying you a visit. Will that be all right dear?"

Sarah's vision fogged over again, and when it cleared, she thought only a few seconds had lapsed, but it had actually been twenty minutes. She realised that a middle-aged man was now standing beside her bed, holding her hand.

He smiled with a doctor's reassuring manner. "Hello, Sarah. Can you hear me? Keep blinking your eyes, and your vision will clear."

Relieved to find the tube removed from her mouth, Sarah blinked as instructed.

"I'm Doctor Bishop," he continued, but before he could say more, Sarah squeezed his hand tightly.

"Where's Russell? Wayne!"

"Shhh, shhh, calm down, don't panic. You've suffered a serious head injury, Sarah. You're very lucky to be alive." He sat on the edge of the bed, still holding her hand, and used his free hand to feel her forehead for her temperature. "You were in a very bad car accident, Sarah. Your husband Wayne didn't survive, and your son Russell is in a coma."

"I want to see him," she sniffled.

"Yes, all in good time. He's just down the corridor. But first, we need to make sure you're well enough, don't we?"

"I feel fine. Just a bit dizzy, that's all."

Dr Bishop's expression turned serious.

"Sarah, you've been unconscious for forty-eight hours. We don't know how your brain will recover from the trauma it's endured." He leaned forward and lifted the edge of a bandage on her face. "I removed half a windscreen from your face and scalp," he said with a smile.

Sarah was stressing. "When will Russell wake up?"

"Calm down, Sarah."

"How long?"

He stood up and spoke with gravity. "We haven't been able to wake him up yet, Sarah. But there's still a slim chance..."

His voice faded away as a thick fog swamped Sarah's vision once more, and she slipped back into unconsciousness.

Sarah woke up abruptly. The fog cleared, and she found herself alone in the hospital room. Judging by the lack of activity, it was the early hours of the morning, still dark. She was free of tubes and beeping machines, and as she checked her arms and face, she noticed only minimal dressings. Gathering her courage, she struggled to sit up and then slowly moved her feet out from under the stiff, starched white sheet, placing them on the cold tiled floor. Despite feeling unsteady, she stood up, gripping the bed to prevent herself from falling. After taking a deep breath, she decided to follow her motherly instincts.

With determination, she moved out of the room and into the

corridor. Her hand brushed the wall for support as she battled dizziness, but soon she spotted a walking brace a short distance away. She focused on reaching it, one step at a time. She finally reached the brace and, holding onto it, walked more steadily with newfound confidence.

Unaware that the back of her nightgown had opened up, revealing her petite naked bottom and shapely legs, she moved down the corridor like a determined but lost geriatric. Guided by instinct and an inexplicable psychic sense, she arrived at a room that felt right to her. She opened the door cautiously, revealing a dimly lit space with a crib and numerous life support machines beeping and whirring.

Sarah staggered to the crib, peering through the Perspex hood to see her son Russell inside. Tears welled up in her eyes as she whispered, "Oh, my poor darling." She wiped away her tears, opened the hood, and reached inside, delicately touching Russell's cheek.

Suddenly, she was jolted backward, as if electrocuted. She was bewildered by the sensation but managed to stay quiet. Tentatively, she reached out again and touched Russell's forehead. This time, she allowed the surge of energy to envelop her, and she began to shake uncontrollably. Her eyes rolled back in her head, and Russell convulsed wildly.

Then, a blinding astral flash burst in her mind's eye.

The next morning, Sarah sat up in her hospital bed, eating breakfast when Dr Bishop arrived. He was clearly pleased with her rate of recovery.

"Sarah, you look absolutely marvellous today!"

"Thank you, Doctor Bishop. I'm feeling a lot better. How is my son?"

Checking her chart, he adopted a more serious tone, "I have to tell you he has made an unprecedented recovery, Sarah. Actually, his recovery is so incredible that several of Australia's leading neurologists are totally baffled by it. Did you by chance visit him last night?"

"Um, yes, I'm sorry, Doctor Bishop, but..." she said sheepishly.

With a grave expression, he continued, "Do you know you violated hospital rules?"

"Yes, but he's my son."

He changed his tone and demeanour, moving closer to her bedside and taking her hand.

"Sarah, we'd like to run some tests on Russell. He has made an anomalous recovery, and—"

But Sarah interrupted him, "No thanks, Doctor. I just want to take him home." All she wanted was to get out of the hospital.

"That, of course, is your prerogative, Sarah," he said, standing and heading toward the door. He stopped and turned to her, disappointment in his eyes. "Such research data could save the lives of other children in similar circumstances, Sarah. Are you certain I can't persuade you to change your mind?"

Sarah simply shook her head in reply.

A few hours later, a crowd of news reporters and journalists had gathered outside the hospital, waiting for Russell. Word of the boy's miraculous recovery had spread quickly: Russell Dixon was big news.

Nurse Peters pushed Russell's wheelchair toward the exit, with Sarah walking gingerly beside her. Sarah noticed the commotion outside.

"Surely those people aren't waiting for us?" Sarah questioned.

"I think they are, my dear," Nurse Peters suggested, slowing down. "They're calling it a miracle, you know?" she explained, then immediately blessed herself.

"Mum, can't I walk?" Russell asked.

"No, not just yet, love. Stop, nurse, I can't face them!" They stopped well short of the exit doors.

"Let's go back, shall we? I've got an idea. Maybe you can make a backstage exit," Nurse Peters said with a canny wink.

They executed a brisk U-turn and then ducked out of a side door.

Thackeray, looking worse for wear from his battle with the bottle the previous night, flicked a Berocca capsule into a glass of water on his desk. Even the sound of the tablet fizzing caused him to wince—such was his delicate state. Parker, looking ever so perky, appeared at his cubicle with a folder tucked under her arm, ready for business. He glanced up at her, guilt-ridden. She gave him a reproving glare and moved on.

Detective Connie Lee walked past with a cup of coffee and noticed Thackeray's state, elbows on the desk, head in his hands.

"Here, Thacka, you look like you need this more than I do."

She offered him her coffee.

"No thanks, Lee. The cure is worse than the complaint. That coffee could kill a man. The makers of it should be charged with attempted murder." He held his chest and winced. "Besides, this heartburn is killing me."

"Nuts."

"Nar... I've had it for ages. I've got a hiatus hernia and an ulcerated esophagitis, which means over acidity in the guts burns the crap out of the ulcers."

"I didn't mean you're nuts; you should eat nuts—raw almonds, instead of chewing matchsticks."

"Almonds?"

"Yeah, my Dad had the same deal. It kept him awake at night; he had to try and sleep sitting up in bed, and you'd know how tough that is. So, when he found out about almonds, he kept a bowl of them on the bedside table... when he felt a burn, he munched a few up. Took away the heartburn."

She shrugged her shoulders and said, "Give them a try... have a good day, Thacka," as she continued to her own cubicle.

"Yeah, thanks for the hint, Connie," he muttered to himself. Just then, his desk phone rang.

"Thackeray. Ah, Superintendent Wilks. Sorry, sir." Hearing from the boss had roused him and magically cleared his head.

"What's that, sir? Yes, Parker... no, I, yes, sir... I'll be there promptly."

Five minutes later, Thackeray stood in front of Superintendent Wilks' secretary, Pamela, and was about to speak to her when a deep voice bellowed out from the inner sanctum of the main office.

"Come in, Thackeray."

In his late fifties, Wilks had the stern "take-no-shit" attitude expected of a superintendent. He was big, broad-shouldered, had a shaven head, and sported a huge handlebar moustache. His sharp, concentrated features suggested he was a shrewd man, which indeed he was. His eyes were not unkind but neither were they forgiving; his lips were pursed as if permanently considering a grave matter. He was seated behind an antique oak desk, mulling over a report. When Thackeray entered the spacious office, Wilks glanced up at him and said with one raised eyebrow, "You look like shit, Thackeray."

"Yes, sir. It seems to go with most anything I wear these days," he quipped, standing rigidly in front of the desk, observing protocol.

But Wilks wasn't amused, and his tone testified to that. "Sit down, inspector."

"Sir," Thackeray said and complied.

"What are we going to do with you, Thackeray?"

In an effort to lighten the mood, he offered, "I don't know, sir. I don't recall applying for a new job."

Still unamused, Wilks said sardonically, "I guess a sense of humour would be mandatory for a bloke in your position."

"Meaning, sir?"

"Get off the piss, Thackeray, or I will relieve you of your duty."

"But—"

"There are no buts. Dismissed!" Wilks went back to reading the report on his desk, thus terminating the conversation.

Thackeray got as far as the door and stopped, thinking better of letting his superior officer belittle him. He turned and said, "Okay, then give me what I need to catch my serial killer."

Still looking at the report on his desk, Wilks replied casually, "And exactly why would I do that?" He looked up at Thackeray, perplexed.

"Because I'm a damn good cop, and because six kids have been butchered... if the press gets hold of the story, there will be hell to pay. I'm your best... correction, your only chance of getting an arrest."

Wilks looked back down at the report and called out, "Pamela!"

The door opened behind Thackeray almost immediately, and Pamela, a middle-aged, portly but well-groomed uniformed officer, strolled in with an iPad under her arm.

"Yes, sir?"

"Take Inspector Thackeray to your desk and arrange for his needs... within reason."

"A car?" Thackeray chipped in.

Wilks glared long and hard at him and then said dismissively,

"Yes, a car."

"Thank you, sir."

Pamela held the door open for Thackeray to pass through and gave Wilks a sly wink for a plan well-executed.

Thackeray was excited; things were starting to look up for him, maybe even his luck had changed. He wanted to share his elation with Parker, so he took the elevator to the basement.

Parker was busy rummaging through her desk drawers, looking for something when Thackeray burst into her office.

"Hey, you're not going to believe this."

When she looked up at him, her hair was in a mess all over her face from bending over, and she was flustered and puffed the hair out of her eyes.

"Believe what?"

He sat on the edge of her desk and announced haughtily, "The super just gave me a car and... get this, an office for us... and he cleared a budget for our case."

She went back to rummaging, "Good," she muttered.

He produced a toothpick and stuck it between his teeth.

She straightened up, "Damn! I can't find Steve's phone number anywhere."

"Steve?"

"Yeah. Oh, I haven't told you."

"Oh, look, I apologise for my untoward behaviour last night, thanks for putting me up."

"No worries. But that was the last time we have a drink on duty— never again. You'd disappeared when I got up this morning. I would've cooked brekkie, you know."

"No, can't confront food after a heavy nigh t... It's a bit of a shame we can't have the odd drink, though."

"No, it isn't. When there's a problem, you just remove the cause. Simple as that, my dear old pappy used to say."

"Must have been a teetotaller?"

"He sure was and proud of it."

"Sounds like a real barrel of laughs... Look, everyone uses something as a wind-down mechanism; mine just happens to be a drink."

"I wouldn't call that performance winding down, Thacka, and I wouldn't call it just a drink. Anyhow, all is forgiven. So, back to the case... I took it upon myself in your absence yesterday afternoon to give a young reporter a mission on the case."

Thackeray stood up from the edge of the desk, incensed, "Am I hearing you straight? Did you say a reporter? ... a mission?"

"Yeah, so? What's wrong with that?"

"For a start, protocol has it that reporters have to go through PR."

"Since when did you become an advocate of protocol, Thacka?"

"And secondly, what the stuff can a reporter do that we can't?"

His face was flushed; he didn't like Parker taking it upon herself to authorise activities related to the case.

She wasn't sure if he was being possessive about the case, a chauvinist about a woman taking control of it, or legitimately concerned.

"I think you're being a tad possessive about the case, mate. I am quite capable of making calls without having to get you to sign off on them first, you know!" she said, standing her ground.

The fist of his mind clenched. "It's not about being possessive, Parker, it's about putting members of the public unnecessarily at risk. You haven't answered my question, what can he do we can't?"

"He's going to get into the occult sects and attend a black Sabbat."

"Oh shit!" he slapped his forehead and flopped into a chair, bummed out. "You'll get him fucking murdered."

"Unlikely. First, he's a smart guy, and second, he will report to me every inch of the way, before he does a thing."

"Yeah? How long have you known him?"

She knew he had her on that one.

"Um, a day."

"Uh, ha! And what paper does he work for?"

"He's freelance."

"Is he experienced?"

"This is his first story."

"Jesus-H-Christ! What possessed you to do that, Parker? I can't believe it!"

"There was something about him, Thacka, a gut feel. Haven't you ever met someone you think is going to be of importance to you?"

"Yes, I suppose so, I married both of them, and where did that get me?"

"Yeah, you told me about it last night."

"I did?" he said surprised. "Oh shit, listen, I didn't try anything on you... did I? You know, funny stuff—la de duh."

"La-de-dah? Is that what you call sex? No, Thacka, you arrived on my doorstep inebriated, told me why you drink yourself into a stupor along with your mushroom theory and a rave about your bad luck, along with a demonstration of it, and that you've been cursed by Wolfen Moloch. Then you fell asleep. No bloody la-de-dah!"

"Oh shit... so I poured my guts out to you, and now you know all my secrets."

"Thacka, what you have been through could turn anyone to drink or worse. But there are better ways of dealing with it, and I'm here to help you."

That got his attention—he'd not heard words of support like those from anyone before.

"Thank you, Parker, so, I told you my mushroom theory, huh?"

She cracked a smile then sat back in her chair, "Work with me on Steve, all right? We both do things outside of the box, don't we?"

"Yes, I suppose so. But we'll have to keep him in tow; we don't want to end up with egg on our faces because he gets necked or something."

"Agreed. Looks like your luck might have changed."

She stuck out her hand to shake and thought, "Lucky he'd been such a bad boy last night or he might have reacted differently to the idea of Steve coming on board."

Steve was at his computer in the spare room, searching the Internet for local covens and getting results. He'd found a bunch of local websites with event calendars and chat forums and joined six of them as Kaspar: a Wiccan magickal name meaning treasured secret. Being an undercover journalist was his treasured secret, and the idea of that thrilled him to the core.

He logged onto The Veil, one of the biggest occult sites, and signed in. Within seconds, he had Rebekah to chat with, who claimed to be a witch. His plan was to earn the trust of someone enough to meet them and then get an invite to a Sabbat.

Kaspar: I have to admit I'm new at this.

Rebekah: The Veil or chatting?

Kaspar: Both.

Rebekah: Well, we all have to start from somewhere.

Kaspar: How long have you been a witch?

Rebekah: We prefer to call it the craft… since I could first walk.

Kaspar: Wow! Were your parents members as well?

Rebekah: You could say that; I come from a long line of Wiccans.

Kaspar: Wish I'd been so lucky.

Rebekah: What interests you about the craft?

Kaspar: I've always loved magic; guess I just want to know more about everything. Inquisitive.

Rebekah: There are many levels.

Kaspar: What, like the Freemasons?

Rebekah: Of understanding.

Kaspar: I want to learn; how can I?

Rebekah: Takes time.

Kaspar: Are you a member of a sect?

Rebekah: We call it a coven. Yes.

Kaspar: Can I join?

Rebekah: It's not a club.

Kaspar: ?

Rebekah: By recommendation.

Kaspar: Will you recommend me?

Rebekah: Takes time.

Kaspar. Got plenty of that. Where do you live?

That was the wrong question to ask, and the immediate response taught him an invaluable lesson.

Rebekah: Got to go. Bye.

Kaspar: Bye. Nice meeting you.

"Damn! Scared her off, didn't I?" he said, flopping back in his chair, disappointed with his first effort. The phone rang, and he answered it.

"Hello. Niki! Hi... Ah, You what! Want to get your things? Why? Can't we talk this over? A break... to think—some space? Oh mate, that's what all couples say when they split up. Look, I'm sorry... Listen! Nik, listen, I got a job! Yeah, I did what you suggested... Freelance for a crime magazine... No, they pay on delivery, but I've got my first case. What do you mean a real job! Come on, Niki, I'm trying."

But he felt his pleading was falling on deaf ears. He figured her mind was made up. She needed space to get her head together, and he had no choice but to provide it.

He acquiesced, "No, Niki, I don't want to argue either. Fine. If you want to pick up your stuff, you've got a key, do it whenever... What? You don't want me here! Fuck why not? So we don't fight...

Huh! shit, more so you don't want to weaken your resolve and stay? Okay, Okay... I'll be out Sunday from ten in the morning, yes all day—at the cricket with Morgan, of course... I know its Tuesday today, please yourself—take it or leave it. I hope he's a nice feller. What? Yes, that's what I said. Well, it sure sounds like you've got someone to me. Where are you staying? Right, you're not going to say. I'd put my money on Jacqui's and I suppose you've been hitting the singles bars with her... You haven't? You know what, Niki, that just doesn't add up, not when it comes to a bird like Jacqui. No, I don't fancy her. Yeah, I'm tired of it as well, goodbye, Niki!" he terminated the call, well pissed.

CHAPTER 5

"First Moloch, horrid King besmear'd with blood
Of human sacrifice, and parents tears.
Though, for the noyse of Drums and Timbrels loud,
Their children's cries unheard that passed through fire
To his grim Idol. Him the Amonite."

John Milton, Paradise Lost

The phone rang at the Dixon house in Randwick. Sarah staggered out of the bedroom, garbed in a flimsy nightgown, and made her way through the house to the phone.

"Hello? Yes, that's me," she yawned. "Oh, pardon me," she looked at the clock on the mantle—it was 9 AM. "Yes, I suppose I can be there by then. What's this about? Oh, the police report for the insurance. Okay, whereabouts?" she picked up a pen to note down the address but didn't need it, "Oh, Surry Hills Station, yes, I know where that is... Officer Lee, right, thanks. Pardon? No, we'll take a cab, thank you. Bye."

Holding Russell's hand, Sarah approached the big Irish Desk Sergeant at Police HQ reception. The Sergeant looked up from reading with a big welcoming smile. He enjoyed dealing with pretty ladies, a change from his usual customers.

"Yes, Ma'am, and how may I help you?" he said politely with a rich Belfast accent.

"I have an appointment with Officer Lee."

He leaned over the counter and peered at Russell.

"Well hello down there, are you meeting Officer Lee as well, young feller?"

"Yes, sir," Russell replied with youthful enthusiasm.

The Sergeant buzzed Officer Lee, and almost immediately, a slender young female Chinese officer appeared through a door in the partition behind the Sergeant's desk.

"Mrs Dixon, I'm Officer Connie Lee," they shook hands. "You'll need these," she handed Sarah a Visitor's pass and bent to fasten a second one on the boy's shirt pocket, "and you must be Russell?"

"Yes, Ma'am," said Russell, his eyes wide.

Officer Lee led them through the security door and into the open plan office array beyond.

Dressed smartly in a severely tailored pale green suit, which did not conceal her figure, and with her rich red hair up, Sarah caused a sudden silence when she entered the austere office setting. Almost all of the male staff had stopped what they were doing to look up and check out this gorgeous woman who had entered their hive.

At five foot ten, Officer Lee was an inch or so taller than Sarah, but because she was so slender, her police uniform made her look even taller, especially to Russell who found her fascinating. He'd not met a Chinese lady before, and her height amplified his fascination.

"Did you have any trouble finding us, Mrs Dixon?" Lee said, gesturing to her cubicle for Sarah to enter and take a seat.

"No. The taxi driver knew where to come."

"Are you Chinese?" Russell asked Lee.

"Yes, but I was born here... as Aussie as you are, mate."

Russell wandered out of the cubicle.

"Russell, come back love."

"Oh, he'll be fine; you can let him wander about."

"I'm sorry for what he said..." Sarah said apologetically.

"Ha, it's the question most people are afraid to ask," she said with good humour.

"Now, Mrs Dixon."

"Sarah."

"Connie," she paused, "this is a rather delicate matter in view of your recent bereavement. You see, we were unable to obtain an accident report from you at the time, for obvious reasons. We need to complete our procedures as regards the accident, and it's in your interest to help. You see, in our experience, without a police report, the insurance company is unlikely to pay out on your deceased husband's policy."

"I understand, so what do you want from me?"

"There's a standard form to fill out."

Sarah held up a flash drive. "I've already written a statement—"

"Well, you're more than just a friendly face, aren't you?" she paused, an embarrassed look on her pretty oriental face. "I'm really sorry to put you through the ordeal again."

"It's okay," Sarah said with a friendly smile, handing her the flash drive.

Sarah sat in a relaxed silence as Officer Lee quickly inserted the drive into her terminal, concentrated briefly on the screen, and transferred the text into her forms. Sarah was more relaxed than she had been in weeks, watching Connie work and hearing Russell's boyish laughter in the distance as he charmed his way through the squad room. The printer chattered, and she shook off her reverie.

Connie handed her the printout.

"Please read it through; I'll go and keep an eye on Russell. Give me a call when you're ready," she smiled.

"Thanks, Connie."

Connie left Sarah to it and went hunting for Russell. She found him in DI Thackeray's new office.

Thacka had fared well from his meeting with Superintendent Wilks. No more cubicles for him; he had his very own suite of offices, temporary as they might be.

Lee stopped at the open door. "Got a new partner, Thacka?"

Thacka and Russell were firing elastic bands at one another

across the room.

"Yeah, he's busy teaching an old dog new tricks, aren't you, partner?"

It was a two-room suite, the second being the Incident Room with its centrepiece, a glass Murder Wall. On it were posted photos and notes referring to the case Thackeray was working. In the centre of the Murder Wall beyond Russell's view in the first office was a photograph of an evil-looking face with a name in marker pen written underneath; Wolfen Moloch.

"You okay here, Russell?" Connie asked.

"Yep."

"Can you handle him for a tick, Thacka? I'm dying for a coffee."

"No worries, we're getting on like a house on fire."

"What fire," Russell asked looking about for it.

Lee and others had noticed a marked change for the better in Thacka's attitude and temperament since he got his office and a car. He even looked younger. They didn't know he was off the sauce, but they had noticed a lack of the familiar odour of Berocca wafting from him.

Sarah finished reading. She stood and peered over the cubicle wall for Russell. His distinctive giggle gave her the direction to search and brought her to the doorway of Thacka's office.

"Hey Russ, who's your new buddy?"

Thackeray swivelled his chair to face the voice and upon seeing Sarah almost swooned. If ever there was a woman to fit Thacka's image of perfect, it was Sarah. Her striking green eyes matched her outfit perfectly, and the severe tailoring of her suit accentuated the curves beneath. Thacka tried not to let his jaw sag open... lost for words.

"We, we were just—"

"This is Bill, mum!" Russell said with a giggle.

"Oh, hello, Bill," Sarah said with a smile that almost caused his crusty old heart to take an unaccustomed leap.

"I'm Sarah Dixon."

Just then, Connie turned up with a steaming coffee.

"Done already, Sarah? These two were having so much fun I left them to play while I grabbed a coffee. If you're happy with the report..."

Sarah nodded, realising she couldn't remember anything that was on the papers in her hand.

"I'll print out the formal version for you to sign. Back in a sec," Connie said with a grin.

An awkward silence fell between Sarah and Thacka, not uncomfortable, but somewhat suspenseful, the suspense when two people are attracted to one another but a little wary of pursuing it.

Thacka was the antithesis of Sarah's husband Wayne in every way, shape, and form. She was attracted to the intelligence in his eyes, his weathered face, and rugged build, and his obvious natural machismo.

While their attention was focused on each other, Russell wandered through the open door into the Incident Room.

"Connie's into data mining," Thacka said with an awkward smile.

He knew his sense of humour was aberrant and wished he'd kept it to himself.

"Guess that comes with the uniform," she quipped.

Thackeray was impressed, not only had she got his gag about Connie's affection for information gathering, but came back with a witty retort. He was becoming more enamoured with her by the minute.

Suddenly, Thacka became aware that Russell had gone into the Incident Room and that was out of bounds to visitors. At the same moment, Sarah realised Russell was missing. She took three steps to the door of the Incident Room and found him staring at the photograph of Wolfen Moloch on the Murder Wall.

"Hang on, Misses Dixon!" Thacka was galvanized. "You can't go in there!"

Russell was transfixed by Moloch's photograph.

"Look at the bad man, Mum."

Sarah glanced at the photo just as Thacka strode up behind her, arm out about to stop her from going further.

"What did you just say?" Thacka asked, intrigued.

"Say what?" she replied somewhat shocked.

"You just told Russell that Moloch hurts little boys, what gave you that idea?" Thacka said, confounded.

The question made Sarah feel uncomfortable. To avoid answering, she diverted her attention to Russell, his face buried in her skirt, obviously upset by the photo of Moloch.

"Right, young man, we need to catch a cab home," she said hurriedly.

She took Russell by the hand and led him out of the Incident Room.

Thackeray couldn't let it go.

"Can't have you doing that, Misses Dixon. Let me give you a lift."

Sarah reacted as if he was asking her on a date.

"No, no! It's not a problem. We can catch a cab... I mean we—"

"No, no listen, I insist. It's peak hour; they're hard to catch... anyhow, I promised Russell I'd put on the flashing blue light."

"No, you didn't!" Russell said, totally giving him up.

Complete with the strobing blue light, Thackeray pulled his new Chrysler 300 SPT Core up outside the Dixon house in Randwick. It was dusk, and the western skyline of Sydney was tainted with the ominous orange glow of bushfires blazing in the Blue Mountains. When they were out of the car, Russell snatched his mum's keys from her hand and raced up the drive to open the front door.

Chuckling at Russell's brash behaviour, Thackeray squared his shoulders, face-to-face with Sarah. He found her eyes hypnotic.

"You can smell the smoke in the air from the bushfires, poor buggers who live up there; plenty will lose their homes over the next few days."

"Yes, I hope none lose their lives. Thank you for driving us home, Bill, it was a nice gesture. You know it's the first time I've seen Russell happy since before the accident that took his dad from us."

"Oh, I'm sorry, I didn't know. Talked too much about myself in the car. How are you coping?" he said with genuine concern. His job had taught him to handle bereavement. He hadn't given any thought as to why she had been at the police station. His infatuation for her had abrogated his natural inquisitive instinct.

"Oh, it's been tough. No relatives or friends here in Sydney to help; we came over from Perth."

"Ah! A sandgrouper!" he scoffed.

"I guess so. Anyhow, thanks again, Bill. By the way, I'm Sarah."

She held out her hand to shake. He took it—and it felt like nothing he'd ever touched before, soft and caring. A special moment lingered while the electricity flowed between them, and they contemplated the next move. When the next move failed to eventuate from him, Sarah took it as a lack of interest, smiled, and let go of his hand. She made off towards the house, feeling as if she had left something behind. When she got to the front door, she stopped, thought better of it, turned, and called back to him, "Got anything planned for dinner, Bill?"

A broad smile broke on his craggy face.

Thackeray was seated in a big comfy armchair alone in the living room. Sarah came in with Russell, dressed in his pyjamas. They'd had dinner, and now it was time for Russell to go to bed. The little fair-haired boy confronted Thackeray and held out his hand to shake.

"Goodnight, DI Bill Thackeray; I'm off to hit the sack!"

They shook hands.

"Good oh, see you, big feller."

"I'll just go and tuck him in," Sarah said with a warm smile. "Help yourself to anything; you know where the kitchen is."

Thackeray was relishing every minute of being part of a family unit again, even if it was only for one brief evening. It had felt like everything he'd wanted and which his former marriages had failed to deliver him.

While waiting for Sarah, he studied the room, as to be expected from a good cop. The mantle over the blocked-up fireplace displayed a collection of framed photographs that provided him with background. They were photos of Sarah's wedding, the honeymoon, the folks, relatives, and pictures of Russell at various stages of his life, from a baby to his last birthday. Thacka's police training had him evaluate the family based on what he could see on the mantelpiece: middle class, been in Sydney a year or so, husband an accountant or lawyer, probably childhood sweethearts, a bit of a miss-match. One of the photographs of Sarah in her youth caused him to conclude her looks had improved with age. She wasn't a stunner in her teens and in fact she looked a tad nerdy in a hippie kind of way.

Suddenly, the dulcet tones of the John Vallins album 'Let's Fly Away' distracted his critical judgment of the history laid out on her mantelpiece.

Sarah glided into the room with a bottle of red and two glasses.

"Profiling the Dixon family, detective?"

"Always on duty, Ma'am... I'm sorry, unfortunately, I can't partake," he said, pointing to the wine.

"Surely you're not on duty now?"

Thacka hesitated. He knew instantly he needed to be honest with this woman, no matter how hard that would be.

"No, no... it's not that."

She sat down beside him,

"Oh, really, not even one?"

"No... one could lead to a dozen for me."

Knowing that she instinctively understood his problem and didn't question him about it elevated her even further in his estimation.

She hopped up and said with a smile, "Back in a sec."

A minute later, she returned from the kitchen with the two wine glasses topped with water, passed one to him, sat down, and offered her glass in a toast.

"Happy days then."

He smiled at her, thankful to be in the company of such an intuitive and understanding woman.

"Indeed. Cheers, big ears!"

They clinked glasses then sipped water, jokingly relishing the taste as if it were vintage wine.

"Big ears?" she said, registering what he'd said.

"Oh, nothing personal, it's just an old saying. Been a while since you've had company then?"

She shot him sad puppy dog eyes and said, "Does it show that much?"

"Not really, but when you've been with the one person for so long..."

"Yeah, I guess that certainly shows," she said looking over at the mantel of photos. "Good work drawing that conclusion from our photo collection."

"Can't help it."

He was deliberately skirting the subject of her bereavement but still desperately wanting to know what had caused her to make the observation at the Murder Wall about Moloch.

"You know, aside from losing Wayne, the toughest thing to deal with was Russell's recovery from the coma. The best doctors in the country had him all but written off as terminal, and then the bloody media circus came chasing the story of a miracle recovery. A miracle mind you... they were relentless, and they haven't stopped hounding me since we got out of the hospital. I get a call from Sixty Minutes or one of the other TV news vultures at least once a day, and you know what?" She was sounding emotional. "I just don't want to lie to anyone."

That caused Thackeray to pause and take another sip of water. It was probably the first time he'd drunk water in years without it containing at least two fingers of single malt. Even that was rare with his personal adage; you don't poison good scotch with water.

"Lie? I don't get it."

"Well, please don't think of me as being mentally defective, but I believe in Karma, and I just don't need any more negativity in my life."

With the subject now open, Thackeray recognised the opportunity to play an amateur psychologist and dig a little deeper.

"What do you mean?"

She stared at him long and hard, assessing him right down to the very core, and he felt it. Once satisfied, she continued.

"Look, I know it's hard to believe, but I had a premonition the day of the accident, not to make the trip to Wollongong, but my husband ignored it."

"Yes, we often get those and—"

She cut him off, sure of what he was about to say; she was used to it.

"Wayne never trusted my ability to... well, to sometimes... see things."

"See things?"

She was a little flustered and took a sip of water. The look in her eyes betrayed a fear that she might have said too much to a man she'd only just met.

"Events coming, you know—future events, visionary. Anyhow, after learning in the hospital that Wayne was gone and that my boy was in a coma..."

He could see the tears welling up in her eyes.

"Unlikely to revive... I got up out of my hospital bed and visited him. It was halfway through the night, it wasn't allowed but I needed to see him," she said, wiping away a tear.

"That's understandable," he said warmly.

"When I touched him on the face, I felt something strange like electricity. It had never happened before, and it frightened the hell out of me. But at the same time, it seemed something I had to do... So, I touched him again and then... I found myself inside... well... I was inside his mind—um, physically."

He was transfixed,

"Go on."

He could tell by the shift in her expression that she'd changed her mind about continuing.

"I found him and... brought him back."

Thackeray was perplexed. He stared at her with his mouth half open, stunned and confused by her claim. He wasn't sure what she meant. Did she believe she had physically brought her boy's soul back from somewhere on the other side? His cop's mind tried to fit that claim into the reality he knew and couldn't, so he put it aside and went back to the reason he'd offered to drive her home in the first place.

"Can I ask you something?"

"Yes, within reason."

"When you saw the photo Russell was pointing at on the Murder Wall at my office, you said, 'he hurts little boys,' why did you say that?"

"I don't know, I felt something from just looking at him, I guess."

"A premonition?"

"Maybe, I'm not sure, but his image is definitely evil."

In the pitch-blackness of his bedroom, Thackeray sat bolt upright in bed with his heart racing at ten to the dozen. He'd been dreaming. To his shock, Moloch was standing at the foot of his bed grinning macabrely at him. Quick as a flash, Thacka twisted, reached under the pillow and grabbed his service weapon and spun back, gripping the pistol in both hands, in the regulation "combat grip'. As he swung back towards his assailant and tried to bring the weapon to bear, Moloch suddenly loomed over him. His hands holding the weapon slammed into what felt like a concrete wall and he glanced down to see his two hands and the pistol clenched in Moloch's huge right hand. Moloch effortlessly held Thacka's hands and arms motionless and squeezed, his vice like grip trapping Thacka's hands with crushing force. They locked eyes and Thacka could feel Moloch's evil burning into his soul. The weapon was pointed towards Moloch's thigh and Thacka knew that was the best he could do, so he fired a deafening blast in the bedroom, expecting to see Moloch crumple to the floor as the .40 S & W hollow-point 'safety slug' tore open his thigh and shattered the bone. Moloch didn't even flinch. With a malevolent sneer, he crushed Thacka's hands around the gun. Crack,

crack, crack the bones of Thacka's fingers and hands splintered and he felt his blood oozing between Moloch's fingers and dripping onto the bed. Thacka's face contorted with pain and he grimaced in a silent scream.

Moloch's stare grew more intense and he snarled, "Spirits of the night and bats that fly by the light of the moon, come forth from the Astral Realm and jinx this person for all time. William Thackeray—Darmastro Aspecti martain."

Despite the ringing in his ears from the gunshot and his temporary deafness, Moloch's words echoed clearly in Thacka's mind. With his hands throbbing in agony, Thacka tore his eyes away from the sinister presence and broke the stare. Instantly, the pain ceased. He looked down at his mangled hands, still tightly gripping the pistol, and then flexed his fingers. They moved freely, and there was nothing wrong with his hands. When he looked up again, Moloch had vanished. It had been a dream—a horrifying dream. This wasn't the first time he'd experienced this exact nightmare. It was why he believed he was cursed, why he was convinced that Moloch was a murderer. But how could he explain that his only evidence was a recurring dream?

Shaking his head in disbelief, Thacka dropped the magazine, cleared his weapon (a Glock 22), and reloaded it, replacing the expended cartridge from the box in his bedside table. He chambered a round and slid the pistol back under his pillow. Although he knew it violated all the rules of gun safety and police procedures, Thacka had formed a habit of sleeping with it there ever since his marriage fell apart.

Swinging out of bed, he made his way to the en-suite bathroom and splashed cold water on his face. It was 4 AM, and he hoped the gunshot hadn't awakened the neighborhood. Staring at himself in the vanity mirror, he tried to determine whether it had been a genuine dream or if Moloch had somehow invaded his mind through occult means. He concluded that being on the wagon made him sleep lightly, and his nightmares were likely a result of this. The last time he had such a visitation was over a year ago, and it hadn't been as violent. Thacka needed something to help him get back to sleep.

He opened the mirrored cabinet and examined his assortment of medications. He opted for a bottle of Melatonin. A former girlfriend, a flight attendant, had praised its ability to reset the body clock. She had used it during her Sydney to London flights, which wreaked havoc on her sleep patterns. Melatonin had apparently solved her problem, and Thacka had inherited the bottle of pills after her last visit.

As he contemplated the bed, his mind wandered to memories of her, lying there naked, waiting for him. He thought, "If it was good enough for you, Lorraine, then it's good enough for me." He swallowed a tablet and stumbled back into bed. The thought momentarily distracted him from the horrors of his recurring Moloch nightmare. The last thing he saw before turning out the light was the blown-out hole in the side of his bedroom doorframe, where the bullet had impacted. At least the gunshot had been real.

The bedroom was a mess, with clothes strewn everywhere. Steve had spent the night sorting through his personal belongings, trying to separate them from Niki's. It was an emotional and sleepless task, symbolising the finality of their separation. On the left side of the bed, he had created a pile of his own clothes, while on the right, a massive heap of Niki's belongings was formed. On top of her pile, he had attached a note that read: "This is your stuff, the other pile is mine— we'll sort the rest out in court." It was a vindictive response to her phone call, fuelled by his belief that she was cheating on him.

Steve, dishevelled and yawning, stumbled into the spare room and sat down at the computer. It was already 10 AM according to the computer clock. He desperately needed a coffee to alleviate the unpleasant taste in his mouth and the sandpaper texture of his tongue. After booting up the computer, he noticed a message from Rebekah, indicating that she was online. He quickly opened the message and greeted her.

Kaspar: Hey!

Rebekah: Hey to you!

Kaspar: What are you doing online so late in the morning, no work?

Rebekah: Tween jobs, just hanging in the house. Got a webcam?

Kaspar: Yeah.

Rebekah: Do you see the little icon on the bottom of the window?

Kaspar: Yep.

Rebekah: Click it.

Steve followed her instructions, and a box opened on the screen, revealing a woman in her thirties with jet-black waist-length hair. A few long white strands framed her face. Her pallid complexion, black lipstick, and heavily painted eyes made a striking impression on him. He couldn't help but think, "If ever I was going to chat with a real witch, then this is it."

Feeling self-conscious, he ran his fingers through his unkempt medium-length brown hair and then smiled at the camera. Now, they didn't need to type their conversation; they had sound and vision.

"Rebekah, I didn't have you pictured as being so pretty."

"Ha! I bet you say that to all the girls."

"No, seriously, this is my first time in a chat room."

"Well, if it's any consolation, you don't look like what I expected either. Most of the guys on Veil chat are pretty ordinary looking. You look like you just woke up."

"You got that right... long night... long story," he said dismissively.

"Are you into the black arts?"

"I'm willing to learn."

"Why?"

"There has to be more to life than what I've been experiencing lately."

"Most dudes take drugs for their kicks," she scoffed.

"Yeah, well, we've all been there, but the side effects can be a drag. There's got to be more to it than what drugs offer."

"Oh, yeah, there sure is. But you need the right partners."

"Do you mean sexual partners or what?" Steve asked.

"Yeah, to challenge your emotional boundaries and take you to places where angels fear to tread."

"Where angels fear to tread! Hey, now you're talking."

"Show me your cock."

"Uh?" he exclaimed shocked.

"Show it to me."

Steve was taken aback but the intrigue and the possibility of a cheap thrill overruled his modesty. He stood up, lowered his shorts and exposed himself to camera.

"Hmm, very nice... give it a rub for me. I want to watch it grow."

He did as she asked keen to see where she was taking him and started to become aroused. Then he noticed she was masturbating. That fired him up big time and they both went for it, feeding on each other's excitement through cyberspace. Without saying another word, she leaned back and raised the front of her black dress to give him to a clear view. He glared at her shaved womanhood and got off on how her slender fingers so sensually massaged it. Both of them were hugely turned on and they quickly climaxed.

Once she'd finished she smiled at him cheekily, completely unembarrassed by cybersex with a stranger. "There, wasn't that fun? Imagine how much further we could take it. Let's chat tonight. Bye."

And the screen went blank leaving Steve panting for more.

CHAPTER 6

Oh visions
Self and selfless, whole and apart
True and fearless, true to my art
I see deep, I see far, oh visions come to me
True to my heart and what I see

Thackeray was seated in a chair in front of the murder wall, gazing at the photo of Moloch when Parker entered the incident room with a folder tucked under her arm.

"Got the report from forensics, no DNA matches on the Willy with anyone on record."

Thackeray ran his fingers through his hair, reclined in the chair, and stretched. He was frustrated.

"Same as always, but it means zip. The DNA database is still in its infancy. What about your reporter, what's-his-name?"

"Steve, yes... he rang in a while ago. He's made contact with a witch named Rebekah. He's going to set up a meet. The first step towards getting into the circle, so to speak."

"Aha," he stretched again. "I hope he doesn't find trouble."

"You look exhausted, not getting enough sleep?"

"Yeah, being on the wagon does that every time."

"Well, you might look tired, but at least you don't look hungover."

"I don't know if there's much of a difference, to be honest," he chuckled.

"Well, keep it up, mate. It's a good look. Connie mentioned there was a little chemistry detected between you and a certain Mrs Dixon yesterday. What was that all about?"

"Good Lord, doesn't news travel fast around here. She's a nice woman. Just lost her husband... but I think it'll be a while before she's ready to see anyone."

"Oh, I wouldn't be so sure about that, Mr Self-conscious."

"Thanks for the advice; you're probably right, but I don't have the best track record when it comes to women."

"Things and attitudes change over time, Thacka, believe me."

"I just don't know how to be myself with her?"

"Yeah, well, the 'me' you think you are might not be the 'me' you really are. There's been a bit of water under the bridge since your last divorce, hasn't there?"

"Yep, I suppose so. Anyhow, tell me more about—"

"Hang on, Mr Trying-to-change-the-subject-person you. I sense there's more to this than you're letting on."

"How perceptive of you—she has a six-year-old son."

"So? Ah! I see—you fear history repeating itself."

"Well, maybe," he admitted.

"You didn't run over your son, Thacka."

"Nope."

"It's what you want, isn't it? A family, a son? It's all you've ever wanted."

"Maybe so." He stuck a toothpick between his teeth.

"So, what do you want me to tell Kaspar?"

"Who's Kaspar?"

"Steve's undercover occult name, apparently it means the keeper of the treasured secret."

"Which is, of course, that he's undercover."

"Precisely."

He stood up and eyeballed Moloch's picture on the Murder Wall. "Kaspar is all we have for now, so let's hope he gets us a lead. Warn him to keep an ear out for the name Wolfen Moloch, just in case it gets mentioned in dispatches."

She joined him at the Murder Wall. "Geez, he's a creepy-looking dude. Look at that scar over his eye down his cheek, looks like he's been slashed."

"It's a pity it didn't kill him."

"How did you learn about him, and what made you suspect him in the first place?"

"The informant that dropped off the radar."

"Not the same informant you were talking to when…"

"Yes, when Ricky was run over, he told me Moloch was the top dog warlock in Sydney and had a reputation for liking little boys. That was only a couple of days before the first penis turned up. When I went to talk with Moloch at his Waverly home, he gave me the creeps—he taunted me. I tailed him for a week, but he was onto me and took me on a wild goose chase. I suppose it's one of those cop things for me, a gut feeling—I know I'm right about him. But we have to connect him to an incident."

"Okay, I'll tell Kaspar. What happened to your informant?"

"Oh, he just stopped calling, and I couldn't get hold of him."

"Didn't you think that was odd?"

"No, it happens a lot with informants. They lose their nerve or they move on. Anyhow, other work distracted me at the time."

"Do you have an address on him?" Parker asked.

"Yes, checked it out a couple of times. He lives alone in Matraville. Never anybody there."

"Might be worth dropping by. When did you last hear from him?"

"A month ago, he was a bit odd."

"Why?"

"I don't know. Never met him in person, always over the phone, and he insisted on ringing me and never gave his number. Got his address when he called once from a cellphone, trapped it, and checked it."

"Still, he went to ground?"

"Look, this case has been almost a hobby to me. You know as well as anyone that I've only kept it open on the side. I still had to do my job. So I just let him go."

"Is he in a witches clan?"

"Said he dabbled. Oh, and thanks for that."

"What's that?"

"Our little talk about my lady problems."

"Ah, I told you, for me, it comes with the partnership."

"Yeah, well, it seems to be all about me. What about you?"

"Don't worry about me; I travel life's journey free of the burden of luggage."

"For now," he smiled.

"For now," she smiled back.

That night, Steve settled into a chair in front of his computer, anxious to chat with Rebekah. He'd been thinking about her all day and this time planned to set up a meeting with her, especially since Parker had told him about their suspect: Wolfen Moloch. But first, he needed to be sure he was on the right track with Rebekah; he couldn't afford to have his time wasted.

As soon as he opened his computer, he found her there waiting for him.

"Hey Rebekah."

"Hi."

"What have you been doing today?"

"Well I shaved my pussy for you. Do you want to see?"

"Sure."

She stood, pulled down her black jeans, slipped off her tiny white panties and showed off her beautiful clean-shaven cleave.

"What do you think?"

"Looks good enough to eat."

"She's been waiting for you."

Aware that if he got into another cybersex session she'd probably sign off before he had a chance to ask some questions, he tried to manipulate the conversation to get some answers.

"Hey, why don't we meet up and take this a little further, you know, in the flesh?"

She tilted the camera up to show a sombre face.

"Don't you want to play on line?"

"Yeah sure, but it doesn't exactly go where angels fear to tread, does it?"

"Uh huh."

"What do you think?"

"I don't know, maybe you won't like me in the flesh."

"I don't think there's any chance of that, your flesh looks pretty good to me."

He poked he tongue out at camera. It was an impressive length.

"Oh wow!" she howled.

"Yes, known in my school days as the windscreen wiper."

"Okay, sold, so when's good for you?"

"That depends on where we meet—your place or mine?"

"A café—in the city?" she suggested.

"Hmm, Okay. Day or night?"

"Day. Soon," she said, with excitement in her intonation.

"Well, today is Tuesday so how about tomorrow at eleven."

"At the Circle Café in Balmain," she said.

"Eleven AM, it's a date."

"Now let me see that big beautiful weapon of yours."

Steve's best friend, Morgan, entered the house through the side gate. Ralph bounded up to him and begged for a head scratch.

"Hey Ralph, where's your master?" he said, rubbing Ralph's head. The patio doors were open, so he let himself inside. Morgan and Steve had been friends for years since they met at the local Clovelly pub. They had many interests in common, particularly cricket; both supported the same rugby league side, the Rabbitohs, and drinking, though not necessarily in that order.

He called out, "Mate, you home?"

Morgan was unemployed and survived on the dole. A rough diamond, nicknamed 'Pencil' for being scrawny, he wore his hair long and unkempt, and he dressed like the pauper he was. His favourite pastime was betting on the horses, and to that end, he spent most of his time at the local betting shop, when he wasn't panhandling to scrounge up pin money. He made his way upstairs thinking Steve would be at work on his computer.

When he opened the door to the study, he found Steve jerking off in front of the computer.

Steve nearly fell off his chair when he realised he had company, and hurriedly fastened up his pants. But it was too late, he'd been caught with them down.

"Spanking the monkey buddy? Hey check her out, she's going for it!" he said pointing at the computer screen.

The camera was still on Rebekah.

"Got to go Rebekah. Bye!" Steve said, as he quickly shut down his computer about to explode from embarrassment.

"Mate, don't stop on my behalf. I can wait downstairs while you take the top off," Morgan scoffed jokingly.

"Just having a bit of innocent fun mate. Let's go down and grab a beer."

"Man, I feel like I've interrupted something magic. I don't mind waiting till yer finish, serious."

"Naw, come on."

Steve led Morgan downstairs to the kitchen.

"So who was the bird then? From what I could see of her she looked a bit of a sort, mate."

"Just one of those webcam sites where you pay for a bit of fun."

"How come? What happened to the missus?"

They arrived in the kitchen, and Steve grabbed two bottles of beer from the otherwise empty refrigerator, handing one to Morgan.

"We've split up."

Morgan unscrewed the top off his beer and offered his bottle for a toast. They clinked bottles.

"Cheers!" Morgan said, then took a big swig from the bottle. "Ah, crap, mate, that's no good. Nik was a real good sort."

"Yeah, she's coming over Sunday to pick her stuff up."

"But we'll be at the cricket."

"Yeah, she won't come here unless I'm out. How's that?"

"Ah, she's got a new fella, then?" Morgan said intuitively.

"I reckon so, but she won't admit it."

"Mate, they never do. Sooner or later you'll be in a bus or somethin', and you'll see her walkin' down the street hand in hand with some ugly dickhead… and you know what?"

"What?"

"Mate, can you turn on the TV? There's a race in a sec, I've got a few skins on it."

"Yeah, no worries," Steve said as he strolled into the living room looking for the remote.

"Where's the bloody remote?"

"Probably under all this stuff," Morgan said, lifting an empty pizza box from the table. "There you go!" He fired up the big flat screen. "S'pose all this stuff will be going then? Who's getting the pad, TV, and all?" Morgan asked.

They sat on the lounge in front of the TV. The next race was about to start.

"She owns everything, and the joint's only rented. I won't be able to afford the rent. I'll have to let it go. I own half the car."

"You can move in with me, mate—my flat's got a spare room. I'm only using it for me dirty washing."

As much as he liked him, Steve couldn't imagine anything worse than moving in with a grub like Morgan.

"No, thanks mate, I'm thinking of finding a gaff in town; I've got a gig there."

"Shhh, they're racing, man."

They watched the race in silence. Morgan practically rode the horse all the way, but it missed getting a place.

"Stuff it! There goes my trifecta. You said you had a gig, doing what, mate?"

"I'm an undercover reporter for a true crime magazine."

"Unreal! That's amazing, man. What does that mean?"

"I'm like a private detective. I go out and find real crime stories, then write them up for a magazine. Then, they pay me."

"Cool. Did they give you any up-front?"

"No, pay on delivery."

"Shit, mate, where you gonna get the dosh to survive?"

"I'm just going to have to make some adjustments to my lifestyle."

"Yer better get on the rock 'n roll, mate."

"I guess so, it'd be my first time on the dole."

"What case are ya working on?" Morgan asked.

"I can't say much, as you would understand, but it's the serial corn flake killer case."

"Sounds like breakfast to me. Got any weed, mate?"

The air was dry from the searing heat of the say. The eerie glow from bushfires lit up the western sky, highlighting the crimson blaze of the setting sun, as Thacka made his way from his car to the front door of the Dixon residence. The porch light was on and had attracted hundreds of Bogong moths—so many that Thacka had to wave his hand to sweep them away from his face. The door opened, and he was immediately awestruck by Sarah's beauty; she looked ravishing.

"Hi Bill. Quick, come in before the Bogong's eat holes in your clothes."

"Howdy, Sarah. Yeah, since the big storm the other day and the heat, they've hatched out, now there's a plague of the blighters," he smiled into her dazzling green eyes. "You look great."

Sarah blushed.

Russell ran excitedly up to Thacka.

"Hi Detective Bill!" he stuck out a hand to shake.

Thacka leaned down and took it.

"Hey partner. Look what I've brought you," he showed off a pizza box.

"But I'm not allowed to eat pizza," Russell said dejectedly.

"Why not?" Thacka cast Sarah a quizzical glance.

"Dad said so."

"Yes, that's right, Russell, but now that you're older, you're allowed," Sarah suggested diplomatically, as she led Thacka into the living room. The 6 PM evening news was on TV with the sound turned down.

They sat down, Bill still holding the pizza box, and Russell ran off to play.

"Have you been busy?"

"Not really. We're at a stalemate with the case I'm on."

"Wolfen Moloch?"

"Yeah, gee, you've got a good memory."

"More a face I'm not likely to forget."

"Yeah, it sticks in your mind, doesn't it?"

Then he noticed something on the television.

"Can you turn the TV up for a second, please?"

Sarah fetched the remote and raised the volume.

A news reporter was standing outside a shopping mall.

"A seven-year-old child was abducted this evening from his mother at Westfield Eastgardens shopping centre. The man, well over six feet tall and wearing a grey hoodie, took the little boy and ran off. Fortunately, a shopper heard the mother's frantic screams for help, sighted the man, and rammed him with a shopping trolley, causing him to free the boy."

Thackeray didn't wait for the news item to finish; he switched into action mode and made hastily for the front door.

"I'm sorry, Sarah, but this could be the break I've been after. I have to go; say bye to Russell for me."

Just as he stepped outside, he remembered he still had the pizza and turned to offer it to her.

"Enjoy."

"Thanks Bill. No problem."

She watched him run to his car and called after him,

"Be careful. Give me a ring later!"

He waved acknowledgment, hopped into his car, and sped off.

It was after 6 PM, and the peak-hour traffic had subsided enough to allow Thackeray to drive from the Dixon house in Randwick to Eastgardens Shopping Centre in no time flat. En-route, he phoned Parker. It would take her longer to get there coming from the office in Surry Hills where she'd been working, back-hunting for leads.

Thacka pulled up at the crime scene that was made obvious by the blue flashing lights from half a dozen stationary police vehicle parked at oblique angles. He didn't bother to find a parking spot; he just left his car and jogged over toward the scene, looking for whoever seemed to be in command. He discovered that Officer Connie Lee was in charge.

"Hey Connie, what's up?"

"Thacka, what brings you to this neck of the woods; late-night shopping?"

He smiled at her joke, "No, I've got enough baked beans in my pantry to last a lifetime. Saw it on the news, and the MO vaguely fits my case, thought I'd better check it out."

Miller ambled over to them filled to the brim with his trademark sarcasm, "Sale on cereals attracted you, Thacka?"

"Didn't know they let you out at night, Miller?"

Connie ignored Miller and filled Thacka in. "Not a lot to tell you really, no clear description of the perp, just a lot of freaked-out folks. That bloke over there talking to the press is Jamie Roddick; he rammed the perp with a shopping trolley. If he hadn't done so, we'd be investigating a kidnapping for sure. He got the best look at him." She paused as they watched the interview wrap up. "He's free now, go and have a chat."

As she watched Thacka sauntering over to the young man she was joined by Miller.

"Hear the old boy's on the wagon, gets a bit grumpy, a sure indicator."

"Why don't you get off his back, Miller? He's a good cop, something you might pick up from him."

Miller turned up his nose, "All he could teach me is how to best get over a hangover."

Thacka assessed the Roddick to be in his mid-twenties. He flashed his ID. "G'day, Mr Roddick, DI Thackeray. Did you happen to get a look at him?"

Roddick was dressed like he'd been at football training. He was a bulky, broad-shouldered lad with short-cropped brown hair and shaved sides.

His forehead wrinkled, "No mate, was all too quick and too dark, wasn't it," he said with a cockney accent. "Plus I was making bleedin' sure I didn't whack the boy."

"Nothing you saw that would allow you to pick him out in a lineup?"

"No guv, he was wearing a grey hoodie, looked just like any uvver bloke, just taller, about six two or three and seriously bulked up, must work out or he's on roids or sumpthin."

"That's good info, thanks. You all right?"

"Yeah, just lucky we got the boy off him then. Why do you fink he was trying to nick him?"

"Dunno mate, body parts, sex, whatever. Here's my card, if you remember anything, give me a bell."

"Yeah guv, talk to the kid; he got the best squiz at him."

As Thackeray made his way through the uniforms, press, and spectators back to Connie Lee, he noticed Parker walking his way.

"I heard on the radio; it sounds like it might have been Moloch. Did you get a description?" Parker said enthusiastically, a little out of breath from the rush.

As Thackeray led her over to Connie Lee, he said, "Not so far, but I've been told the boy might have got a look at the perp."

They came to Connie, who was consoling the distraught mother of the boy.

"Howd'ya go, Thacka?"

"Not much joy, he gave me a general description which helps a bit, but not much more... any chance of having a chat with the lad? Roddick thinks he might have got a look at the perp?"

"Yeah, sure but..."

"What's the problem, is he too upset?" Parker asked.

The teary-eyed mother of the boy spoke up, "No, he has Asperger's... it's difficult to get him to talk."

"Ah, I understand. Are you all right?" Parker asked her with a sympathetic tone.

The mother nodded her head and wiped tears from her eyes. Connie put her arm around the woman's shoulders and then nodded in the direction of the boy.

The mother looked up and said, "Richard, his name is Richard."

Thackeray and Parker made their way over to the ambulance where a paramedic was attending to Richard. Parker made the first move.

"Hello. Your Mum told me your name is Richard; my name is Parker."

The boy was sitting in the rear of the ambulance wrapped in a blanket. He sniffled and looked the other way, distant, as though Parker didn't exist.

Parker mumbled to Thackeray, "That was my best shot."

"Hey partner, looks nice and warm in that blanket?" Thacka tried.

The boy glanced at him, it was something... at least the boy had acknowledged his existence.

"Did you see the man's face, Richard?" Thackeray asked.

The boy looked away.

"I don't think you'll get him to talk. Too difficult for him to describe the kidnapper." The female paramedic explained.

A nod from Thackeray and Parker betrayed their agreement that pursuing it any further seemed to be futile.

"Thanks Richard, catch you later," Thacka said.

Just as they turned to head back toward Connie Lee, a single word from the boy stopped them in their tracks.

"Star."

Galvanized, Thacka turned back to Richard and asked gently, "A star, Richard, where?"

Richard hesitated, then opened the blanket, stuck out his left hand, and touched Thackeray on the forearm. Thackeray smiled at the little boy.

"Thank you, partner," he returned to Parker.

"A star?" she inquired.

"Yeah, a tattoo, I'd say, on the perp's forearm. We've got a lead, Parker. Let's get back to the office. We'll need to check some photos of our buddy Moloch. This might be enough to arrest him on suspicion."

"I should have brought a photo of him. Could've shown it to Richard," Parker said regretfully.

"Nah, it's okay."

Getting into her car, parked opposite Eastgardens Shopping Centre on Bunnerong Road, Parker looked up at a street sign pointing south, reading Denison Street, Matraville—and it rang a bell. That was where Thackeray's informant lived. She speed-dialled, "Hi Thacka, it's me. What's your informant's address? I'm heading towards Matraville and might as well stop by... Uh-huh, forty-two Perry, yeah, why not? No, I'll be fine—meet you at the office. Yeah, well, you never know your luck in the big city. I'll be careful. Bye."

Driving north through Kingsford en-route to Surry Hills, Thacka ended Parker's call and mumbled, "Keenest cop I've ever known." He dialled Sarah, "Hi there, how was that pizza? Great, oh, I'll grab a burger or something when I get to the office... Yes, it might be a long night. We got a lead; the boy saw a tattoo on the kidnapper's forearm... No, he's autistic and couldn't describe the man. Yes, it's something, but it will mean sifting through stacks of records to see if we can find anything about Moloch having a star tattoo on his forearm... No, we'd need more solid grounds to arrest him—can't arrest people on suspicion anymore, unfortunately. Parker will be there to help. Okay, talk to you tomorrow. Good night."

Parker stopped outside 42 Perry Street. The house was a ramshackle old weatherboard affair with a rusted corrugated iron roof and a horribly overgrown front lawn. It looked as though it had been vacant for a considerable time. Parker noticed the letterbox was full of leaflets. After inspecting them, she determined it had been last emptied about a month ago, which tallied with Thackeray's last contact. She was about to open the wooden gate in the mostly dilapidated front picket fence when a gruff voice stopped her.

"Hasn't been anyone there for weeks."

Parker turned her attention to the neighbor sitting in a chair on the veranda of the house next door. He was in his mid-seventies, bald, wearing a grubby white singlet and khaki shorts, and resting a stubby on his huge beer gut.

"Detective Parker, and you're?"

"Eric Gilbert, lived here seventy-six years."

"When did you last see the owner?"

"Riley? Oh, 'bout a month ago. Guy's a pain in the butt, never mows the bloody lawn—look at the state of the bloody joint, it's a disgrace and it stinks! Me and the missus reckon he locked his cats in there when he blew through, and they died in there—he had four of 'em, you know? Big bastards too! Haven't seen 'em or heard 'em— you know what cats are like in spring, on heat looking for a mate and all, well, we've heard nothing."

"Why didn't you call the police?"

"Kept expecting him to come back... it's not the first time he's gone bloody walkabout, and I'm not his keeper. If you ask me, he's on drugs, a bloody weirdo."

"Does Mr Riley own the house?"

"Yeah, he inherited it about six years ago from his mother when she died; she was a good old stick. They found her dead in there sitting in her chair in front of the TV with a look on her face like she'd seen the devil." He genuflected, nearly knocking over his beer in the process.

"Thanks, Mr Gilbert, I'll just take a look around."

"Sure enough, I'll be here when you're finished if you need me."

Parker went to the front door and tried the door handle— locked—she didn't really expect it to be open. Even though it was dark, she decided to walk around the side of the house to try and get a glimpse through a window.

He was right about the smell, phew! Something was dead. Is it time for her to call backup? But she decided to just take a quick look first. One of the side windows had a gap in the curtain. She took her trusty penlight from her pocket and put it up to the glass. Suddenly, a snarling cat with a huge pair of glowing red eyes smacked against the window. The fright caused her to stagger backward.

She yelped, "Shit!"

With her hand on her chest, she took a couple of deep breaths, trying to ease her heart rate down from one hundred and twenty beats per minute. Once she'd collected herself she thought, I've got to let the poor thing out. She continued to the back of the house and tried the back door—surprisingly, it was unlocked. She hesitated a second, then pushed the door wide and stepped back. Lucky she did, almost instantly two cats came hurtling toward her from inside, and she leapt back out of their way as they zipped past her exactly like proverbial scalded cats, out into the yard and into the waist-high grass and were gone. Then the stench hit her—the place reeked of abandonment. She turned back to the doorway, framing the blackness inside. The other two cats must be dead—they've probably been eating them... a month and in this heat. Oh, well, in for a penny...

With those brave words and her nose covered with a handkerchief, she set her handbag down on the step, took a couple of deep breaths, and slipped her Glock from her waistband holster. Then she called out sternly, "Hello! Police, is there anyone here?" With no reply, holding her penlight torch, pointed forward in her reversed left hand, she braced her right gun hand on her left wrist and stepped inside. The stench was so foul it got past her perfumed handkerchief—she fought back nausea. The narrow beam of her penlight shone on the steps and doorway that led from where she was in the back veranda to the kitchen, and the muzzle of her pistol tracked the beam as she scanned back and forth. She went up three steps into the filthy dilapidated kitchen—a tap was dripping in the kitchen sink. That's where the cats had got their water. There were cat faeces all over the Linoleum—the entire kitchen floor had been used as a giant kitty litter. She saw a light switch and flicked it with her left hand, the pistol in her right pointed toward the rest of the house. A fluorescent light blinked on. Well, at least there's power... she muttered into her handkerchief, surprised and still edgy. The glow from the kitchen light allowed her to see into the living room. As soon as she stepped on the carpet there she was overcome by a feeling of dread. In the dim light, she could see the body of a dead cat on the floor, half eaten and alive with maggots. She swept the room, muzzle and torch beam locked together and her penlight found the light switch for that room. Dodging more cat droppings on the shagpile carpet she turned on the light. There was only one active globe in the old six-globe candelabra light fitting slung from the centre of the ceiling. Other than the maggot-swarmed dead cat and the scattered cat crap, there seemed to be nothing else out of the ordinary, furniture undisturbed, windows all sealed shut. Then she noticed that the phone had been wrenched out of the wall, and in the hallway leading to the main front bedroom, there were cat prints in the shagpile—bloody cat prints. She followed them, past the door to the small bathroom toward the door of the master bedroom. It was slightly ajar, enough for a cat to enter, and she could hear a soft buzzing noise.

Her tension was increasing—her heart rate was back to drumming at 120 bpm. There was something wrong in the main bedroom—she could sense it, and she could hear it. She raised her pistol and penlight, placed the muzzle of the Glock on the door, and softly pushed. It swung open, and a cloud of blowflies immediately hit her. She frantically waved her arms in front of her face, conscious of the loaded firearm. With her nose uncovered, she recognized the stench—it was the distinctive sickly, sweetish, smell of human decomposition, so thick in the air she could taste it. She spotted the light switch inside the door, flicked it on, and was immediately overcome—her gorge rose, her arms dropped and she leaned forward and vomited on the carpet at her feet. As the spasms passed, she slowly and reluctantly raised her head. On the bed, naked, on his back and spread-eagled, lay Riley—his hands had been severed at the wrist and left on his chest. Cats had eaten his cheeks and lips down to the bone giving him a ghoulish skeletal grimace—his genitals had been cut off, as had his tongue. Razor wire was looped around his throat and fastened to the headboard of the bed. There was died blood everywhere —the floor and the bedclothes writhed with maggots and there were blowflies buzzing all over the room. Riley had been tortured—the blood spatter on the walls was from him waving his handless arms about. Parker stood back from Riley's corpse careful not to step in blood pooled on the floor. She swallowed sour bile that rose with each breath she took of Riley's putrid decomposing flesh, and then she used her phone to snap half a dozen digital photographs of the crime scene. Thacka sat back from his computer to check his buzzing cell phone. It was an incoming text from Parker. The text asked a single question: is this Riley? He opened the first photo.

Parker was making her way along the gloomy hallway of Riley's house when her mobile rang. Caller ID said it was Thacka. She stopped and answered. "You got the pics then? Okay, we have to assume it's Riley, better send mop-up team and forensics. I'm on my way back. No, I need to get out of here before I throw up again. Yeah, it's gross all right!"

Parker entered the office pale, drawn, flopped into a chair, and put her face in her hands. Thackeray got out of his chair and put a consoling hand on her shoulder.

"Kitty and forensics are there; it must have been terrible."

"You've got no idea, Thacka. He'd been there for a month, his cats had been eating him—and he'd been mutilated. Argh!" she shivered at the memory, sat up straight, and sighed. She had to accept it because it came with the job. "Can't get the smell out of my nose... Was there anything for Kitty?"

"No," he shoved a toothpick between his lips and paced. "Not a bloody print—blood from one end of the bedroom to the other and not even a shoe print—un-bloody-believable!"

"A ritual slaying I'd say."

"For talking too much?" he said.

"I think so. How did you get on here?"

"I'll need glasses if I have to look at the screen any longer. There's not even an arrest description of him!" he stretched, "Let's call it a day."

"There's only one thing left to do, Thacka."

"What's that?"

"Put an eyeball on him."

"Last time I tried that, he dry-cleaned me."

"Dry-cleaned?"

Thacka took the toothpick out of his mouth and shot her his customary sardonic grin with one raised, thought you'd know that, eyebrow.

"Left me at the cleaners so to speak. Look, I've never been able to pin anything on the bastard. Closest I got was what Riley told me, but it was never enough to get me a warrant to make an arrest—just like this time."

"You tried, of course."

"Sure, I tried so many bloody times it made me the laughing stock of the magistrate's office. Even with Riley murdered, there's only hearsay Moloch was involved—my word, and for too long, that ain't been worth crap round here."

A pregnant pause fell between them while they took count of each other. She knew he was right—they needed something concrete to get a warrant to arrest Moloch.

"I'll get on it tomorrow, but I'm over it for now, I'm going home," Parker groaned, rising tiredly to her feet.

"You think Moloch did Riley, don't you?" he asked.

"It sure adds up, but why? Why would he torture him and leave him like that?" she could feel the bile rising in her throat, the image of the corpse, the putrid smell.

"I reckon it was a warning for me to butt out, a demonstration of his power... his savagery and his cleverness. He's challenging me," Thacka barked angrily.

Without having to say so, they both knew that the casual brutality and audacity of Riley's murder meant they were up against a monster even more dangerous than they had believed, and what made that thought even worse—was knowing Moloch was a cunning monster.

It was 11:15 AM, and Steve was running late for his rendezvous with Rebekah. He was lucky to find a parking spot for his rent-a-wreck VW Beetle, a stone's throw from the Circle Café in Darling Street Balmain. He raced into the café front garden and stopped dead, realising he'd attracted the attention of the patrons. He scanned for Rebekah and sighted a dark-haired lady garbed in a gothic black dress seated at a table under an umbrella—it had to be her. He hurried over.

"Rebekah?"

She looked up through round rose-coloured sunglasses, and her black-painted lips parted with an ever-so-slight smile. "Kaspar," she purred like a cat.

He sat on the log seat and sighed, "Phew! I'm sorry for being late, never been a punctual kind of guy."

She sipped on a black coffee with a cute smile, then removed her sunglasses and fixed her deep black heavily made-up eyes on him.

"That's okay, I only just arrived myself."

He felt her eyes reach into his very soul, and it chilled him to the bone.

"I'll get a coffee," he said nervously, looking about for a waiter.

She raised a pointed finger, and a waiter materialised as if out of thin air, ready to take the order.

"A soy latte, thanks," he ordered, wondering where the waiter had come from.

"What happened last night? It felt like coitus interruptus," she said sexily, licking the corner of her mouth.

"Oh, a friend barged into my room and caught us in the act."

"So you live with friends, then?"

"No, on my own, but he just wandered in."

"Don't you lock the door?"

"I've got a dog, so I leave the back door open."

"And didn't the dog bark?"

"Probably not, Ralph knows my mate, but then maybe I was a little preoccupied at the time to hear him if he did knock."

They exchanged knowing smiles.

The waiter brought Steve's latte and placed it in front of him. It was then that Steve noticed the jewellery the waiter was wearing and recognised he was a Goth.

"He one of your flock?"

"You mean coven."

"Sorry."

"No, another coven."

"Do they all meet here?" he said, looking around in case there might be a vampire present.

"As the name implies."

"Are there many covens in Sydney?"

"Yes, quite a few. Not all dark, some are different shades of grey."

He knew she was talking figuratively.

"Which end of the colour spectrum is your coven?

"Nuit noire," she said with smiling eyes.

"Is that satanical?"

"Would that frighten you?"

"Not really."

"You did say you wanted to experience where angels fear to tread. Like what? What haven't you experienced?"

"Well, I've been reading about Pagan and Wicca rituals, and maybe it's my imagination, but I get the impression there could be a lot of free love going on at them, and I'd like to experience that."

"You mean a sex orgy at a Sabbat?"

He noticed that when she mentioned the word sex or anything

to do with sex, her eyes opened a little wider than normal and she licked her lips ever so slightly. He thought to himself, hell, you're a sexy little thing.

"Well... Yeah," he said tentatively.

"Where witches dance naked around a fire, working themselves into a frenzy, before indulging in wild coitus with each other or whoever else might be present?"

"Yeah, that's it, that's the menu."

She smiled devilishly and took his hand.

"Do you really believe that sort of thing happens—here—in Sydney?"

"I hope it does," he said with a cheeky smile, as he lifted her hand and licked the webbing between two of her fingers.

Just then, something large loomed over them, blocking out the sun—they had been all but consumed by a dark shadow. Steve peered up at the giant silhouette of a man.

Rebekah smiled at the silhouette in a manner that would suggest they had been lovers or perhaps still were.

"Kaspar, this is a friend of mine, Oscar.

CHAPTER 7

As the moon waxes and wanes,
and walks three nights in darkness,
so the Goddess once spent three nights
in the kingdom of death.

Parker walked into Thackeray's office on a mission. She flopped into a chair and swivelled it to face him at his computer.

"How goes it, boss?"

He looked at her with one eyebrow raised, "I used to be indecisive. Now I'm not so sure."

Parker sat silently for a moment.

"That's a paraprosdokian, isn't it? I'm impressed."

Thacka's jaw dropped. Damn, she's NOT just a pretty face. Thacka stammered, "Good enough for Churchill to collect, good enough for me."

"Any more news from the Riley crime scene?" she asked.

"Yes, according to Kitty it took him an hour or so to die."

"But both his hands were..."

"The killer had put a tourniquet around his arms—there were ligature marks above the elbows—to make sure he died slowly—he actually bled out from the severed tongue. Oh, it actually wasn't severed, his tongue had been ripped out."

"Argh, cripes... Glad I had a light breakfast. Nothing else?" she groaned.

"Not a print or a hair follicle other than Riley's—wiped clean—the two cats died of natural causes. You?"

"I finally heard from Steve."

"Oh really, well it's about time, here it is Friday afternoon and you've heard nothing since when—Tuesday?"

"Okay, okay, settle down, he's done well. He's been invited to a witches Sabbat on Saturday night at midnight."

Thacka folded his arms in front of him. "What's that, a bunch of ratbag hags getting together to exchange herbal remedies or is it the real thing?"

"He reckons it's the whole naked ritual orgy full moon box and dice number—in fact, he said it's the prelude to the witches' equivalent of the academy awards, Beltane, the festival of fertility and love at the end of the month."

"Isn't that Halloween? Doesn't sound like Moloch's speed unless there's a ritual sacrifice on the menu."

"Well, I reckon we should just put a tail on him Saturday night to find out. What do you reckon?"

"I think that's a bloody good idea, Parker, did you have anything planned?"

"Guess I do now."

Steve was excited—he reckoned it didn't get much better than being undercover at a witch's coven but deciding what to wear, now that was tough. He found a black dress shirt. Ah, yes! I remember this. Wore it to a fancy dress as a Vampire—there's the black tie here somewhere. He found the tie and a pair of black jeans. Righty-Ho! He checked the time and panicked—Shit, I'm running late!

A few minutes later, he emerged from the townhouse dressed in black jeans, a black shirt, and a thin black necktie—with his longish brown hair slicked back—he looked the part. He climbed into the green VW Beetle and headed off to pick up Rebekah en route to Seven Hills in Western Sydney.

The waxing moon was bright in the night sky over the Sydney seaside suburb of Waverly. But to Thackeray with his partner in her car outside a creepy old house that overlooked Waverly cemetery, it felt more like a scene from a Wes Craven horror flick.

"How's the sobriety going? I must say you're looking good."

"If that's a compliment there's no point coming onto me, Parker. I'm taken..." he scoffed past the toothpick clenched between his teeth.

"Sarah Dixon?"

"You know nothing is private with cops, born snoopers, comes with the territory."

"It's written all over your boat-race mate—I'm very happy for you," She grinned.

Silence prevailed. She was wondering whether to talk more about his new relationship. While he was hoping she wouldn't. She chose not to.

"What do you make of all this witchcraft stuff?"

"Oh, I don't know. It's probably not so much about what we believe but what they believe, you know, the likes of Moloch. Not much different than religion. Are you religious Parker?"

"No, my folks were agnostic. What about you?"

"My folks were serious foot-stampers."

"What's a foot-stamper?"

"It used to be a secret code exchanged by Catholics to identify one another. Came about during the reign of Elizabeth I in the 1560s when the Crown was persecuting Catholics because they supported the Catholic Queen Mary. That's why they devised the secret identifying code."

"Like a Masonic handshake?"

"Yes. Don't see much foot stamping these days, but in my folk's day, they still did it. No, I'm not religious at all, can't you tell by the way I take being cursed so seriously?"

"Well, I did a little extra research on the whole Moloch warlock premise, and there are some very strange cases bearing some similarity in various police records, especially on the Scotland Yard database."

"Yeah, like this one?"

"In 1931 a penis was found in London's Hyde Park, then another one in 1932."

"Any bodies turn up?"

"Not a one."

"Did they solve it?"

"No. They didn't even have a suspect. Cases like that were just filed away under 'occult stroke suspected ritual killings,' so it seems they were on the same track as us, only the trail went dry."

"Were they adult penises?"

"No, same MO, thought to be aged six to ten."

Thackeray removed the toothpick from his mouth and dumped it in the ashtray, "I wonder if there's any connection?"

Parker thought a bit, "I think that would be tough, too long ago and not enough to go on. I wish he'd hurry up and leave, this place is giving me the creeps."

"We'd save ourselves a shit-load of drama if we could just go and knock on his door and order the prick to show us his forearms. Bloody rules—bloody rigmarole—too many civil liberties these days."

"What if he's not at home? What if he's already at the Sabbat?" she considered.

He checked the car clock; it was 11 PM.

"You know, you've got a point. We've been sitting here since sunset and seen nothing but lights going on and off inside like on timers. If he left now, I doubt he'd make it to Seven Hills before midnight."

He opened the passenger door, waited for Parker. They strode across the street to the house, and Thackeray hit the doorbell. There was music coming from inside the house.

"Only the lonely, someone's into Roy Orbison," Thackeray noted.

It was obvious to Parker he was a fan by the way he was humming along with the tune.

Roy stopped singing, and Thacka stopped humming the moment the door opened. Parker and Thacka found themselves staring down at a very angry dwarf.

Thacka flashed his ID as said sternly, "Officer's Thackeray and Parker, we're doing a house-to-house check on your block, there's been a break-in a few houses up."

The little man glared up at them like they'd pinched his lunch money. He was wearing blue overalls and a weird curly orange wig. He ripped the wig off angrily and snapped.

"Is that why you've been sitting outside casing my house since friggin' sunset?"

Thinking on her feet Parker chimed in,

"Just doing point duty at the end of the street, sir, while other officers have been sweeping the neighbourhood. Are you the only resident, sir?"

He seemed to accept her explanation.

"No, three of us live here!" he answered savagely.

Thacka figured he was in his forties and he certainly had a nasty attitude, which caused him to wonder if that was mandatory for little men—the ones he'd met seemed to be permanently pissed off.

Parker drew a notebook and pen from her pocket,

"Names please?"

"I'm Jason Little."

Thackeray nearly exploded with laughter at his name, and only just managed to quickly conceal his hysterics behind a hand, his eyes, however, failed to cloak his mirth. Jason had heard and seen it all before and so continued without his feathers ruffled.

"And, Dorrie Wilson and Mr Moloch."

"Full name?"

"Wolfen Moloch... I don't see how—"

"Are they home?" Parker cut him off while diligently jotting notes.

"Um, Dorrie's inside but Mr Moloch is out, why?"

"Okay, just for the record, do you know the whereabouts of Mr Moloch?" Thacka asked, having contained his jocundity.

"No, he hasn't been home for a couple of days."

"Does he do that often?" Parker queried.

"Yes, but I don't see what that's got to do with your investigation."

"Does Mr Moloch have a star tattooed on his forearm?"

The little man's features hardened again—he wasn't going to answer that and he slammed the door in their faces.

"Little bloke has a big chip on his shoulders!" Thackeray remarked.

Parker glanced up at the house in time to catch sight of an obese woman peering at them from behind a curtain in the front window.

"That must be Dorrie."

When Thacka gazed up, Dorrie raised an iPod and snapped a photo of them.

"I guess Wilks will have that photo on his desk tomorrow..." Parker said.

"Harassment no doubt."

Steve pulled up outside a terrace house in Newtown. It was a ramshackle affair in desperate need of repair. He beeped the horn twice... the porch light came on... the door opened, Rebekah appeared in the doorway and waved goodbye to someone inside. She was garbed in obligatory Goth black. Steve thought she looked taller than he expected. When she got into the car, the pungent aroma of Sandalwood overcame him.

"Hi, head to Ryde, I'll direct you from there. You look nice... how are you?" she said with a cute smile.

"You too, oh, I'm fine but nervous," he admitted, moving the car out into the traffic that was crawling along King Street like a monstrous metal centipede with headlights for eyes.

"Nervous about going to the Sabbat or meeting me?"

"The Sabbat, not sure what to expect I suppose."

"Here take this," she handed him a heart-shaped pink pill.

"A Molly?"

"Yeah, MDMA—the best!"

"You flying?"

"Nope, hasn't come-on yet."

"Might wait till we're a bit closer, I don't like driving when I'm out of it."

"If you drop it when we get to Ryde, you'll be soaring by the time we get to Seven Hills."

"Cool," he said, slipping the pill into the top pocket of his shirt.

"Don't be nervous, you'll have the time of your life there, I promise."

"How long have you been doing the coven thing?"

"Oh, as long as I can remember, my mother is a witch and so is her mother."

"I feel disadvantaged with you having the craft in your genes?"

"Don't worry about it you'll be fine. If you like to fuck then you'll get your fill tonight!"

"How many will be there?"

"Normally six or seven women and one or two guys."

"Six or seven! I hope I won't be expected to do all of them!"

"Nah!" she chuckled. "Most of them are lesbians but a few aren't. One of them you'll get a kick out of, Vivian, she's nearly seventy."

He nearly gagged.

"Seventy! No, I couldn't..."

"You'd be surprised, guys love giving it to her."

A big man wearing black leathers and a black bike helmet emblazoned with a red devil icon, walked over to a huge Harley Davidson chopper parked outside the Seven Hills North 7-Eleven gas station. Out of nowhere the Roy Orbison song "Only the Lonely' started playing: it was a message alert on the biker's iPhone. He drew it from his side pocket, removed his left glove and then tapped the screen to open a file he'd received from Jason Little. The note said: The two cops in the pics came to the house tonight asking weird questions about you. Jason. He clicked the first of two photos. It was of Parker and Thackeray: the shot Dorrie had taken from the window. He clicked the second photo—it was of Parker's car. A zoom in revealed the number plate. He zoomed in further and panned to clearly show Parker as the driver. A tighter zoom revealed a parking sticker on the windscreen and that gave him an idea.

When they reached Ryde, Steve dropped the ecstasy. Within fifteen minutes, due to the lack of traffic at that time of night, they were on the outskirts of Seven Hills, forty kilometres from Sydney.

"Turn next left into Beethoven Street," Rebekah said.

Steve found the street and made the turn. Not far down, he glimpsed a park through the darkness.

"Just park over there with the other cars," Rebekah said pointing to several cars parked by an entranceway to the park. Steve felt the Molly coming on, his nerves had gone; he was ready for anything. When they got out of the Beetle, Rebekah produced a blindfold from her pocket and flashed it at Steve.

"Sorry, but that's the rules."

"No worries, it adds to the intrigue. Nice Molly, I'm feeling as horny as hell."

"That's good. So am I."

Only a little shorter than Steve's five foot eleven, she rose up on to her tip toes and blindfolded him. Then she took his hand and led him along a bush track into the forest. After a few minutes of stumbling along the narrow track in the dark, they arrived at their destination. Rebekah stopped and removed Steve's blindfold.

"There you go," she grinned, stoned.

Steve was amazed by what was before him. It was a circular clearing lit by six flaming torches around its perimeter. In the flickering torchlight, gathered around a stone edifice at the centre of the clearing stood six women with their eyes fixed on him.

"Hey everyone, Merry meet, this is Kaspar!" Rebekah announced.

"Ah, Kasper, so what is your treasured secret oh wondrous one?" Chortled an old lady with waist length grey hair glaring at him as though he was wearing something that had once belonged to her.

"Perhaps that I'm not who you think I am!" he replied.

"And so it is for all of us young Kaspar... Witches!—The time is nigh!" she declared.

The women surrounded him and began peeling off his clothes.

Within seconds, he was left standing naked with his hands covering his manhood, feeling a little bashful but thankful it was a warm night. All seven women then stepped out of their dresses to stand proudly naked. With MDMA pulsing through his veins, he felt himself rising to the occasion.

The old lady spoke up, "Now we are as one with the earth in the flesh, now we speak our given names, I am Vivian."

Another older lady stepped forward, "I am Raven."

A younger woman Steve estimated to be in her early forties, buxom with ample curves, stepped up and announced, "I am Lilith."

Steve thought to himself, there's obviously a pecking order here, with Vivian the oldest and then Raven.

Next, a stunning woman Steve estimated to be in her mid-thirties stepped forward.

"I am Luna."

The next to step out was in her early thirties, with a body that seriously turned him on.

She couldn't take her eyes off Steve's manhood, which he stopped trying to hide now they were all naked. It had pretty much gotten away from him anyway.

"I am Nissa."

The last to step forward was Rebekah, the youngest member of the coven, exhibiting what Steve considered being her signature provocative smile.

"I am Rebekah."

He was admiring Rebekah's shapely body when Vivian began to prance about and chant. Her movements caused her shrivelled dugs to flap about like socks on a clothesline. The others joined in and chanted in unison.

"By earth, by wind, by land, by sea, I summon a lover to come to me. By witch's dance and Goddess tree, I summon a lover to come to me. By earth, by wind, by land, by sea, I summon a lover to come to me. By power raised I send my plea; I summon a lover to come to me!"

Steve was awestruck by the seven witches prancing about in their birthday suits. He wondered which he'd take first. Aside from Rebekah two others looked inviting, especially the blonde haired Nissa, with her full breasts, shapely body, a beautiful butt and big blue eyes that hadn't stopped flashing amorously at him since he got naked.

Suddenly, two of the coven stopped dancing and led Vivian by the arms to the edifice. Rebekah and the Nissa walked Steve over to Vivian. Rebekah stroked Steve——his head was swimming with arousal. Vivian leaned back against the altar to receive him. Driven by primordial desire, he coupled with her. At first, it felt awkward, like he was taking his grandmother, but then when she began to writhe and gyrate under him and he felt a sort of magic that emanated from within her, he was driven to pump harder and harder, in a sexual frenzy.

Vivian moaned and groaned with euphoria.

Attracted by groans of pleasure coming from beside him, Steve glanced down at Raven, Luna and Lilith fornicating as a threesome on the ground. He erupted with a climax of epic proportions.

Vivian immediately slipped out from under him and disappeared into the darkness, and before Steve had time to think, Nissa the blonde, replaced her. She turned and placed her hands flat on the altar presenting for Steve. He coupled with her and pumped with even more enthusiasm. She let out a orgasmic shriek. Steve had never experienced a sensation quite like it. With her chest heaving, Nissa slipped away from him and was immediately replaced by Rebekah, who was high on ecstasy and eager for fulfillment. She faced him, a devilish look in her eye... it brought out the animal in him. He was seriously aroused by her graceful calisthenics. Without warning two big hands gripped his shoulders. He shuddered and turned his head sharply to look behind— the hands belonged to a big brute of a man—naked, with the horned head of a goat—and... he was going to enter him! Before he had a chance to stop it, Steve felt a rush of blinding pain—his inner sanctum had been violated.

Steve woke the next morning and sat up in bed confused by his surroundings. He was naked and adrift in a sea of black satin sheets. A door opened and Rebekah entered. She was also naked and carrying two steaming mugs of coffee.

"Ah, the king but hath arisen. Fare ye well oh lord?"

He knuckled his eyes, "Yeah, I guess so. Is this your place? I don't remember coming here."

She sat on the edge of the king size bed and passed him a coffee.

"You passed out—all that exertion."

He smiled and took a sip of his coffee. He arse hurt.

"Who was that guy?"

"Oscar. Remember you met him."

"At the Circle Café—is that his real name, thought I heard someone call him something different last night?"

"Oh, probably Wolfen."

He almost choked on his coffee. Wolfen was the name Parker had cautioned him about. His very reason for being at the coven suddenly flooded back, you're undercover remember? But his mind wouldn't let go that the guy the cops wanted had given it to him last night.

"I was expecting to be the giver, not the receiver. I was a virgin up until then."

"All part of going where angels fear to tread, don't you think?"

"I understand why angels don't go there it hurts. What's the time?"

"About eight thirty."

"I need to make a call. Where are my pants?"

He found them on the floor beside the bed and wrenched his cell phone from the pocket.

To give him privacy Rebekah wandered into to the en-suite bathroom and closed the door quietly behind her.

Steve rang Parker.

"Hello, Parker, yes, Moloch was there... Yes, I'm certain of it... Oh, I'm going to the cricket today, tomorrow at 10 AM, Surry Hills sure—see you then. Bye."

He put his phone away, flopped back on the bed and took a sip of coffee. A feeling of self-accomplishment came over him... undercover true crime reporter Blake had checked in.

After a few minutes, Rebekah cruised out of the bathroom wrapped in a black satin robe. She collected his coffee mug.

"Another?"

"Oh please, excellent coffee."

"Thanks. Back in a tick."

While she was downstairs getting the coffee, Steve studied her bedroom. An array of occult paraphernalia decorated the room; black candles, upside-down crucifixes, a couple of framed posters; one of them a classic of the band Black Sabbath and the other Black Magik, a more obscure American heavy metal band.

In the kitchen brewing the coffee, Rebekah was talking conspiratorially on her cell phone. "He was talking to a cop named Parker. I don't know. Okay, I'll text it to you. Bye."

Rebekah floated back into the bedroom with two mugs of freshly brewed coffee. She let her robe fall open at the front as she handed Steve his.

He feasted his eyes on her voluptuous body and felt the remnants of the Molly he taken last night kick in a little.

Rebekah sat on the edge of the bed. With a smirk she set her cup down on the bedside table and turned her attention to the lump in the sheet.

"Are you erecting a tent?" She said with a smile as she lifted back the sheet to reveal his pulsing member.

He melted into the pillows and placed the coffee mug beside hers.

"First, tell me your real name big boy."

"Argh, that feels so good... Steve Blake."

Being erotically massaged had dimmed what little restraint he had. He was blinded by the demon of desire, and his already limited ability to reason jammed. Suddenly, he realised that he had just let the secret slip. The treasured secret was no longer concealed. What the hell, no harm done, he thought. What could possibly go wrong?

CHAPTER 8

*But I'm spellbound
Haunted by a demon of hell
Spellbound by a supernatural
Devil from a Witch's hell.*

gk

Sarah went to answer the front door just as Russell called out from upstairs.

"Mum, someone's at the door!"

"I know, love, I'm getting it."

She opened the door to find Thacka holding a bunch of flowers.

"Hello, a peace offering for having to head-out the other night."

"Oh, there was no need, Bill," she said with a warm, slightly embarrassed smile. "I know you're busy on a case." She took the flowers. "But thank you anyway, very considerate of you. Come in. Russell has been busting to see you. Russell, it's Bill!"

Russell came thundering down from upstairs.

"Hey Bill!"

"Hi there, partner, what's the latest?"

"Not much, I'm on school holidays."

"How was that pizza the other night?"

"Nine out of ten, partner!" Russell said and followed that up with a well-executed salute.

Smiling at Russell's antics, Sarah led Thacka into the living room.

"He's been playing cops and robbers on his iPad ever since he met you. He's into saluting today, aren't you?"

"I've got an iPad... maybe you can teach me how to use it sometime? I'm hopeless," Thackeray admitted to the boy.

"I'll just go back upstairs to finish my game. Got a few more crooks to wipe out."

"Sounds good. When you finish, bring it down and show me how to play."

Russell took off upstairs, and the two adults sat down together on the lounge. Suddenly sure of himself, Thacka leaned over and gently kissed Sarah on the lips. After a moment, she opened her mouth to him, and he was lost. Time stopped for both of them.

She opened her smiling eyes after the kiss and remained staring deeply into his and said softly, "That was nice. I've been thinking about you."

"I'm glad. Hate to think I failed to make an impression."

They cuddled in contented silence for a moment. Sarah brought him back to the real world.

"How's the case going?"

"Slower than a wet week."

"Why, what's the problem?"

"All cases need a break, and this one just refuses to come."

His phone rang; he checked the caller ID. "Sorry, Sarah, I have to take this."

"No worries."

He answered the call, "Hi, Parker. Good," he stood up and paced the room excitedly. "Well done! Could be just what we need. Okay, tomorrow then. Bye." He slipped the phone back into his pocket and raised a clenched fist. "Yes!"

"Sounds like you've got your break."

"Sure does. How about you get that little man of yours organised, and I'll take you both to lunch."

"You've got a date. Give me a few minutes to put my face on."

"What, another one? I'm more than happy with the one you've

got."

They both laughed, and she shot upstairs.

When Steve pulled the Beetle into the driveway of his home, he was surprised to find Niki's BMW still there. It had been a big day at the cricket with Morgan. He was tired and hungry and didn't feel like arguing with her. He was about to get back in his car and drive off when he changed his mind and decided to go inside and confront her.

When he opened the side gate, he was surprised Ralph wasn't there to greet him as usual.

"Ralph! Hey fella!" he called out, but Ralph failed to respond. Huh, must be in the house with Niki, he mumbled to himself.

When he rounded the house to the patio and the pool, he discovered why Ralph hadn't responded. His dog was floating in the pool with entrails hanging from a huge gash in his gut. The pool water was stained red with blood.

The pit of his stomach dropped out; he fell to his knees and cried out in despair, tears running down his cheeks.

"Oh, Ralph. Oh, why...? What happened mate?"

Suddenly he thought of Niki.

He stood up and raced in through the open patio doors, calling out in a panic, "Niki! Niki!"

He stopped dead, wondering, what if there's a robber in the house? With his heart racing, he looked about for signs of a break-in or damage or worse: a robber. The lights were off—dusk was coming, it was getting dark—he couldn't see any signs of a struggle or anything broken. He crept through the living room into the kitchen and found everything in order. She must be in the bedroom. He had to check the bedrooms upstairs. Slowly and nervously, he made his way up the staircase—with every creak underfoot, his heart faltered—the house was utterly silent—he was so on edge the slightest sound was like thunder.

His tears over Ralph had been replaced by a nameless dread. He imagined that every little creak could be someone waiting upstairs with an axe. When he got to the landing at the top of the stairs, he saw that the doors to both the main bedroom and guestroom were closed. He confronted the door to the main bedroom—placed a shaky hand on the doorknob, then, put his ear to the door to listen for sounds inside the room. Is there a killer waiting in there? Maybe Niki is still packing her things—but why is Ralph dead? With confused thoughts running through his mind, his heart beating at then to the dozen, he felt the iron fist of fear gripping his guts. He needed to calm down. Wait, Steve, just settle down, don't panic. A deep breath to muster some courage, and he gently turned the doorknob. The door opened. The only light was coming from the en-suite bathroom. His eyes were immediately cast to the bed—where Niki was face down, stark naked.

"Niki?" he asked quietly with a lump in his throat. She must be sleeping—he didn't want to startle her. But he had a hollow feeling in his gut—reluctantly he moved closer. His ears began to whistle: tinnitus brought on by nerves. He felt sick to the stomach—something was wrong—something was terribly wrong.

"Niki?" he called again, this time a little louder.

He moved closer, and then the horror of what was before him registered: Niki was spread-eagled face down on the bed—dead. He reached out a nervous hand and touched her hair.

"Oh, Niki," he mourned. With his heart in his mouth, he gently turned her head to face him. The look on her face frightened the hell out of him—her big blue eyes were wide open—staring, bulging, lifeless—her face was a frozen grimace of terror—her mouth agape in a permanent scream—her tongue protruding, swollen and blue. He buried his face in his hands. No, no, no! Who could have done this? Why? He looked up suddenly from his hands, realising he hadn't seen any blood—he needed to know what had happened and gently turned her over onto her back. A pair of pantyhose was tied tightly around her throat: she had been strangled. The sudden realisation caused him to jump backward in fright, and he struggled to fight back nausea. He wobbled, battling against passing out, but managed to steady himself against the bed and catch a breath. Then he noticed there was something etched in the skin on Niki's abdomen. On closer inspection, he found words carved into her flesh! He mouthed them, "Seducer be warned." He doubled over and threw up.

When Parker got the panicked call from Steve, she was in the car on her way home from the office. She instantly made a conscious decision not to alert anyone to the murder other than Thackeray. She wanted to have some quality time with Steve before the crime scene started crawling with cops.

Parker and Thackeray arrived at Steve's Clovelly townhouse within seconds of each other in the front yard, and Thackeray asked to be brought up to speed before going inside.

"This isn't going to go down well with Wilks, you know that, don't you, Parker?"

"You're right about that, but there's nothing I can do about it now. Here's what happened. Steve went to the witches' Sabbat last night. It was a sex orgy. He woke up at Rebekah's house in Newtown this morning and called me to report in. Moloch was at the Sabbat."

"Remind me, who is Rebekah?"

"The bird he met in a chat room on a witchcraft website called the Veil—she invited him to the Sabbat. Rebekah is a witch."

"Right. Did she overhear him talking to you?"

"I don't know. He went to the cricket and was there all day. Steve and his wife Niki had split up; she turned up to pick up her things, she was moving out—it was organised to happen while Steve was out—to avoid conflict. Steve came home from the cricket, found the dog floating in the pool butchered, and then found Niki upstairs strangled."

"Does he think there's a link between the Sabbat and the murder?"

"Yes. Said he's got something to show us."

As Parker rang the doorbell, she said gravely, "Leave me to deal with Wilks."

The door opened. Steve looked terrible.

"Come in," he mumbled, clearly he cared little about anything anymore.

Thackeray and Parker slipped on latex gloves and shoe covers then moved inside the house.

"Any sign of a break-in Steve?" Thackeray asked looking about.

"No, the house was open. I turned her over. She was lying on her belly—I didn't know she was dead," Steve said glumly and then began to weep.

"Did you notice anything else Steve?" Parker asked while Thackeray searched the room.

"There's something written on her body."

Thacka could tell he was too emotional to be questioned any further and turned to Parker.

"Take him outside for some fresh air. I'll comb the place. Where's the body Steve?"

Parker put a consoling arm around Steve's shoulders and walked him towards the open patio doors.

"She's upstairs in the bedroom. I turned her over... I didn't know..." he said with his voice breaking.

Thackeray started up the staircase.

When Parker got Steve out to the pool area and sighted Ralph floating in the blood-stained water, she stopped in her tracks. Steve took one look at Ralph and threw up again, the empty bile burning his throat. Parker changed her mind about sitting outside, and walked him down the side of the house to her car out front.

Being careful not to touch anything and spoil the crime scene for forensics, Thackeray entered the bedroom. Niki's naked body was face up on the bed. He carefully made his way closer so he could read the words etched in her flesh. Seducer be warned, he muttered to himself contemplating the meaning. The look on Niki's face and the panty hose wound tightly round her neck made the cause of death unmistakable. Clothes were spread all over the floor and there were two open suitcases, one partially filled with women's clothing. Thacka surmised Niki had been packing her things to move out, as Parker had mentioned. There were no signs of a struggle. He assumed the perpetrator had surprised her. The light was on in the en-suite bathroom. He thought perhaps the murderer caught her there. In his mind's eye, he recreated the scene: Niki collecting her things in the bathroom with her back to the bedroom. Suddenly, a black-gloved hand gathered up a pair of pantyhose from the pile of clothes on the bedroom floor, twisted them tightly around each fist, and then flexed them between both hands. Thacka noticed that the top drawer of the vanity table in the bathroom was open about five centimetres and there was a plastic supermarket carrybag on the floor. He visualised Niki opening the drawer with her back to the bedroom, the plastic bag ready to fill with her things from the drawer. Thacka took a pen from his pocket got down on his haunches in the bathroom and used it to lift the plastic bag—it was empty. He managed to glimpse inside the drawer without opening it any further and found women's items still there—he concluded she had been attacked before she had time to put the items in the plastic bag. He stood back and looked at the mirror above the vanity table—and envisaged Niki opening the drawer but failing to notice the dark shadow of her assailant looming up behind her. The pantyhose whipped around her throat and tightened, so tight, unable to scream—gasp—or even draw a breath, she fought wildly to prise her fingers under the noose that was choking her. But she was no match for her attacker—he dragged her fighting and kicking backwards out of the bathroom, across the carpet and then fell backwards onto the bed with her on top of him.

Thackeray noted two indistinct lines indented on the carpet, which he deduced were caused by Niki's heels as she was dragged backward towards the bed. He carefully made his way to the bed, lifted Niki's right hand, and checked the state of her fingers. He was right in his assumption: her fingernails were torn and bloody from her battle with the ligature—a battle that had taken her last breath.

He considered her body on the bed then imagined the big man

falling backward on the bed, on his back with Niki on top struggling while he choked the life out of her. Once she was dead, he slid out from underneath her then stripped off her clothes. Thacka glanced at the pile of the clothes on the floor and speculated: He would have cast her clothes among this lot. Then he imagined the killer positioning Niki's limp body on the bed so he could carve the curious message into her flesh with some sort of blade. When he had finished, the killer then turned her face down on the bed—But why face down? He questioned, baffled.

He leant over Niki's corpse, closed his eyes and then gently sniffed the air. It was a habit of his. Inadmissible as evidence but of immense value to him: he prided himself on a keen sense of smell and in this case detected an odour foreign to the bedroom and the general perfume of the household: incense. A feint but nevertheless presence of incense and it was not ordinary incense, it was unique and—he'd smelt it somewhere before—but where? The fragrance wasn't actually on Niki's body. He sniffed the bedclothes—nor was it on them, he straightened up with a sudden realisation—no, it was hanging in the air like a skein of mist, just floating above Niki, so slight, ever so feint but there nonetheless—and he knew that scent had been left behind by Niki's murderer.

One last check for anything out of place that he might have missed, found nothing, and so decided to investigate no further. He wasn't prepared to risk compromising any evidence. The entire house now needed to be handed over to the forensics specialists to do their job.

On his way back down the staircase, he phoned Homicide HQ to report the crime and arrange for investigation team and forensics to cover the crime scene.

When Thackeray met with Parker by the car in the driveway, she was still keeping a keen eye on Steve, concerned he might go into shock at any moment.

"A word, Parker."

They moved away from Steve to discuss the case in private.

"I'd say it was a surprise attack in the en-suite from behind. She'd been dragged onto the bed and strangled. Two things have me stumped, one, the cryptic message? And two, why she was turned face down? Did you get any more out of him?"

"No, I'm worried he might go into shock."

"Hmm, best to keep him talking then."

They returned to Steve.

"Steve, do you know any of the neighbours?" Thackeray asked.

"Only the old bag next door."

Thacka turned to Parker, "I've called HQ, they'll be here soon with forensics. I'll do a door knock to see if anyone saw anything. Steve, you'll need to come with us to the station; your house will be a crime scene for a couple of days. He won't be able to take anything, Parker, and that includes the Beamer. Mate, what do you think 'seducer be warned' means?"

"I've been running it over and over in my head, I've got no idea," Steve replied.

Parker and Thackeray exchanged a look of consternation; the message seemed pretty obvious to them.

First thing in the morning, Thackeray and Parker were summoned to the office of Superintendent Wilks. It wasn't difficult to assess Wilks' mood by the dour expression on his face. Parker and Thackeray were seated in chairs facing the big man's desk, looking for all the world like defendants waiting for the jury's verdict. Time was standing still for them—Wilks hadn't acknowledged their presence; his eyes remained down, silently studying the contents of a file on his desk.

Finally, his head rose slowly, he looked Thackeray square in the eyes and bellowed, "It's difficult to believe I'm reading a report about the conduct of an officer with your experience Thackeray. What have you got to say for yourself?"

"Sir, it was..." Parker tried to answer but Wilks shut her down with a slight gesture of his hand.

"The question is not for you, Parker."

"Sir," she said acquiescent.

"We all make mistakes, sir. Blake came to Parker after a story. We didn't set him up as a patsy; we were just using him as an informant."

"You don't seem to have the best record with informants, Thackeray, and in this bloke's case, you placed his and his wife's lives in jeopardy. And look what happened. The press will have a field day with this, Thackeray."

"Sir, may I speak?" Parker asked courteously.

"Go on then if you must."

"If you can just keep the lid on it for a few days, sir, we have a suspect and Steve Blake is our witness."

"So did Blake witness the murder of his wife?"

"No, sir, but we have a link between his wife's murder, the possible murder of six little boys, and Thackeray's suspect, Wolfen Moloch."

"And the link is?"

"Steve Blake, because he saw Moloch the night before the murder and a message that was left on the corpse, which referred directly to that meeting."

"What was the message?" Wilks asked.

"Seducer be warned," Thackeray said.

"Which means?"

"We're not sure, sir, but we believe it to be a threat against Steve Blake."

"Why was Blake at a meeting with Moloch?"

"It was a Sabbat, sir," Parker said reluctantly.

"A Sabbat... Who else was there?"

"Six women, sir, um witches. There could also be more evidence once forensic finishes with the crime scene and the body of Mrs Blake," Parker added hastily, hoping Wilks might have missed the reference to witches.

"Witches... That sort of Sabbat—so you believe there's some sort of black arts occult thing happening in Sydney?"

"A coven, sir," Parker answered hesitantly.

"Does Blake have a solid alibi?"

"Yes, sir, time of death was estimated at between 1 PM and 4 PM yesterday, which was while Blake was at the cricket with a friend."

"You've confirmed that?"

"Yes, we have, sir," Parker said more confidently.

"Better do background checks on Mrs Blake—where she was staying and with whom."

"Yes, sir," Parker scribbled on a small notepad.

"And what about the Riley murder?"

"No evidence," Thackeray said despondently. "But lack of evidence is never enough to remove suspicion."

Parker interrupted, "We think Moloch killed Riley."

"Suspicion will do you no good—doesn't work in a court of law, you know that, Thackeray," Wilks snarled, eyeballing him.

"Yes, sir," Thackeray and Parker said in unison.

Wilks mulled over what he'd been told, and his demeanour appeared to soften a tad.

"I tell you what you two, I'll give you one last shot at this one, you have a week to make an arrest, or I'll give the case to Miller. Is that absolutely clear, one week, not a minute more."

"Yes, sir," they again answered in unison.

"I want nothing leaked to the press. Keep Blake in a safe house under your surveillance and light years from the press."

"Sir, I want an arrest and search warrant for Moloch."

"On what grounds?"

"Um, drug trafficking."

"Come on, detective, you know better than that!" Wilks hesitated a moment. "You've got enough to bring him in for questioning; if you get something solid on him, or forensic turns up something, then we can proceed."

"Yes, sir." Thackeray knew it was a win for them. They could easily have lost the case to his nemesis Miller.

As they walked along the corridor to the elevator, Thackeray said, "Leave Wilks to me, huh?"

"Well, I called him, but he needed to hear it from the horse's mouth."

"Nnnhhhhhh!" he neighed like a horse. He got an odd look from a uniformed policewoman passing.

Thackeray and Parker walked from Surry Hills HQ to the City Crime Lab only a block away. Thackeray felt something plop onto his shoulder, stopped, and looked.

"Bird shit. Damn!" he cursed, as he drew a handkerchief to wipe it off. "There's Moloch's bloody curse again."

"Nah," Parker said with a grin. "That's good luck."

But Thackeray wasn't convinced and looked grumpy as they made their way inside the Crime Lab building.

Once past reception, they were met by an old friend of Thackeray's: middle-aged, gruff, and dry-witted Dr Kathleen Hawke—known to her mates as Kitty, a play on the famous World War Two fighter plane, the Kittyhawk.

Chief forensic pathologist Kitty was internationally renowned as one of the best in her field. Before Parker joined up with Thackeray, Kitty was Thacka's only ally, often running under-the-table DNA tests on boys' genitals and such for Thacka and then burying the costs. DNA testing was a high-ticket item at homicide and needed to be requisitioned. Thackeray had no budget for anything relating to his Corn Flake killer, but with Kitty's support, he at least had forensics on his side.

Thackeray knew Kitty would have Niki Blake's corpse at the lab. After donning personal protective equipment, they entered the autopsy room, and found Kitty seated at a bench peering into a microscope. It was the first time at the crime lab for Parker. The smell of formaldehyde reminded her of a funeral parlour she had visited during police training. It wasn't a pleasant memory; she'd almost fainted during the demonstration of the undertaker preparing a corpse for burial.

"Checking the racing guide, Kit?" Thackeray scoffed. He enjoyed teasing her.

"The only race the thing I'm looking at under here might've won would be to an ovary."

She looked up at Thacka with a grin, then lowered her glasses from the top of her head to focus on Parker.

With shortish grey curly hair, a round face, and a little overweight for her five-foot-eight height and her fifty-seven years, Kitty nevertheless had a very cheerful face and demeanour. Everybody has an Aunty that looks like Kitty—but no-one would have one that does what she does.

"Hi Kitty, I'm DI Parker, please call me Jess."

"Hi Jess. You must be Thacka's new offsider—I'm surprised."

"At what?" Parker queried.

"Well, let's say his partners don't last very long. Do they, Thacka?"

"Hard to find class these days, Kit—but this one's doing alright, she's lasted a few days now," Thacka teased.

"Is that Niki Blake?" Parker asked.

"No, it's the sperm I found in her clacker."

"Her butt?" Parker said with a furrowed brow.

"Yep, looks like the bastard who choked her gave her one up the bum after he'd killed her."

"So nothing in the front door then?" Thacka asked.

"Rape, no. Only an embryo."

"She was pregnant!"

"If that's a question, Jess, then yes, three months."

"That would probably explain the fall-out she had with her hubby," Parker surmised.

"Do you think he knew?"

"No, I don't think so."

"If it's any consolation we've got a DNA fingerprint from the sperm, and that's more than I can say for all the willies you've brought me over the years," Kitty said with a grumble.

Thacka and Parker exchanged a knowing look—DNA could get them a step closer to nailing Moloch.

"Oh, and he used the point of a knife, a big one, I'd say, like a bayonet, to do the engraving, similar to what was used on Riley, probably the same, I'd guess."

"How can you tell?" Parker queried.

'The cut marks—would have taken him a while to do it, he was very particular about getting it right."

"Good grief!" Parker gulped.

"He needed a seriously sharp knife and a lot of time. The lettering was very precise."

"Left-handed, right?" Thackeray suggested.

"A lefty giving a brazen warning."

"Seducer be warned!" Thackeray muttered.

"Yep, but it doesn't necessarily mean seducer as in sex. The dictionary definition is a bad person who entices others into error or wrongdoing, or someone who leads away from duty or proper conduct."

"That's as clear as mud, Kit," Thacka said.

"No, it's a riddle—if it is Moloch, then he's playing with words," Parker concluded.

"A game," Thackeray stated resolutely.

"An erroneous metaphor maybe," Kitty added.

"An erroneous metaphor... how do you come up with words like that? Makes me feel like a mental re-tread!" Thacka complained.

"Enrich your word power," Kitty said with a cheeky smirk.

"How's that?" Parker asked.

"A by-product of a tertiary education—I used to read Reader's Digest concealed inside my textbook during boring anatomy lectures. Enrich your word power was my favourite. Learn a new word a day, my dad used to say."

"Must try that. So anything else to go on?" Parker asked. She liked Kitty.

"Not a single print or hair follicle left behind at the Blake's or Riley's, not a thing to go on," Kitty looked Thackeray square in the eye. "So why on earth did he leave a sperm sample? Either he wants to get caught or he's damned sure he won't."

"So are you saying, with what you've seen, you think the same killer did Niki Blake and Riley?" Thackeray questioned.

"I'm saying there are certain similarities but just not enough to be conclusive. We need the murder weapon Thacka," Kitty frowned at the two detectives.

They came out of the Crime Lab knowing the answers to their questions had only led to more questions. Before Parker could start for the car park to collect her car, Thackeray stopped her.

"Where's Blake?"

"When he finished his statement with Connie, I had him taken to his mate's place."

"Okay, get onto him, get him over to your apartment, he'll have to prop there for a few days until this blows over."

"My place! Why me? Why do I have to put him up?"

"Because he's your responsibility, you brought the guy in, unauthorised, unofficial, and untrained and you heard Wilks, that's why..."

"Not on your life, mate, I live alone!" she complained.

"As far as I can see, we only have one life, Parker, over which for you, I currently have seniority."

"You sir have a messiah complex."

"So my ex-wife cautioned me, but I learned to live with it in my own humble way."

Was he being facetious, she wondered. But now wasn't the time nor place to pursue it, so she changed the subject.

"Why not one of those cheap hotels the department uses as a safe house?"

"Because we don't have the budget, do you think Wilks will authorise it once he finds out how Blake got involved? Do you want to pay for it? Besides, he's all we've got to get Moloch... I don't want him dead."

"Okay... okay, but just for a couple of days until his house is cleared."

"Good, but keep your bedroom door locked, you know how

much he likes an orgy?" He said with a devilish smile.

Parker folded her arms defensively, "Not likely. So, how do we proceed from here?"

"First, we need the murder weapon. None of the Blake's neighbours saw anything. So, let's verify Niki's movements. We'll need a list of her friends and whom she was staying with. We have to bank on the DNA, but I'm pessimistic about it."

"Yeah, I'm with you. Okay, I'll get a list from Steve."

"I'll sleep on the next move. Let's meet at the office at sparrows fart in the morning."

"You sure? I don't want to turn up early just to sit on my big butt for hours waiting for you!"

"I'll be there, I promise... and Parker, it's not a big butt."

"You know something tells me Moloch definitely did Niki."

"Why do you say that?"

"The message, after Kitty's definition, I reckon it was a warning for Steve. I think Moloch wants his identity kept secret."

"Maybe. Both murders are all so clean, it's got Moloch's MO all over it, he's as cunning as a fox. I'll see you tomorrow." He walked off.

"Thacka?" Parker called after him.

He stopped and turned to her, "Yes?"

"You've been right all along. Moloch is going to be a tough nut to crack, isn't he?"

"Parker, if I was to agree with you, we'd both be wrong."

"I love your confidence, Bill."

"It's the only thing that keeps me going."

Thackeray crossed the road, entered Police HQ, and took the elevator down to the car park.

While driving home, Parker phoned Steve.

"Steve, it's Jess Parker. You can't stay at your mate's place; we need you to be safer than that... yeah, you'll have to stay a couple of days at my apartment... in the city. I'm on my way there now. Okay, forensics will be done with your Vee Dub by tomorrow, but not the

Beamer. Okay, I'll send a taxi for you, what's the address? Aha... aha... Okay, done. See you in half an hour or so. Bye."

She finished the call as she arrived at the driveway to her apartment building. As she drove into the underground car park, a single headlight flashed in her rear-view mirror: a motorbike had followed her in through the automated doors. As she continued down the winding driveway, she could hear the bike close behind. Constantly checking the rear-view mirror, she drove through the dimly lit car park to her designated parking place and slowed. The omnipresent rumble of the bike engine and the light in the mirror was beginning to worry her. Suddenly, the bike pulled into an alcove, and the headlight shut off.

Her remote opened the door to her parking space, and she slotted the car into the bay. She slipped her standard-issue Glock from her belt holster, dropped the magazine, and checked the loads. She re-seated the loaded magazine, cracked the slide, and confirmed a round in the chamber, then re-holstered the weapon.

Stepping out of the car, she set the car alarm and exited the parking bay, hitting the inside button to close the tilt door. Then she began the long trek through the dimly lit car park to the elevators.

An underground car park is a cold and scary place at the best of times worse when you're alone—worse at night when there's a killer on the loose. Parker's footsteps resounded through the cement cavern, trapped by the low ceiling—the damp, musty smell seemed more obvious to her than usual. She came to a narrow passage that wound like a snake to the elevator. As she entered it, she felt claustrophobic, as though it was closing in on her and so increased her pace a little. When she rounded a corner, she slowed, her heart racing—though the elevator landing was only a few metres away, the single fluorescent light in the false ceiling outside the two elevator doors was flickering and that made the moment even more chilling for her. She slid a shaky hand under her jacket and onto the butt of the holstered pistol—the touch of the cold grips provided some comfort. She took her hand off the gun butt and pressed the elevator call button. Only one elevator was operating. She watched the floor counter tick laboriously down in its descent to her. It was taking an age. Suddenly, she was startled by the sound of a crunch—a footstep—and it came from the corridor behind her—someone was coming. Panic rose instantly in her. A loud flutter came from behind, and before she could react, something covered her head—darkness—she fought madly to get it off her—but two huge powerful arms wrapped it so tight around her head and upper body, she couldn't move her arms. It smelt like a leather jacket, and the overpowering stench of perspiration confirmed that thought. Her arms were pinned to her sides, and she tried desperately to free them but it was no use, he was just too strong. She tried walking her hands and fingers towards her pistol but could only touch it with the tip of her finger, couldn't grip it. Then she felt her attacker's face push hard against the side of her head—and the panic made her dizzy—she felt faint. Then he spoke with his mouth close to her ear quietly, menacing—in a frightening tone, a voice like sharpened gravel.

"Detective Parker."

Again, she tried with all her strength to shake him off, but he countered by gripping her even tighter—he was far too strong for her. She could tell by his grip he was over six feet tall with powerful bodybuilder-like biceps.

"What do you want, Moloch?"

"Who? This is just a demonstration how easy it would be to kill you."

He squeezed her in a bear hug—tighter, tighter—until she couldn't breathe—her panic was at fever pitch—tighter—she was about to pass out. She had visions of Niki being strangled.

"Takes your breath away, doesn't it, Parker?"

"Wha... wha... what do you want, Moloch?" she managed to squeeze out.

"I will cut off your tits and eat them if you continue to harass me or my friends—that I promise..." he grabbed her breasts roughly.

She was about to pass out when, ding! The elevator sounded its arrival. The jacket flipped off her, and she gulped the fresh air in a desperate bid to regain her breath.

The elevator doors opened, and a man dressed in a dinner suit stepped out. With one look at Parker, he realised she was about to collapse. He stepped forward and caught her as she was about to slump to the floor.

"Hey! I've got you!" he said warmly. "I'm a doctor. Are you having a seizure?"

"No, no..." She was battling to get it back together. "I, I, I've been attacked... police officer... I'm a detective... I... live here."

He checked her pupils.

"Just take long deep breaths... There you go... good. The colour is returning to your cheeks. Feeling better?"

She nodded, holding her throat.

"Yes, thanks, he was strangling me."

"Who was?"

"Didn't you see anyone?"

"No, when the door opened there was only you standing there about to collapse. I thought you were having an epileptic seizure."

She pulled her pistol.

He stepped back, shocked by the sight of it. "Whoa!"

She turned and hurried back along the corridor with the pistol up and called back to him, "Thanks, doc!"

While on the run, she heard the distinctive sound of a Harley Davidson crank up and changed direction, running for the exit. When she got there, she was just in time to catch the big automatic doors closing. It was too late. The sound of a motorbike accelerating in the street outside was proof her attacker had escaped.

When she finally made it to the safety of her apartment, her cell phone rang. It was Steve calling from the entrance to the apartment block. She buzzed him in.

When he arrived at the door, she was surprised to feel relieved to see a friendly face.

"Hi Jess, you look like shit. What happened?"

"Moloch just attacked me in the car park."

"Christ! Are you alright? Sit down... sit down."

He led her over to the sofa and helped her onto it. He could tell it must have been traumatic by how pale her face was and her trembling hands.

"I'll be all right in a minute; it's just the shock... comes a little later..."

"How about a cup of tea?"

"Great idea."

He made his way to the kitchen and called out. "Shouldn't you call the cops? I mean, I know you're a cop, but... you know?"

"Yeah, I'll ring Thacka once I've got the nerves under control."

She leaned back and tried to slow her panicked heart. The sound of Steve preparing a pot of tea helped ease the stress; the adrenaline was dissipating. She fumbled in her pocket for her phone, found it, and dialled Thacka.

"Bill, sorry to disturb you. Yes, he's here now, just arrived. Listen, Moloch attacked me in the car park of my apartment block... yeah, came up behind me and threw his stinking leather jacket over my head then locked me in a bear hug. He said it was a demonstration of how easy it would be for him to kill me... No, I'm all right. Someone came out of the elevator in the nick of time, a doctor... yeah, one of the residents. No, no I didn't get a look at him... by the time I got it together, he'd gone... on a motorbike, a Harley I reckon. I think he followed me from the station. Oh, of course, the bloody photo! Dorrie Wilson! ... That's how... And she probably took more. Yeah, I was lucky. He said he'd do me in if we continue to harass him and his friends... Yep, a direct threat... I know, we'll have to do it tonight, exactly... Okay, see you then. Yeah, I'll be alright, just a bit shaky. Thanks. Bye."

Steve brought two cups of tea.

"Couldn't find any biscuits. There's bugger all in the fridge. Don't you cops ever do any shopping?"

"No. Do you?" she grinned, as she took a cup.

"Nope."

"Sit down Steve we need to talk."

She was going to have to broach an emotional subject with him and needed to gauge whether he could handle it or not.

"How are you Steve after all you've been through?"

"Bearing up I guess, feels like I'm nearly over the shock of finding Niki like that. I need to be doing something. I want to start writing?"

"I'm sorry to tell you this mate but Niki was three months pregnant."

He flopped into the sofa beside her dispiritedly.

"Ah no! Fucking hell!"

She patted him on the shoulder.

"I'm so sorry, Steve."

"Can they check if it was mine?"

"Why? Do you suspect…?"

"We were having troubles… I don't know what to think."

"Let me see what I can do. I'll give forensics a call tomorrow. But we finally have some positive news."

"Yeah, what's that?"

"We might have enough to bring Moloch in for questioning."

"How's that?"

"There was sperm, Steve?"

"In Niki? You mean he—?"

"Yes."

"He raped her… Oh God!" he put his face in his hands.

"But not while she was alive."

"Are you saying after he'd killed her?"

"Yes. Do you think you could identify Moloch if you saw him?"

"In a line-up or something?"

"No, that's on TV, in reality under Australian law, he has the right of silence and not to appear in a line-up. If we brought him in for interrogation, we'd let you see him through a one-way mirror."

"Yeah, I got a good look at him at the Circle Café, is that

enough?"

"What about at the Sabbat?"

"No, he had a goat's head."

"Damn, we'll have to rely on DNA, but we'll need a sample from him," Parker was thinking out loud.

"Didn't you see him in the car park?"

"No. He'd put his jacket over my head. But I smelt him."

"Wait, I saw a mark on his arm at the Sabbat, a tattoo, a star—a pentagram. Is that any good?"

"Enough grounds to arrest him that's for sure; we've got a little boy who saw the same tattoo."

"When will you arrest him?"

She checked her wristwatch, "I just spoke with Thacka, and he's picking me up here at 9 PM."

"Tonight, wow! You're not mucking around then?"

"No, not with this bastard, especially now he's threatened me as well. A hot shower, a frozen pizza, and I'll be ready for him. Listen, I'll need the name and number of Niki's best friend?"

"Jacqui... Okay, I've got it on my iPhone. Listen, do you want me to throw a pizza in the microwave?"

"Yeah, there's one in the freezer. Turn the oven on to 220 degrees, better than nuking it, that'd be great, mate, thanks." She went to her bedroom to shower.

She was busy enjoying the steaming hot water relaxing her when Steve called from the bathroom doorway.

"Why do you think he killed her?"

She flinched with fright.

"Argh! You frightened me, Steve. Let me finish showering... then we can talk."

To Steve, the opaque glass of the shower recess was distorting her naked form.

"Sorry, I didn't mean to. I guess I'm a bit freaked out by all this."

She turned the shower off.

"Go back to the living room, Steve, we'll talk there."

She was beginning to feel a little uncomfortable with him being there and ignoring her request to leave. If he was still there when she opened the shower door to get her towel, she was set to give him a blast.

"I've finished showering, are you still there?"

Even with no reply, she wasn't confident he had gone and still felt uneasy. A grizzly thought entered her mind: What if he killed his wife? What if he's a psychopath? What if it was his sperm? There she was naked in her apartment with a man she didn't even know, a man who couldn't be ruled out as a suspect in a murder investigation. The thought caused goose bumps to rise on her forearms. She grabbed the shower door handle, took a deep breath for courage, and then slid it open. A sense of relief came from not finding him standing there. She snatched a towel from the rack and wrapped it around her body. As she wandered into her dimly lit bedroom, she was immediately taken aback—Steve was lying on her bed, back against the headboard, holding her pistol.

"Have you ever shot anyone?" he said, staring at it in his hand.

"I think you better put that down, Steve, and wait for me in the living room. Please get off my bed," she said firmly.

He sat up, swung his legs off the bed, moved to the edge of the bed, and sat there with a look on his face like a little boy in trouble. After a pause, with her waiting patiently, he slid the pistol back into the holster on the bedside table, got up, and walked silently out of the room.

Parker made a beeline for the door and locked it behind him, her heart was pounding so hard that the sound of it seemed to have an external source, as if someone were thumping on a timpani in another room.

A little while later when Parker strolled into the lounge room, she was pleasantly surprised to discover Steve had set the dinner table, complete with a burning candle. She could hear him in the kitchen.

"This looks a bit romantic, Steve," she said, trying to relieve the tension.

He called from the kitchen,

"Take a seat, one pizza à la Blake coming right up."

He hurried from the kitchen carrying a hot pizza tray wrapped in a couple of tea towels and placed it on the table.

"A couple of plates and we're in business."

"No, no, let's eat traditionally Italiano style with our hands, saves on washing up."

"Ah! Spoken like a true bachelor."

"Bachelorette is the popular female equivalent; spinster or maid is more grammatically correct."

"I stand corrected, lady of the realm. Shall we indulge?"

They tore into the pizza, both suddenly ravenous.

"I didn't mean to frighten you. Sorry."

"Okay, you're forgiven this time but only because you cooked the pizza."

"Thanks."

"But you're on notice. You're here for your safety. You'd be under guard in a cheap hotel if it weren't for Thackeray's generosity and mine. Please leave my things alone while you're here—and stay out of the lady's boudoir. Do not, I repeat, do not talk to anybody, especially the press. Are we on the same page, Mr Blake?"

"Can I use your computer?"

"No, but if you promise to stay out of chat rooms and not to send emails to anyone, especially your publisher or any witches, you can use my iPad. Here's an access key card for the apartment. Do not lose it!"

He saluted her, "Scout's honour."

CHAPTER 9

If you're looking for a thrill or two
I've got a place for you
to chill you through.
They say Satan walks the floors at night,
looking for someone to feed his appetite.

gk

Steve waited for Parker to leave and then rang Jacqui. After finding out Niki was three months pregnant, he was determined to find out for himself if Niki had been seeing someone. He didn't give a second thought to his promise to Parker not to talk to anyone.

"Hi Jacqui... Steve... no, no, please don't hang up! I know... that's what I'm ringing about... I need to talk to you about her. Please... I know we have problems, but maybe you can help... I, I've got no one else to talk to Jacqui."

His attempt at snivelling was getting through to her, and she took pity on him.

"I can be there in fifteen minutes."

"Oh, thanks, Jacqui, you don't know what this means to me... I'll see you then," he hung up, with a smug smirk of accomplishment on his face.

For the second time, Thackeray and Parker found themselves stationed outside the Waverly home of Wolfen Moloch. It was an eerie night as before, with the waxing moon now and again breaking through the clouds in the inky sky to light up the old Waverly cemetery overlooking the Pacific Ocean. The pungent smell of the sea from the spray of surf hammering the rock platforms below the cliffs was omnipresent. Thacka was confident that this time, things were going to be different. Countless times before, he had sat in his car alone in the same spot for hours on end, waiting for a chance to tail Moloch. Every time, bar none, Moloch had taken him on a joy ride to nowhere, it seemed probably just for the hell of it. This time Thacka was armed with enough to arrest him on suspicion of murder. His six-year wait to put Moloch behind bars was almost over, all they needed was a DNA sample, and the thought of that had him fired up and ready to go.

"I've got back-up on standby," he told Parker, who looked decidedly nervous. "You okay?"

"Yeah, I'm just not used to this."

"Come on. You'll be all right. Just think about getting even for the way the bastard treated you earlier tonight."

As they got out of the car, Moloch's garage door opened, and a bright light temporarily blinded them. Then the distinctive rumble of a Harley Davidson starting up broke the serenity. Thacka immediately realised what was happening,

"Quick! He's making a run for it!"

They took off on the double back to the car. Just as they got there, the Harley roared out of the garage onto the driveway and left a smoking trail of rubber as it accelerated up Trafalgar Street.

"That was him all right!" Thackeray shouted.

"Same bike as earlier!" Parker confirmed.

There was no missing Moloch's huge frame on the bike. They hopped back into the car with Thackeray behind the wheel—he revved it—slammed it into gear, and the wheels spun in the gravel as they shot after the bike.

"Much tougher to chase a bike than a car, tighten your belt, kiddo, this'll be a rough ride!" Thacka warned Parker, who was wide-eyed.

Moloch hit the throttle as soon as he saw the cop car in his rear-view mirrors. The big bike sped away from its pursuers.

Thacka fumbled in his pocket for a toothpick, found one, and clenched it between his teeth.

Parker gripped both sides of the seat, white-knuckled—she hated high-speed car chases in movies—it was even worse when it was for real.

"Shouldn't we call for an intercept to cut him off?" she suggested tensely.

"Not until I can get him isolated on a road we can block. Call in and tell Ops we're in pursuit, call sign Raygun."

Moloch was getting away from them—the bike easily out-cornered and out-accelerated them.

Parker opened the window and placed the blue flashing police light on the roof, then hit the switch. She was hoping the strobe light would get them safely through traffic lights.

"No siren?" she asked.

"Not yet, it looks like he's heading for the airport. I reckon he's going for Airport Drive to get him onto the M5 Motorway. If he gets on that, he'll leave us for dead. Get Ops to set up a block at the traffic lights, junction of Joyce Drive and O'Riordan Streets in Mascot."

"Roger that!" she replied.

Steve stepped out of the elevator, found apartment 217 and knocked on the door. It opened to reveal Jacqui dressed in a red and green robe with rollers in her hair, clearly she was getting made-up and ready to go out.

"Steve, hi, come in. I've been worried out of my brain about Nik, she hasn't been answering my calls—I've left stacks of messages. I thought she was with you? Sit down."

Steve took a seat in the posh white leather lounge of the small city apartment and Jacqui sat opposite. He looked at the splendid view of Darling Harbor through the glass balcony doors, then back at Jacqui who was sitting opposite with her legs crossed. Her feet were bare, he checked them out—pretty, toenails painted red—turned him on.

She felt his stare and self-consciously covered one foot with the other—obviously not proud of her feet.

He looked her in the eyes. She held his gaze.

"I don't know how to tell you this Jacqui... but."

A tear trickled down his cheek.

Jacqui was flustered, she thought he was going to have a cry about Niki leaving him.

"Niki's dead."

"What?" she shrieked.

"I came home from the cricket and found her on the bed strangled."

Jacqui just stared at him, her eyes the size of dinner plates unable to process what he'd said. Then the thought struck her that Steve had killed her.

"What? Um, how...? Um, who?" she stammered.

"The police have a suspect but will need to question you as well. She was staying here right?"

"Yes... but."

"Jacqui, I need to know if she's been seeing anyone, you know, another guy. He might have..."

"No, Steve! You know Niki, she's not like that... why?"

"Because she was pregnant."

"What?"

"Yes, three months—I need to know if it was mine."

She was on her feet running her hands through her hair unable to cope with the story.

"Oh, Steve... how can you think that... Niki was—"

"You telling me that you two haven't been out while she's been here?"

"No, oh we had an after-work drink at a pub the other day but nothing... no..."

He jumped up, grabbed her by the wrists and yelled at her

furiously.

"Tell me the truth Jacqui!"

"Let me go Steve you're hurting me!"

Not content, he pulled her out onto the balcony and pushed her up hard against the railing forcing his body against hers. The robe fell open—she was naked underneath. She had large breasts and an hourglass figure. He had fancied her for years and despite his anger, he found himself hardening to the feel of her.

"Tell me truth Jacqui... You don't know how much this means to me!"

"Look, Steve I know you're upset but cut the violence... just calm down. We can go inside and talk this over."

That seemed to placate him a little—he looked her over—her big green eyes. He reached his hand down to feel her.

"No Steve, don't!"

He put his hand over her mouth and forced her back against the railing. With his other hand, he fondled her. She struggled against him. He kissed her neck and ground his pelvis against her. He could hear her panting hot breath in his ear—she was aroused—he undid his pants and let them drop—he was hard—he needed it now—having her was something he'd always wanted but had been denied by Niki. She opened her legs to take him. They made it—hard, fast and furious. He wanted to make it last. He pulled out, turned her around, bent her over the railing and entered her from behind. She worked hard with him enjoying every thrust. He pulled out again— he wanted to look in her eyes—she turned and lifted a leg into his hand— he could feel her trembling—her legs began to shake, she threw her head back—her eyelids fluttered—she opened her mouth and yelped as she climaxed... again, and again... he closed his mouth over hers and probed the inside of her warm cavity with his tongue. He was determined for this to be a moment she would never forget— and to make sure, he kept on going making her scream with ecstasy as she kept climaxing.

Moloch was well ahead of Thackeray, speeding due west on

Wentworth Avenue, one of the main arterial roads to Kingsford-Smith airport. A traffic light turned red and stopped him. He couldn't run it because there were too many cars ahead of him. Thackeray pulled up a half a dozen cars behind the Harley, just as the lights changed to green.

With precision, Moloch worked his bike between the cars so he could speed off as soon as they moved. Thackeray couldn't help but admire how well Moloch handled the Harley; he leaned it over like it was a toy as he zigzagged through the traffic at speed, leaving Thackeray in his wake. But Thackeray knew his chance was waiting up ahead.

"Not far to the roadblock—You armed?"

"Yep!" Parker replied, still looking nervous. "I suffer from anxiety without it." She managed a chuckle.

They sped through a red light onto Botany Street and then took a sharp left into General Holmes Drive that would traverse a level crossing. The traffic lights at Joyce Drive on the other side of the level crossing turned red.

When Moloch hit the level crossing, he was travelling so fast that the hump launched him airborne—he landed with a thump and a shower of sparks on the other side of the tracks. The jump had unsteadied him—he was off balance.

On his right, a big Mack semitrailer fully laden with freight containers bound for Port Botany was bearing down on the green light. The red light wasn't going to stop Moloch.

Thacka hit the brakes hard, and he and Parker watched in horror as Moloch leaned the bike over and slid through the red light directly under the oncoming semi. The big truck's airbrakes locked up with an unearthly shriek.

Thacka's car shuddered, and they fishtailed to a halt.

When the truck braked, it almost jack-knifed, its big rear tyres smoked and bounced until it finally came to a stop.

"He didn't come out the other side!" Thackeray groaned.

He and Parker were out of the car in a flash.

On the far side of the truck, the Harley was a twisted smouldering mess—there was no sign of Moloch.

The truck driver was out of his cab, standing with his hands on his head in shock.

Thackeray and Parker ran over to him.

He pleaded, "Jesus mate, I didn't even see him. He came through the red light like a rocket... I... I..."

"It's okay fella, we're cops, we were following him and saw it all. You did nothing wrong!" Parker said to placate him.

She led the big tattooed driver by the arm onto the median strip.

"Just sit down and take it easy mate, you've had a helluva a shock."

"Thanks I..."

She put a finger to her lips to quieten him.

"Shh, shhh, just take it easy mate, alright?" She had been trained how to handle shock victims.

Thackeray leaned down and peered up under the truck for some sign of Moloch. When he felt something drip on his forehead, he touched it and checked his fingers—it was blood. He looked up into the dark undercarriage of the trailer—something was caught up in the chassis—his vision resolved the mystery, and he realised he was staring at a mangled mess of flesh and bone that had formerly been Moloch.

Thackeray flopped onto his backside on the road, devastated. It looked like the bastard had gotten away from him again.

Parker arrived.

"You all right, Bill?"

She wouldn't have normally called him by his first name, but he was clearly overwhelmed.

With his head in his hands, he grumbled,

"Six years of hard work down the bloody gurgler just like that. No, I'm not alright... He's bloody minced meat..."

Parker climbed under the trailer for a look. After a couple of seconds, she called back to him with urgency, "Maybe not Bill. He's still alive."

It was past 3 AM when Parker quietly opened her apartment door. Barefoot, she entered, tiptoeing with her shoes in her hand as if she was coming home late to her husband from a girl's night out. She was expecting to find Steve asleep, but the TV was on, and he was glued to it sprawled out on the couch.

"Hey, I thought you'd be asleep," she said.

He sat up abruptly and said, "No way Jose! Not with you guys out there busting the dude who threatened to kill me. So what happened?"

Parker flopped into an armchair like a rag doll and put her tired feet up on the ottoman.

"Moloch got himself mangled under a Mack truck."

"You're having me on!"

"No, we went to bust him, he fled, we chased him on his Harley, he ran a red light straight under a dirty big Mack loaded with containers en-route to the Botany Bay container wharf."

"Is he dead?"

"All but—he's on life support but unlikely to make it."

"Well, I suppose that's a win, divine providence, right?"

"Well, the threat has probably gone, but it means we won't get closure on the case."

"What do you mean?"

"If he dies, then finding out whether he killed the six boys or even if he did, what he did with their bodies... well, that will be buried with him."

"I see. Do you think he might regain consciousness long enough to confess?"

"Unlikely, he's seriously busted up, lost most of his right arm—he's basically minced meat from the waist down. It's only a matter of time before he croaks."

"So it's all over then?"

"Yes, I guess you could say that," she admitted with a tired sigh.

"Then can I start writing my story?"

"I don't see why not. I'm off to bed."

"Want some company?"

"Cut it out Steve, you can probably go home tomorrow, you're safe now."

"No harm in asking, right?"

"I suppose not, but I'll be locking my bedroom door in case you get randy."

"Don't worry Jess, you'll be safe."

Jacqui had already satisfied his sexual appetite for the night. Parker got up, collected her shoes, and plodded tiredly off toward her bedroom. She stopped at the doorway and turned back to Steve.

"Oh," she yawned. "Sorry, um, when you speak to your witches next, ask if they know a Richard Riley."

"So I take it it's okay to talk with them now?"

"I suppose so," she waved and closed the bedroom door.

Steve immediately booted up Parker's iPad and went directly to the Veil chat room. As soon as he logged on, he found Rebekah online.

Kaspar: Hey! I didn't expect you to be on line at this time.

Rebekah: You either. What's up?

Kaspar: A lot has happened since I left your place.

Rebekah: Turn on your webcam.

Kaspar: Okay, but I have to keep quiet, I'm staying at a friend's house.

He booted up the webcam.

"What's new?" Rebekah asked.

"Heaps, wanna catch up for a coffee tomorrow? I'll tell you then."

"Cool. At the circle?"

"Yeah, at 11."

Running late after not enough sleep, Parker rushed into the office in a flurry.

With a toothpick clamped between his teeth, Thackeray was busy typing on his computer.

"Good morning, sorry I'm late."

"That's a first, normally it's me," Thacka said as he swivelled on his chair to face her.

"Any news on Moloch?"

"He's still battling, while there's life there's hope."

"Hope for what?"

"I don't know. I keep hoping he's going to start talking. I know it's mad," he admitted, looking about his desk as if he'd lost something.

"Yeah, I suppose," she answered with furrowed eyebrows, wondering what it was he'd lost.

He looked up at her, "You seen my pen? It was here yesterday."

She picked it up from her desk and handed it to him, "Name's Parker, what can I say?"

He snatched it possessively from her, "Pen thief, I ought to call the police!"

"Ooo, childhood problem emerging?"

"When you grow up with only one pair of shoes, with a mother who used to buy your clothes from the markets because they were cheap factory seconds, which meant they mostly never fitted—like shirts with one sleeve shorter than the other, then you learn to appreciate what you've got, Parker."

"Must've looked funny wearing a shirt like that."

"Especially having a mother with a weird sense of humour—just lean left and pull your left arm back a bit, so the sleeve matches the other one love, she'd say. One day I was walking down the street like that and an old lady offered me some money—thought I had a disability."

They both had a chuckle.

"Anyhow," he smiled studying his pen. "Wilks is impressed."

"Good, want me to have Kitty DNA fingerprint Moloch at the hospital?"

"Good idea," Thackeray acknowledged.

"What else?"

"Has Steve asked the witches about Riley?"

"Not yet."

"Okay, you'll need to write up your accident report. I'm doing mine now. You better add in the assault."

"Will it matter that I didn't report it?"

"You did report it, to me."

"Of course."

He turned back to his computer and continued typing.

"Where's Blake, by the way?"

"Oh, should I tell him to go home?"

He took the toothpick out and thought about it for a moment.

"No, let's wait a day or two until the dust has settled."

"You mean wait till Moloch's dead?"

"Yeah, you could say that."

"Even in his condition you still don't trust him, do you?"

"He's a warlock, capable of anything. I won't be content until he's nothing more than a column of smoke rising from the crematorium smokestack."

"I'll be with you applauding that day."

"You all right with having Blake at your place for a bit longer?"

"He put the word on me last night."

He shoved the toothpick back between his teeth and grinned through it cheekily. "What? You're kidding me. Did you take him up on it?"

"Huh! Not likely! Why is it when you're nice to a guy they take it as a come-on? The next minute they're all over you like a cheap suit," she snapped.

"Nothing wrong with a free no-strings-attached shag or a cheap suit. Anyhow, if you looked like the rear end of a bus, you wouldn't get the come-ons."

"Mate, he just banged half the witches in Sydney. Never know what a girl might catch."

"Oh, nostalgia isn't what it used to be."

"You and your damn paraprosdokians!" she chuckled, enjoying his witty remark.

"Oh, damn, I forgot to get the contact for Jacqui."

"Who's Jacqui?"

"The girl Niki Blake was staying with. Do we still need to interview her?"

"Don't worry about it for now."

Steve looked up at the sun. The sky was blue, and it was a lovely Sydney spring morning. The waitress set down a soy latte on the table in front of him, and he beamed her a big smile, receiving one in return. While he amused himself people-watching the patrons of the Circle Café, a woman in black, sheltering herself from the sun under a black Japanese parasol, arrived. A picture of feminine gracefulness, Rebekah sat opposite Steve and gently closed her parasol.

"Sorry I'm late."

"No complaints, it's nice here. I just ordered you a black coffee."

"Thank you."

"You look lovely as usual."

"Why have you been staying at your friend's house?"

"Because there was a murder at mine."

"A what?" she reacted, shocked.

"Remember when I left your house, I was going to the cricket?"

"Yes."

"When I got home after the cricket, I found my dog floating in the pool, butchered, and my wife, who'd come home to collect her things in the main bedroom, dead."

"My goodness! What happened?"

"I can't say anything yet since the cops are still on the case, but she was strangled."

She reached across the table, took his hand, and said compassionately,

"I'm so sorry, Steve. How long had you been together?"

"Three years, but it was all over. I'd told her to move out. I was tired of supporting her. She'd moved in with some guy, so I told her to pick up her stuff while I was at the cricket. I didn't want to see her."

"It must have been terrible for you to find her like that. Are you all right?"

"Yeah, it was a shock, but I'm pretty much over it now, thanks. I heard your friend was in a bad accident."

"Who's that?"

"Wolfen Moloch. He was in a police chase last night and got himself mangled under a Mack truck. He's on life support, but not expected to live."

"Oh my goodness! Are you sure?"

He could see that the news had really rocked her.

"Absolutely."

"How come you know all this?"

"I have to be honest with you, Rebekah, I'm an undercover crime reporter."

"What!"

The waitress brought Rebekah her coffee. Steve observed a more than friendly smile between Rebekah and the waitress.

"You know her?"

"Yes, she's into threesomes. So, you're a crime reporter you say?"

"Yes, I go undercover on serious crimes like serial killings and such, working with the police, then when it's all done, I write the story. That's what I wanted to talk to you about. Do you think I can get an interview with Nissa and Vivian?"

"What about?"

"Moloch."

A worried look crossed Rebekah's face.

"I don't know; you know how private the coven is."

"I wouldn't expose anyone or the coven, I'll give you my word on that. I just need to know a few facts about him."

"Is Moloch suspected of something?"

"Yes, murder."

"You're kidding me! Who is he suspected of murdering?"

"My wife and a number of little boys over the last six years—all six-year-olds."

A radical change came over Rebekah; she was suddenly more cooperative.

"Look, it's Beltane tomorrow night, our biggest event of the year, and there'll be about twenty of us at the altar in Seven Hills. With Moloch out of the picture, you could well be the only guy."

"Sounds inviting."

"You could ask Nissa and Vivian whether they'll do an interview then."

"Okay, here..." he handed her a hundred dollar bill. "Get us a couple of Molly's for the big night?"

She took the bill and stashed it.

"Sure, no worries."

It was mid-afternoon by the time Steve entered the offices of Paragon Press in East Sydney—publishers of True Crime Magazine. He asked the receptionist to speak with the editor of True Crime about a story he'd been commissioned to write and was told to wait. He took a seat and thumbed through a copy of True Crime. After fifteen minutes, the receptionist told him to enter the offices where he would find the Editor-in-Chief Eric Kingston, waiting for him.

As Steve ambled through the open-plan office, he studied the staff hunched over their computer terminals, oblivious to him. Then he spied a set of offices at the rear of the big room that seemed the most likely haunt for an editor. As he approached the offices, feeling a little self-conscious about appearing lost, he sighted the name 'Eric Kingston - Editor in Chief' stencilled on an office door, exactly where he expected it to be. With his confidence restored, he tapped his knuckle on the door, and the response, "Come" bellowed from inside. He opened the door.

Behind a very messy desk stacked with papers, was seated an extremely large man, who immediately reminded Steve of a bespectacled version of Jabba the Hutt.

Steve stuck out a hand and approached the big man.

"Hi, Mr Kingston, Steve Blake, crime writer."

Kingston ignored Steve's offer of a handshake and replied

grumpily, "Never heard of you. What do you want, son? Can't you see I'm busy?"

"I phoned last week with a story and was told to write and submit it."

"Yes, that's our policy here, so?"

"Well, my story is special, I've got an exclusive."

"Listen, every journo with a Pulitzer Prize bee in his bonnet tries that one on me, son. They all claim a tacit arrangement with the cops. Get on with it."

"No, not on this one, I have the exclusive from homicide, it's the story of the Sydney serial killer."

"Hmm, nice title, go on, humour me."

"Six little boys murdered over the last six years, the killer now on life support after a police chase that went wrong and got him pulverised by a Mack truck. The killer is the warlock of a witch's coven in the Western suburbs... I attended a witch's Sabbat undercover for the police—the killer found out, and murdered my wife only days ago, threatened to kill me, then attacked a female detective... Need more?"

"Jesus, son! It sounds like the plot for a B-grade Hollywood movie! What do you want from me?"

"A full-time crime reporter's job here in exchange for the story exclusive... and... an advance... for expenses."

"I tell you what, get me a draft of the story with sworn witnesses, photos of a Sabbat, you know paparazzi style, and you've got yourself a permanent job, plus I'll backpay you for the story... and I'll give you a hundred bucks cash for expenses. Deal?"

"A hundred won't buy me a tank of gas and a hamburger, four hundred."

"Yeah, you're right, money ain't worth shit these days, three hundred then."

"Deal!" Steve said, offering his hand to shake. Steve had cut himself a deal, and this time Eric Kingston took his hand.

Later at sunset, Thackeray and Sarah were seated at the window table of the upmarket Woolloomooloo Pier Restaurant Manta, on Sydney Harbour. They were sipping mineral water while waiting for their entrees. Sarah noticed Thackeray staring into space, reached across the table, and gently shook his hand.

"Hey, are you there or off with the pixies?"

He snapped out of it and locked eyes with her.

"I'm sorry, I don't know where I am."

"What's wrong?" she held his gaze.

"We agreed I wouldn't bring my work home."

"Perhaps this time there's nothing you can do to prevent it coming with you. Tell me."

"You're so perceptive."

"A casualty of our liaison perhaps."

"This case has torn my life apart. It cost me my marriage and robbed me of my self-esteem. It made me the laughing stock of the precinct. I tell you, I don't think I could cope with not knowing Moloch is the murderer. This had been so much a part of my life, I need closure."

"I understand, love. What brought this on?"

"Moloch had an accident last night, he's on life support with no chance of recovery."

"Sounds like Karma to me. What goes around comes around. If he did those terrible things to all those little boys, then he's got what he deserved."

"It's not that. I won't get closure, Sarah. How can I go on not knowing whether he's the killer or not? Not just of six boys, but Niki Blake and Richard Riley. What if he isn't... what if the real killer is still out there?"

"There's nothing you can do about that, darling. Nature will take its course."

"You're so special to me, I don't want this to get in the way of what we have."

"It won't, love—what can we do?"

"I know you're right... but there is something that only you can do."

"And what could that be?" she removed her hand from his suddenly overcome by a sense of foreboding.

"He's in a coma."

Suddenly she realised what he was getting at and reacted badly, "No, Bill... I—"

"You could try going inside his mind like you did with Russell."

She lurched back in her chair and crossed her arms protectively across her chest.

"No! I can't do that, Bill. I won't."

A deathly silence descended. Both avoided eye contact—both uncertain what to say next.

Sarah finally broke the spell, locked her eyes fiercely on his, and said defiantly, "End of discussion, Bill."

He leaned back in his chair and mirrored her defiant body language. "Okay, okay... Sorry for asking."

The waiter arrived with their entrees, but they didn't even notice; they were both far too busy searching their respective innermost thoughts—a galaxy apart.

The silence continued after dinner while they were driving towards Randwick. Sarah staring out of the passenger-side window while Thackeray chewed on a toothpick, humming "Only the Lonely'.

The humming was driving her crazy, so she finally broke the ice and demanded, "Pull the car over, Bill."

Once the car had stopped, she continued. "It's unfair of you to ask that of me."

He took a deep breath to gather his thoughts. He didn't want to argue. "Look, Sarah, the last thing I want is to fight with you over work issues, but I wouldn't have asked if it wasn't... Look, have I ever mentioned what happened since you told me about it?"

"No, but that's not the point, Bill. You've put me in an impossible position by asking me."

"I know, and believe me, I wouldn't have asked at all if it wasn't my last option."

"I'll be honest with you, Bill, there was a lot more to bringing Russell back from a coma than I told you. Enough to scare the life out of me—I'm still recovering."

Again, there was a pregnant pause while he considered what she had admitted.

"I need to understand, Sarah, so tell me."

She contemplated confessing nervously, chewing her knuckle. He noticed her expression suddenly change—she had made the conscious decision, and took a deep breath. "Okay, Bill, I'll tell you what I have told no-one else. I think somehow that night, standing beside Russell's crib, seeing him dying and feeling so... so helpless, I was able, by some freak of nature, to summon up a way to enter his mind... no, no, not his mind, his dreams."

"His dreams?"

"I know it sounds impossible, Bill, but hear me out... Somehow his dreamscape was a physical place; a place Russell had created."

"Go on."

"As I reached out and touched Russell's forehead for the second time, well, one minute I was standing there beside his hospital bed and the next..."

She closed her eyes to picture what had happened; it was as clear as if it were yesterday.

"I was standing in some sort of surreal world. Everything about it felt very odd. It was a dark place. The sky was yellow—the moon and sun were in the sky together. Clouds were scudding through the sky impossibly quickly. There was a pungent smell—the sort you get just after it rains... and there was lightning... purple lightning on the horizon... I could hear a low rumble—but it wasn't thunder, it was more like the sound car tyres make on the road."

In her mind's eye, she remembered looking around and realising she was standing in a field dotted here and there with giant-sized toys—they were distorted—They're Russell's toys, she thought with a sudden familiarity. The toys were a comfort to her as they provided an emotional connection with her little boy. She called out, "Russell!

Russell!" Her words resounded in the strange world, as from a mountaintop, but the echo was too long, unreal—it repeated as if she was at the bottom of a deep chasm. The sun was setting unnaturally quickly, and suddenly the ground beneath her feet began to shake... an earthquake! She fought to keep her balance against the violent trembling. The rumbling sound was growing louder and louder... it was now almost unbearable. She covered her ears. Then came an even louder roar, and the earth directly in front of her opened up like a cavernous mouth and spewed a two-storey house—like a giant children's pop-up book. The front door of the house swung slowly open, beckoning her inside. The roaring noise ceased, and she slowly lowered her hands from her tortured ears.

"Mummy! Mummy!"

It was Russell, and she began to panic. She screamed out soundlessly, "Russell baby, where are you!"

Sarah paused and returned to reality.

"The house looked vaguely familiar, like our house in Randwick. All I could think was that Russell must be inside," she told Thackeray. He was staring at her intently, thunderstruck by her story. Sarah took a deep breath and cast her mind back to continue her gruelling tale.

Without hesitation, Sarah charged in through the front door of the house and suddenly wary, turned sharply to see it slam shut behind her. The house shuddered from the slam as if it was alive, and it scared the hell out of her. Lightning flashed brightly outside the window, and she flinched.

"The house groaned, creaked... and then began to move," she said, to a spellbound Thackeray.

She raced over to the window and looked out. The house was moving over the terrain like it was on an air cushion, heading towards a huge metal high-tension tower that was arcing in a fury of violent purple plasma discharges, a short distance away.

"It was then I realised I was inside Russell's memory at the time of the car accident. The house was a representation of the car interior—the way Russell understood it from the perspective of his safety seat, and it was about to collide with the high-tension tower—just like it had before. It was like history repeating itself. I just wanted to get out of there."

She raced back to the front door and pulled at the handle, but it wouldn't budge. Now she was in a real panic. She heard Russell again.

"Mummy, mummy."

"I'm coming sweetheart—keep calling me!"

"I couldn't get a fix on where Russell's voice was coming from, but I knew I had to find him before the house crashed into the tower."

She swallowed her fear and began a frantic search of the house for Russell.

"I was sure the room was pretty much an exaggerated representation of the inside of the car... but seriously distorted."

She looked up and recognised the car interior light in the centre of the ceiling—it was huge. Then she noticed the far wall didn't quite reach the ceiling.

"I could see the console gap between the two front bucket seats... I felt if I could climb through the gap, I'd find Russell on the other side."

The gap was like a crevasse. Looking back over her shoulder while she climbed through, she could see through the window that the house was closing quickly on the high-tension tower.

"I had to get to Russell before the collision."

Then she sighted Russell strapped into his safety seat, cheerful as ever, totally unaware of the impending crash.

"Hi Mum!" he smiled.

"Hello darling, let's get you out of there."

She released him into her arms, gave him a big kiss, and then squeezed back through the seats and rushed to the front door. The room began to rock about, causing her to run like a drunk. It must be the car bouncing over the field. When she got to the door, she pulled at the handle with all her strength, but it still wouldn't budge. She went to the window and belted the glass as hard as she could with her fists—but couldn't smash it.

The house was only seconds away from colliding with the tower.

"Then I had an idea."

"Maybe only Russell can open the door—it's your dream... give it a try love. Open the door."

Russell grasped the handle and gave it a twist—it opened. "That's my boy!" she looked down and saw the ground speeding under the house, then up at the looming tower. They would have to jump. "Here we go baby, hang on!" Then, with Russell grasped firmly in her arms, she closed her eyes and bailed out.

When she opened her eyes, Sarah was back in the field where she first arrived, but now with Russell safely in her arms. "Right, now all we need to do is find our way out."

"I sensed somehow that finding a way back to reality would revive Russell from his coma."

Russell pointed to a cluster of pine trees on the far side of the field where there was a strange glowing light.

"A light!" Russell exclaimed.

"That might be the way out, baby."

"As we raced towards the light, I suddenly felt a presence—it was a feeling like something terrifying and evil was near."

She stopped—there was an acrid sulphurous stench in the air, like rotten eggs. Over the ground, a dark sinister shadow was creeping slowly towards them.

"It was like the shadow of a man, but no ordinary man—he had long extended clawed fingers, like the shadow of Nosferatu in that old 1922 black and white horror movie."

"It's only a shadow, Sarah, it can't harm us!" she told herself, but then she noticed that the grass the shadow had touched had shrivelled and died, and she was overcome by an ice-cold dread.

"It dawned on me that the shadow was the coma or even death itself coming to take Russell."

She held on tight to her son and took off as fast as she could towards the light.

Suddenly a voice called out to her.

"It's a Dreamraider! Don't run towards the light, run for the toys!"

"The voice sounded familiar and friendly, so I obeyed."

She ran towards the giant toys dotted about the field. The closest toy was a giant flying saucer she recognised as one of Russell's favourites. She headed for it. On the run, she looked back over her shoulder—the shadow was gaining on them!

"Then from out of nowhere, a man dressed in black materialised, like he'd stepped from the set of a Hollywood Western, right between the Dreamraider and us. I realised he had called us. He was wearing a big black cowboy hat, but I couldn't quite make out his face under the brim."

She stopped dead in her tracks aghast.

"He was a comic strip character, a 3-D animated version of my dead husband Wayne! I realizsd that this must be how Russell saw him."

"Hello Daddy!" Russell said.

"Wayne?" Sarah questioned tentatively.

He looked up at the two of them from under his hat, with the sort of broad smile that was totally out of character for the real Wayne, more like Clint Eastwood.

"Hey Sarah, Russell. A Dreamraider—that's what we call 'em down here, pardner—shadow demons, they smell like sulphur just as they appear, cool huh? Like a computer game." Wayne spoke with a Hollywood Western drawl that she thought he must have acquired along with the outfit.

He casually produced a sawn-off shotgun from under his black full-length coat, thumbed the hammers back, and aimed it at the Dreamraider shadow as it flowed towards them. He was just about to fire with Sarah and Russell watching in amazement, when the Dreamraider shadow suddenly solidified into a man-sized version of the high-tension tower and with clawed steel arms, reached out, and ripped Wayne to pieces.

"Wayne, no!" Sarah screamed.

"I shielded Russell's eyes from the bloody dismembering of his father and repeated out loud to myself... this can't be real... this isn't real!"

'This isn't real!' The tower blurred into the shadow and started towards them again, and she ran for the flying saucer, clutching a strangely weightless Russell to her hammering breast. They got to the base of the ladder leading to the turret of the saucer and started up. Sarah looked down at the Dreamraider—it was coming up after them.

"Where's Daddy?" Russell asked, close to tears. And then he leaped out of her arms onto the ladder and disappeared into a bright light that had appeared at the turret of the saucer.

"Something was telling me to follow Russell into the light and that everything would be all right. So, I climbed up into the light. The next thing I knew, I was back in the hospital room, still looking down at Russell in his crib, with my fingers on his forehead. I looked at the EEG monitor beside his bed, and the lines on the screen were moving up and down—it showed brain wave activity."

Thackeray was totally absorbed in her story.

"It felt like only seconds had passed since I'd first touched Russell's head. I honestly don't know if it really happened or if I was only dreaming, but I tell you something, I can remember the fear— I can taste it—I remember the sheer terror of the place, wherever it was, the smell of sulphur, and Wayne being there." She was weeping openly now. "Whether it was real or not, Bill, I will remain terrified of shadows and petrified of the dark forever."

He leaned across from the driver's side and took her into his arms. After a quiet, calming few moments while her sobbing faded, he held her at arm's length, locked eyes with her, and said tenderly,

"Now I understand."

She fell gratefully back into his arms, and they kissed.

CHAPTER 10

You touched me
And I'm under your spell
You're the magic of Christabel
And those sweet angel eyes
They hypnotise
Lips of fire
Sweet burning desire.

gk

In a black suit that screamed 'copper' and sticking out like a sore thumb, Thackeray battled the throng of scantily clad Bondi Beach sidewalk pedestrians, a man on a rendezvous mission. When he sighted the sign for Beachbums Café, he navigated through the alfresco setting, spotted the person he was there to meet, and flopped into a chair under a big umbrella, opposite her.

"Terri!" he smiled, loosening his tie.

An attractive indigenous woman in her early thirties, Terri was dressed for spring, not beachwear but a tasteful print dress. She took a sip of what looked like iced tea and peered at Thacka over her Ray-Ban sunglasses. He looked as if he was about to expire from heat exhaustion.

"You look like you need a drink," she said.

"You're not just whistling Dixie, Terri. Is it table service or…?"

A waiter appeared, took one look at Thacka, and rolled his eyes.

"So what will it be, sir? A new wardrobe perhaps?"

"Very funny, dearie. An iced latte, thanks, make that two," Thacka said.

The waiter turned up his nose and waddled off.

"You let him off the hook, that's not like you, Thacka?"

"Never argue with an idiot; he will drag you down to his level and beat you with experience."

"Yes, well, at least take your coat off."

He saw the logic in that but couldn't. He slyly opened his coat and flashed Terri his belt holster.

"Oh, now that wouldn't be a good look, would it?" Terri said with a pearly-toothed smile.

Terri noticed a slim young lady in smart-casual dress and wearing sunglasses, making a beeline for them.

"This must be your partner. Thought no one wanted to work with you, Thacka?"

Parker arrived puffing, flopped into a seat, and announced, "Gawd, it's hot!"

"At least you're dressed for it," Terri said, leaning over and offering her hand to Parker.

Thacka piped up, "Dr Terri Nulla-Nulla Parsons, meet DI Jess never-never-on-time Parker."

"Ha! Very funny, that's the pot calling the kettle black!" Parker scoffed.

"Don't mind her racism, Nulla Nulla," Thacka returned the service.

"Just ignore him, Jess, he loves stirring the pot."

The waiter arrived with two lattes, put one down in front of Thacka, and rolled his eyes. The other went to Parker, who nodded once, and the waiter smiled at her, pursed his lips at Thacka, and waddled off.

"Is he an old flame of yours or something, Thacka?" Parker quipped.

"I think he's in love," Thacka said with a chuckle.

Terri took a sip of her tea.

"So you obviously invited me here for something more than a nice morning chinwag. To pick my psychologist brain about something other than men without hats, yes?"

"Men without hats?" Parker queried.

"Thacka is always going on about how men don't wear hats anymore. But take a look around, they're all wearing hats."

"Those baseball caps aren't hats! Anyhow, a top band that... Men without hats, Canadian." He sang, "We can dance if you want to. Safety dance circa 1983."

"Give me a break, Thacka, singing in the morning. What's in this coffee?" Parker lifted her sunglasses and peered into her latte jokingly.

Thacka focused on Terri. "You're the only psycho I know, so..."

Terri removed her sunglasses, and her smiling green eyes added to her enchantment.

"Funny, I would have thought otherwise!"

"You're probably right—most of my clients are psychos, right, Parker?' he turned back to Terri. "I told you over the phone about Sarah's experience."

"Yes, amazing."

"Well, we need to know what enabled her to enter the mind of her son Russell. Was it all in her imagination or was she in Russell's mind or, 'dreamscape' as Sarah calls it?"

Terri took a sip of her tea.

"Well, since we spoke, I've done some research, and there are plenty of recorded cases of people who, when faced with a life-threatening situation, have performed superhuman feats, even miracles to save a loved one. Things such as lifting a car off someone crushed under it. But dream psychology... now that's something completely different. In a nutshell, my view is this: something probably happened physically to Sarah's brain to enhance her latent psychic abilities, and that allowed her to enter the unconscious mind of her son."

"Unbelievable!" Thacka said.

"That is as opposed to her son's brain being an open portal for her to enter?" Parker added.

"Yes, well put... The condition might have resulted from head injuries she'd sustained from the car accident, but more likely... it was the bombardment of electromagnetic energy from the storm and the high-tension tower... that seems likely to me anyway."

"Was she struck by lightning?" Parker asked.

Thackeray lounged back in his seat. "Yes, actually, the lightning struck the high-tension tower that the car was tangled up in. But I guess the question is... could it work again with anyone, especially someone other than a relative?"

"Possibly," Terri said, scratching her scalp through her short brown hair. "Perhaps she has gained use of an area of her brain that is normally dormant in others; an area that permitted her to access another mind, like a physical mind reader. To the average mind, that part of the brain is a closed door that might only open if triggered to do so by endorphins, but then closes again once the endorphins have worn off. Follow me?"

"Yes," Thacka nodded. "Go on."

"During that state, the subject might be able to perform feats of superhuman strength only to return to a normal state once the hormone inducement has ceased."

"So maybe in Sarah's case, the door mightn't have closed," Thacka said and then took a sip of his latte.

"Perhaps her injury has kept it open. It's only a theory, mind you."

"Wow!" Parker said.

"Yep, that all makes perfect sense. Especially with her already being gifted with the power of premonition," Thacka added.

"Shit, don't get me started on psychics or we'll be here all day. So Thacka, are you and Sarah an item?"

Parker nodded with a grin, while Thacka threw down the dregs of his latte.

"You're good—thank you, police psychologist Parsons—send me the bill."

"You're Bill already, so how can I?" she joked. "That's how he always gets my services for free, Jess."

"Just one thing, guys, what's this all about?" Parsons said, peering intently at Thacka over her sunglasses.

Thacka shot Parker a sly look, seeking her agreement to say more about the case. Parker nodded her approval and spoke up.

"We're close to cracking Thacka's serial killer case, but the perp met with an accident, so... um."

Thacka chimed in, "I'm exploring ways to draw a confession out of him."

"So, he's conscious then?" Parsons asked.

"Um, no," Thacka said dismissively.

"You're not thinking of using Sarah's abilities, are you Thacka?"

The penny dropped for Parker; she looked at Thacka, astonished. "That's not what you're thinking, is it?"

"Look, this guy is a warlock, involved in black magic, capable of doing anything unconscious or not. I just can't rest on my laurels."

Terri pursed her lips and thought silently for a moment.

"I'm just a psychologist with a little more knowledge about psychic matters than most. You need more than my opinion, Thacka, you need an occultist, and I've got just the guy."

"No, we'll be—"

Parker cut Thacka off from being negative, "That'd be great, Terri, thank you," she glared at Thacka, who averted his eyes, seemingly uncomfortable about involving another specialist.

"We don't need any more new-age ratbags involved," he protested.

"Who said anything about a new-age ratbag, Thacka? He's the real thing, a respected academic with scores of published papers on all matters of the psychology of the occult in many respected journals. I've followed his work on-and-off for years and have met him at mainstream conferences. He's a tenured Professor at the University of NSW. You have murders to solve, don't you?"

"What murders?" he said, feigning ignorance.

Taking out her mobile, Parker lightened things up, "Okay Terri, give me the contact, and don't worry about old cranky-bum here.'

Thacka stood, leaned over, and gave Terri a peck on the cheek.

"Thanks, mate, I owe you one," he said with a curt smile.

Parker stood and whispered to Terri. "Don't think he's had a drink since he met Sarah."

"Outstanding, it must be serious. Nice to meet you, Jess."

They smiled at each other as they shook hands. Thacka hadn't heard the whisper, but he knew what they had been talking about.

"Like I've always said, ladies, when you come to the fork in the road of life... take it. See ya, Doc."

"Hey, you're leaving me the bill again?" Terri complained jokingly.

"No, I'm leaving!" he chortled.

Parker and Thackeray left Terri sipping her latte. As they were on their way back to their respective cars, Parker wanted to sum up the meeting.

"Terri's occultist contact will be valuable—I don't know why you gave her such a hard time over it."

"You can pursue it if you like; I've got another idea that might just give us the break we need."

Parker came alongside her car and hopped in. As she watched Thacka walk further along the street towards his vehicle, she dialled the number Terri had given her.

"Hello, this is DS Parker, I'd like to speak to Professor Aleister Klein please... Hello, Professor Klein? Detective Sergeant Parker, of the Metropolitan Police. I hope you can... Dr Terri Parker suggested I call you regarding a case my partner and I are investigating. Yes, it's a murder investigation... a suspected serial killer. Would it be possible for you to come to Police HQ in Surry Hills for a briefing? Yes, today... In an hour, that'd be fine, yes Homicide division, thank you professor... yes, DS Jess Parker. Bye."

Parker entered the office and sat down in her chair with a sigh, glad to be out of the heat of the day. Thacka glanced up at her from his monitor.

"So?"

Parker checked her cell-phone, "Professor of Occult Sciences Aleister Klein will be here in about fifteen minutes."

"And just what do you expect us to learn from him?"

"If I knew that, Thacka, there wouldn't be any need for us to talk to him, would there?"

He swivelled back and faced his monitor.

"Point taken, Parker, but to avoid a waste of his time and ours, it might be prudent to compile a list of questions."

Before Parker could reply, her desk phone buzzed. She picked it up.

"Okay, thanks," hung up and stood. "He's here."

"Oh great," Thacka grunted, irritated by having to conduct what he considered an unnecessary briefing.

"Can we trust this professor?"

"Do you trust Doctor Terri Parsons?"

"Yes, she's a member of the force, but you're right, Parker, she's too professional to give us a bum steer. Go get him."

Parker returned with a tall, rake of a man dressed in the obligatory professor's brown corduroy jacket with leather elbow patches, beige drill pants, and dark brown suede desert boots. With his drastically receding hairline, shoulder-length thin greying brown hair, and round John Lennon spectacles, Thacka thought this academic looked the part. He rose and offered his hand. Parker did the honours.

"Professor Klein, Detective Inspector Bill Thackeray."

They clasped hands.

"Please call me Aleister," he said with an almost British accent.

Parker had moved to the murder wall and set up three chairs. She returned to Thacka and Klein.

"Gentlemen, shall we?" she motioned for them to follow her.

Thacka led Klein to the murder wall, and they sat facing the display of grisly photographs.

"Professor... Aleister, we are investigating two murders and six suspected murders by a person we suspect to be responsible for all of them," Thacka said. "The suspect is a known warlock, a member of a group of witches..."

"A coven," Klein chipped in.

"Yes, in Western Sydney. We have been unable to make an arrest due to lack of evidence."

Klein sat back, studying the photographs on the murder wall and listening intently to Thacka's narrative of the investigation. When he had finished, Parker stood, walked to the murder wall, and took over.

"The top row of post-mortem photographs were taken at the crime scene of the murder of Mrs Niki Blake. The next row of photographs were taken at the crime scene where Richard Riley was killed; we believe both murders to have been committed by the same perpetrator. This photograph is of a young boy's severed penis found recently in Centennial Park. There have been six young boys' penises found over the last six years but no bodies or reported missing persons. This is a photograph of our chief suspect, Wolfen Moloch."

Klein rose slowly to his feet and moved in for a closer look at Moloch's picture. When he turned to face Thacka and Parker, his face was ashen grey.

"Are you certain this man's name is Wolfen Moloch?"

Thacka and Parker exchanged looks; it seemed something must have touched a nerve in the Professor.

"Yes," Thacka said standing. "Why?"

Klein flopped into the chair with a dispirited look on his weather-beaten, fiftyish face. He held his chin deep in thought.

"Professor?" Parker tried to snap him out of his malaise.

He suddenly looked up at them, removed his glasses, wiped them clean with a handkerchief he pulled from his pocket, replaced them, and said nervously, "Moloch was a god worshipped by the Phoenicians and the Canaanites. He had associations with a particular kind of child sacrifice. Throughout the ages, those of the dark arts have sought to resurrect Moloch, along with his demonic assistants, to do their evil bidding."

"But it's only a name, surely?" Parker questioned.

"Wait, Parker, go on, Professor," Thacka was intrigued.

"Apart from the fact that Moloch worship involved parents sacrificing their own children, often by fire, there's not a great deal more I can tell you without further research." He stood still, looking very nervous. "But I'm afraid I won't be able to help you."

"Why not?" Parker asked, miffed by his sudden backpedal.

"This is all quite out of my depth."

Thacka recognised fear when he saw it.

"Professor, I get the sense you're frightened? Are you afraid of Moloch?"

"No, no... not Moloch, but it's what he might or might not represent. Look, I think you are dealing with ritual black magic here, these photographs show all the signs," he took out his handkerchief again and wiped sudden perspiration from his brow. "The ramifications of delving into this are, to be quite frank, not worth risking."

"Are you saying Moloch is some sort of real magician with evil powers?" Thacka inquired.

"Inspector, the occult is more complicated than you could possibly imagine. A warlock such as Moloch is capable of the darkest, most demonic acts... I... couldn't... I mean it would be risking my life to get involved."

"But he's on his deathbed!" Parker added with enthusiasm.

"What do you mean?" Klein said, putting his handkerchief away and appearing to calm down.

Thacka put his foot up on the chair and stuck a toothpick between his teeth.

"He was in a near-fatal car accident, he's on life support, unlikely to last more than a few more hours. Look, all we need from you is as much background on Moloch, his coven, and his supposed demonic assistants as you can give us. I can see no harm in that, can you?"

"What do you need this information for?"

"Because we need to work out where to look for the bodies of the little boys this evil bastard has mutilated and murdered," Thacka said.

"It's the only way we can put this case to bed," Parker added.

Klein thought long and hard about their request and after some moments, which felt like an eternity to Thacka and Parker, he slowly nodded his head.

"I understand what you are trying to do and it's totally commendable. These children and the two murdered adults deserve justice. But I warn, if Moloch is what I think he is, half-dead or even in death, he could continue to be a serious threat... However, I'll do what I can."

Thacka took Klein's hand and shook it.

"Thank you, Professor."

"Aleister. Call me Aleister. I'll get back to you."

Parker showed him out while Thacka went back to his computer.

When Parker returned, she sat on the edge of her desk and candidly said to Thacka, "So what do you think of our professor then?"

"Parker," Thacka announced swallowing his pride, "I stand corrected. As eccentric as he is, I think he will be of value to us."

"You just liked him turning green at the mere mention of Moloch."

"Yep, you're spot on there. His reaction certainly added to the intrigue. Anyhow, more info on the occult side of things certainly won't go astray; we need all the help we can get. Did he add anything else on the way out?"

"No, just that he'll call me when he's got something worthwhile."

"I'm going to catch up on some bookwork here," Thacka said. "How about you drop by St. Vincent's and get an update on Moloch?"

Parker picked up her car keys to go, "Good-oh, see you back here then?"

Thacka nodded.

Professor Klein sat back in his big comfy antique leather chair in his small, dimly lit office, staring at the shelves of reference books that took up an entire wall. He was almost willing the book he needed to identify itself. His office at The Theosophical Society in Kent Street, downtown Sydney, was like an anachronism—a remnant of 19th Century London. Aged wood panelling, old books, the musty smell generally only attributed to old libraries and rustic colonial buildings—papers were strewn all over the antique oak desk. Antiques they might be, but in age only, far too dilapidated to be worth anything, only if they were to be restored to their former glory—but that was unlikely to occur around Professor Klein, who was himself a living, walking vestige of the 19th Century. The one thing out of place in this virtual time capsule, standing on the oak desk and positioned in a place of reverence, was a black, ten-core, dual CPU, Apple Mac, attached to a ViewSonic cinema monitor.

The chair creaked in protest when he tipped himself out of it to reach one long arm up enough to withdraw a book from a high shelf of the bookcase. The book was 'The Revival of Magick and other Essays' by Aleister Crowley. He then selected a second book, it was red, and printed on its spine was 'Studies in Occultism' by H. P. Blavatsky. The founder of the Theosophical Society, Madame Helen Blavatsky, had authored the book in 1887. Klein sank back into his chair with the books on the desk in front of him. This was where he would begin his research into Moloch and his dark universe.

Parker was standing outside Moloch's hospital room with PC Richards behind her, posted as a sentry. She dialled Thacka on her mobile.

"Thacka, doctors say Moloch has lost all vitals and they'll take him off life support soon. Yep, it's all over. Well, in the absence of family, there needs to be a court order for termination... yes, it was applied for this morning and has been issued to the police medical examiner... Yes, that's him... CME Badger, you know him? What's that? He's what? Well, if he's a difficult person like you say, then we're as good as sunk. No, they won't say when they're pulling the plug.

Badger is at his office... Okay, yeah, I know where that is... I'll meet you there in twenty."

She ended the call on the fly out of the hospital.

Thackeray was waiting outside the East Sydney Morgue for Parker. He saw her approaching and opened the door for her.

They walked down the narrow corridor until they came to a door marked CME Badger MD, MBBS. Thackeray knocked, opened the door and ushered Parker in ahead of him.

Behind a plain steel desk was a man with a solemn look on his face, an expression worthy of an undertaker. His head was down reading a document. Close to retirement, Badger disliked Thackeray with a passion. Thacka considered this put him in good company, as he believed Badger probably disliked most people. Skinny, thin-faced, and balding with a gruff monotone voice, Badger spoke without looking up at them.

"I knew Moloch was yours," he glanced up with a dour look. "But then everyone in the force knows about your obsession Thackeray."

"Then you obviously know why I'm here," Thacka reacted sharply.

"You probably want to buy some time so you can try and pin all your unsolved crimes on him, clean up your books."

"Just exactly whose side are you on Badger?" Parker barked.

Badger ignored her.

"Face it Thackeray, you haven't been able to pin a murder on him so far, so what makes you think you can do it now?"

"I need time Badger," Thackeray said stubbornly.

Badger went back to dismissively flicking through papers on his desk—intimating the conversation was over.

"No. He's fresh out of time Thackeray... the decision is made."

"I'm the arresting officer, I have the right to at least know when you're pulling the plug."

"So what was the charge, you incompetent imbecile. You have no rights here Thackeray, only the Coroners Court has rights! Clear? Now, good day!"

Parker saw Thacka's face darken—he was about to explode—she had to step in.

"I'm sorry, Chief Examiner, but perhaps you're ignorant of the law. Moloch is not only a murder suspect but he was exceeding the speed limit. He ran a red light and collided with another vehicle. We were the arresting officers and have every right to know when his life support will be discontinued. Clear?"

An ever-so-slight smirk broke on Thacka's otherwise sullen face. He was proud of Jess.

Badger continued studying papers on his desk, more as a put-down than anything else, then, he casually checked his wristwatch.

"From twenty hundred hours tonight, you have forty-eight hours unless he checks out of his own accord—which is more than likely," he grumbled, like someone had twisted his arm to make him talk.

Parker turned her back on him and stoically led Thackeray out the door—a door they didn't bother to close behind them.

Walking along the corridor, Thackeray gave Parker a playful 'well done' jab in the ribs with his elbow. She giggled.

"Meet you back at the office, I'll pick up some donuts," he said cheerfully.

"Don't be too long; Kitty's meeting us there in ten minutes."

When Thackeray entered his office carrying a box of donuts, he found Parker chatting with Kitty.

"True to form," Kitty sniggered as she peered at her wristwatch. "Late as usual, would've stood me up if it wasn't for Parker here being punctual."

Thacka ignored the wisecrack, flopped into his chair, and handed Parker the box of donuts.

"Had to wait while they cooked them—what's up?"

"Donut, Kitty?" Parker said, offering her the box.

"Absolutely," Kitty said, helping herself to one and then handing Thackeray a folder.

Chewing on a chocolate-coated donut, he casually opened the folder and after a cursory glance sighed morosely.

"I can't bloody believe it—it says here that you took a DNA swab from Moloch, but it doesn't match the sperm sample taken from Niki Blake's rectum. Jesus H. Christ! Why not?"

"That'll make it impossible to get a stay of execution!" Parker said glumly.

Thackeray got up and paced the floor, donut in one hand and running his other hand through his hair—frustrated.

"Why on earth does everything have to be so bloody hard with this bastard Moloch?"

"Bill, take it easy old son," Kitty was an old friend and knew him well. "You'll pop your cork with all that stress. Look, the sperm belongs to someone... let's just find out whom? We can start by getting a swab from other suspects like the husband, just to rule him out."

He knew she was right and flopped back into his chair.

"I'll leave that up to you, Parker."

"Wait a minute," Parker interrupted. "I might be a slow learner but what you're saying is someone gave Niki Blake a shot up the backside post-mortem, and it wasn't Moloch!"

"Yes, that is correct," Kitty confirmed.

"So hey, that leaves our case against Moloch in the shit doesn't it? Who else could it have been for heaven's sake?" Thacka said.

"You sure it was post mortem, Kitty, like she couldn't have brought it with her from somewhere else?" Parker said.

"Ah! It's a bloody dog's breakfast!" Thacka moaned.

"Nope, it was post-mortem all right. But there was something a little odd about it." Kitty said.

"What's that?" Parker questioned.

"Well, normally you see lesions inside the rectal canal after anal sex, and there were none."

"What does that mean?" Parker asked.

"It's difficult to say. With her being dead—there wouldn't have been a struggle. Normally the external anal sphincter is damaged, and it wasn't. There were no signs of lubricant, so the rectal rape is a mystery."

"Would it have been easy for someone to enter the rectum of a dead person? Wouldn't it have been slammed shut tighter than a waterproofed duck's arse?" Thackeray asked.

"No, the opposite applies especially after strangulation. When someone is hung, for instance, they generally release their bowels at the point of expiration." Kitty said.

Thackeray scowled at the donut he was about to bite into. He quickly changed his mind and put it back in the box. "That's enough to turn anyone off a chocolate donut!"

"Sorry, Thacka," Kitty chuckled.

Parker jumped in. "Thacka, you told me you were concocting something to break the case."

"Yes, I've been trying to convince Sarah to enter Moloch's mind."

"You've got to be joking! What for? Terry warned you..." Parker said shocked.

"To find a clue as to how he disposed of the boy's bodies, that's why!" he barked contrite.

"But this guy's teetering on death and he's probably one of the most dangerous killers in the world!" Parker said perplexed.

Kitty had sat through this exchange with her jaw getting progressively wider.

"What the hell are you two talking about? It sounds like the plot to a science fiction movie. What is it to be—superstition or forensic science?" she was utterly confused.

"Laughing clairvoyant!" Thacka fired back.

"What's that? Now I'm confused too!" Parker admitted.

"Pay no attention to him, Jess; he's nuts. Laughing clairvoyant: a happy medium. Means he's going to approach the case both ways," Kitty said with a grim smile.

"That's what I was afraid of—are you sure about this with Sarah?" Parker questioned.

"Well, she hasn't agreed to it yet. Look, you and Kitty get Steve's DNA sorted out. Let me know the results."

The DNA being a dead end irritated him, and Parker knew it. She glanced at Kitty, who was still puzzled by their bizarre conversation about mind travel.

"I'll tell you the sci-fi plot on the way to get a sample from Steve; he's at my place."

Kitty and Parker both stood to leave.

"Now that should be enlightening. Catch you later, Thacka," Kitty said with her signature chuckle. "Stay off the caffeine; you already look more highly strung than Roger Federer's tennis racket."

That got a modest chuckle out of him.

Parker ushered Kitty into her apartment where they found Steve on the lounge with her iPad.

"Hi Steve. This is Kitty. She's the chief crime lab pathologist."

"Hi Steve," Kitty said with her usual brash good-humour, plopping her medical bag down on the sofa.

"Pathologist? What, like CSI?" Steve asked.

"Yeah, that sort of thing, only not dressed as well or paid as generously, and our results come through a lot slower than theirs!" Kitty scoffed.

"Surely you're not suggesting CSI isn't factual?" Steve joked.

"Well, put it this way, they fit more into 48 minutes of television than we fit into a month of true toil."

"Steve, Kitty's here because we need to take a DNA fingerprint from you."

"Me! How come?"

"To exclude you from our inquiries," Parker said, trying to make light of it.

"That's what they say on CSI when they're trying not to freak out a suspect!" Steve said, concerned. "Was there something wrong with Moloch's DNA sample?"

Kitty sat on the lounge beside Steve and opened her bag.

"Wait, was the sperm taken from my wife Moloch's?"

"No, Steve, it wasn't," Kitty confirmed.

He jumped up and started pacing the floor. He stopped and

yelled at Parker. "So now you want to test me in case I screwed my wife, what... after I killed her?"

"No, Steve, we want there to be no reason why you should be suspected," Parker countered.

"Look Steve, either we do it the easy way with a swab now, or Parker will have to take you to the station," Kitty said being pragmatic.

He flopped onto the sofa with his mouth open.

Kitty had a swab ready and took the sample. After she'd locked it away in a sterile tube in her bag, she got to her feet. "That's it from me, I'm out of here."

"I'll run you to the lab," Parker offered.

"No, Jess, I get a cab-charge. Don't worry yourself. I'll give you a bell in a couple of hours with the results. A little advice Steve, if you've got nothing to hide: don't look so worried. Cop you later."

Parker walked her to the door. "Thanks, Kitty."

When she came back to the lounge room, Steve was looking more relaxed.

"Sorry I got a bit riled up, it just feels bad that someone might think that I—"

"No one believes that, Steve. But what other course of action can we take? We have to eliminate everybody to try and sort this out. It just doesn't make any sense."

"What if there was a guy with her when she came to pick up her stuff? What if they had some fun in the place where she used to live and then he split? After that she got murdered."

Parker sat on the sofa.

"I suppose that's possible, but there were no prints anywhere to suggest someone else was with her, Steve. Besides, was she like that?"

"Did you get prints from Moloch being there?"

"No."

"Well, then there could've been someone, couldn't there? Maybe Moloch didn't act alone. Did you think of that? Like I've always thought, how could one person have butchered my dog without Niki hearing it? I know Ralph, only three people could come to my place without him going off his head, me, Niki, and Morgan... and mate, when Ralph went off, everyone in the neighbourhood heard it!"

"Ralph was baited, Steve."

"What?"

"Forensics found meat poisoned with cyanide in his gut. The killer threw him a bait, waited for him to eat it and die, then entered in silence."

"So he came prepared then? He knew I had a dog and all?"

"Yes, I guess he did."

"So if it was Moloch, how the stuff would he know that?"

"Not difficult: he turns up at your house to leave something to frighten you, sees Niki's car out front. Goes to the side gate, sees Ralph. Moloch lives in Waverly, only five minutes' drive from Clovelly. He slips back home and makes up a bait—returns—Niki's car is still there. He baits Ralph—waits a couple of minutes, then enters, goes upstairs, finds Niki. Does the deed. Goes back down stairs and butchers poor Ralph's carcass, then leaves."

"It would have taken him ages to do all that."

"He knew you were at the cricket mate. He had plenty of time."

"How did he know that? Come on, I said nothing about the cricket to anyone at the Sabbat."

"No, but you might have told the girl you stayed with?"

"Rebekah?"

"Didn't you phone me from her place?"

"Yes."

"So it could be assumed Rebekah overheard you talking to a cop and called Moloch. He is her friend, isn't he?"

Steve had gone quiet. It was all making too much sense for him. He suddenly realised he'd been set up.

"Fuck! You know, that's exactly how he knew; she told him about the cricket and Ralph. How could I be so stupid? Now she knows he's dying."

"What? Have you spoken to her?"

"Yeah, I met her today for a coffee."

"Where? Here!" she exclaimed angrily.

"No, at the Circle Café in Balmain."

"Steve, you were told to stay here and you promised not to talk to anyone!" Parker scolded.

"But you said it was over with Moloch, as good as dead."

"There are still loose ends to be tied up, Steve. We've got an occultist specialist, Professor Klein, to help with the case now... We have no idea how the coven might be implicated in the murders; there are people living at Moloch's house, we don't know what part they might have played in it all. We'll need to investigate all of them including Rebekah, that's if she hasn't blown town now that you've let the cat out of the bag." She got up. "Right, I'm going back to the office. You stay put and don't talk to a living soul! Okay?" she said reprimanding him like a school headmistress.

He sank into the lounge.

"No problem."

She let herself out.

Steve immediately booted up the iPad mumbling to himself, "Not likely sister. No-one sets up this little black duck and gets away with it!" He opened The Veil web site and went to the chat room. Rebekah wasn't online but he saw Nissa's name. He typed a message to her.

Kaspar: Hi Nissa.

Nothing...

Kaspar: Is that you Nissa? Remember me, met you with Rebekah.

Nothing... then,

Nissa: Hi Kaspar, sorry I was talking to someone. Yeah, how could I forget you?

Kaspar: Haven't seen you online before. Do you have a webcam?

Nissa: I don't do it much. Yep, wait.

A window opened with Nissa in full frame; he pressed record. Her long blonde hair was tied up in an old-fashioned bun with two black lacquered chopsticks holding it together at the back. She wasn't a Goth like Rebekah, more an earthy hippie type of witch. She didn't wear any makeup and really didn't need to—she was dressed in a dark blue smock dress decorated with moons and stars, nothing flashy and unlike Rebekah, nothing revealing.

"Well look at you, pretty as ever!" Steve complimented.

"Thanks, are you coming to Beltane?"

"No, sure yet, got a few problems to deal with first."

"Yeah, is everything all right?"

"Did you hear about Moloch?"

"Who?"

"You know, Moloch?"

"Oh, yes, I know him, what about him?"

"After he was at the Sabbat the other night, he was in a terrible accident."

He was trying to trick her into admitting Moloch was the He-goat.

"Really, is he all right?" she asked.

He got the answer he was after.

"No, he's in the hospital on life support. They say he won't make it."

"Oh dear, that's shocking news."

"Yeah, so I wouldn't count on him being the Horned God at Beltane."

"Oh, he wouldn't be there anyway."

"How come?"

"Hey look, I've got to go, it's been nice chatting to you."

He knew she was trying to cut the conversation short.

"Wait. I'd like to see you."

"Maybe at Beltane."

"Is it going to be at the same place in Seven Hills?"

"Yes."

"But I'd like to see you before that."

"Oh, when? Why?"

"Tonight."

"Why?"

"I just want to see you tonight."

"Where do you live?" he asked.

"No, you can't come here; I've got flatmates. Do you have a car?"

"Yeah. Want me to pick you up?"

"Are you in the city?" she queried.

"Yes."

"Okay, let's meet at the Archibald Fountain in Hyde Park at 9 PM."

"Okay. See you then."

"Park nearby, okay?"

"Yep, will do. Bye. Oh, do you have a cell number in case..." It was too late; she had gone.

Excited about the prospect of obtaining the information he was after, he decided to send Kingston, his Paragon Press editor, an email update. He thought of a good buyline, then came up with: "Van Helsing-like Demon Slayer Leads Witch Hunt in Western Sydney." Proud of the headline, he quickly typed a two-hundred-word story that stopped short of mentioning Moloch, the murders, or the police, but did mention Professor Klein, a name he remembered from when he was a kid, and a relative from Germany who used to call him his "klein boy." He pressed send without considering the consequences.

Thackeray was in bed reading 'Hide and Seek' by Ian Rankin, one of his favourite authors.

Sarah came from the en-suite bathroom garbed in a black, see-through negligée.

Thacka peered amorously at her over his reading glasses and then reached across the bed took her by the arm and then dragged her onto him. They kissed passionately and their excitement for each other increased. This was their first time in bed together.

Lightning flashed outside and thunder sounded.

"Sounds like a warning from mother nature!" she said with a cute smile.

"Jealous, that's all," he said.

Looking deeply into her eyes he whispered, "I can't believe I've wasted half my life looking for you."

"Seems you're always looking for someone detective Thackeray."

She touched the small tattoo of a snake on his left bicep.

"Why the snake?"

"I've got no idea, a beer too many on a night when I was young and stupid."

"I can't imagine you ever being stupid. I didn't think I'd be able to do this so soon, but it's difficult to resist something as handsome as you."

"I think it's been longer for me than you. I can't remember when Mr Happy last performed."

"Mr Happy is it? Nice to be introduced."

Suddenly, they both heard floorboards creak. They froze, looked up sharply at the bedroom door and were shocked to see Russell standing there in his striped pyjamas.

"Mum, I'm a bit scared of the thunder."

Thacka locked eyes with Sarah and whispered with a smile, "See, I told you the Gods were jealous."

Blushing a little at being caught in the act, Sarah said, "Okay darling, go back to bed, mum will come and tuck you in."

"Funny, that's what I had in mind—different spelling!" Thacka whispered through a cheeky grin.

She slipped out of the bed, donned her robe and looked back at her man in bed.

"Hold that thought, big guy."

Bill went back to reading about Rebus.

Time passed—he'd nodded off flat-out on his back, still wearing his reading glasses, snoring, with 'Hide and Seek' open on his chest.

Sarah crept in, removed the book, stepped out of her robe, and slipped silently into bed beside him.

Bill opened one eye and peered at her. "You forgot my glasses and you owe me one."

She propped herself up on one arm and said with a warm smile, "Sorry it took so long, but he wanted a story, and you're right, I owe you the first one."

He sat up, "Okay, I'm ready to collect. I want you to try and enter my mind while I'm asleep?"

Her expression changed from light-hearted to darkly serious—she wasn't impressed. She had hoped they had moved on from the heated discussion they had had at dinner the other night.

"I thought we agreed not to talk about that again."

"Hey, no harm... I'm not in a coma, I'll just be asleep."

"But why, Bill?"

"To prove a theory."

"What theory?"

"I promise to tell you once you've given it a go. What do you say? Pretty please," he said, using all the leverage in his arsenal, including sad puppy dog eyes. Then, to top it off, he gave her a cute peck on the cheek.

She caved in.

"Okay, but just this once."

He removed his glasses and put them on the bedside table, turned off the light, then lay back with eyes closed.

"Promise you'll wake me afterward?" he mumbled.

Lightning flashed and thunder rumbled; the storm outside was gaining momentum.

After a few minutes, Bill began to snore gently.

Sarah took a deep breath, tentatively reached out two fingers, closed her eyes, and touched Bill on the forehead.

A sudden astral light in her mind's eye jolted her, and she quickly pulled her fingers back. Regaining her composure, telling herself that it was all right, she again touched Bill on the forehead. There was a blinding astral light in her mind.

She was standing in a bathroom that she didn't recognise. There was a young man showering behind a glass partition. He was singing 'Only the Lonely.' It was Bill, but a lot younger and somewhat trimmer—a leaner version of the man he would become.

"Bill?" she enquired with some hesitation.

He stopped singing and looked sharply in her direction. Wiping the glass feverishly for a clearer view, he was clearly shocked and in disbelief that a woman could have appeared in his bathroom.

"Who the hell are you? What are you doing here?" he said, totally flummoxed.

The shower recess door opened enough for him to peer out.

"Remember the word nascent," she said intently.

She quickly reached out two fingers and touched his wet forehead.

A blinding astral flash, and she opened her eyes. She was in bed beside Bill with her fingers resting on his forehead. She lowered her hand then gave him a gentle shake.

"Bill... Bill."

He sat bolt upright with a start and in a reflex action turned on the light.

Turning to face her, he looked her directly in the eyes and said, "Nascent."

They hugged.

"I told you to say that."

"You would have had to, I've never heard the word before."

"It means to display signs of future potential."

"Way too academic for me, I'm an autodidact, lost in a world that only values degrees."

They laughed.

"When was that?" she asked.

"I don't know, describe what you saw."

"A small glass partition shower with a door that opened outwards. Um, a tiny bathroom, tiled half way up the wall with green tiles and then painted pale yellow to the ceiling."

"I've got it—my flat at Kingsford when I was a twenty-five-year-old bachelor."

"Were you a cop then?"

"Nearly, I'd just dropped out of Uni—shame that."

"So what's your theory then?"

"Okay, you, Sarah Dixon, have a gift. It wasn't a dream of Russell's you entered. It wasn't a moment of great love that allowed you to do it... it wasn't Russell having an open, receptive mind... It was all you. Tell me, what if you met someone else in the dream, would you be able to return to reality by touching them?"

"I don't know but it feels to me like the visitor can only return through the host."

She pecked him on the cheek, suddenly exhausted and ready for sleep. Deep down inside she appreciated him accepting her psychic ability without question—something she never had with Wayne. "Goodnight, Bill."

He was still thinking. "How come it doesn't happen when we kiss or if you shake hands with someone?"

"Who says it doesn't?" she said sleepily.

He looked at the alarm clock on the bedside table. It was almost 9 PM, and he reached to turn the light out.

"Goodnight, love," he said, but he knew sleep wasn't going to come easy to his racing mind.

Parker called in to the Crime Lab to see Kitty before heading home.

Kitty was in her office at her desk catching up on paper work when Parker knocked at the door.

Kitty looked up surprised at Parker's face framed in the window of her office door. "Come in Jess, it's open."

Parker entered and sat in a chair opposite Kitty.

"You look buggered," Kitty cracked, peering over her reading glasses.

"This bloody case just won't go away!" Parker said with an element of frustration in her tone.

"Well, I'm not going to be very helpful I'm afraid. The bad news is the sperm sample is a match for your Mr Steve Blake."

"Christ!" she erupted shocked. "How can that be?"

"Take it easy girl, I said that was the bad news, the good news is: I thought, seeing you seemed to believe in this bloke's innocence, that

I'd better check the sample for other fluids."

"Other fluids? I don't understand?" Parker had calmed down somewhat.

"Well, the thought struck me that it was most unlikely Mr Blake would have given his dead wife a shot in the butt... it also struck me that when he claimed so vehemently, at your apartment, that he hadn't had sex with his wife, he had no idea the sperm had been taken from her anus."

"Yes, I picked up on that as well."

"So, I decided to check the sperm sample for contaminants, and I found other female DNA."

"What! From another woman?"

"Yes."

"Wait, so are you saying there were three sets of DNA present, Niki's, Steve's and another female?"

"Precisely. Vaginal fluid contains DNA, so that would suggest the sperm actually came from another woman and that it had been planted in Niki's rectum," Kitty said with a self-satisfied grin.

"A set-up?"

"A set-up," she confirmed.

"But how? Wait a minute... he'd had sex the night before at the Sabbat and maybe even again the morning of the murder. So if he had protected sex with a woman it could have been in a condom or if it was unprotected, the woman could have purged his sperm and given it to Moloch—then he could have planted it in Niki to set Steve up."

"Yep, that's the most likely scenario... and the unprotected version, otherwise we wouldn't have found female DNA other than Niki's."

"Of course—but wouldn't the sperm be dead?"

"Sperm only lives for an hour outside of the body, but no, it doesn't need to be alive for me to extract a DNA fingerprint."

Parker sank back in the chair astounded, "Oh my God! That confirms Moloch had an accomplice, a woman, or maybe even a whole coven of accomplices. Rebekah!" she jumped up in a panic. "This isn't going to end with Moloch dying! There's something else going on here big time. I've got to speak to Steve. Better go. Thank you Kitty, you're a diamond."

She blew her a kiss and then rushed out of the office.

When she reached her car parked in front of the Crime Lab, she immediately pulled out her phone and dialled Steve. She got no answer until his voicemail kicked in.

"Steve? Ring me back urgently, the sample was yours but the sperm sample had been taken from another woman... it was planted on Niki. It was a set up Steve! Be careful of Rebekah!" she hopped into her car and sped for home hoping to find him there.

Steve parked the VW Beetle on College Street, across from St. Mary's Cathedral. Just as he was about to exit the car, his phone alerted him to an incoming message. Presuming it was Nissa to inform him she was running late, he checked it. His face immediately drained of colour when he read Parker's message. Then bitterness overcame his dismay, and revenge overpowered his disgust. He chose not to call Parker back; instead, he stepped out of the car with an uncharacteristic determination: he wasn't going to let a group of witches deceive him.

It was a sultry night, and the Bogong moths were swarming in abundance, dive-bombing the Hyde Park lights.

After briskly walking for a minute or two through the park, Steve spotted a solitary woman sitting on the edge of the low wall surrounding the massive Archibald Fountain.

Nissa looked up and greeted him warmly.

"Ah, it's Theseus—the conqueror of the Minotaur. The spirit triumphed over bestiality—the monster sacrificed itself for the good of humanity!" She was clearly referring to the remarkable bronze sculptures in the fountain behind her.

Steve sat beside her, unconcerned about the classical reference. She looked stunning, with blonde hair cascading onto her shoulders from a colourful Mexican print summer dress that fell just above the knee, adorned with tassels hanging from the elbow-length sleeves like pom-poms. Her dainty feet were elegantly displayed in sleek high-heel sandals. The overall effect was hippie-like, feminine, and exceedingly elegant.

"Not much difference between a man with a bull's head and a man with the head of a goat."

"A he-goat, you mean? Do you see yourself as Theseus, Kaspar?"

"Call me Steve."

"Steve?"

He knew the Minotaur was a metaphor for Moloch.

"No, Nissa, I didn't slay the beast, but I wish I had."

"Why?"

"Because then I would be the hero."

She stood, took both his hands in hers. They kissed, her mouth warm and sweet. All of a sudden, water dripped on his hair and dribbled down his forehead. Then Nissa burst into hysterical laughter—he sensed she was mocking him.

A noise came from behind him, and more water dripped on his hair—he looked up sharply and saw Vivian standing behind him—she had risen from out of the fountain. Her hands were outstretched and clawed, and water dripped from her long grey hair—she looked like a demonic spectre, a ghoulish banshee. He gasped in sudden terror, feeling all of his strength suddenly drain away as Nissa clamped his arms to his sides. A hood cut off his view as other hands grasped him. Before he could draw a full breath through the hood to try to scream, a gag was shoved under the hood and into his mouth. He was powerless, blindfolded, gagged with his hands lashed behind his back.

Parker was on the sofa in her apartment, wondering where Steve was. She worried that he might have reacted badly to her message and gone to confront Rebekah. Whatever turned out to be the case, there was little she could do about it now. She decided to get some sleep and talk to him in the morning.

Steve was tied to a chair in a dimly lit room with a black hood covering his head. In the distance, he could hear the sound of waves crashing, indicating that he was near the ocean. Faint voices echoed from an adjacent room, but their words were indistinct. Among them, he could distinguish Nissa's voice and possibly Vivian's, though there were others present as well. Steve braced himself for what seemed like a long and uncertain night.

Bill and Sarah sat at the kitchen table, with Bill lost in thought. Sarah poured fresh coffee into their mugs and attempted to engage him in conversation.

"So, which distant planet is Detective Thackeray visiting this morning?"

"Oh, I'm sorry, Sarah. I've got work-related issues, and they're gnawing at me. I barely slept."

"Want to talk about it?"

"Ah, I don't think it would help."

"Try me," she said with a mischievous grin.

"Last time, it only led to an argument."

"Oh, I see... go on then."

Taking a deep breath, he continued, "I have a little more than forty-eight hours to prove that Moloch murdered Niki Blake, Richard Riley, and six children."

"Why forty-eight?"

"Because the Chief Police Medical Examiner obtained a court order yesterday to terminate Moloch's life support in just over forty-eight hours. That's why."

"So, what can you do in that time?"

"Nothing now that you've withdrawn your..."

Cutting him off, she said, "Ah, so that's what this is all about... me, is it?"

She rose to her feet, livid. "Your little test last night was nothing more than a ploy to find a convincing way for me to risk my life, huh? For what? Bloody Wolfen Moloch! Well, no thanks, Detective Thackeray!"

She burst into tears and rushed out of the kitchen into the

backyard.

Bill sank back into his chair, feeling like a first-class heel. He knew she was right and asked himself, How could I be prepared to have her risk her life for my obsession? He got up and trudged to the front door to leave, deservedly ashamed of himself.

Sarah was sitting on the back doorstep, crying, when she heard Bill's car start up and drive off. She took a deep breath—the air smelled of freshly mowed lawn.

When Parker wandered into the living room in the morning, she half expected to find Steve there. She went to the spare room, knocked, then opened the door—he wasn't there—he hadn't come home. Concerned for his well-being, she pulled her phone from her handbag to call him. As she retrieved her phone, she found a text from Steve. She blinked several times, suddenly frightened for his life as she read out loud: "If Moloch's life support is cut off before Beltane is over, Steve will be sacrificed." She rose slowly to her feet and read the message repeatedly in disbelief. "No! This is going from bad to worse." Then she noticed her iPad under a cushion on the lounge. "That's funny, why would he leave it here?" She booted it up and noticed a saved movie file on the desktop Steve had left for her. It played back a video of his online webcam discussion with Nissa. She watched it through. "You silly fool, Steve, how dumb are you. So..." She murmured to herself, "you went to meet Nissa, the witch at Archibald Fountain last night. She's one of the coven, and somehow she captured you. The coven wants to keep Moloch alive until after Beltane. But why?" She had missed the email that Steve had sent to Kingston, Editor-in-chief of Paragon Press.

CHAPTER 11

If you're game enough to take the risk
not afraid to taste the devils kiss
understand you're a better man than I,
go and look Satan square in the eye...

gk

Parker was already at the office when Thackeray came in, and he was in a foul mood. She figured he'd had a domestic.

"Morning. Looks like you're not in the mood for it, but you'd better sit down; we've got a problem, and it's a substantial one," Parker said sternly.

Without saying a word, he sank back into his chair and listened.

"Kitty got a positive match on the semen from Niki with Steve Blake."

"What?"

"Wait, let me give you with the complete picture. We knew he wouldn't have killed his wife and then had intercourse with her."

"Why not? I've heard of worse things."

"Unlikely then... at least we felt so."

"Go on."

"Kitty felt the sperm had been planted by Moloch to frame Steve, and so she examined the sample for other substances, including vaginal fluids, and she got a hit. The sperm had been taken from a female with whom Steve had intercourse, and then it was inserted into Niki's anus."

"Unbelievable, but it does explain why she was face down on her stomach."

"Hold on, it doesn't stop there. Steve was worried we suspected him, so I called him from the lab to give him the good news. He didn't answer, so I left a message. He must have received the message, flipped out, and then arranged to meet Nissa, a witch from the coven... then I received this."

She displayed the text message on her phone. When he finished reading it, he lowered his face into his hands; it was all becoming overwhelming for him.

"Damn. Damn. Damn. So let me get this straight," he sighed, "we now have a coven as possible accomplices in the murder of Niki Blake and maybe more. They have now kidnapped Steve Blake and are trying to ransom his life for Moloch's until Beltane is over... that's tomorrow night. The plug is due to be pulled on Moloch before that. Why do they want Moloch kept alive until then?"

"I have no idea. I got onto the tech guys, and they tried to triangulate Steve's phone, but no go, it's turned off, with the battery probably removed."

"Okay," he stood up and said firmly. "We've got two questions to answer: one, why do they want Moloch kept alive, and two, where would they have taken Blake?"

"Keeping Moloch alive must have something to do with Beltane."

"Okay, get the nutty Professor to research that."

"You mean Professor Klein? Okay, you realise if we make a move on any of the witches, they might kill Steve?" Parker offered, genuinely concerned despite her anger at Steve's foolish behaviour.

Thackeray's mood had changed—his face had lit up, and he was onto it with enthusiasm, his hunter's instincts overwhelming his earlier gloom. He moved quickly to the Murder Wall. Parker joined him. He took the black felt-tip pen and began scribbling on the board while talking.

"Let's assume everything we know already is somehow

connected: the boys, Riley, Niki's murder, the coven, the Sabbat, Moloch, Rebekah, Missy, Steve's kidnapping, and Beltane."

"That's Nissa, not Missy."

"Fine," he irritably rubbed out Missy—reluctantly changed it; he wasn't fond of being corrected; it broke his concentration. He drew lines connecting each name and questioned, "Who or what do we have to link all this together?"

"Um, how about the Circle Café in Balmain? Or the boy with autism... the Veil chat room, um, Sarah?"

He wrote it all down on the Murder Wall, then turned to face her. In doing so, he noticed Miller staring through the glass partition at what he'd written on the murder board. Miller shook his head and ambled off.

Thacka turned his attention to Parker. "Right. Well, Sarah's not looking good," he turned sharply to the board and angrily crossed out her name. "We might be able to get something on Rebekah from the Circle Café, but there isn't enough time—the chat room might give us a lead, there are no leads on Riley's murder yet, the boy only had the star tattoo connection—what about—" he scribbled on the wall. "Jason Little and Dorrie Wilson!"

He faced her with an amazed look on his face. It was as though light bulbs had illuminated simultaneously above their heads.

"Moloch poisoned the Blake's dog with cyanide."

"Yes, he probably prepared the bait at his home," Parker said with enthusiasm.

"We need to search it for cyanide. We'll need a 46A search warrant under an indictable offense—accessory to the murder of Nichola Blake before the fact should do the trick. Do you have the cyanide poisoning lab certificate?"

"Yes."

"Good, give it to the desk sergeant and have him start the process. It'll take a couple of hours to get a magistrate's approval. I'll book a SWAT team for 3 PM."

"Are you sure we'll need SWAT?" Parker questioned.

"You bet, I don't trust that little bloke, and Moloch's probably got an armoury in the house. Besides, this needs to be short and sweet—over in a flash—for Steve's sake. Otherwise, they might tip off the kidnappers."

She rose and stood for a second, deep in thought, then made a private decision and turned to Thacka. "So why the sad face first thing today, boss?" Parker said with a warm smile.

"Mate, there are two types of people in the world, those you want to drink with and those who make you want a drink."

"I get the picture, woman problems. Don't let it get to you; we're a weird mob. If you could work us out, you could retire from being a cop, write the definitive book, and make a squillion."

He cracked a smile; she had cheered him up.

"Right, go!" he ordered, breaking the bonded moment.

She jumped to it, picked up a folder, and rushed out of the office bound for the Desk Sergeant at reception. On her way, she phoned Professor Klein on her mobile.

"Hi professor, it's Jess Parker, fine. No, I'm not expecting your research already... I just have a question. Members of the coven we mentioned have kidnapped someone and are holding him ransom... no, not for money, they want Moloch kept alive until after Beltane. Yes, well, he's scheduled to be taken off life support tomorrow afternoon. It's an order from the coroner's office. Yes, it's normal procedure in a terminal case such as this... Well, we think there must be some dark reason why they want Moloch kept alive, and we thought it must be to do with the day itself—Beltane. Okay, I appreciate your help, just give me a call as soon as you know anything."

Thackeray and Parker pulled up a few houses short of Moloch's home in Trafalgar Street, Waverley. The street ran east-west towards the sea, with a sharp slope down towards a park and cliffs overlooking the Pacific Ocean. This time it wasn't so scary; the sun was shining, the sky was blue, and the azure Ocean waters were glistening as though they had been sprinkled with diamonds.

A SWAT Lenco Bearcat armoured vehicle pulled up behind Parker's car. Inside, Parker and Thackeray checked their weapons then, as they stepped from the car, four heavily armed SWAT troops, dressed in black, helmeted and clad in Kevlar armour, charged Moloch's house.

There was no mucking around—they went straight in through the front door as if it was made from paper mâché. The crash as the door burst open was followed by the shouts and commands as the SWAT team searched the house.

Thackeray and Parker followed, guns up, but by the time they got inside, the front rooms had been efficiently secured.

Jason Little and Dorrie Wilson were face down on the living room floor, their hands clenched behind their heads with two SWAT troopers standing over them. The other two SWAT troopers were still searching the house.

"Clear!" A loud call came from the senior SWAT officer, and Thackeray and Parker holstered their pistols.

Two uniformed support police entered the room.

"Cuff them and take them downtown," Thacka ordered the uniforms.

They walked Jason Little and Dorrie Wilson out of the house to the police wagon parked outside.

"Right, Parker, let's search for cyanide."

The other two SWAT members joined them in the living room.

"There's a vehicle in the garage, the rest of the house is clear, sir," the senior Swat officer reported.

"Good, give us ten minutes with the place before you leave."

"Yes, sir," the tall bulky SWAT leader said.

To Parker, he looked to be as tough as goat's knees.

The SWAT team took some time out while Thacka and Parker went on the hunt for poison, congregating on the porch and lighting cigarettes.

"You check the garage... I'll do the kitchen," Thacka instructed.

Parker was only gone a minute when Thacka heard her call,

"Thacka! Thacka!"

He raced through the interior doorway into the double garage and found Parker staring at an old VW Beetle.

"That's Steve's car," Parker said.

"He must be here somewhere!"

They hurried back to the lounge room.

"Sergeant!" Thacka bellowed.

The SWAT team had removed their helmets and was loafing about on the porch. The Sergeant jumped up as soon as he was addressed. "Yes, sir?"

"The car in the garage belongs to the kidnap victim, search the house again, thoroughly this time, every bloody nook and cranny!"

"Yes, sir! Snap to it!" he ordered his men.

The other three SWAT officers jumped up and moved on the search like greased lightning.

After a few minutes, a loud cry of "Sir" resonated throughout the house. They all converged on a room at the back of the house where the sergeant was standing by a locked door he'd uncovered. It had been hidden behind a tall kitchen cabinet on concealed casters, which the SWAT lads had pushed aside.

"We noticed wheel marks on the floor, sir," the Sergeant reported pleased with himself.

Thacka amused the SWAT team by standing near the door and sniffing the air.

"The same smell, Parker, the same smell of incense I smelt in the bedroom at the Blake's. Can you smell it?"

Unlike the SWAT team, Parker didn't think Thacka was off his rocker, and she sniffed the air as well.

"Yes, some sort of exotic incense, all right."

A grin of gratification broke Thacka's intensity, he yelled. "Bust it!"

Snapping to it, the Sergeant drew a tomahawk from his belt and with one powerful, precise blow, knocked the padlock and chain from the bolt that was securing the door. He holstered the axe, unslung his Heckler and Koch submachine gun, jerked back the charging handle to chamber a round, flicked on the torch attached to the barrel of the weapon—and flicked off the safety, then led the way through the doorway into an abyss with a wooden staircase leading down. At the base of the stairs, his sweeping torch beam suddenly illuminated a man tied to a chair—bolted to the floor—in the centre of the room. He was motionless, breathing shallowly, with a black hood over his head.

Parker rushed to him and removed the hood.

Steve gasped and blinked a few times, trying to focus while being untied and having his gag removed.

Shielding his eyes from the torchlight, he said, "Is that you, Parker?"

"Yes, Steve."

"Fuck, am I glad to hear your voice!"

One of the SWAT team found the light switch and flicked it on. What they saw astonished them.

They were in a large windowless chamber. The walls were painted crimson and inscribed floor to ceiling with black painted occult symbols. A white pentagram in a circle was emblazoned on the floorboards. An altar stood at one end of the room, on it were a golden candelabra, with seven black candles, a large golden inverted crucifix and a ceremonial dagger. In various places around the room, chrome chains with leather hand straps dangled from the ceiling.

"This is where Moloch butchered those little boys, I can feel it!" Thackeray said, darkly sniffing the air.

"Here, sir!" One of the SWAT team said.

Thackeray strode over to a black, gothic-looking cabinet, which the trooper was pointing to. It looked ancient. Perched scowling on top was a one-metre-high statue of a gargoyle. The cabinet was ajar and inside Thacka could see bottles containing various S&M items including whips and chains, as well as surgical instruments—bone saws, scalpels, and other medical paraphernalia, he didn't recognise.

There were bottles containing different animal and human

foetuses in formaldehyde and bottles of chemicals—it was a regular alchemist's apothecary. Then he saw a bottle labelled cyanide.

"Don't touch a thing!" he said abruptly. "This is a crime scene; we'll need to lift Moloch's and maybe his accomplices' prints from everything here, in particular, this bottle of cyanide."

"Should I call Kitty?" Parker asked.

"Yes, do that. Let's get out of here—this place gives me the creeps!" Thackeray said as he made for the staircase.

Two of the SWAT team members helped a badly disoriented Steve up the stairs.

Later, back at Homicide HQ in Surry Hills, Parker and Thackeray were sitting outside the interview rooms. Thackeray was checking his wristwatch.

"Late for something?" Parker queried.

"We're still on countdown for the plug to be pulled on Moloch. We might have enough to stop it now."

"And why would you want to do that for God's sake? Inside of an hour, we'll probably have a confession from Little and Large, then we can round up the witches tomorrow night at the Beltane orgy, and we'll have it done and dusted. Next thing, we'll be in court."

"I'm not as confident as you, Parker. Once Moloch's gone, so have our chances of determining the fate of those boys."

"Thacka, have you ever given any consideration to the idea that because you lost your six-year-old boy you might be obsessing over Moloch's victims?"

"What, seeking retribution? Venting my guilt? You sound like a psychoanalyst, Jess."

He pulled a toothpick from his pocket and jammed it between his teeth.

"Where there's smoke, there's fire, DI Thackeray."

"If I was to agree with you, we'd both be wrong."

"Maybe, maybe not."

"All I'm saying is Moloch still might be our only hope. We've got enough to delay Badger flicking the switch; he's going to die anyway—what's to lose?"

"Has Sarah agreed?"

"No."

"So, end of argument, Bill."

"There comes a time in everyone's life when the seconds mean more than minutes ever had. I don't want to spend those last seconds still wondering if Moloch killed those boys."

Parker nodded; she understood exactly what he was saying. They both went back to staring at the floor, killing time.

"Tell me, how many toothpicks do you carry in your pocket?"

"Enough."

"Give us one."

Thacka raised an eyebrow at her, then reached into his pocket and with a deep flourish, handed over a toothpick as if it was his most prized possession. She gripped it between her teeth and went back to studying the floor.

The next time Thacka looked at his watch, he showed concern.

"Something's wrong. We've been here for over an hour."

Parker whipped out her phone and was just about to dial and complain when footsteps alerted them to someone approaching. Officer Lee appeared with Dorrie Wilson and, after a slight nod to Parker, pushed the hefty woman into Interview Room one. Soon after, a uniformed officer showed up with Jason Little and took him into Interview Room two. Thackeray followed.

After Jason Little sat down, Thackeray took a seat and then switched on a recorder on the table. Little was locked and loaded.

"You must be nuts, copper? I'm saying nothing until my lawyer gets here, and even then you'll get zilch out of me."

Thacka casually flicked off the recorder and called out, "Officer, send in the gown."

The Officer smirked at Thackeray's play on words, referencing the song "Send in the Clowns". Thackeray didn't like lawyers. He closed the door then sat back in his chair with his arms folded, chewing a toothpick, staring the little man down.

Dorrie Wilson's lawyer was with her, so Parker turned on the recorder, date-stamped the interview, and proceeded. "Miss Wilson, how long have you resided at 23 Trafalgar Street, Waverly?"

"No comment," Dorrie said, rolling her eyes defiantly.

"Miss Wilson, how long have you known Mr Wolfen Moloch?"

"No comment."

"Miss Wilson, you are required by the law to answer my questions."

Her lawyer cut in, a supercilious, thin-lipped, balding overtly gay man in his mid-fifties.

"Incorrect, DI Parker, and you know it. Until my client has been formally charged, she doesn't have to cooperate at all."

"Fine. So I presume you will be happy with the charge of accessory to the murder of Mrs Nichola Blake, before and after the fact then?"

Lawyer and client exchanged a grimace of disbelief.

"I presume you have evidence to support that charge," he countered.

Parker stood, switched off the recorder, and collected her folder from the desk.

"I'll send an officer with the formal charges for you to sign, then you can make up your mind if you want to answer my questions or not."

Bryson the lawyer whispered in Dorrie's ear, "She's bluffing."

Parker opened the door and was about to leave when Bryson spoke up.

"DI Parker?"

She looked back from the door,

"Yes, Mr Bryson?"

"Will Mr Little be charged as well?"

"Now, now, Mr Bryson, you know I can't answer that."

"Can a deal be done here?" Bryson asked coyly.

"That depends on the quality of your client's answers. So, what's up, am I leaving or staying?"

Again Dorrie and Bryson exchanged glances along with a clandestine whisper, and then Bryson said, "Please stay, Miss Wilson is willing to cooperate."

Parker paused for effect then went back to the desk, sat down, opened her folder on the desk in front of her, and triggered the recorder.

"Shall we start again, Miss Wilson? How long have you resided at 23 Trafalgar Street, Waverly?"

"Six months," Dorrie answered.

"How long have you known Wolfen Moloch?"

"Same. I was brought to the house by Jason; he said I could stay there."

"During that time have you ever attended a black mass or any occult ritual involving Mr Moloch?"

"Don't know whatcha mean by occult, but he chained me up a few times... you know in the cellar... he liked to watch Jason, well you know, giving me one or two."

"You mean he watched you and Mr Little copulating while you were chained up?"

"Yep?" she admitted.

"I see... Um, have you ever seen any little boys at the house?"

"Nope."

"Do you know the name Richard Riley?"

"Nope."

"On Sunday, October 25th, last, were you at home between 10 AM and 6 PM?"

"Let me think... Sunday a week ago... Um, yeah, think so. I don't usually go out on Sundays."

"Was Mr Moloch?"

"Um, lemme think... he was in and out a bit."

"Do you remember if he went out, came back, went down into the basement, and then went out again?"

"Yeah, well, he came into the basement, I remember that because me and Jason were in there having... well, you know..."

"Why did he come into the basement, was it to get something?"

"Yeah, I remember because Jason was getting the whip from the monster cabinet when sir came in. He took a jar of something out of the cabinet and took it upstairs... he brought it back later before he went."

"Could that have been cyanide?"

"Oh, I dunno, could've been anything, really."

"I see. When Mr Moloch came home, was there anything different about him?"

Now it's funny you should say that 'cause there was, aye. Me and Jason were on the lounge room floor playing piggies."

"Is piggies a card game?"

"No, I get on my hands and knees and, well, he's gotta catch me first..." She chuckled, and her jowls and quadruple chin shook like a jelly on a plate.

"Did you see Mr Moloch's clothes?"

"Yes, I had to wash 'em 'cause they had blood on 'em."

"Did you ask him where the blood came from?"

"Don't be stupid, you don't ask sir questions like that, he's gonna belt you."

"Were you a sex prisoner of Moloch and Jason Little?"

"S'pose you could say that."

"So were you permitted to leave the house?"

"Nope. Wasn't brave enough to run away. They'd only get me again and then give me a beating."

Parker was feeling sorry for Dorrie; she wasn't the sharpest tool in the shed, and she'd obviously been terribly abused.

"Do you know Rebekah, Nissa, and Vivian?"

"Yeah, and Lilith, Raven, and Luna, they're all sir's witches."

"Who brought Steve Blake to the house last night?"

"Nissa and Vivian did."

"Why did they bring him to the house?"

"For Beltane."

"What's that?"

"They said for the Halloween party. Tomorrow night."

"Where?"

"Dunno."

"Are you going to the party?"

"No, sir was gunna lock me up."

"Why?"

"He's got guests, I s'pose. He does that when he's got company."

"You and Jason?"

"No, Jason helps sir."

"How long have you known Jason?"

"Same, six months—I met him when I was visiting graves at Waverly cemetery."

"What a relative's grave?"

"No, just visiting all of them one night."

"I see. Last question to you, Mr Bryson, if your client wants leniency, she will agree to take me to the Beltane Sabbat?"

Dorrie and Bryson exchanged looks then Dorrie nodded to Parker.

"Is that a yes?"

"Uh-huh, but I dunno where it is." Dorrie said vaguely. "I don't go to them things."

"Okay, that will be all for the time being," Parker stood, switched off the recorder, and collected her folder.

Thackeray was getting nowhere with Jason Little. The little man was arrogant and uncooperative. His thin-lipped, dour-faced, plain-Jane lawyer Doretta Lowenstein, who insisted on being addressed as Miss Lowenstein, would have been better placed working as a prison guard. Her reputation for being obstinate had earned her the nickname Sudor, from Thackeray, because he thought she had the personality of an armpit.

There was a knock at the door, it opened, and Parker handed in a note to Thackeray. He rolled his eyes at her, a testament that he was doing it tough.

"Sudor?" She mouthed knowingly.

He whispered, "Put it this way, women will never be equal to men until they can walk down the street with a bald head and a beer gut and still think they are sexy."

"Got ya," Parker said and then disappeared behind the door, which closed. Thackeray sat down and read the note from her, making sure his uncooperative guests caught his theatrical reaction of smug success.

"Hmm, Little, how long have you known Miss Dorrie Wilson?"

"Five or six months, why?"

"What is your relationship with her?"

"We do stuff, you know...."

"Right."

"Can we go now?" Little snapped.

"How long have you been living with Moloch?"

"A few years—I've already answered that."

"Yes, but I have some information Miss Wilson has given my partner that I'd like to check with you. Have you ever seen a little boy at the house?"

"No... no... no, I've already answered that before. You got a bad memory or something?"

"Are you going to the Beltane Sabbat?"

"No, I don't do that stuff."

"What do you normally do during Beltane?"

"Moloch and I sacrifice a lamb and eat its liver raw! What do you want me to say? We have our own celebration trick or treating."

"Does that entail human sacrifice?"

"Don't answer that Jason!' Lowenstein jumped in. "Mr Thackeray, if you're going to continue badgering my client, then this interview is over."

"Keep your blouse on Miss Lowenstein, I've already got enough on your client to put him away for a long holiday at the State's expense. We can call it a day now or your client can cooperate for a change and perhaps earn some leniency," he paused to let the message sink in. "Your call."

Lowenstein and Jason went into a huddle.

"What exactly do you want to know Thackeray?" Lowenstein asked bluntly.

"Three questions: one, does your client know if Wolfen Moloch killed any children? Two, did Wolfen Moloch commit murder last Sunday, October 27? And three—did Moloch kill Richard Riley or Niki Blake or her dog? I'll give you a few minutes to think those questions over and prepare your answers."

He left the room.

CHAPTER 12

Folks tell of sulphurous smells
of death and decay
if you end up with the walking dead
then you're there to stay.
No-one returns to tell
of what's inside
It might be paradise it might be hell...

gk

Thackeray and Parker met in the corridor outside the interview rooms.

"Thanks for the note—it worked a treat. But you could have at least written something on it!" he joked.

"Wilson said that Moloch gave her some bloody clothes to wash. Must've been from the dog he gutted. Might find traces in the laundry to match up with the dog. She also agreed to direct us to the Beltane Sabbat, though she's never been to one before, so I wouldn't put my house on that happening."

"We'll need to firm that up to bust the witches."

"Seven of them in the coven, they're all in it up to their necks in my book. If she falls through, we can use Steve," Parker said sternly.

"Still, we don't have what we're after."

"No mention of the boys from Little?"

"No, but he reacted when I mentioned them."

"How far can you go before Sudor shuts you down?"

"It's already getting too close for comfort."

"Why not try the old play one against the other trick? Tell him Dorrie told us he helped murder a little boy. Either Sudor will pull the plug or you'll get something."

"Yep, that's worth a try," Thacka said. "I left them to mull over a few tough questions. You done with Porky?"

"You're terrible Thacka. Yeah, she can bake in a cell for a while."

"What about Jason bonking her, wouldn't that be a sight for sore eyes?"

She grimaced, "Ten times a day she said!"

"Bloody hell, he must something going for him."

"Yeah well, looking at her, size would have to matter."

"It's hard to picture, there'd be a lot of folds of fat before you could find the right groove."

"Urr, Thackeray, the mind boggles, that's disgusting—no more thanks."

"Speaking of that, where's your mate?"

"Steve? He's at my place, I told him to sit pat. I think after the kidnapping ordeal he might do as he's told this time."

Thacka chuckled to himself as he ambled back to the interrogation room.

"Well," Thacka said, flicking on the desk recorder and then taking his seat. "I'll ask the questions again just for the record. Does your client know if Wolfen Moloch killed any children? Did Wolfen Moloch commit murder last Sunday October 27? And did he kill Richard Riley?"

Lowenstein gave her client a feeble nod to answer.

"Never heard of him killing anyone," Jason answered spitefully.

"Okay, well, that just about does it, my partner has concluded her interview with Miss Wilson, we'll be holding you both until further notice."

"But—" Lowenstein protested, but was stopped from speaking by a hand motion from Thacka.

"Take up the legal inquiries at the front desk Miss Lowenstein," he said caustically.

He leaned across the table to turn off the recorder but paused and then mentioned nonchalantly, "Oh, by the way, Miss Wilson told us you bragged to her about attending a human sacrifice. We're getting further details from her, so we'll certainly have more to talk about later."

"That's just bullshit! I'm saying nothing more!" Jason sneered.

"You can turn off the recorder now Detective, the interview is over. If you want to ask anything more of my client, then you'll have to charge him first."

Thackeray leaned across the desk, switched off the recorder, and then eyeballed Jason Little.

"You'll have time to think in a cell... Because in a few hours they'll flick the switch on your boss, so he won't be doing any more little boys or anything else for that matter."

"I wouldn't be so sure of that copper!" The little man snarled with an evil grin.

The statement chilled Thackeray to the bone.

Parker was driving home, mentally reviewing the events of the day when the ringtone sounded on her mobile, snapping her back to reality. She picked it up from the front passenger seat, saw it was Professor Klein, and pulled over to the kerb to take the call.

"Professor Klein. No, I haven't, what! You're kidding!" she blushed with anger. "I'm just on my way home from HQ but I can meet you... Where? Sorry, bad signal... four eight four, ah-ha, The Theosophical Society third floor, yep, I know where that is. No don't worry I'm a cop, we don't get parking tickets. I'll be there in fifteen."

It was 7 PM, the peak-hour traffic had subsided, and the city had been all but emptied of its weekday visitors. Daylight savings time meant a red-orange glow from the setting sun in the west beamed dying rays, which cut scythe-like through the high-rise buildings dominating the skyline of Kent and Sussex Streets. Kent was one-way northbound, and Parker found a parking place in a taxi zone right outside the hole-in-the-wall café, next to the entrance to Theosophy House. She displayed her police parking permit on the dashboard for the parking Nazis, then got out and went to the left-side entrance of Theosophy House. She looked up at the carved, six-pointed star over the arched entrance for a long moment—she distinctly felt it was warning her to enter at her own risk. She felt the hairs rise on her forearms and the back of her neck, as if someone had walked on her grave. She shook off the feeling and ascended the six stairs to a cramped foyer where she found a small old-fashioned elevator. It was like a trip into the past for her, she hadn't been in an old post-war Sydney building for ages. She pulled the grill aside and stepped into the elevator. It was licensed to carry only four passengers, and as she closed the grill, she noticed a peculiar smell and was instantly cast back to memories of her grandfather. She pressed number three on the control panel, and the old machine came to life with a sudden jerk. It rose slowly, as hesitant as she had felt earlier.

When she stepped out of the elevator into the dimly lit wood-panelled hallway, the Goosebumps returned. It was a spooky place. Void of life and eerily silent, it felt like a scene from an old B-grade horror movie. She told herself she was just being silly but was uncomfortably reminded of her ordeal with Moloch, in the underground car park of her apartment block. That caused her to hurry to the office door marked Prof A.B Klein—Occult Research, knocked briskly once and entered, relieved to find a familiar face inside the messy office. Professor Klein stood up from behind his desk to greet her.

"Detective Sergeant Parker, please take a seat," he said, quickly removing a stack of folders from a chair facing his desk and then offering it to her.

"Please pardon the mess, I, well, it's how I work, organised chaos."

"Don't worry Professor, you're expected to be a bit eccentric, it goes with the bow tie you're wearing."

He unwittingly touched his maroon bowtie with a bashful smile;

he wasn't used to being complimented. Sinking into his big old leather chair, which Parker thought had seen better days, he picked up a newspaper from his desk and passed it to her to read. She opened it at the page he'd marked and immediately spotted a short article with the headline: Demon Slayer leads Witch-hunt in Sydney's West. It took her a few moments to scan.

With a dour expression, she looked up at the professor and protested.

"I can't believe this could have leaked out... and it mentions you by name, but how?" As she spoke the words, the answer simultaneously dawned on her, "Steve!"

"I beg your pardon?" Klein questioned.

Parker was embarrassed.

"I think I know who leaked it."

"To tell the truth, I don't know whether to be angry or not. For now, let's just say that I'm a little concerned."

"My apology isn't enough Professor; this article has possibly placed you in danger."

"That is what I feared you would say. Should I panic?"

"I don't know. I used to be indecisive, now I'm not sure!" she mumbled to herself, shocked at being deceived by Steve yet again, more than anything else.

"Ah! You like paraprosdokians."

The word snapped her out of her revelry.

"You and DI Thackeray have more in common than meets the eye, professor."

"Please, call me Aleister. What do you mean by that?"

"Thackeray prides himself on his library of paraprosdokians."

"It would be fun to trade a few with him once we get through this, or should I say if we get through it."

"Look Professor, I think we need to put you in a safe house until the case is over. I can't risk..."

He interrupted, "No, Miss Parker, that will not be necessary. I will simply work from home for the next few weeks. There is no way anyone will be able to obtain my home address. I had some trouble with the press some years back and had to move. Now I am very careful with my privacy."

"I'll put an officer outside your..."

"No, no, no, that won't do either... it would simply attract unnecessary attention. Now, let me tell you what I've uncovered so far in researching Moloch. I think I can suggest where he might have buried the bodies of his sacrifices, they were unusable, you see—"

"Wait a second Professor," remembering something, Parker drew a notebook from her inside coat pocket. "A few nights ago Thackeray had a sort of spectral visitation from Moloch."

"By spectral, you mean in spirit: an apparition in a dream?"

"Yes, I guess so, anyway he woke up in the middle of the night and found Moloch standing at the foot of his bed."

"And did Moloch say anything?"

"Yes, Thackeray dictated it to me to tell you," she read from her notepad. "Darmastro Aspecti martain."

Klein immediately knew which book to select from his library to check the phrase. He quickly pulled a large old leather-bound volume from the shelf, returned to his chair, and flicked through the big book for a few moments, suddenly stopping to stare at a page inscribed with what appeared to be illuminated Latin Script.

"This is The Academy of Sorcery Book of spells, rituals, potions, demons, and necromancy... basically Darmastro Aspecti martain is a curse in an early version of Latin, a revenge spell if you like, and it translates thus: 'You have wronged. Now you must be revenged.'"

He went on, "There's more to the curse: All the wrong you have done to me will be bestowed unto you. You have wronged. Revenge is near. You have done wrong towards me. You will be punished! The Curse of Bad Luck—Spirits of the night and bats that fly by the light of the moon come forth from the astral realm and jinx this person for all time! Darmastro Aspecti martain!"

The Professor's incantation brought back the Goosebumps to Parker's arms.

"Hmm," the Professor looked thoughtful. "Your antagonist Moloch certainly knows his stuff when it comes to curses; it's a good one!" he said, peering over his spectacles at her with an encouraging smile: a schoolteacher to a bright pupil.

She was pleased, suddenly she thought of something he'd said earlier.

"Aleister, before we discussed the curse, you said the sacrifices were unusable. What did you mean by that?"

"It's just a theory I'm working on; it would be premature to reveal it just yet."

That night, still not talking, Bill and Sarah turned in. They both lay awake unable to sleep, their minds in chaos. After a minute, Bill leaned over and gave Sarah an apologetic peck on the cheek. But it had no effect, and she turned her back on him to go to sleep. He switched off the light.

When Sarah closed her eyes, there was a sudden flash in her mind's eye.

She found herself in the same field she had escaped from in Russell's dreamscape coma. The sky was the same: dark and foreboding. The sun and the moon were in the sky together, and the sounds were the same—the giant toys were the only things missing. She felt someone behind her, turned sharply, and found Wayne dressed in his cowboy outfit. He got in her face but was looking down. Then, he slowly tilted his head up and peered macabrely at her from the shadow under the broad brim of his black hat.

"Dreamraiders can follow you back into your world. Be careful, Sarah Dixon, be real careful; they are of the Gaap."

It was a chilling warning. Suddenly she could smell sulphur— Wayne's eyes darted to one side—a shadow suddenly reared up out of nowhere with its hands clawed! She felt wrenching terror, then... a bright flash and—

Sarah sat bolt upright in bed and screamed at the top of her lungs. The shock almost catapulted Bill out of the bed onto the floor. He dived for the light switch and sat wide-eyed staring at her, his heart pounding so hard in his chest he could hear it.

"Sorry," she said, then quickly turned her back to him, pulled the bedsheet up to her chin, and closed her eyes.

The weak apology did nothing to slacken Bill's heartbeat from galloping like a champion thoroughbred. He lay there staring at the ceiling as his pulse gradually slowed, wide-awake, reliving the Jason Little interview.

Chewing on a Doner kebab, Parker fumbled the keys to her apartment door. She was exhausted. It was a juggling act between the keys and the kebab, but she managed finally to get the door open. She expected to find Steve working on her iPad or watching television, but instead found the room dark and Steve nowhere to be seen. She noticed a light showing under the door to the guest room— he was there and awake. Lucky for him he's in the bedroom, she mumbled sleepily to herself, wanting to give him a piece of her mind for again ignoring specific orders to stay put and for getting himself kidnapped. She checked the time on her Blu-ray player under the flat-screen TV; it was 22:20. Steve's reprimand could wait—it had been a long day for her, and a good night's rest took precedence over dealing with an idiot.

Next morning with Russell on the bus to school, Sarah, garbed in a pink dressing gown, was seated at the kitchen table with her head in her hands: the dream about Wayne from the previous night was plaguing her.

A newsreader on the radio warned of a heat wave and that a total fire ban was in force. Dressed for work with a cup of coffee in his hand, Bill was leaning up against the kitchen bench listening to the newscast. The air between them was tense.

"So tell me about the dream."

There was concern in his voice as he turned off the radio.

After a lengthy pause, she spoke,

"It wasn't so much a dream as a premonition," she looked up from her hands at him. "It was Wayne. I was in the same place where I found Russell before... that weird, weird other-world with the sun and moon in the sky at the same time... I felt someone behind me, turned round and found Wayne dressed like a cowboy again. He warned me that Dreamraiders could follow me back into the real world, this world. He said to be careful and that they were of the Gaap. It was terrifying."

"What's a Gaap?"

"I looked it up on the net this morning while you were in the shower. The Gaap is a transporter demon of hell. It commands a legion of followers and takes a semi-human shape. The pictures of it on the net aren't nearly as frightening as seeing the thing live. We're dealing with forces greater than just Moloch and stronger than nightmares here—this is dark evil... this guy is in league with the devil."

"It was only a dream. It wasn't a conscious journey into a subconscious mind because you hadn't touched anyone. So it's probably best left ignored, love," he said, trying to trivialize it.

Her head sank back in her hands, and she groaned,

"That's easy enough for you to say Bill, but I think there might be a link between a normal dream state and this other-world... and those creatures can traverse it... and that gives me the heebie-jeebies."

He stopped pacing, bent down, and kissed the top of her head. He lifted her chin with his index finger and met her eyes caringly.

"You'll be fine, love... don't worry. Now, it's time for me to get a move on; work calls."

"Undo your tie; it'll be sweltering outside."

The ice had finally been broken. She stood up and undid his tie for him, then with her arm draped around his shoulders, walked him to the front door. It was obvious he was still brooding over Moloch. Deep down inside, she wanted him to have closure but was afraid of the consequences if she were to help.

"I'll catch you later, kiddo," he said gloomily.

He opened the front door, turned and kissed her. She looked into his eyes, feeling like a little girl. Her resolve suddenly crystallized.

"One condition... If anything goes wrong and I decide to pull out, you have to accept my word as final."

Light returned to his eyes—hope—a chance.

"Yes, yes," he said excitedly. "It would be your call, but we can only do it around 6 PM this afternoon, around the nurses' shift change."

"Okay, set it up, Bill. I'll call you mid-afternoon once I've thought through my modus operandi."

He took both her hands, looked deeply into her eyes, and said wholeheartedly, "I love you."

They kissed tenderly.

As she watched him get into his car, she wondered why she had given in after opposing him so vehemently. Because I love him, I guess—I know he'd do it for me. And to her, that was a good enough reason.

Thackeray was on Anzac Parade well on his way to the Hospital to visit Moloch when his mobile rang. He answered it hands-free.

"Thackeray... Good morning, Parker, what! You've got to be kidding me!" He angrily pulled over to the kerb. Cars behind him honked in protest of him blocking the left-hand lane—there was no stopping on Anzac Parade. While talking, he opened the window and put a flashing blue strobe light on the roof as a warning to other drivers. The horn blowing ceased.

"Steve. I'll break his bloody neck when I see him! What on earth possessed him to do that? I know, I know. We'll have to put him in a safe... He won't, mate I can hear Wilks blowing up about this now. All right, I'm on my way there now. See you there." He ended the call, but something else was gnawing at him. He loaded a fresh toothpick into his mouth, a habit that had replaced his need for cigarettes after quitting years ago. He chewed thoughtfully for a second, wondering what was bothering him when a feeling of gloom suddenly descended on him, and he questioned himself—How can you risk Sarah's life for the sake of closure—the idea suddenly felt very selfish—because that's what it will take, he decided. Gaap, demons, for crying out loud! He hit the car radio—and was immediately barraged with heatwave warnings and an announcement that the Sydney region was under a total fire ban. The Royal Fire Service was already fighting twenty bushfires in the Blue Mountains west of the city. He took down the strobe light and continued on at a more sensible pace in the direction of St. Vincent's Hospital.

When Thackeray entered the guarded hospital room, he found Parker standing beside Moloch's bed. The big man was still hooked up to life support machines, bubbling with a mix of different digital blips, beeps, and bloops.

"Hot enough for you out there?" Thacka said with a smile.

It occurred to Parker something had changed; this was totally out of character for him first thing in the morning.

"Hotter than hell and made worse by what Steve has done. So, today's the big plug-pulling day then?"

"Not if I can bloody help it," he growled.

"Hello, am I in need of an update here?" she said with a furrowed brow.

"Sarah has agreed to do it."

"What?" Parker gasped, stupefied.

A pregnant pause suspended their conversation while they both contemplated the ramifications of what he'd disclosed.

Parker glanced at Moloch's ugly face then back at Thackeray.

"Are you sure that it's the right thing to do Bill?"

"No, I'm not bloody sure of anything, but what choice do we have?"

"Well, you could just let the bastard die and keep your lady safe from harm."

"Don't you think I've been telling myself that? But what about those six little boys?" He said, racked with indecision and self-directed anger.

"Well, we've got Little and Large in the can, aren't they enough?"

"Little claims he has no idea where the bodies are—we need

evidence Parker. Look, in my time as a cop, I've seen far too many cases thrown out of court because of a lack of critical evidence. People like Little and Large will lie under oath; if we rely on them, they will let us down. You can bet your arse on that. Look, in everyone's life sometimes a small window of opportunity opens to do something that means a whole lot more to you than anything else, and to undertake it means foregoing the easy way out—to me this is one of those occasions."

"But Moloch will be dead Thacka. Look, Wilks wanted a suspect and we've delivered one. Besides, Professor Klein said he's close to working out where Moloch might have buried the bodies."

"But there's no time Parker—and there's something Little said that really frightens me."

"What's that?"

"When I told him I wouldn't be worried about Moloch being a warlock anymore after he's dead, he said, "I wouldn't be so sure about that.""

"What do you think he meant?"

"He's scared Parker, scared of Moloch, even with the bastard on his deathbed he's still scared. What if there's more to this magic, witchcraft, warlock, or whatever-the hell shit-it-is than meets the eye?"

They both glanced at Moloch and both imagined him smiling knowingly at them.

"Now you're really scaring me!" Parker admitted tensely.

"I don't like talking about this in front of him... he gives me the creeps. It's like he's listening to us."

"He probably is," Parker said with a shiver.

"Let's talk outside then," Thacka said with trepidation. He got no argument from Parker, and they stepped out into the corridor.

"I know it's a risk, but there's now more to this case than just Moloch. We need a body, and we need it before they pull the plug on him. One will do for now... but we bloody-well need one Parker! Only then will we be able to put away the witches, bitches, ghosts, and all!" Thacka contended.

"Okay, granted, a body is what we need and no-one, including Klein, is likely to deliver us one in such a short space of time. How will what you're proposing work then?"

"Let's get back to the office; I'll fill you in there."

"Okay," she was about to walk off to the elevator when she noticed Thacka had gone back into Moloch's room. She followed after him.

She found Thackeray at Moloch's bedside. As she moved closer, Thacka leaned close to Moloch's left ear and yelled venomously.

"I'll get you, you fucking mongrel! Your curse hasn't beaten me yet; you hear! You hear me!"

"Come on Bill," Parker wanted out of there; it was getting a little insane with Thacka shouting at a comatose body like a lunatic. Thacka realised the futility of his outburst, put a toothpick between his teeth, and grinned at Parker.

They left the room together bound for the elevator.

"Don't worry, Jess; I haven't lost it. I just needed to vent a little frustration on the prick. Sarah will phone me at the office this afternoon. Now we need to work on a stay of execution."

They stopped at the elevator, and he pressed the call button.

"Oh... and Sarah learned that these Dreamraider creature monsters that she's come across in her astral travels are actually an ancient race of demons called the Gaap. Can you get the Professor to research them?"

The elevator arrived, and they stepped inside.

"Monsters? What, like biblical demons or something? You're telling me she has to deal with that as well?" Parker was shocked.

"Yeah, not for the faint-hearted."

"The Gaap you say, okay I'll phone the Professor on my way to the office. Do we still need info on Niki's friends?"

"It's not a priority for now, but we'll have to follow up when there's time. I'd really like to know if any of the witches knew Richard Riley."

"Okay, I'll try to look into it. Maybe I can get Steve to ask one of them on the phone or in a chat room without getting him any deeper into this."

"Speaking of Steve, I think you better get him into the office as well, don't you think? And how's the professor handling it? I know you like him."

"Yeah, I guess I have a thing about academic types, must be something to do with a crush I had on a teacher once."

The elevator door opened at the car park.

They hadn't been at the office long before Wilks cold-called them. He entered without knocking and closed the door quietly behind him. It was an ominous sign—Wilks rarely made house calls.

Through the window, Thackeray noticed DI Miller gossiping to another detective with an expression of smug satisfaction on his face. That said clearly that he knew that because Wilks was there, he would soon inherit the case—well, at least that's how it seemed to Thacka.

Without a word, Wilks ambled into the incident room, his hands clasped behind him like Prince Philip, and came to a halt in front of the Murder Wall. He studied it intently while Thacka and Parker watched him silently. There were dozens of photographs on the wall, mostly grisly crime scene shots but others of suspects and potential links to the case.

"So, is this your main suspect?" Wilks tapped a full-face photo of Moloch. "You have made two arrests, I'm told."

Parker and Thackeray had moved to stand behind him.

"Yes, that's Wolfen Moloch, sir. We suspect him of murdering Niki Blake, Richard Riley, and possibly six boys, plus a dog. These two women," he pointed to names on the wall, "Nissa and Vivian, are members of a coven in Seven Hills. They and Rebekah, here, we believe were accomplices to Niki Blake's murder. Nissa and Vivian and perhaps other members of the coven kidnapped Steve Blake," Thackeray explained.

"We rescued Blake yesterday, sir," Parker added.

"Yes, SWAT briefed me. Charges?"

"Not yet, the kidnap might have been a Halloween prank,"

Thackeray admitted.

"Of the two suspects we have in custody, we expect one of them to lead us to a witches' coven tonight, to arrest the possible accomplices."

"Evidence?"

"Forensics is turning over Moloch's house as we speak. They drew a blank at the Blake residence and at Riley's. Sir, we found a jar labelled cyanide at Moloch's, in the room where Blake was held, we're waiting for the lab to confirm it was cyanide and if that's what killed the Blake's dog," Parker said. "Once we have that and the witches, we'll hopefully get DNA evidence to support the theory that Moloch planted Steve Blake's semen in Niki Blake's rectum to frame him," Parker explained further.

Wilks was intrigued.

"Clever, and the murder evidence on the boys?"

"No bodies yet, sir," Thacka reported apologetically.

"With your experience Thackeray you know you have nothing for a conviction. Your main suspect is on life support and the only thing he can be charged with is running a red light."

"You gave us a week, sir, we'll have it done and dusted by close of play tomorrow," Parker said with conviction.

"You had better do so, Parker, because if you look outside, the vultures are circling."

They both looked up in time to catch Miller peering at them from the other side of the glass partition.

Wilks made his way towards the door, and then turned back towards them.

"And what's with the demon slayer story? Who is Professor Klein?"

Thacka took a deep breath, but before he could answer, Parker spoke up.

"Steve Blake leaked the story, sir. He was under the impression that because Moloch was on life support which would be terminated tonight, the case was over with."

"And just how did he manage to come to that conclusion DS Parker?"

"He's been staying at my apartment, sir, and—"

"Probably overheard our phone conversations, sir," Thacka chimed in to cover for Parker.

"And why was he staying at your apartment, Parker?"

"He is an important witness, sir, and we thought—"

Wilks cut Parker off.

"Shut him down, I don't enjoy having to explain press leaks to the police commissioner, Parker—and Klein?"

"He's an expert on the occult, whatever that is and whatever any of us believe, a consultant recommended to us by Dr Tess Parsons. Whatever any of us may think we know, there is a huge link to the supernatural in this case," Thacka said.

Wilks snorted, "Witchcraft my arse!' he paused. "Tess, a smart lass that one... then make sure this professor is kept out of harm's way... something you haven't got a good track record of doing, Thacka!"

"Yes, sir... sir, can we get a stay of execution on Moloch?" Thacka asked.

"Only Badger can answer that."

Wilks closed the door behind him, leaving Thackeray and Parker confused and worried. Miller and his mates were still smirking outside. Had Wilks accepted their wild theories? They were both heartened somewhat that he hadn't shut them down outright.

"You were right about the fallout," Parker admitted. "So, how are we going to play this?"

"We've got to stop bloody Badger?"

"Time is against us. If something turns up from forensics, we might have a lever but for now, Badger's intent on pulling the plug tonight. Once we bust the witches and get a DNA match with the semen, we'll have motive, but that'll be too late to stop Badger."

"None of that will stop him. What time are they pulling the plug?"

"About twenty hundred hours by my reckoning," she said, glancing at her wristwatch.

"Then Sarah has to do it at eighteen hundred hours tonight."

"Why then?"

"Change of shift, fewer hospital staff to contend with."

"Okay, then we bust the Sabbat at midnight: the witching hour."

"Yes, get with DS Lee and organise a squad of uniforms for the raid... and arrange for Dorrie to lead us in. Where is the Sabbat?"

"Seven Hills, I expect."

"Hmm, a good forty minutes from here. Better have the troops muster here at twenty-three hundred hours sharp."

"Roger that!" Parker said on her way to the door. She stopped in the doorway and added, "Oh, I called Klein this morning about Gaap, the so-called mighty prince of Hell. And yes, he's a bad demon. Necromancers sacrifice to Gaap and his legions of many. He can appear in hell and on Earth in many shapes and can walk through dreams. Scary shit."

"Walks through dreams, okay, thanks. Off you go. Oh, and get Klein to call you ASAP if he works out where a body is. Let him know the urgency... and bloody-well sort Blake out, will you? I ought to cut his nuts off for leaking that story!"

As Parker closed the door, Thacka stuck a toothpick between his lips, thinking to himself, Maybe Sarah did get a warning, maybe these Dreamraiders or Gaap are a serious threat, maybe we're out of our depth here. It made him realise just how much he was banking on Sarah being successful, but even if she was, and she determined where Moloch had hidden the body of the last boy murdered, they would still have to get to it, probably exhume it, and ID it, before Wilks handed over the case to Miller. He watched Miller walk past his office window and silently cursed, No way you're taking this case off me, buddy, stuff Moloch's bad luck curse.

Thackeray got the call he was expecting from Sarah, and they discussed their plans. They agreed to meet at the hospital reception at 5.45 PM, just fifteen minutes before the change of shift for nurses and staff.

Thackeray entered the hospital lobby, puffing out of breath from the heat more than anything else, and found Sarah and Russell waiting.

"Howdy partner, am I late?" he said to the boy.

"No, but you've got leaking armpits!" Russell said with a giggle.

Thacka checked his underarms and chuckled—the boy was right.

"That's what you get for rushing during a heat wave. I must teach you about time management, Detective Thackeray!" Sarah said cheekily.

"Good idea, come on, let's go to the playroom before I melt."

They moved to a waiting elevator. Inside, Thacka hoisted Russell up to reach the floor button.

"Number seven please, partner."

Russell pressed the button.

"Where's Jess?" Sarah asked.

"She's probably busy planning tonight's raid," he said, checking his watch. "Said she'd try and drop in."

"Oh good, I'd like to meet her."

"She's got to pick Steve Blake up after she's done with planning the raid."

The doors opened on the 7th floor, and they disembarked.

While walking towards the playroom, Sarah asked, "Is he going on the raid?"

"Blake? Yeah, I was opposed to it at first, but Parker convinced me he'd be good backup in case Dorrie Wilson pulls a swiftie and backs out. He's been to a Sabbat before and knows the location; he also knows the witches—intimately. We'll need him to identify whoever was at the Sabbat he attended last week, to bust them."

"Are you going?"

"Well, I'm hoping I'll be too busy uncovering the remains of the boy after you get the locale from Moloch."

"Let's hope so."

Once in the Children's Playroom, Russell checked it out and wasn't impressed.

"Mum, this is all kids' stuff!"

"Here," she handed over his iPad. "I thought you might need this; they've got Wi-Fi here."

"Great. Thanks, Mum."

He sat happily on a chair and started playing a game on his device.

Thackeray put his arm around Sarah.

"You all right?"

"Yeah, just a little nervous... where's Moloch's room?"

"8th floor."

"Can you give me a minute with Russell, Bill? I'll meet you there."

"Sure, no worries, out of the lift on eight, turn right and you'll see the guard outside his room."

He gave her a peck on the cheek and left, understanding that she needed time with her son to muster her courage.

"I'm just going to visit somebody with Bill, love, and I'll be back in a few minutes. Will you be all right?"

Russell looked up at her from his iPad and smiled. "No worries, Mum. See ya."

She gave him a big warm hug and then bravely left him, knowing she was about to risk her life.

PC Richards was on guard outside the doorway of Moloch's room. He was expecting Sarah and he opened the door for her to enter as she approached.

She found Thacka and Parker standing at Moloch's bedside and said, "Hi, you must be Jess. I didn't expect you to be here."

"I got everything done at the office, and I sure wasn't going to miss out on this. Good to meet you, Sarah."

Sarah couldn't help but stare at the hulk of a man in the hospital bed. With his face and clean-shaven head decorated with satanic tattoos and ears that had been surgically altered to points, he was the epitome of evil.

"My God, I've never seen anyone so scary!" Sarah said aghast. "He's a ghoul."

"Hey, don't throw my nickname around lightly!" Parker said with a chuckle. That was the name her peers gave her when she formerly inhabited the lost and found office in the basement of police HQ.

Bill piped up, "Sorry, I should've introduced you two."

"Don't worry, Jess, Bill's social skills leave a little to be desired."

"Ganging up on me, huh?" he complained jokingly.

"You're not wrong about Moloch, Sarah; he's one ugly mother!" Parker admitted.

"Death will suit him," Sarah said solemnly.

"I checked his forearm; the one missing had the star tattoo I reckon, he's got bloody everything else under the sun tattooed all over him, mind you!" Thacka said.

"I know, I checked for the arm at the scene of the accident, then I asked the medic if they had collected it, but they told me it had been mangled beyond recognition."

"Damn!" he placed his arm around Sarah's shoulders. "After seeing him, are you sure you want to go through with this, kiddo?"

"No, not at all, so let's get on with it before I chicken out. Listen, Bill, if something goes wrong and I don't make it—"

He cut her off, "Shush, don't say that."

"Be a realist, Bill; if I don't make it back, promise me you'll look after Russell."

Thacka looked deeply into her eyes and confirmed, "That goes without saying, love."

Parker saw that there was obvious unequivocal love between them.

Tears welled up in Sarah's eyes. "Okay, are we all ready?" she said, wiping her eyes.

"Sarah, I'm here as a formal witness. You're so brave doing this," Parker said, taking a seat and readying a notebook and pen.

Sarah moved to Moloch's bedside. "Shit he's gross!"

Bill leaned across and lifted Moloch's top lip to expose his teeth: they had been sharpened to points.

"They match his ears," he chuckled.

"Yuck! That's enough, Bill."

The moment had come.

"Jess, I've already told Bill, when I do my thing, it will look like I'm a Madame Tussauds wax dummy, the lights will look like they're on, but there will be nobody home."

"Got it. Can you be moved in that state?" Parker asked concerned.

"I don't know, I need to return through the host, so I'd have to remain close to him, I think. Mind you, all of this is pure speculation—I'm not speaking from stacks of experience."

"Sarah, I—" Thacka choked on his words.

She recognised he was having doubts about what she was about to undertake and so took his hand and said warmly, "You know, a friend who understands your tears is much more valuable than a lot of friends who only know your smile."

They held eye contact for a long moment until she finally released his hand, sighed, and added, "Okay, enough said, let's do it."

Slowly she extended two shaky fingers, closed her eyes, and touched Moloch on the forehead.

A blinding astral light flashed in her mind's eye, as it had before.

When she opened her eyes, she was face to face with Moloch and realised immediately that he couldn't see her. The grotesque man was looking right past her as though she wasn't there. She quickly ducked aside to let Moloch move off. Taking in her surroundings— in the dim light, she could see a stone altar in the middle of a clearing, stretched out on the altar was a young girl, naked with long blonde hair, lying still. She was adolescent. The sky overhead was unnatural, surreal—a huge full moon cast a dull yellow glow on the Stonehenge- like monolith. Standing stones, which encircled the edifice, cast long thin shadows on the ground.

A figure garbed in a hooded, blood-red caftan suddenly stepped out from behind one of the dolmens and moved to the foot of the altar.

Sarah took a couple of hesitant steps closer the altar to see if it was Moloch under the hood, but before she could get close enough to find out, the red caftan fell open revealing a naked man underneath with an erect phallus. She looked at his face but instead of it being Moloch, she was horrified to see the head of a he-goat and she knew it wasn't a mask—there was plenty of life in its goat's eyes with frightening horizontal pupils.

Two women in white caftans suddenly appeared from the darkness beyond the dolmens and ceremoniously made their way into the circle. Each took hold of one of the girl's ankles and then spread her legs for the he-goat to manoeuvre between them. The girl was conscious but not struggling.

The he-goat let out a roar like a bull. One of the women slapped a sacrificial knife into the girl's open hand. She sat up, took hold of the he-goat's genitals and in one strong stroke sliced them off. The creature bayed in agony and staggered backwards with blood squirting from the gaping wound.

With the prize held aloft blood trickled down the girl's thin white arm and dripped off her elbow.

The he-goat, still howling, sank to its knees on the ground and bled out.

Sarah couldn't avert her eyes from the sickening sight of the he-goat on its knees in the shadows of the cyclopean standing stones with it head bent down, bleeding to death. Then before her unbelieving eyes, the he-goat morphed into a young boy who collapsed and died. Stunned by the vision, Sarah suddenly realised this is was the boy Thackeray needed to find.

A demonic laugh issued from the darkness behind the dolmens— it was Moloch. He strode over to the young girl snatched the boys genitals out of her hand, and cast them into the darkness. Then, he slowly turned to face Sarah, his eyes aglow and he bellowed at her, his deep voice resonating from the surrounding stones.

"You dare violate the sanctity of my sacred realm, bitch! Bury the sacrifice at the seventh stone, then cut this fool bitch up piece by piece... let her be alive to watch you bury her body one piece at a time!"

Sarah took off as fast as her legs could carry her. She came to a thicket of dark woods, stopped, and steadied herself. Puffing out of breath, she tried to pull herself together, "Wait, Sarah, you're inside Moloch's mind. You're not in control of your surroundings; he is! Now, where am I? I've got what I came to get, the body of the boy is under the seventh stone—now all I need do is get out of here—I need to find the light."

Taking in the terrain, she saw she was surrounded by sinister, craggy black tree trunks, as after a bushfire. Each tree seemed to be reaching out branches towards her like arthritic fingers. Through one cluster of them, she caught a glimpse of a light—A light—head for the light! That's what Wayne had told her before, and it had worked. But just as she was about to follow her instincts, the moon changed colour from yellow to red and cast a ghastly crimson glow on everything. She looked again at the light through the trees and noticed that the tree trunks were actually naked bodies of men and women, their limbs twisted, enmeshed and grotesquely contorted into the craggy branches. "What sort of nightmare is this?" She questioned. "These people seem to be tormented, imprisoned, and in tortuous pain. This must be hell—it's Dante's Inferno!"

A flapping sound from above had her look up in time to see a huge bird-like silhouette pass between her and the crimson moon. A feeling of imminent danger engulfed her, and she ran towards the light.

A man clad in black suddenly materialised directly in front of her and stopped her in her tracks. Her heart skipped a beat when she recognised him.

"Wayne?"

He looked about as though expecting someone else, "Shhh!"

He took her by the hand and led her quickly away from the light into the forest.

"Humans are drawn to light like a moth to a flame. Why is that?"

"Humans?" Sarah questioned.

Sarah noticed that this time Wayne looked less like the comic character in Russell's mind, though he was still dressed as a cowboy. "How can you be in Moloch's mind?"

But before he could answer, there came another flapping sound, and once again, the shadow of a huge flying creature passed overhead.

"What is that thing?"

"That thing is what we are running from!" Wayne said urgently.

"I'm running from Moloch!"

Wayne increased the pace. It wasn't Wayne's or Sarah's world; it was Moloch's, and he suddenly appeared out of the darkness just ahead of them. They stopped instantly and stood in frozen panic.

Flapping wings sounded again, and Wayne looked sharply behind. "There!" he said.

Sarah spun back and saw that an evil-looking, winged creature— a four-metre tall bat, was blocking their retreat. Sarah couldn't believe it. The bat was part reptilian with a dark scaly skin that looked crimson in the light of the blood-red moon. Apart from a massive maw showing an impossible number of teeth, it had spikes protruding from both cheeks that continued over its snake-like head down its spine to the tip of its long tail, which flicked about like an angry cat. It was sitting on its haunches, snarling ready to pounce.

Suddenly Sarah could smell rotten eggs, and she caught sight of something out of the corner of her eye on her left... then something on her right—two grotesque, gargoyle-like Dreamraiders were materialising on either side of them—any chance of escape was out of the question: Moloch had them surrounded. A thought struck Sarah—she looked down at the ground, found a rock, picked it up, and clouted Wayne on the head with it. He hit the deck out like a light. Immediately she knelt down beside him, reached out two fingers, closed her eyes, and touched his forehead.

CHAPTER 13

Death walks with you at night
Gliding like a ghost
In the full moon light
Chanting to your prince of darkness
You sold your soul to power
You were possessed.

gk

Sarah felt a cool breeze on her face and so opened her eyes. The sky was blue—she could smell the ocean—it was a beautiful summer's day. She was sitting with Wayne in a small boat. Wayne wasn't in cowboy attire this time; instead, he was dressed in casual fishing clothes, with a vest and floppy hat and had a rod in his hand.

It was all very familiar to Sarah; she said to herself, "This is the Swan River in Perth... we're on our honeymoon, he's about to catch a fish." The rod suddenly bent, quivering.

"Sarah, I've got one! Quick, the net!"

Sarah grabbed the landing net from the deck of the boat and stood vigilantly with it, looking into the depths of the clear, blue water for a sign of the fish. Wayne stood up to best fight his catch; the rod was thrumming—it was a big one! Sarah glimpsed a shadow from the depths. Suddenly it broke the water with a huge splash, but it wasn't a fish; instead, something with clawed hands reared up at them—a

Dreamraider! Wayne immediately reverted to the comic caricature clothes, cowboy hat and all. In a flash, he dropped the rod, pulled open his black trench coat, whipped out a sawn-off shotgun from underneath, aimed, and let go both barrels. Boom-boom! And the Dreamraider exploded, showering Sarah with pieces of gory flesh and dripping blood.

Wayne casually blew smoke from the barrels, then broke the weapon open one-handed. Sarah watched in amazement as two empty, smoking shells popped out of the breach and splashed into the water over the side of the boat. Wayne gave her a lazy, John-Waynish smile, snapped the breach closed, then spun the shotgun on his finger like a true Hollywood cowboy and in one smooth motion, had it stashed back under his coat.

Sarah stared at the mess on her and all over the boat.

"Ew! How come there was a Dreamraider in your mind?"

Suddenly, the blood and gore on her clothes and the boat mystically evaporated, leaving her perplexed.

"They can move from dream to dream, no matter the host—there is a passageway like a wormhole connecting everyone's dreams—and they can exploit it—they can even materialise in reality, outside of dreams if they want!" Wayne explained.

"But how is that possible?"

"You're in a real place, Sarah. It isn't just imaginary."

"But, I, you—" she was confused.

"There are portals in every dream but more so in the dreams of children—because their dreams are more vivid and pure. For example, if a child was in your dream, a Dreamraider in that same dream could enter that child to get to reality—a child is a direct portal to reality."

"I suppose that's why kids see things, ghosts, apparitions, fairies, things that most adults don't see—maybe the bogey man is really a Dreamraider. I don't like that at all Wayne. Russell could easily turn up in our dreamscape. I've got to go now?"

She felt as though she was losing it. Then the entire scene

surrounding her suddenly shimmered, and she found herself seated at the kitchen table opposite Wayne in their Randwick home. Somehow, she had been transported to another event in the memories of Wayne.

Wayne looked up over his coffee cup and his horn-rimmed glasses and said, "Get Russell up and dressed, we're going to visit uncle Charlie today."

Sarah suddenly felt terribly dispirited: it was always the same after she'd had a premonition. Sarah's father had castigated her mother for her insight, consequently, over time, Sarah had learnt to file her visions in a mental junk drawer along with a collection of "I told you so's' from previous visions. But having Russell had changed all of that; now she was convinced that her insight was a valuable tool for keeping Russell safe from the perils of the world. That view was, however, unacceptable to Wayne.

"Wayne, I've had a vision. It turns out very badly. We shouldn't go to visit Charlie. Please, let's just stay at home."

Short on tolerance, he stood and stared up at the ceiling as though looking for heavenly guidance.

"No Sarah! We've been through this before..."

"I know what you're going to say, but believe me... this is a very strong vision. Please Wayne, trust me."

He stared at her with contempt and barked,

"I've made my decision Sarah, we're going to Charlie's. Now get the boy ready."

Sarah felt she had no control over what she was saying; she thought she must be reliving a past event, or was it? Then she smelled sulphur; it meant a Dreamraider was coming—she saw it materialising behind Wayne. It began as a small pulsating shadow floating in the air about chest height, then it suddenly expanded until it was the size of a man six feet tall, the shadow's edges beginning to coalesce into the shape she had learned to hate. Wayne hadn't noticed. Sarah backed slowly away—she felt the urge to rush to Russell upstairs and enter his dreams; she bolted past the

Dreamraider while it was still manifesting. She raced upstairs into Russell's bedroom. Russell was sound asleep. She looked at the door—the Dreamraider was there, outstretched claws clutching at her, teeth bared. Wasting no time, she closed her eyes and touched Russell's forehead with her fingers.

A blinding astral flash sliced through her senses.

When Sarah opened her eyes she was in a room surrounded by giant toys. It meant she had left Wayne and was now in Russell's mind. A sulphur-stinking shadow floated near her—another Dreamraider was manifesting! She had to divert it—she saw a window, ran over and looked outside—the house she was inside was floating in mid-air! She remembered she'd been in the same situation before. Frantic, she searched for an alternate exit, but when she turned round, she was jolted by the sudden arrival of Wayne dressed in his cowboy outfit. He shot her a big cheesy grin, drew his shotgun and fired. Ka-Boom! The Dreamraider exploded leaving only wisps of black silk threads hanging in the smoky air.

"Wayne, I need to get back to reality. Our son's life depends on it."

"You can only return through your original host Sarah."

"Moloch! But how?"

"First, we need to find him. When I concentrate touch my forehead," he closed his eyes.

She touched him.

There was a bright astral flash in her mind—she opened her eyes and found she had returned to the weird dark forest under the light of the crimson moon. She saw a light glowing on the other side of the trees and resolved, being human, I'll do the moth to a flame thing, and she headed for the light. As she closed on it, she noticed it was pulsing an evil throbbing. I wonder if this is Moloch's beating heart. Then deep within the light a ghostly phantasm materialised, silhouetted and distorted. She recognised it was a man and he was striding towards her. As it drew closer she saw it was indeed Moloch— and then she realised he was dragging something—it was the dead body of a boy, and it left a gory blood trail on the ground behind him. She panicked and yelped—Russell! The sound of large wings flapping suddenly filled the air, and Sarah instinctively looked up. A flock of grotesque-looking vultures was perched on the branches of the trees above her waiting for a feast of carrion.

Moloch stopped a few feet from her and casually discarded the boy's carcass for the vultures. He glared at her. "You're next, bitch!"

As the vultures descended to feast on the pathetic carcass, Sarah realised it wasn't Russell.

"Was that the body of one of your innocent victims Moloch?"

"No one is innocent!" he bellowed maniacally.

But Sarah wasn't going to be intimidated by him; she felt an unfamiliar strength well up in place of her fear as she stepped towards him and barked back, "You wouldn't know the meaning of the word innocent, you bastard!"

He wasn't expecting her to punch him in the face. As her fist made contact an astral flash blinded her.

Thackeray and Parker were observing Sarah standing motionless with her eyes closed and her fingers pressed against Moloch's tattooed forehead. Suddenly, her eyes opened, and she turned to face them.

"I'm back!"

The two detectives jumped with fright.

Unsteady on her feet, Sarah swayed, and Bill rushed forward to catch her before she fell.

"You all right, love?"

Parker dropped her notebook, leaped from her chair, and went to assist.

"You've been gone less than five minutes!" Parker said.

"Hell, they don't make minutes like they used to; it felt like hours," Sarah said, struggling with her equilibrium. "Time must be different in there."

"Sit down, Sarah; you look pale," Bill led her to Parker's chair and sat her in it. "Just take it easy for a minute."

Sarah sat back, took a deep breath, and then let it out with a long sigh.

"Moloch is your serial killer all right Bill. You'll find the body of the last missing boy, minus his genitals, buried at the base of the seventh stone."

Thackeray was so overcome with relief he flopped on the edge of Moloch's bed.

"The seventh stone?" Parker queried.

"Um, yeah—there were standing stones, Stonehenge-like. That's all I know, really."

"Is there a Stonehenge in Sydney, Bill?"

Pinching the bridge of his nose, he mumbled tiredly, "Um, no, I don't think so—no, not to my knowledge—we'll have to check."

Parker nodded. "Were they real monolithic pillars or something else, Sarah?"

"I honestly don't know; I didn't pay a lot of attention to them, Jess. There were other things more important at the time, but they looked real enough to me."

Bill could tell by Sarah's eyes that the ordeal had taken a mental and physical toll on her. He stood and offered a hand to help her up.

"Come on, love, let's get Russell and go home. You can fill me in on the rest on the way. Jess, do some quick smart research on Stonehenge, call Klein, he might be able to help... call me with what you come up with. Is everything set for operation Beltane?"

"Yes, twenty-three hundred hours," Parker placed her hand tenderly on Sarah's shoulder. "Brave of you to do what you did, Sarah," she looked at Moloch. "I couldn't have done it. At least it will be all over for the evil bastard in a couple of hours."

"Thanks, Jess, Bill, how can you leave now with so much at stake?" Sarah asked Thacka.

"Let me worry about that. You've done what I asked of you, love; it's time for you and Russell to go home."

Sarah took one last look at Moloch.

"He's even more wicked where I met him. At least in his hospital bed, you know he'll be dead soon, but in there..." she shivered, not from cold but from remembering her fear.

"Bye, Jess, good luck, and keep safe."

The two women hugged warmly, and then Thackeray walked Sarah out of the room past PC Richards.

Russell was still playing with his iPad when Sarah and Thacka entered the hospital playroom. Sarah rushed over and gave him a huge hug. For Thackeray, the enormity of what Sarah had just done for him rang home when he saw how passionately she held her child. At the risk of her own life and everything in it, she had literally been to hell and back for him. He looked at them lovingly then joined in on the hug.

He whispered in her ear, "Thank you for what you did for me, love."

In the car on the way home from the hospital, Sarah was quiet, her head back, resting her eyes. She opened one eye and peered at Thacka, concentrating on his driving.

"You know, with each trip, I learn a little more about this other world that exists in our minds."

A newsreader on the car radio was reporting a huge number of bushfires burning around Sydney. Thacka turned it down.

"Yeah, how's that?" he said, somewhat distracted negotiating the traffic on Anzac Parade.

"Well, rather than it just being a figment of the imagination, I think it's actually a real place like another world or dimension. Could even be what we refer to as heaven or hell."

"That's a scary thought."

"Try this hypothesis, say a person is about to die and is dreaming at the very second of death—and then dies during that dream—what if that means he remains in that dream for eternity?"

"That's it, no more nightmares for me! What a frightening thought, Sarah!"

Making light of the moment brought a smile to both their weary faces.

"You know it might explain why priests give the last rites to people on their deathbed. The imagery of what the priest preaches could well put the dying person in a place they imagine to be heaven."

"Or hell... so you think the dreamscape is a physical place then?"

"Could well be... but in a form we don't yet understand."

"Moloch obviously understands it... What happened in there, Sarah?"

"It was horrible, I saw a girl of about fourteen, with blonde hair on an altar about to be sacrificed. There was a creature with the body of a man and the head of a goat, with horns and all, that was about to rape her, but he turned out to be the one sacrificed. When he... he..." She squared her shoulders and continued. "She stabbed him, cut off his... parts... After he was cut, he fell to the ground, bleeding and then he suddenly turned from being a goat into a boy. That's when Moloch appeared and ordered him to be buried under the seventh stone."

"Couldn't they see you?"

"Well, that's what was very strange. During the sacrifice, it was as though I was allowed to be a spectator. Then suddenly, once the boy was on the ground dead, Moloch turned on me. It was horrifying... I was petrified, if it hadn't been for Wayne..."

"Wayne? Was he there again? But how come?"

"I don't know, I was in Moloch's mind and then Wayne turned up like he had been watching over me as a guardian angel or something. He explained how Dreamraiders, awful rotten-egg-gas smelling creatures that look like gargoyles, can jump through children's dreams into reality!"

"Seriously? Well, that sort of explains all the myths about gargoyles and why they appear on old Churches and gothic buildings?"

"Maybe, it certainly puts another spin on the bogeyman that's for sure."

"What's the relationship between Moloch and these Dreamraiders?"

"They seem to do his bidding for him."

The last few hours had been such an emotional drain on her that she rested her head in her hands. Thackeray recognised she was exhausted and patted her on the knee to comfort her.

"Just relax, love, we'll be home in a jiffy."

Sarah and Russell were cuddled up on the lounge asleep. Thacka was in a comfy armchair reading the newspaper, waiting for the call from Parker. He turned the page and noticed an advertisement that read: Halloween—Beltane—The Druid Festival of Fertility and Love—an open-air play in Centennial Park, Midnight, October 31. He stared blankly at the photograph in the ad, a night shot of Stonehenge dolmens in Centennial Park with the lights of Sydney in the background. He lowered the newspaper slowly as it dawned on him. That's tonight! Forgetting that Sarah and Russell were asleep, he called out loud to them.

"Sarah! I found it!"

Sarah woke with a fright and sat up, confused and disoriented. Then, without thinking, she accidentally touched Russell, who was asleep, on the forehead.

A lightning astral flash zapped her optic nerve.

She was sitting in a grassy field with Russell asleep in her lap, in the same position they had been on the couch in the living-room. It was a beautiful summer's day. She looked at her sleeping boy admiringly and smiled, realising what must have happened. Then a putrid sulphurous smell filled the air, accompanied by an ominous feeling. A towering shadow fell over them, and she gazed up at a Dreamraider. Her heart was pounding—there was no time to escape on foot. Wayne wasn't there to save them; she was left with only one option: to jump back to reality through Russell. The Dreamraider snarled, and she quickly rolled to her side, then bounced up onto her feet. Then she jumped at Russell with her fingers pointed at his forehead. The Dreamraider jumped at the same time.

Bill could smell something gross like rotten egg gas, he thought, then noticed a strange stream of black smoke rising from Russell's body. Suddenly the smell registered in Thacka's mind—Sarah had said the smell of sulphur meant the arrival of a Dreamraider. He threw down the paper and called out, "Sarah!" But Sarah was frozen with her fingers resting on Russell's forehead and didn't respond. The sulphurous smoke manifested into a dark, evil, almost human form. Bill leapt to his feet.

"Jesus, Sarah! Wake up... Sarah! Something Is... What is this?" he drew his pistol. The creature had now fully materialised. It snarled at Thacka like a Velociraptor, and then before Thacka could squeeze off a shot, it grabbed Russell and held him up as a shield. Thacka realised the thing was intelligent; as nightmarish as it looked, it wasn't just an ordinary animal. He studied it—it was naked with dark olive-green reptilian skin and a grotesque head reminiscent of the gargoyle statues he had seen on churches. Its mouth was packed with pointed teeth, its arms and thighs thickly muscled, and it was obviously male. Wayne had warned Sarah about this creature. It had travelled from the dream world through Russell and was now snarling at him with saliva dribbling from its ugly mouth in a slimy string—it reminded him of H.R. Giger's monster in the movie Alien.

With his Glock 22 up, Thacka inched closer to the creature, hoping to get a bead on its head. Caution was necessary with Russell in the line of fire, the fear of hitting the boy a hindrance to a clean shot.

The Dreamraider snarled and gnashed its teeth as it backed away from Thacka's advance towards the living room front window. The couch with Sarah on it was between Thacka and the creature, preventing him from taking a shot at its legs. There was only one thing left to do: holster his weapon and attack it with his fists. He held up his gun in surrender, then carefully holstered it with his other hand, making a halt sign for the Dreamraider to understand that the threat was over. Then, with both hands held up in capitulation, he inched around the lounge. Now that the gun was gone, the creature held its ground.

"Hey, Gaap, that's your name, isn't it? How about putting the boy down?"

The Dreamraider snarled in reply, and Thacka realised that talking to a monster might not be a sensible option.

He dived at its legs, hoping to bring it down and make it drop Russell, who had been strangely comatose throughout the encounter. But the creature was too quick for him, too agile; it simply side-stepped him and struck him with a powerful backhand blow that sent him spiralling backwards over the couch and Sarah, landing on the floor with a thump. The impact took the wind out of him and left him seeing stars. But it was going to take more than that to defeat Thackeray; he bounced back up, his head still spinning, and charged the beast. It was too late—the Dreamraider anticipated his counter, turned, and dived through the window, shattering the glass.

Thackeray charged to the window and looked out but could see nothing—it had vanished with Russell into the night. He was left torn with indecision—should I go after him or not? He chose not to and went to Sarah.

"Sarah! Sarah!" he shook her, but there was no response. "Shit!" he growled in frustration. Biting his knuckle, he pondered his next move. He had no experience dealing with a supernatural creature— it wasn't in the police-training manual. What to do? He questioned himself, who'd believe me if I called it in? He looked at Sarah, Okay, so you must have jumped inside Russell, now, what did you say? The visitor has to return through the host... but what if the host has been moved? Like Russell has..."

Sarah murmured, "Hmmm, ah... Bill?"

He held her by the shoulders, relieved. "Oh, Sarah thank Christ you're all right."

Jumping simultaneously with the Dreamraider into Russell had saved her.

"Sarah, a weird black smoky thing came out of Russell, turned into a monster then snatched him up, dived through the window, and ran off with him... I couldn't stop it."

She had to restrain herself from crying out in despair. "Bill, I think I know what's going on. It was a Dreamraider. It has taken

Russell to Stonehenge... I think Russell is to be the next sacrifice!"

"Beltane. Tonight," he mumbled.

"What about Beltane?"

"The Druid celebration night, sacrifices."

He pulled out his mobile and dialled.

"What are you doing?"

"I'm calling Parker; Stonehenge is in Centennial Park, we'll have to meet her there. Come on!"

He started to move towards the door, punching the numbers on his phone, but Sarah stopped him.

"No, Bill, wait, don't call her, we're doing this my way, remember? No complications."

He stopped dialling and pocketed his phone.

"Okay, your call."

"Let's go."

Parker was at her computer terminal in her office. She rocked back in her chair as she dialled Klein on her mobile.

"Hello Professor Klein—Jess Parker, are you at home? Hey, I thought we agreed you'd work from home and not at the office. I know your library is there but... Okay, but please be careful. We have a lead on where a boy's body might be buried, and I wanted to check in with you. We were told under the seventh stone at Stonehenge. I know Stonehenge is in England, yes, on the Salisbury Plain, but we were told Stonehenge here in Sydney. Yes, at midnight tonight we're raiding the witch's coven in Western Sydney. No, we don't need a Demon Slayer, thank you. You have? ... Great, so you expect to hear back from him tonight, oh, that soon—okay, excellent, call me when you find out. I better let you go then, please be careful, don't talk to any strangers, and go home soon. Gosh, I sound just like my mother when I was a teenager. Right, bye."

Klein was almost hidden behind piles of books on his desk. As he put down the phone, his computer alerted him to an email he was expecting. He quickly opened the reply from a colleague at the London Theosophical Society and read it out loud to himself, "Death nor desecration of the body or remains of this Warlock Moloch will not destroy his vital source. Should he fail to possess a new host at Beltane, he will lay dormant in a sub-host until, by the light of the Waxing Moon at the next Beltane, an incantation of communion will raise him to as the incarnate to possess a new young host: evil incarnate. There is only one rite to terminate this Warlock, but he must be alive for it to be performed. See: The Corpus Hermeticum under rites of possession."

He had his answer; it would require a black magic exorcism. He knew the power of this sacred book. Though there were many forgeries of it around the world, there was an original in London and a copy here in the Theosophical library on the next floor.

Driving at speed heading for Centennial Park, only ten minutes away, Bill glanced at Sarah. She was deep in thought. Suddenly, she had a revelation.

"Bill. No!—I'm wrong. I'm wrong! Drive to the hospital—it's not taking Russell to Stonehenge; it's taking him to Moloch—That's it Bill! That's it! Moloch needs Russell. He plans to transfer into Russell just before he dies—that's what this has all been about!"

"Wait a sec, let me get this straight. You think just as they're about to pull the plug on Moloch, he's going to enter Russell's dream-state so he can live on as Russell in reality. Moloch gets a new body—he's reborn... This is serious witchcraft—you're right, now it makes sense. That's why they wanted Moloch kept alive until after Beltane, so he could make the transfer."

"Exactly."

"Do you realize what you're saying Sarah? This could be how this evil has been reincarnated down through the ages! This is what the sacrifice rituals are really about; rebirth of one evil soul into a new innocent host!"

"We have to stop Moloch from being terminated Bill, we've got to keep him alive—it's the only way to ensure Russell's safety."

She was biting her nails now that the enormity of the situation had dawned on them. If they failed to stop the transfer, she would not only lose her son, but Moloch would possess him, and the evil demon would live on. Without hesitation, still speeding through light traffic, Thackeray drew his cell phone and dialled.

"Badger... Hello... DI Thackeray... I need you to delay the termination... No, I don't have fresh evidence of... But... Damn!" he glanced at Sarah through angry squinted eyes. "That was the Terminator; the bastard hung up on me. He said without solid evidence it will go ahead in a little over an hour!" he trod on the gas.

CHAPTER 14

Stones forever
Here we stand and reach up to the Heavens
Here we stand and reach down to the Earth
Here the Stones and the people stand together
To heal and grow. To heal and grow.

Sarah and Bill ran into the hospital and dashed into a waiting elevator. They stood in panicked silence as it ascended to the 8th floor.

"Your ear is bleeding," Sarah said.

"Copped a backhander from your Dreamraider. I'll be fine."

The elevator stopped, and they charged down the corridor. Thackeray stopped in front of PC Richards, still on guard at the door to Moloch's room.

"Has anyone been in Moloch's room?" he asked, panting.

"No sir."

Desperate to find Russell, Thacka led Sarah into Moloch's room, but the only one there was Moloch. They stood motionless, accompanied only by the incessant pumping sound of the heart-lung machine artificially keeping Moloch alive. They were just about to leave when a premonition caused Sarah to freeze. She looked towards the window... it was partly ajar. She turned back to Moloch's body, realisation dawning.

"Wait Bill, he's under the bed!"

She dropped to her knees, peered under the bed, then reached under and dragged Russell out. The boy was as limp as a ragdoll—unconscious. She tapped his hand trying to wake him.

"Whatever you do don't touch his forehead!" Thacka warned.

"He's gone Bill, I think we're too late."

Crushed, she sank to the floor with her son on her lap and wept. "He's inside Moloch. He's taken him!" she whispered with watery eyes.

"Come on!" Thackeray said and took Russell from her. He offered her a hand up.

"Let's get him out of here." With the boy in his arms, he led Sarah past PC Richards, standing open-mouthed, into the room next door. It was empty. After gently laying Russell on a bed, he turned and made sure the window was locked, then went back to Richards. Sarah gave her son a kiss on the cheek then followed Bill.

Richards tensed up when Thackeray confronted him.

"Sir, I don't know where he came from, no one went past me..."

"Never mind, guard the boy, don't let anybody in there, and keep one eye on that window, got that?"

"Yes sir!" the young officer moved into position.

Thacka joined Sarah.

"I wonder where that ugly, foul-smelling monster is? Would it have gone back?"

"I don't know... What are we going to do, Thacka?" she appealed teary-eyed.

He wiped the tears from her eyes.

"You're going to stay here and make sure Moloch stays alive while I get the evidence we need."

"That won't work, Bill, there's not enough time. Now that he's got Russell, he wants to die, don't you understand that?"

"I honestly don't think we've got any choice, Sarah."

She looked at him solemnly. "I've got to go back inside Moloch to get Russell—it's the only option."

"No Sarah!" he insisted, the thought of losing her now a serious issue. "It's getting out of hand. They're going to pull the plug on him in under an hour and if they do that while you're in there, you won't be able to make it back!"

"Bill," she said gravely. "If they pull the plug I will lose my boy—gone forever—Moloch wins. Is that what we want?"

They looked deeply into one another's eyes.

"No, no... no we don't, but I don't want to lose you either. After seeing that monster now I understand what you'll been up against in there and I've got to tell you, it scared the hell out of me."

"It has never been a good situation Bill. Look, while I'm in Moloch's mind I will be trapped there, you'll need to get the evidence to stop them pulling the plug or neither of us will be coming back. How's that for incentive?"

"More than enough, though I'm not keen to do any more rounds with stinky the monster!" he said, with a reluctant but acquiescent grin. He knew she was right; it was the only choice left.

"And remember while I'm in there it will look as though we're both in a coma, so watch the hospital staff or they might dump both of us in the morgue."

"Done. I'll need to exhume the boy's body from the 7th stone. Only solid evidence will buy you the time you need, so I won't be able to watch over you."

"We'll just have to take that risk, Bill."

They kissed, passionately, knowing it might be their last time together.

Thackeray approached PC Richards.

"Richards, also keep an eye on Moloch's room, let no one but Parker or me in or out for the next hour. Mrs Dixon here will be staying beside Moloch, and don't let anyone disturb her. That goes for doctors or nurses. You got that son?"

"Yes sir."

Thackeray raced down the corridor dialling Parker on the fly.

Sarah walked soberly over to Moloch with her fingers extended, desperate to save her son, but she knew it would be an almost impossible task without Wayne's help.

Parker was about to open the door of her apartment when her cell phone rang.

"Parker. Hi Thacka, just got home... Who did? What! You're kidding, Centennial Park, how weird is that. Yes, I spoke with Klein and he didn't know anything more. Hey remember when we were dragging the lagoon at Centennial Park for the body? PC Richards wanted us to check out the Druid set in the park. Yeah, that was it— we should've listened to him. All right, I'll bring him. Where's Sarah? She's what? Back inside with no-one looking over her! — Thacka do you think that's wise? Richards, okay, do you want me to call the hospital and check... no, okay, see you at the park then."

She opened the door and found Steve on the sofa, shirtless and intent on the iPad. He looked up as Parker entered.

"Get your gear on buddy, we're off on a dig."

He put down the iPad, got up, and pulled on a T-shirt.

"What do you mean a dig?" he queried.

"Thackeray called, we know where Moloch buried a boy's body, and we're going to dig it up. And have I got a bone to pick with you... What was that about with Demon Slayer, huh?"

"Oh that!" he blushed. "Sorry."

"Sorry isn't the word Steve, you've made me look like a fool to my boss and you've placed Professor Klein in serious danger."

"How? I don't get it."

"Think Steve, irrespective of whether Moloch is in hospital or even dead, we are still dealing with real witchcraft and we don't know how involved in the murder the witches are. So Professor Klein could well be in danger from them."

"Oh, the witches, um, I better tell you that Rebekah invited me to the Beltane Sabbat, and I said yes."

That fired her up big time.

"You agreed not to talk to anybody Steve! You know the trouble you got into last time with those bloody witches. Don't you listen to anything I say!"

"She said the kidnapping was just a Halloween, Beltane prank."

"Yeah right, like giving your sperm to Moloch to plant on Niki or informing Moloch you were going to the cricket. Not pranks, Steve, deliberate—they helped kill your wife, for Christ's sake... they're in it together... don't you get it? Moloch is the warlock, and they are his witches. Them and little and large."

"Who are they?"

"Jason Little and Dorrie Wilson are the two weirdo's who were holding you prisoner at Moloch's house. I was already planning on taking you with us to the Sabbat bust tonight anyway."

"What do you mean bust?"

"We'll be arresting the witches to check their DNA to see who matches the sperm sample..."

"That'd be Vivian; she split with my first load, although it could have been Nissa or Rebekah."

"My my, you are a horny young idiot, aren't you?" she checked her watch, not sure whether she was disgusted or amused. "Come on let's get out of here; we've got a big night ahead of us."

They made for the door.

"Wait!" he ran back to the sofa and collected the iPad.

Standing with the door open, Parker asked, "What do you need that for?"

"I'm keeping a record of everything."

Professor Klein was the only person still at the Theosophical Society—everyone else had vacated the building at the stroke of five. He could never relate to workers who didn't seem to enjoy their work as much as he did. He opened the mahogany double-doors to the library, stepped through, and turned on only the decorative lights— obsolete incandescent bulbs, casting a dim illumination from wall sconces. The big old room with its high ornately decorated ceiling was his favourite place. He liked the Theosophical Society star emblem emblazoned on the Kent Street facing wall with its slogan underneath: there is no religion higher than truth. Then he cast his eyes over the other three walls, stacked to the ceiling with books ancient and contemporary on everything occult. The room had a particular smell of aged leather that appealed to his eccentric taste. It always called up in him memories of his parents. As an only child, he had lost both his parents in a horrific car accident in Sydney in 1976—they had both been academics. At the time, he had been at Oxford in the UK studying Ancient History. Questioning the deaths of his parents compelled him to begin to explore the occult, which led him to ultimately complete a PHD in Occultism and Paganism. Following his PHD, he joined the Hermetic Order of the Golden Dawn and then The London Theosophical Society. In 1980, at twenty-eight years of age, he returned to Australia to take up residency as a professor at the Sydney Theosophical Society. Years later, still in residence, here he stood admiring the vast collection of knowledge in front of him and aware that the many books and papers on occultism which he had authored were scattered on those hallowed shelves, in humbling company. The low lighting at night, in place of the full overhead fluorescent lights, gave the library a certain mystical ambiance. But it was the quietness that Klein loved most—it gave the room the feeling of peace—it was his inner sanctum. He made his way over to a sliding ladder that would allow him to reach the book he was after. It was just below the top shelf, which was almost ten metres from the floor—a dizzying height. As he carefully ascended the ladder, he caught a whiff of sulphur.

This was the moment Sarah hated most, arriving eye-to-eye with her host, Moloch. She felt vulnerable, even if he couldn't see her for those first few seconds. She knew he soon would—it was only a matter of a very brief time.

Moloch was standing at the edge of a sheer cliff with a stiff sea breeze blowing in his face. He was staring at a crimson full moon rising over the ink-black ocean. Waverly Cemetery, a veritable sea of bleached Gothic tombstones, was spread out behind him, in decay.

It was a fifty-metre drop below Sarah's feet to a rock platform being hammered by an angry swell. She took a quick peek downwards, and the fall spooked her; she hated heights. She looked sharply back at Moloch and caught the crimson moon reflected in his black, soulless eyes. While he was still blind to her, she carefully manoeuvred around him and away from the precipice.

The move took up precious time, and the freeze moment ended. Moloch saw her and barked, "Now!" and Sarah was immediately seized from behind.

"I was wondering when you'd turn up again, bitch!" he growled. "You think you can defeat me, what a joke. And you think I'll let them find the boy's body and stop me, ha! My demons will destroy the Professor and your detectives."

Sarah was being restrained by three old witches with cadaverous faces, long grey hair, and garbed in soiled, white caftans.

"Let go of me... You and your stinking demons are no match for my friends, Moloch, you'll die and rot in hell."

"Hell, ha! A religious concept, you've got no idea, you stupid ignorant woman."

Moloch motioned to the witches, and they dragged Sarah kicking and fighting along the ground, up on top of a stone slab. It was the same slab she'd seen the young blonde girl on when she had killed the beast. Exhibiting great strength for their size, age, and build, the gnarly old witches forced Sarah down onto the slab where two of them pinned her down, while the other drew her dress up past her waist and stripped her of her panties. Sarah squealed, but her wrists were gripped too tightly for her to move. One witch bent her arms back over her head while the other two took hold of her ankles and forced Sarah's legs, holding them apart.

Wide-eyed and desperately resisting a rising hysteria, Sarah realised she was about to be raped. Struggling against the steely grips restraining her, she watched a huge obviously male figure step out from the darkness. She froze—she didn't want to be raped by Moloch, she didn't want to be raped by anyone! Dressed in a red caftan, a hood was covering his face. Then the caftan fell away, and to her horror the crimson moonlight revealed a horned, goat-headed monstrosity brandishing its huge erect phallus.

She conquered her panic and tried to rationalise the situation—
I can either give in to avoid injury or fight like hell to stop him
entering me. She chose the former but as the diabolical creature
moved in between her open legs, her panic returned ten-fold.
Suddenly, two shotgun blasts resounded—leaving gaping holes in the
chests of the witches holding Sarah's ankles. The holes were so
cavernous Sarah could see through them as the witches collapsed.

Bang! Bang! Two more shots and the witch holding Sarah's
wrists dropped like a sack of potatoes.

Boom! A fifth shot took the head clean off the he-goat. Its legs
crumbled and it went down.

This time Sarah wasn't concerned at all by the blood and gore
sprayed all over her. She sat up and swung her legs off the slab.

"Thank you Wayne," she said to the dark figure with a smoking
shotgun rested on his shoulder. She had seen him through the
gaping holes in one of the witch's chest before she collapsed.

Wayne gave her a hand down from the slab and noticed her
nakedness.

"Not a good look Sarah."

"Nothing you haven't seen before Wayne," she said smoothly,
picking up her panties and slipping them on. "We need to find
Moloch, he's got our son," she said urgently.

Her dreamscape experiences to date had casehardened her
resolve, she realised she had found the guts to confront anyone or
anything thrown up against her in this weird world—and nothing
was going to stand in the way of her getting Russell back.

Klein carefully descended the ladder, clutching the Corpus
Hermeticum, when suddenly, the lights went out. In the ensuing
darkness, he muttered, "First that smell… now the lights, something
must have short-circuited." He paused on the ladder, allowing his
eyes to adjust to the faint light filtering through the windows from
Kent Street. Proceeding with caution, he continued down the ladder.

But just as his foot touched the red, carpeted floor, he detected
movement out of the corner of his eye. Suspicion gnawed at him, and

he whispered, "Is someone there? Is that you, Walter?"

Walter, the night security guard, had become a friend to Klein over the years due to his late-night work. However, an instinctual unease nagged at Klein, suggesting that the figure wasn't Walter. This was precisely what he had feared most since becoming involved in the case.

A rustling noise persisted, and Klein made out the silhouette of a shadowy figure, a ripple in the darkness, moving near the entrance doors. In his search for something to arm himself with, he implored, "Who are you? What do you want?"

The only response was a deep, menacing purring sound, akin to that of a massive cat. Horror coursed through Klein as he realised that he wasn't dealing with a human; this was, in fact, a demon. He carefully set down the book on a nearby table and picked up a wooden chair. The creature moved past a window, briefly silhouetted by the faint glow from the streetlights below, allowing Klein to catch a glimpse of the terror before him.

In a trembling whisper, Klein muttered, "Gaap! I know you... you are the mighty prince of hell."

A deep growl emanated from the creature, and Klein took it as a form of acknowledgement—a chilling indication that he was indeed facing Gaap, a demonic force beyond comprehension.

"Amaymon is your King, not Moloch. Why do you take your orders from a warlock? You can carry men from one Kingdom to another. You rule over the sixty-six Legions of Spirits! In the shadow world, you are a great philosopher. You are not a killer!" Klein spoke with desperation, hoping to reason with the creature that had him cornered.

For a moment, the creature halted its advance, and a faint glimmer of hope stirred within Klein. He believed he might be getting through to it and continued, "You can't talk because Moloch has put a spell on you to deny speech in this world. That's because he doesn't want you to speak with your targets. Look, in another, more reasonable form, you could teach me so much. You could help me speak to my parents. We don't need to be enemies."

However, Gaap, in its current embodiment, had no intention of entertaining reason. It resumed stalking Klein with menacing intent, ignoring his pleas for reconciliation. In a final, desperate attempt to fend off the terrifying creature, Klein screamed loudly, "Oh demon Gaap, I banish thee back to hell. So mote it be! So mote it be!"

The Dreamraider, outraged by the curse, roared with fury and launched itself out of the darkness at Klein, its sharp claws extended. Klein raised the chair, bracing himself for the impending impact. Yet, in a display of overwhelming strength, a single powerful blow from Gaap's heavily muscled arm shattered the chair, sending it spinning into the obscurity of the room.

Gaap's cruel claws slashed at Klein, inflicting searing pain as they tore through the side of his face. It was a harrowing realisation for Klein that this was no contest. With ease, Gaap reached out, gripping Klein by the throat with one hand and slowly lifting him off the ground as though he weighed next to nothing. The dire situation had reached its climax, and Klein faced an uncertain fate in the clutches of this malevolent entity.

Klein stared into its malevolent eyes and at its gnashing teeth... He knew his time was up. It drew a breath and flung Klein onto a table with such force that it shattered into pieces, leaving him sprawled on the floor, battered, bleeding, and unconscious. The massive, grotesque creature, snarling like a rabid dog, stooped down, lifted him, and hurled him through the air like a limp ragdoll, crashing into the wall of books that Klein held in such reverence. The impact caused the bookshelf to collapse, showering down books on him, burying his almost lifeless form.

The foul creature was poised to deliver the fatal blow—growling in a frenzy of bloodlust, it clawed at the books in a desperate attempt to reach its prey. It seized Klein's broken body and began dragging it from beneath the mound of books when the lights suddenly illuminated the scene. The creature blinked in the abrupt glare, then turned its gaze sharply towards the entrance, where a security guard, terror-stricken, trembled while aiming a revolver at it.

The Dreamraider snarled at the elderly Walter, contemptuously releasing Klein's arm, and swiftly leaped towards the street-facing window with inhuman speed. Walter clutched his trusty old Smith and Wesson .38 special with both trembling hands and emptied the cylinder at the monster. However, from that distance, he missed all six shots. The Dreamraider did not pause at the window; it plunged straight through, shattering glass in every direction.

Walter hurried over as fast as his seventy-year-old legs would allow and peered through the broken window onto Kent Street below, but the creature had vanished without a trace. He withdrew uncertain if what he had witnessed was real or a delusion, then rushed to summon an ambulance for Professor Klein, who remained unconscious on the floor in a spreading pool of blood.

On the way to Centennial Park, Thackeray made a stop at a hardware store to purchase a couple of shovels for the Stonehenge excavation. He was loading them into the boot of his car when his mobile rang. "Hello, Parker... I'm at the hardware store getting shovels. What's that? The show starts at eleven! I thought it was midnight. Oh, I see, that's when the audience arrives. Alright, try to clear everyone out so we can get to work. He's requesting what? Paperwork! Well, inform him that if he doesn't allow us... Okay, put him on... Hello, Senior Detective Inspector Thackeray here. You're Mr Greg Pearce? What's that? The producer. Okay, Mr Pearce, if you can't give us an uninterrupted hour, I'll have to come with a warrant and close you down completely. We might need to bring in a forensics team... yes, that could take up to 48 hours. I understand tonight is Beltane, yes. Work with me, and the show can go on. Look, it's seven o'clock now. Give me until eight thirty without any interruptions, and then I'll return Stonehenge to you... I realise that's an hour and a half. Do we have a deal, Mr Pearce? Excellent. Put DS Parker back on. Parker? Alright, it's settled. He'll have his production team withdraw until eight thirty. Please, for heaven's sake, don't tell him that if we find a body, we'll have to shut everything down. Get started... I'll be there in say ten minutes. Have Blake start digging; he's a robust young lad, or so the witches claim. See you soon."

Parker and Steve were accompanied by a large Maori security guard in charge of the Centennial Park set. The replica of Stonehenge was arranged in the round, with portable amphitheater seating around it. Powerful overhead lights illuminated the area. It was an impressive structure and a convincing replica.

"How long did it take to construct?" Parker inquired as they walked from the guardhouse to the set.

"It's spray-crete... took 'bout three or four months, maybe," he replied, scratching his bearded chin.

"It's massive!" Steve exclaimed, gazing up at one of the enormous trilithons.

"It's to scale, bro."

"Dead-set. What's it constructed from?"

"Like I said, spray-crete over wire and timber reinforcement. We had to build it all on-site."

"Okay, well leave us with it Mr Williams. DI Thackeray is about ten minutes behind us, so let him in please."

"No problem, Miss. I'll grant him access, aye."

The towering guard, standing at six-foot three and likely weighing around 125 kilos, gave the impression that he might moonlight as a front-row forward for a Sydney rugby team. Parker couldn't help but notice his muscular physique as he headed to his post at the temporary guardhouse by the stage entrance.

"How on earth did Moloch manage to bury a kid here?"

"Would have been early in the morning during the construction stage I'd reckon. There wouldn't have been much security then."

"Yeah, I guess so. It might not be real blue stone but it sure looks convincing," Steve said, admiring the replica monolith.

Parker handed him a shovel she'd borrowed from the guard.

"Here you go."

"Geez, I feel like a grave robber from the nineteenth century."

"And you look the part. Alright, it's the seventh stone, so we're standing at the heel stone... counting the stone directly in front of us as number one, and then counting only the inner stones, I'll count clockwise," Parker explained, somewhat uncertain.

"Okay. I'm glad you worked that out, I'm a slow learner when it comes to maths."

"Good, then this is the seventh stone," Parker said, indicating the largest sarsen stone.

"But what if you count counterclockwise?" Steve asked.

"Then the seventh stone would be a different one. Hmm, okay, let's count the outside stones using the heel stone as number one."

They counted the outer stones.

"So, the outer stones are a bit of a challenge because there are more of them. Let's dig the seventh one clockwise from the inside."

"Alright, front or back? ... Which side?"

"Is that construction terminology or something?" she asked, raising an eyebrow.

They walked over to what they believed to be the seventh stone, and Steve sank the shovel into the ground.

"So what'll it be?" he said ready to dig.

"Let's approach this logically. Where would you bury a body?"

"Well, assuming this is the seventh stone, then right on the inside of the circle, directly in front of it."

"Yep, me too, but I'm still not convinced this is the right stone."

"Okay, off you go."

Steve started digging. Parker looked up at the big full moon rising in the east. The time of the waxing moon was over, the moon was full - it was nearly Beltane.

"Follow me," Sarah ordered Wayne, and they set off towards the craggy forest.

"Is your perception driving you?" Wayne asked.

"Yes, why is that a problem?"

"No, should it be?"

"Well, it was when you were... I mean... before."

"You were about to say when I was alive."

Sarah wasn't going to buy into that discussion; it was tough enough trying to make sense of everything else, let alone getting into a life-after-death debate, especially with a dead man.

Moloch's Waverly house was in the dreamscape, though decidedly more sinister-looking. Its roofs and towers seemed to shimmer in the crimson moonlight. Inside the house, in the centre of a dimly lit room, bare of furniture, Russell was strapped into a single chair with his mouth gagged, guarded by a Dreamraider. Moloch stormed into the room, grabbed Russell by the chin, stared into his eyes, and growled at him with a harsh, gravelly voice.

"Soon, I will be you, boy!" He tilted his head with a macabre smile, showing his pointed teeth, and peered at the Dreamraider with one eye. "You stopped Klein, now go and stop them from opening the boy's grave. There can be no more interference!"

Russell flinched, frightened by the big, ugly man. The Dreamraider moved in front of Russell then jumped at him.

PC Richards was in the hallway, looking towards the lifts, and Russell was on the hospital bed when a sinister shadow emerged from his comatose body. It slowly coalesced into the grisly Dreamraider Moloch had dispatched to further his bidding. With long hind legs and clawed feet, it strode silently over to the window, opened it, and dived out into the night. Richards felt the draft and turned, incredulous at the open window but relieved that the boy was still there.

Creeping with dread through the forest of dead craggy trees, Sarah spotted something up ahead and held up her hand to stop Wayne.

"Wait."

It was a house with a light burning inside.

"Russell is in that house," her sixth sense had led her there, and she trusted it.

"It doesn't look very friendly," Wayne said.

"I will have to kill Moloch; it's the only way to save Russell."

"Too hard—way too hard, he is protected."

"What if I were to take your shotgun, get to Moloch, make an astral jump through him back to reality, then immediately jump back through him again—then, in that moment when he's blinded to me... blow his head off?"

Suddenly, an astral flash of lightning in her mind's eye completely obliterated everything.

Sarah looked down at her feet—she was balanced on the very edge of a precipice, a tiny ledge high up on a mountain! Heights were her mortal fear—she froze and closed her eyes tight. If it weren't for the powerful updraft pressing her flat against the cliff-face like a giant hand, she would surely fall. Mustering her courage she opened one eye and peered down at the toes of her shoes—they were overhanging the narrow ledge—she was up so high there were clouds below and beyond the clouds, nothing: an abyss. The height literally took her breath away. To Sarah, there were few things scarier than heights. Oh, how she hated heights—she shut her eyes tight and screamed out.

"Wayne! Don't look down!"

It was like something out of a dark and frightening fairy tale— she peeked through a half-opened eye directly ahead. The mountains surrounding her were 2-D, like in a photograph or in a painting.

"Wayne?" she opened the other eye and peered beside her. Wayne wasn't there—she realised she was alone.

"Wayne? Oh, shit!"

Panic swelled to delirium—her mind warned her she was going to fall. Then, as if that wasn't enough, a loud crack erupted from the rock wall behind her—it cleaved open on either side of her, and from the clefts, six clawed hands emerged. They mauled at her. Two fastened to her thighs and dug their claws deep into her flesh. Two seized her by the waist, and two grasped her shoulders. She was paralysed with fear and horror, utterly helpless. In a panic, her left foot slipped off the ledge and was left dangling in mid-air—only the clawed hands prevented her from slipping into the abyss below—if they were to let go, she was gone. With her heart in her throat, she managed to pull her foot back onto the narrow ledge, fighting back the horror. "God! What is this? Think, Sarah, think... calm down, you're in Moloch's mind, this can't be real—he's controlling your every thought, your every move—he's controlling everything."

With the updraft howling like a thousand wolves, clawed hands simultaneously tearing at her body, she took a brave deep breath, closed her eyes, and yelled at the top of her voice, "This isn't happening, Sarah!" Her last word—echoed—and then a bright astral light flashed in her mind's eye.

Sarah opened her eyes slowly, uncertain of what to expect. She was pleased to find herself back in the dark forest close to Moloch's house with Wayne beside her. As her pulse rate dropped and the unwanted feelings drained from her, she recognised the irony of being pleased to be back in a more familiar nightmare than the one she had just left. Wayne was continuing the conversation as though nothing had happened.

"But how would you get back? You can only exit through your host," he said.

"Wait a minute, Wayne. What just happened? Didn't I just disappear in the middle of talking to you?"

Wayne looked about and shook his head, bemused. "No, when?"

"I was standing on a ledge on a mountain."

"Oh, one of those—jumps like that can happen if the host doesn't like what you're saying or doing."

"Wait a minute, Wayne, are you saying Moloch knows what I'm thinking and can hear what I'm saying?"

"Of course, you're in his mind, aren't you?"

The revelation seriously unnerved her.

"No, that's just too scary. Okay, I'm not saying another word about what I'm planning to do. And while we're at it, how come you know so much about this place? It's like you're Wiki-dream or something?"

"I don't know—I just do," he admitted.

Steve had dug down about a metre and was still going strong. The soil was loose and fairly easy digging but it was still hard work. He stopped, drenched in sweat, and glanced up at Parker supervising with her arms folded.

"Whew, this is hard work and it's bloody hot. Why did we pick a heat wave to dig halfway to China? Want a turn?" he leaned on the shovel puffing and wiped sweat and grime from his brow. "How deep you reckon?"

"I have no idea, Thacka will be here soon, maybe he'll know. Just keep digging, I guess."

But before Steve could get started again, he smelt something putrid.

"Phew, what's that? Smells like rotten eggs…"

Before he could finish the sentence, two shadowy arms sprung out of the ground beneath him and clawed at his legs. With eyes the size of dinner plates, he screamed and swiped at them wildly with the shovel.

"Parker!" he yelled frantically, dropping the shovel and scrabbling backward from the hole like some sort of giant pink and sweaty crab.

Parker drew her pistol, and with both arms extended, took aim as the creature rose from the hole, but she couldn't risk a shot without possibly hitting Steve. Somehow sensing her movement and the threat she represented, it whirled at nightmare speed and sprang out of the hole like a jaguar. It stood in front of the hole, six and a half feet of monster, snarling at her like a rabid dog. Steve was clear.

"Got you, you ugly mother!" She laid the front sight in the middle of its chest, took a breath, held it… and…

Steve, having recovered some semblance of manhood as it had turned on Parker, leapt up, into the line of fire again, seized the shovel, and took a mighty swing at the creature's head but missed.

Afraid she'd hit Steve and struck by the shock of the unearthly creature before her, Parker was paralysed. It sprang at her, as fast as a striking snake, and she pulled the trigger, just as the thing's unearthly long arm smashed at her wrists. The Glock discharged, but the blow had knocked the pistol off target, and the round went low and wide. The jolting impact had loosened her grip on the weapon, and the recoil of the shot made her completely lose control of it. It spun out of her hands, and she watched it drop, almost in slow motion—time had slowed for her. She looked up at the monster towering over her. Its teeth parted in a terrible smile, and a streak of greenish saliva slowly oozed from its lower jaw. She was facing death in its pitiless eyes, and she knew it. A calm resignation descended on her as the monster paused, seeming to savour its triumph.

Steve swung the shovel at it but missed again. In response, the Dreamraider turned and slapped Steve with an almighty backhander that knocked him out of the hole. He staggered to his feet, his mouth bleeding, and swung at the creature again with the shovel. It struck across the chest, but the blow didn't bother it. Its claw-ripper arm moved invisibly fast and seized the shovel handle, ripping it out of Steve's grasp. It stepped forward, grabbing him one-handed by the throat and swung him through the air, hurling him at the big sarsen stone. His back struck it hard, and he dropped to the ground, out cold.

It turned its attention to Parker, seized her two-handed by the hips, and picked her up, raising her above its head. It was about to smash her onto the heel stone when it saw Thackeray rounding one of the stones with two shovels in his hand.

When he saw it, Thacka froze for a long moment, then immediately went into attack mode. He dropped the two shovels he was carrying, drew his pistol, took aim with both hands, but couldn't fire because the creature lowered Jess to shield itself. Thacka moved stealthily closer, gun up, and glanced quickly at Steve on the ground, unconscious. The only way to stop the creature from throwing Parker against the stone and smashing her skull would be to keep his gun trained on it. He knew from the experience back at Sarah's house that the creature understood the threat that the firearm posed.

Parker shivered and revived from her shock somewhat. Through her panic, she caught sight of Thackeray.

He yelled at her, "Stay cool, Jess, poke it in the eye!"

Suspended in the air and gripped by the hips, she twisted sharply and gouged its left eyeball out of its socket with her sharp fingernails. The Dreamraider let out an unearthly shriek and flung her sideways—her training kicked in and she broke her fall with a well-executed parachute roll.

Bang! Bang! Bang! Shots resounded and the creature went down. Thackeray holstered his smoking pistol and rushed to Parker's assistance.

"You all right partner?"

He helped her to her feet.

"Ahhh... shaken but I'll survive. Look out!" she screamed.

Thackeray turned in time to see the Dreamraider towering over him with it sharp claws poised to strike. There was black slime oozing from its empty eye socket—but none of the damage including the three bullet holes in its chest had done any more than delay the next attack. Before Thackeray could fire, it struck him across the face knocking him against one of the trilithons. He took the impact on his right shoulder but the blow and the collision left him dazed, a sharp, burning pain in his right arm and shoulder. He shook his head and drew his pistol, but when he tried to raise the weapon, the pain in his shoulder slowed him—the creature saw it and capitalised. It picked him up as if he weighed nothing, and then smashed him hard against the sarsen stone like a toy it didn't like. The impact was so fierce it rocked the huge stage-set sarsen stone—it swayed—and then... it toppled—the domino effect—one after another the trilithons toppled against each other until the entire inner ring had collapsed. A huge sarsen stone crashed down on top of Thackeray but lucky for him, it jammed on the heel stone and that saved him from being crushed under its weight. But he was trapped under it.

The ruckus caused by the collapsing stones brought the guard running.

The creature went for Thackeray trapped under the big stone—

it grabbed his protruding leg and tried to drag him out from under it—Thacka braced himself—it was a tug-o-war with his leg as the rope. The big Maori guard saw what was happening, charged over and smacked the startled creature in the back of the head with an almighty blow that would have destroyed the jaw of any mortal man—but not this creature, it just stood its ground, shrugged off the blow, then turned and threw a massive counterpunch that knocked the big Maori into the middle of next week. He hit the deck out like a light. The Dreamraider turned back to Thackeray's leg and this time dragged him out from under the fallen stone.

Thackeray was battered, his clothes were bloody—he was still hanging in there—but only just.

The monster grabbed him—lifted him two-handed high above its head, set to bring him down on the fallen dolmens and smash him, when a salvo of gunshots resounded, Bang-bang! Bang-Bang! A split-second pause, Bang-bang! Four of the rounds punched into the Dreamraider's back—the last two blew off the top of its head. It stood still for a moment, then folded and collapsed on the ground with Thackeray on top. He looked up at Jess standing with the smoking pistol held limply in her hands.

"Jess? Jess... you all right?" Thacka groaned.

She shook her head, she couldn't answer—she was in shock.

Thackeray struggled to his feet, took her gun, cleared it, and guided her to sit on a fallen stone.

"Take it easy Jess... At least we know where the body is don't we?" he said, staring at the hole Steve had dug. Suddenly his attention was diverted when the repulsive corpse of the monster evaporated in a puff of sulphurous smoke. Thacka shook his head.

"There's nothing left to amaze me anymore after what I've seen of late!" he mumbled to himself, turning his attention to Steve. Thacka saw he was breathing and gave him a shake to try to revive him, to no avail. He turned and checked the Maori guard who was just coming around.

"Parker, you'll have to help me here. Walk this guy back to his office; he doesn't need to see any more, and call medics."

"Are you all right? Your head is bleeding," Parker said.

"Not leaking any brains, I'm alright. I'll worry about the cuts and bruises tomorrow. Meantime, I've got a body to dig up."

In pain, gripping his badly bruised ribs, his right shoulder burning, he groaned as he bent down to pick up one of the shovels. Then, after a deep breath, he went to the hole, gingerly hopped in, and started digging.

CHAPTER 15

Whatever it takes, whoever you are.
Heal the wounds erase the scars
Allow your hearts to be wide open
Shed, release, return unbroken.
How many times have you gone within
Only to find yourself there again.
Shed, release, return unbroken
Know thyself this truth be spoken.
Shed, release, return unbroken
Know thyself this truth be spoken.

Cocksure and accompanied by a brace of elderly doctors named Spira and Felstead, Badger strode down the hospital corridor en route to Moloch's room. PC Richards stopped the three doctors at the door.

"Sorry, gentlemen, but I have orders not to allow access until further notice."

"And just exactly who issued those orders, officer?" Badger barked.

"DI Thackeray, sir."

"Well, I am Chief Police Medical Examiner Badger, and I have superiority over DI Thackeray—so I'm countermanding that order. Let me pass, officer."

PC Richards, face red with embarrassment, obediently stood

aside to permit their entry.

When Badger found Sarah standing beside Moloch's bed with her fingers rested on his forehead, he inquired, "Excuse me, miss." And when no reply came, he moved closer and repeated, more loudly, "Excuse me, young lady."

Unable to get a response from her, he passed his hand in front of her open eyes and got no reaction.

"What's going on here? She appears to be suffering from narcolepsy."

The two elderly doctors in white lab coats studied Sarah.

Spira removed a pen light from his top pocket and flashed it on her pupils, one at a time.

"No response," he reported, shaking his head gravely.

Felstead checked her pulse then listened to her heart through his stethoscope.

"Pulse and heart are fine. I'd have to agree with you, Dr Badger, narcolepsy or perhaps encephalitis, whatever the case, she requires hospitalisation."

"Officer!" Badger called out loudly.

PC Richards poked his head in through the doorway.

"Yes, sir."

"Get a couple of orderlies down here on the double to remove this woman."

"Yes, sir."

Badger proceeded. "Fine, we'll just ignore her for the time being and proceed with the job at hand."

He checked the digital readout on Moloch's life support monitor.

"No brain activity, so in accordance with the court order issued, I am authorised by the state of New South Wales to discontinue the life support of Mr Wolfen Moloch at," he checked his watch. "Nineteen forty-seven hours, are we in accord, gentlemen?" he glanced at his associates for their nods of approval.

"Good, I note there has been no objection from witnessing Doctors Spira and Felstead," he scribbled a note on Moloch's medical chart.

Just as Badger was about to flick off the life support, Doctor Spira noticed movement on the brain wave monitor.

"Wait a moment, Doctor, there's a spike."

In pain but still digging strongly, Thackeray struck something with a different texture, soft and yielding. He paused digging.

Jess was helping the big security guard to his feet.

"Sorry, I wigged out, Bill," she called to Thacka.

He glanced up at her, wiped his brow with the back of his hand and with a pearly-white grin cracking his dirty face said, "You're entitled to a wig-out after a scene like that, partner!"

The security guard was holding his aching jaw. "Shit, that dude in the lizard suit could sure punch aye? Nearly took my freakin' head off. Who was he then?"

In an effort to dispel the reality of the attack by a monster from another dimension, Thackeray leaned on his shovel and said, "Ah, just some clown in a Halloween suit, a nutcase, plenty of them around, second one tonight. I've got officers on his tail—they'll pick him up."

"Oh good. Hey, what you digging for, bro?"

"A body."

"Geez, Mr Pearce is gonna be pissed when he sees all them stones down."

"Better tell him to have a crane on standby," Thackeray said, shaking his head.

"Okay, I'll just leave you with it then, aye."

Parker led him a part way back to the gatehouse to ensure he wasn't going to see any more of what they were up to, and then returned to Thackeray.

Steve stumbled over to Thacka, rubbing his head, still dazed after being knocked out. "Bloody hell, what was that thing?" he quizzed.

"That was the demon Gaap, a monster from someone's dreams, Sarah calls them Dreamraiders. That's what she's up against inside that dickhead's brain!" Thackeray said, digging more carefully.

"You mean there's more of 'em? Shit. It sure packed a punch for a dream. Nearly took my head off. What happened to it?"

"I shot it, and it disappeared in a puff of stinky smoke," Parker said flatly.

"You serious? Any more of them around here?" he said with a shiver, glancing about nervously.

"Hope not!" Parker said with a frown. She was engaged in swapping her half-empty magazine for one of the full spares she carried.

There was a rush of foul odour, and Thackeray exclaimed, "Pay dirt!" He tossed the shovel aside, squatted down in the hole at his feet, and carefully brushed the remaining dirt off what was obviously a badly decomposing body encased in a large plastic bag. The empty dead eyes of a small boy peered back at him.

"Phew! Pretty bad decomp, but at least the plastic has preserved it a bit," he covered his nose from the fearful stench and took Steve's shaking hand to climb out of the hole.

With a handkerchief covering her nose, Parker studied the pathetic face in the hole as well.

Steve backed away, holding his nose and fighting back nausea.

"The genitals have been removed," Thacka said, as he slumped on the ground and wiped his brow, relieved but exhausted.

A huge weight had been lifted from his conscience, all his efforts had been vindicated, as well as finding the boy's body was also helping him deal with the loss of his own son.

He leapt to his feet with renewed resolve and said, "Right-O, Parker—get onto Badger and stop the termination; I'll call Kitty."

They both drew their phones and dialled.

Sarah and Wayne were close to Moloch's house, but the closer they got, the more anxious Sarah became.

"Time is running out; we need to find Russell soon."

She was worried that back in reality, they could pull the plug on Moloch at any moment.

"Chill, Sarah, time progresses at a much slower rate here. An hour to us is like a few minutes in real time."

"Good, I sort of thought that might be the case. Now look, we've got to get into that house, but first tell me this Wayne, how come you're in Moloch's dreamscape? I need to understand."

"I'm not, I'm in yours and Russell's."

A large flying bug the size of a cockroach landed on Sarah's forearm and bit her. She slapped at it but missed.

"Ouch!" she shooed it away.

"What?"

She peered at the tiny bite mark the bug had left on her forearm.

"Nothing, a bug just bit me; look there's a mark. So, if I saw somebody, anybody, in this dreamscape, could I enter them?"

"Jump, Sarah, we call it jump, not enter."

She noticed the bite mark had swelled into a small lump.

"Oh, sorry, jump."

"Yes, you can jump into anybody, provided they're not dead in real time."

They were moving towards the house at a dawdle. Sarah had slowed, intrigued by the lump on her arm. It appeared to be getting bigger by the second, and she thought she saw it move under her skin—like it was alive.

"Why, what's the difference? You're dead, and I jumped through you."

Suddenly the lump moved up her skin, stopped at her bicep, and began to swell bigger—faster. She stopped abruptly, horrified.

"That was because we are connected. What are you looking at, Sarah?"

"That bite on my arm—it moved and it's getting bigger!"

"We share many of the same memories—you actually jumped into your own memory of us when you thought you jumped into me. We share that memory."

"Wayne?"

"Whereas children are open portals, until they hit puberty, then it's all over... unless they're psychic, of course... like you."

Sarah couldn't take her eyes off the thing swelling on her arm—it was now the size of an orange.

"Never thought I'd hear you say that, Wayne. Argh!"

"Now what?"

Suddenly the lump erupted like a huge pustule and spewed out live maggots.

Sarah panicked, "Wayne! Wayne! What is this?"

She showed him her arm—then froze, her eyes wide open in shock—she gagged, choking... something hairy and spiky was caught in her throat. She coughed hard, doubled over and then vomited up a huge, live cockroach. Then she quickly straightened up and grabbed at her left ear—a cockroach crawled out of it—she caught it, threw it away in disgust and she shivered—insects especially cockroaches, were another of her pet phobias. When she opened her mouth to tell Wayne, cockroaches poured out—the egg on her arm had hatched into thousands of cockroaches and they were pouring out of her every orifice. She was truly freaking out as she lifted the front of her dress and found cockroaches crawling down her inner thighs, they were coming out of her private parts. In a panic, she swiped them off her legs, but the more she swiped, the more materialised. Then she felt a buzzing sensation on her face—giant pustules erupted—weeping sores exploded pus like mini volcanoes—and from the boils poured maggots. Choking on cockroaches and almost insane with the terror of the ordeal, she pleaded with Wayne.

"Help me, Wayne, please... there are cockroaches all over me. Argh, help me!"

Wayne stared at her—he saw nothing, just his wife contorting like an exotic dancer.

"Sarah, there is nothing there," he said calmly. "It's only Moloch again!"

She immediately stiffened up, and feeling stupid, closed her eyes to collect herself. Through clenched teeth, she growled loudly, "Another phobia—he's exploiting my inner fears. This isn't happening," she shouted, "this is not happening! ... This is not happening!"

When she opened her eyes, they had all gone—not a bug, a maggot, or a sore to be seen or felt anywhere.

"I can't deal with any more of these psychological games, Wayne. I don't even know if that was the last of my phobias!" she almost cried, hand on her chest, willing her heart to slow down before she suffered a cardiac arrest.

"Just be prepared for anything, Sarah. Now, can we move on?"

They started again towards the house, but Sarah needed more answers.

"Why does he want Russell?"

"Because Russell is like you."

"What, psychic? Russell? Really?" Sarah said shocked. Finally, it was beginning to make sense to her. She stopped to gather her thoughts.

"Wait a minute... Right, I think I've got it... for fifty years Moloch has practiced occult, goetic necromancy, to prepare himself to be reborn through a child, but it couldn't be just any child, no, the host had to be psychic. That's why he chose Russell, and maybe that's why he killed the other boys because they hadn't come up to scratch."

She looked sternly at Wayne. "So let's go get our son; this bastard Moloch isn't going to have him. I'm going to win this battle if it's the last thing I do!"

As she took a step towards Moloch's house, he appeared right in front of her. She leapt back in terror—he had scared the living daylights out of her.

"It probably will be, bitch. I have your son to do with as I please."

She stiffened at the mention of her little boy.

"Get out of my face, you pathetic arsehole!" she screamed.

Her statement surprised Wayne because he couldn't see anyone there but her.

"What?" Wayne questioned.

Moloch evaporated.

Sarah realised Wayne hadn't seen Moloch, "This is getting

tougher by the minute; that was Moloch I was talking to."

"Sarah, this all might appear like a simple deal for you, like killing Moloch and taking Russell back to reality, but what about me?"

"What do you mean, love? You're dead."

"Only in real time."

Sarah sensed possessiveness from him and shrewdly determined he needed to be consoled.

"I'm sorry, love, I shouldn't have been so cruel. Both of us miss you like crazy, darling."

"You wouldn't think so by the way you're talking. I've got both of you here now, so why should I let you go?"

Sarah wrapped an arm around him, pulled him close, and gave him a big warm hug.

"You have to, love—and you know it. We're inside Moloch's mind, remember, and that's no place for..."

He pushed her away angrily.

"Don't patronise me, Sarah! I'm the one who died in that crash while you and Russell live on."

Sarah put her hands on her hips to confront him. "Mate, if you had listened to me that day, we wouldn't be having this conversation right now, wasting valuable time, would we?"

But before their argument could escalate, Sarah smelled the foul stench of a Dreamraider materialising. She kept her cool—then saw it behind Wayne.

"Wayne, behind you—a raider!"

In a flash, Wayne whipped around, drew his shotgun on the turn, and fired both barrels. The creature exploded into a cloud of putrid black smoke.

Sarah reached her hand into the black smoke and let it drift through her fingers.

"It feels like a spider's web. I wonder where they go?"

"Oblivion."

"Is that a place?"

"Yes."

"Where do you get the bullets? Is there a shop here or something?"

"No," he cracked the breech of the shotgun open, and the two spent shells spun into the darkness. He snapped it shut again, then opened it halfway and showed her,

"See, it's always loaded."

CHAPTER 16

Goddess of the Moon
Goddess of the three-fold
Moon Maiden, Mother, Ancient One
My voice, Goddess help me find my voice
What I ask is my choice.

Thackeray leaned against his car. He was hurt, aching, and physically exhausted from all the digging. The city was still in the grip of a heatwave, and it was frighteningly hot. He watched Kitty and her staff rushing towards them to deal with the crime scene.

"You both look terrible," she announced on joining Thacka and Parker. "And you look a bit rough as well!" she said, looking at Steve sitting on the ground, head in hands.

He looked up and scoffed, "Not every day you get into a fight with a monster and live to tell the story!"

Kitty looked surprised but ignored the monster reference.

"Took us all day at Moloch's house, and we're still not done dusting."

"Find anything of use?" Thackeray said tiredly.

"A lot of dried blood traces in the cracks in the cement floor of the basement, had samples taken for analysis. After a cursory check, I'd guess we'll get DNA matches for all the penises Jess has in that fridge of hers."

"That's excellent news," Thackeray said.

"Kitty, have you got any pull with CME Badger?" Parker asked. "He's not cooperating with us."

"That so and so, he's a stick in the mud at the best of times. We used to call him Bad-Arena because he grandstands so much. Can't help you love." She glanced at Thacka's bloodstained shirt. "I'd change that if I were you, Thacka; red and white tie-dye went out with the hippies. Where's the John Doe?"

Parker pointed her in the direction of the fallen stones, and Kitty hurried off with her assistants. Parker considered her own rumpled and stained jacket and blouse.

Thacka sighed, "I'm getting too old for this. Lucky I carry a change of clothes in the boot."

"Well, don't hold your breath, boss; it's not over yet. We better get to the hospital and nail Badger because he's still insisting on pulling the plug on Moloch."

"Can't I take a shower first?" Steve groaned.

Williams, the security guard, arrived and presented Thackeray with a clipboard and pen.

"Hey, chief, Mr Pearce said I have to get your autograph on this, aye. It's for all the damage and all. He didn't half go off, mate."

Thacka took it and signed.

"I don't know what that was all about back there, but I said on the form here some dude in a Halloween lizard suit caused them stones to crash."

"That'll be fine, Mr Williams," Thacka said with a grim smile.

"Can't wait to tell the boys at the pub about this after my shift, aye."

Thacka handed him back the clipboard and pen. "They probably won't believe you, mate."

"Yeah," he chuckled. "Probably, might wait until they've had a few."

Williams shook hands with Thackeray, Parker, and Steve then wandered back towards his shed.

Thackeray opened the boot of his car, threw in the shovels, and retrieved a fresh white shirt still in a plastic wrapper.

"Well, aren't you the boy scout; what else you got in there?" Parker joked.

"A spare tire!" he grinned while buttoning up his fresh shirt. "Right, let's move. Sarah's been left standing in a trance beside Moloch for long enough."

When Thackeray, Parker, and Steve entered the lobby of St. Vincent's hospital, Thackeray immediately sighted Badger at reception talking to doctors Spira and Felstead.

"There's Badger," he muttered.

Steve was his usual focused self, "I'm going to get a falafel, anybody want one?"

"Yeah, get me one," Parker said, handing him ten bucks. "But don't disappear off the planet; I'll meet you back here at reception. Right?"

"No worries, nothing for you, Thacka?"

"Nope," Thacka hadn't taken his eyes off Badger.

Steve left, and Thacka confronted Badger. "Excuse me, Examiner Badger, what's the story with Moloch?" Thackeray asked coldly.

Badger's irritation at the interruption was all too obvious from his contemptuous glare. He answered coldly. "You got what you wanted, Thackeray, but it's unlikely he'll last more than an hour."

Thackeray and Parker had heard what they wanted and silently headed for the elevator.

"Oh, detective, those two you left there, Sarah Dixon and her son Russell, we suspect they had lapsed into a coma. I've not seen anything like it before. We're discussing them now; it seems from their medical records they both recently recovered from comas, so we suspect a relapse. The Neurologist that tended the lad at Wollongong Hospital is on route to do some tests. We suspect Mrs Dixon might be suffering from MPD."

Thackeray turned back and bolted over to Badger in a panic.

"No, no, you're wrong; it isn't—"

"Oh, so now you're a doctor... you know, you truly amaze me, detective! You've got a lot of nerve for a second-rate cop!" he turned up his nose at Parker, who had walked over to join the discussion, and then turned his back dismissively on both of them.

"You rude, insensitive bastard, Badger!" Parker hissed.

Badger turned back to her indignant, "I beg your pardon, are you addressing me, officer?"

"Just when do you get off treating fellow officers with such contempt?"

"Oh, go away now before I report you for insubordination! I've had a belly full of the pair of you."

Thackeray pulled her towards the elevator, but Parker was too wound up; she shrugged him off, drew her cell phone, and hit speed dial.

"I'll fix this bastard once and for all!" she muttered angrily. "Uncle Dan, it's me, yes, we're getting unnecessary resistance from Badger. Yes, he's a rude pig... Okay."

She marched over to Badger. He glanced at her from his conversation with Spira and Felstead and arrogantly sneered, "Now what?"

Parker handed him the phone. Badger looked at her with hostility.

"I'd take it if I were you. It's your boss!" she growled.

The look on Badger's face changed from hostility to apprehension as he reluctantly took the phone. "Hello, ah yes, Superintendent Wilks... Good... er... but Thackeray... yes, so... thank you, sir." Seriously embarrassed, he handed Parker back her phone. "I apologize."

Fighting back a victory cheer, Parker walked over to Thackeray standing at the elevator. They stepped inside, and just before the door closed, she let loose with one last verbal jab at Badger. "You pompous, ignominious, pretentious, pen-pushing old fool, Badger, time you retired and let someone competent take your job!"

As the door closed, Thackeray casually slipped a fresh toothpick between his teeth and grinned past it at Parker.

"A pompous, igna—hoozigagga, pretentious, pen-pushing old fool... Poetic justice, Parker, well done... and Uncle Dan? Wilks? So, the super is your uncle? I'll be damned."

"How do you think you got your car?" she said smugly.

When the lift door opened, they were facing the reception desk on Moloch's floor.

As they approached the duty nurse, Thackeray questioned Parker. "What is MPD, by the way?"

"Multiple personality disorder."

"Oh, so Badger thinks Sarah's schizophrenic?"

"Sort of."

"The man's an idiot."

After getting directions from the nurse as to where the hospital staff had taken Sarah, they re-entered the elevator and descended two floors.

The ward was void of people. They quickly checked room after room and found them all vacant—it seemed the ward was for special cases. At the end of the long corridor, they came upon a room with Sarah in a bed and a nurse standing over her. They entered and were struck by the array of medical machines plugged into Sarah. Without announcing himself, Thackeray immediately began removing all the attachments, which caused the attending nurse to go ballistic.

"Sir! Back away! You have no right to—"

Parker flashed her ID at the nurse and said sternly, "This woman is not ill, and she is not in a coma. Where is the boy?" she peered at the nurse's nametag. "Nurse Stuart!"

The nurse fired back the most obstinate glare she could muster and ignored the question—that was a mistake. Parker lost patience and barked angrily, "I said where is the boy?"

The nurse flinched at the ferocity of Parker's demand and replied indignantly. "He's in the children's ward, one floor up."

"Right, take me there. We'll bring him back here, Thacka."

When Nurse Stuart hesitated, Parker demanded, "Now!"

Parker fired Thackeray a sly wink as he left with the irate nurse.

Thacka sat on the edge of the bed, leaned over, and gave Sarah a delicate peck on the cheek. Then he lapsed into deep thought. Now that he had slowed down, the aches and pains from the fight with the Dreamraider were registering. With Badger out of the way and a stay of execution for Moloch, he needed to come up with a way to get the comatose man to a controllable environment. He felt sure it was only a matter of time before Moloch sent another Dreamraider to do his evil bidding. He considered himself lucky to have defeated the last one and wasn't in the best shape for a second round.

Parker had the same problem with Russell that Thacka had had with Sarah. The boy was attached to all sorts of medical gadgets monitoring his brain activity, heart, and vitals. Fortunately, there was no nurse tending, so she only had to deal with Nurse Stuart, whom she had under control. "Unhook all that machinery, and we'll wheel him down to his mother."

"Listen, Detective Parker, I'm going to get into serious trouble doing this."

"Not while you've got me to blame you won't. Now get on with it!"

The rusty old front gate of Moloch's house squeaked when Sarah pushed it open. Wayne was lagging behind, so she stopped for him to catch up. It was then she noticed that not one but two Dreamraiders were materialising behind him.

"Wayne! Behind you."

He swung around, drawing his shotgun on the move, but this time he was too late. The Dreamraiders ripped him to pieces, and the shreds of him just evaporated into thin air, almost the same way Dreamraiders vaporised when shot.

Sarah was stunned—she'd seen her husband killed several times now, but no matter how often, she couldn't get used to it. Suddenly she realised she had two Dreamraiders to contend with, and Wayne wasn't there to protect her. It was then the thought struck her that perhaps while she was inside another's mind, in a world of Moloch's creation, she couldn't be physically hurt in reality—it was as if she were a virtual being and cognisant of the difference in her separate realities.

The Dreamraiders were staring menacingly at her but not attacking. She wondered whether that was because she represented such a threat to Moloch and his plans that he was only trying to scare her off. But that didn't really make sense. Perhaps there was another reason the Dreamraiders had not attacked?

Suddenly, both Dreamraiders vanished. Now what do I do? She wondered. The sound of flapping wings chilled her, and she was suddenly driven by an impulse to take cover from whatever it was. She sighted a stormwater drain at the side of the house, partially overgrown by vegetation. It looked like it could be a safe haven, and she made a run for it. When she took off, the sound of flapping increased—whatever it was, it was gaining on her—closer, louder, closer and closer. The crimson moonlight cast a huge bat shadow that was overtaking her. Instinctively, she knew that whatever it was, it was about to strike, so she crouched down and ran as fast as she could into the drain. She felt a gust of wind from the wings of the huge creature as it swooped overhead, only a metre or so above the drain.

Trembling, she climbed further into the foreboding dark drain. Claustrophobia had troubled her since she was a child, and cursed by a vivid imagination, she felt a panic attack coming. To go on would be to leave the comfort of the light and enter a deep, malevolent darkness—a darkness in which she would be as fully visible to evil as if it were daylight, and all the evils of the dark drain would be invisible to her. Although she seemed to be the only occupant of the lightless passageway in which she sprawled, she envisaged unwanted company in countless grisly forms: slithering snakes; spiders by the hundreds; bugs; rats; colonies of blood-drinking bats. She tried to rid her mind of the thoughts, knowing Moloch could cause them to materialise— she kept reminding herself they were only her phobias.

Eventually, concentrating on Russell to distract herself from the terrors of the dark drain, she began to wonder about the dead boy Moloch had been dragging behind him the last time she had been in his mind. As the thought struck her, so the boy was animated before her in the gloom. This isn't happening, she reminded herself. But the hideous, naked, decomposing corpse, a ghastly void where its genitals should be, came staggering towards her, scraping off pieces of flesh on the rough wall of the drain. It lurched along—classic zombie, frightening glazed-over milky eyes fixed on her. She closed her eyes tight, willing the spectre away and screamed out loud, "No! this is not happening!"

"What are you doing in there?"

Sarah opened her eyes, recognising the voice as belonging to her late husband. The shambling corpse was gone. Wayne was peering into the drain with a bewildered expression on his face. Sarah smiled at him.

"I just watched you being ripped to pieces, so I thought I'd take an intermission."

He offered his hand for her to climb out of the smelly, mildewed drain.

Now that they had Russell and Sarah together in the same room, Parker and Thackeray headed for the elevator. The door slid open, and they entered.

"Nurse Stuart will be screaming blue murder to the hospital administration by now, so we can expect an irate tap-back real soon," Thacka warned.

The elevator door opened to Moloch's ward, and they made their way to his room but were stopped by PC Richards still on guard.

"Richards?"

"Sir?"

"You allowed Badger pull rank on you, didn't you?"

"Yes, sir," the lad had the grace to blush.

"Right. He's off the case now due to his actions, so enforce my orders. Do not let a nurse, a doctor, or a friggin' cockroach into this room. Have you got that, Richards?"

"Yes, sir, only you and Detective Parker."

"Good, that can't be countermanded. Now, back on guard."

As Thacka joined Parker beside Moloch's bed, he growled at Moloch, "I think your number is almost up in the lotto of life, pal... but just hang in there a bit longer... I want my family back."

"Be careful what you say to him, Thacka. Just because he's unconscious doesn't mean he can't hear you."

"You're right."

Parker watched him draw his mobile and dial.

"Hey, Dr Nulla Nulla... yep, it's me all right, how you doing, Terri? Listen, I need a mega-favour. I know I already owe you ten thousand of them, but this one's so big I'll owe you twenty."

Parker realised he was talking to Dr Terri Parsons, the police psychologist they had met at Bondi Beach only a few days ago—it felt like weeks.

"I need to bust someone out of the hospital. St. Vincent's, can it be done quickly? Excellent, yes, if you need that, I think Jess will be able to get Superintendent Wilks to sign off on the order. Great!"

He hung up and turned to Parker. "I'll stay with Moloch until the cavalry arrives. You get back down to Sarah and Russell and keep the hospital staff away from them."

CHAPTER 17

A divided self
In parallel worlds
Fire and brimstone
A private hell.
She stalks the shadowed dream.

gk

Sarah detected the presence of a Dreamraider as it began to materialise right beside Wayne. She squawked, "A Dreamraider... beside you!" Wayne drew his shotgun. Sarah grabbed his arm. "No don't shoot. Wayne, can you jump though a Dreamraider?" she asked urgently.

Wayne rested the gun on his shoulder and thought. "I don't know. Why would you?"

The Dreamraider was materialising fast.

"Can you jump?"

"Don't know."

"Have you tried?"

He tucked away his shotgun, "Never needed to."

"Soon as it takes form, jump with me, okay?"

He nodded his head, and they waited. When the creature's form began to solidify, Sarah took Wayne by the hand, and together they jumped at the Dreamraider and disappeared.

The big ugly Dreamraider looked about for them, confused,

gnashing its teeth.

Sarah and Wayne appeared inside the old house right in front of Moloch. They were in a dusty, dimly lit room, with black drapes covering the windows—the living room of Moloch's house. A cobweb-covered bookcase took up one end of the room, with a big, old gothic chandelier also ensnared in cobwebs, taking up the centre of the ceiling overhead.

"See, Wayne, this is the moment of blindness I told you about. Moloch can't see us, I could blow his head off right now... but I won't, I've got to get Russell first. Quick, move!"

They raced across the room, trying to escape through an open doorway, just as Moloch's vision cleared. He bellowed at them, and they froze. "You pair are stupid. You're only here because I wanted it so. I allowed you to jump through my demon!" he laughed.

Sarah moved closer to him and snarled, "What do you want from me, Moloch?"

"I like your tits, I'd like to eat them... first." He stressed it by licking his lips to further gross her out. She noticed his tongue had been bifurcated and he had command of both sides of it. It moved about in his mouth like a pair of worms. His tongue, his tattooed face, pointed ears and chiselled teeth filled her with horror. She fought it down.

"Where is my son?" she barked at the big man.

Her tone was demanding—she was well over her fear of Moloch and not about to take any more crap from him.

He was not perturbed. He casually perched on the arm of an old weather-beaten Chesterfield lounge in the centre of the room, and nonchalantly studied the pointed tips of his long, black-lacquered fingernails.

"I'll tell you what, bitch, you jump back... pull the plug on me in real-time just at Beltane, and we can call it a day. What do you say, honey, do we have a deal?"

"Okay, but only if I can see my son first."

"After all this, you still think I'm an imbecile, Sarah Dixon? What is that, a superiority complex? No, bitch, dumb is the definition of your dead cartoon husband there. No-fucking-deal!"

Wayne pulled his shotgun and aimed it at Moloch.

Moloch jumped up and raised his hands in a parody of a panicked surrender.

"Oh no! Cartoon cowboy is threatening me."

Boom! Boom! Wayne let fire with both barrels. The first blast blew open the right half of Moloch's head and the second tore his right shoulder clean off. The room steamed with Moloch's blood. Sarah wiped chunks of bone, brain matter, flesh and blood spatter off her face.

Moloch stood agog, his remaining eye darting this way and that as if searching for something missing—which was half of his head. His brain protruded from the cavity in his skull, dripping fluid. His right arm hung from his shattered shoulder, suspended only by a few strands of torn muscle and ligament.

With the smoke from the shotgun blasts still suspended in the air, the three of them were stupefied.

Sarah hadn't expected Wayne to shoot Moloch and Wayne knew he had acted impulsively.

"I didn't want him dead Wayne!" Wayne gave her a ghastly smile.

"Now you are with me Sarah, it's where you belong."

Moloch hadn't dropped onto the floor and that held Sarah's attention. Then, right before her eyes Moloch's features began to re-animate—the ugly wound in his head filled in and his shoulder reformed. Within seconds he was back to normal and laughing at them acrimoniously.

"Nice try Cartoon Cowboy—Are you two lovers having a domestic over moi?"

All the blood and muck evaporated in sudden a flash.

'See, good as new. Idiot, you can't kill anyone, you're dead already. Now where were we?"

Before Wayne had the time to react or say anything, Moloch snatched the shotgun out of his hands, shoved the barrels up under

Wayne's chin and glared at Sarah. "Watch him blow his top."

Boom! Wayne's head exploded. Moloch cast the shotgun aside and exhibiting great strength lifted Wayne's lifeless, headless body off the ground with one hand, gripping what was left of his throat.

"See, nothing left under the hat! Here bitch, have a husband!" he flung Wayne's body at her.

Sarah dodged the flying flaccid carcass and caught a whiff of a Dreamraider manifesting. She turned sharply to find it behind her with its claws raised to strike. Without hesitation, she closed her eyes and jumped at it.

An astral flash blinded her mind's eye.

When Sarah opened her eyes, she was in a small room, face to face with a Dreamraider guarding Russell, tied to a chair. She had jumped from one Dreamraider to another. She only had seconds to untie Russell and get out of the room before the Dreamraider's vision cleared, and so she leapt at the chair and scrabbled at the knotted rope. Russell was unconscious. She'd just finished untying him when she became visible to the Dreamraider. Curiously, the creature seemed paralysed.

"You won't get away with this, bitch, this is my mind!" Moloch's voice bellowed from the corridor outside the room she was in. Then came heavy footsteps—Moloch was approaching. With no time to lose, she picked Russell up, ran at the Dreamraider full pelt, and jumped.

There was a blinding astral flash.

She found herself with Russell still in her arms standing in the hallway of Moloch's house, eye to eye with another Dreamraider. At the end of the hallway, she saw Moloch enter the room they'd just been in.

Moloch's voice roared when he found Russell missing. "Where are you, bitch!"

Again, she only had seconds before the Dreamraider would see her, so she took off with Russell in her arms along the hallway in the opposite direction, away from Moloch. At the end of the corridor, she came to a fork with one way leading back to the living room where Wayne had been shot, and the other leading upstairs to the second floor. She needed to decide, and she needed to do it quickly; she could either keep running away from Moloch or she could make a stand.

Moloch appeared at the end of the hallway and bellowed at her, "This is fun, isn't it? We could do this for hours, but you know what, bitch? I will eventually win!"

Sarah looked into the living room and smelt a Dreamraider materialising, then she glanced at the staircase where she could see the tell-tale puff of rotating smoke that meant another was about to materialise. A steely resolve welled up in her. She knew what she had to do, and she set her trap.

Moloch strode emphatically down the hallway towards her, followed by the Dreamraider that had been guarding Russell. She waited until he was halfway, then she turned and ran at the Dreamraider that had almost fully materialised in the living room... and jumped.

A bright astral flash, and she appeared behind Moloch in the narrow hallway. Unable to see her, he growled, "When I catch you, I'll let your son watch while I hack you up piece by piece, bitch!" He strode towards the living room. Sarah wasted no time... she stepped up behind Moloch and shouted, "Hey, arsehole!"

Moloch stopped dead in his tracks and turned slowly with a foul grin on his ugly face to face her as she became visible. But he didn't expect what came next—with Russell cradled safely in her arms, she jumped at him. There was a blinding astral light in Sarah's mind.

CHAPTER 18

I tried to have you exorcised
You laughed like Satan
But to your surprise
I staked you
Right through the heart
But for murdering you
I'm now locked
Behind bars – Spellbound.

gk

Thackeray was resting his weary body in a chair beside the king-size bed in Sarah's bedroom. The lights were dimmed. Sarah and Russell were on the bed unconscious. Sarah woke abruptly—she was disoriented, expecting to be in the hospital room facing Moloch, not at home in bed. She calmed herself, got up, went to Bill and said in a whisper so as not to startle him, "Bill, Bill."

The whisper didn't help—he still woke with a jolt. "Huh! Argh! Sarah, honey. Did you get Russell?" he said, knuckling the sleep from his eyes.

"Yes, but why are we here? How? I expected to be at the hospital."

He stood, embraced her, and gave her a peck on the nape of the neck. "We pulled favours from a doctor pal of mine, and from Superintendent Wilks for custody over you and Russell. The doctors and staff at the hospital figured you both had relapsed into comas.

They'd taken you to a different ward and hooked you up to all sorts of gadgetry, we had to bust you out."

"What about Moloch?"

"We found the body of the boy you saw at the 7th stone, like you said we would, and Wilks accepted that as prima facie evidence to release Moloch from Badger to us. With help from a friend of mine, we moved heaven and Earth to have him brought here along with you. He's in the guest room with Jess."

"Here! You're kidding me? Listen to me, we've got to pull the plug on Moloch now before he goes after Russell again."

"Sarah, why Russell? What makes him so special?"

"Because he's a psychic, Moloch needs a boy with psychic abilities, the others over the years were either not psychic enough or they died during the transfer process. I think he's been refining the process, but now, since his bike accident, and he knows he's going to die anyway, he has no alternative but to proceed. For him, it's a race against time!"

"That makes sense. Come on then."

When they entered the spare room, they were immediately assailed by a sulphurous odour—two Dreamraiders had hold of Parker. Her head was lolling, semi-conscious, there was blood on her arms from the creatures' claws, and her holster was empty. Thacka spotted her weapon on the far side of the room. The creatures were strangely motionless, as if waiting for orders.

Thackeray drew his pistol took aim and shouted at them. "Let her go... Now!"

All he got in response were snarls and menacing looks. Parker's head came up slowly, and she produced a wan smile, clearly stunned and frightened. "Take it easy Bill, I don't think they're very happy," she said.

Sarah looked about the spare room—it had been converted to a simpler version of Moloch's hospital room, complete with life support equipment, including monitors, various drips, an oxygen tank, and the ventilator that was keeping him breathing. She glared at the ugly unconscious monstrosity in the bed and visualised him killing Wayne. "Pulling the plug on him would be doing the world and the dream-world a massive favour!" she snarled.

Suddenly the room began to shake. "What the? It's an earthquake!" Thacka said startled.

Sarah steadied herself against the wall and had to shout to get above the ruckus, "No... it's an illusion. You all right, Jess?"

"Nothing that a week in Tahiti—alone—wouldn't fix!" she had recovered some of her spirit with them there, and was now struggling against the powerful grip of the Dreamraiders.

Moloch's bed began to shudder and then slowly levitated. It floated a metre above the floor. Alarms on the monitors all started shrieking.

Thacka blared in disbelief. "What the...?"

The bed began to rock turbulently, a coracle in an invisible psychic sea. Amidst the chaos, the bedroom window suddenly exploded as if a brick had been thrown through it from the outside. Shards of broken glass sprayed the centre of the room, over Parker and the Dreamraiders. A gale force wind roared through the smashed window, picking up everything in its path not fastened down. A wickedly powerful, swirling tornado whipped up glass, papers, and other debris and filled the centre of the room. Thackeray and Sarah were hurled backward into the wall with such force that the impact jolted the pistol from Thacka's grip, and it slid along the floor and under Moloch's bed. A bed lamp, magazines, papers, and books were being whirled around the room in the wild twister. Sarah and Bill had to duck and dodge the flying objects—things smashed into the walls and shattered, the lights flickered—it was a gale of supernatural force and it howled with the voice of a thousand wolves. Daggers of glass had peppered Parker's face and arms but had had no effect on the Dreamraiders restraining her.

Amidst the mahem, Moloch suddenly opened his foul mouth and let out an almighty roar, despite the ventilator tube. "Arrrrghh!"

The howl scared the living hell out of Thackeray—the last thing he expected was for Moloch to be conscious. Thacka yelled at Sarah trying to compete above the cacophony. "Sarah! This can't be! He's all but dead!"

Flattened against the wall by the sheer force of the whirlwind, as if pinned in a centrifuge, Sarah screamed in reply. "It's not him! That's the other Moloch... The one from his dreamscape... He's talking though him!"

Bleeding from cuts on her face and arms Parker screamed at the Dreamraiders, "Let me go!"

All of a sudden Moloch sat bolt upright and the sheet covering him dropped to reveal an ugly bloody stump, all that remained of his right arm and his heavily bloodstained bandaged chest. He glared at Thackeray with white, lifeless eyes, and then spoke in a deep demonic voice. "You've hunted me for six years, Thackeray, you scum... but now the hunter becomes the hunted. How does it feel? Ha! More than just a curse of bad luck, now I'll have total revenge!"

"Ha, Ha, what about this guy?" Thacka yelled back, intent on taunting the demon. "Twenty years ago, a priest would have been called to exorcise you, now we know you're nothing but a ventriloquist's dummy!"

Thackeray's attention was swiftly distracted by the arrival of a third Dreamraider. It materialised next to the two holding Parker. Thacka checked Parker—she was in bad shape, bleeding from lacerations on her arms and cheeks, her face white with shock and a renewed fear, her hair and clothing blowing wildly in the tornado.

The whirlwind continued to deliver mayhem, but it had no effect on Moloch or the Dreamraiders.

Moloch raised his only hand and pointed a finger at one of the three life support monitors. "Here, idiot... you should be on television—have one!" He swung his hand to point at Thackeray, and the monitor shuddered—then by some mysterious force, it tore from its mount and flew through the air at Thackeray.

Thacka realised he was seeing telekinesis in action, just as the monitor slammed into his chest and pushed him even harder against the wall.

"Bill!" Sarah screamed, thinking it had hit so hard it might have killed him. She wanted to help, but the whirlwind had her pinned against the wall. A sinking feeling overcame her as she watched Thacka slide down the wall onto the floor, his chin dripping blood. Emotion got the better of her, and she screamed, "Stop it, Moloch!" and then she pleaded. "What on earth do you want of me?"

His white eyes shot to her. A deep growl issued around the ventilator tube.

"I told you before, bitch, I want to eat your tits!" Let my total will be done!"

Upon his command, the wind abruptly ceased, and everything that had been suspended by the tornado crashed to the floor. The chaos was over. The monitor and life support alarms stopped whining.

Moloch spoke in a different voice—in another tongue—he was in a mystical trance. "Zirdo... Iadnamed... Elila—Micalzodo...Sannir... Madriaax—Finis... Balziziras... Iada... Lo...Kia!"

The words chilled Sarah and Parker to the bone.

On the floor with his back to the wall, blood dripping from the cut in his chin, Thackeray watched Moloch's bed slowly come to a rest back on the floor—the levitation was over.

"What are you going on about? Shut up, Moloch, nobody cares what you've got to say. You're only a murderer of little boys. You're nothing!" Thacka yelled though the pain in his chest. "Nothing! You hear me, Moloch? Nothing!"

Staring ahead with expressionless white, glazed eyes, Moloch spoke again in the demonic voice of the possessed. "I am Moloch, God of the Ammonites—beguiled for millennia by your moralistic orders that slaughter in the name of your God—You have burnt me at the stake numerous times only for me to rise again as does the Phoenix. You and your Vatican hypocrites who preach against idolatry while holding a golden cross, you who preach against tyranny while obliterating entire civilizations from the surface of the earth—I speak of the Cathars, the Aztec, the Inca, the witches. By the side of Thoth, I will fell the tree of life and bring to an end the reign of the false Son of God. No matter what you do, you cannot prevent the rise of the order of the Golden Dawn and the invocation of Choronzon—He who dwells in the abyss. If I give the order, your friend here will die. My faithful servant Gaap will snap her neck like a matchstick. Bring your son now to me now, bitch, or else she dies!"

Sarah's eyes flashed towards Thackeray for guidance.

"Don't do it, Sarah," Parker gasped. The Dreamraiders tightened their grip on her arms, and she yelped from the pain.

"We'll do nothing for you Moloch!" Thackeray said solemnly.

"Fine, have it your way. Kill her!" he ordered.

Gaap grabbed Parker, forced her to her knees and then gripped her in a headlock—it would only take one sharp twist to break her neck and end her life.

Sarah screamed, "No! Wait!"

Gaap froze and then shot Moloch a stare awaiting his orders.

Moloch nodded and Gaap relaxed his grip on Parker.

On her knees on the floor gasping for breath, Parker realised she could see Thackeray's Glock under Moloch's bed. She tried to catch Thackeray's eye to alert him but he was looking at Sarah.

"All right! All right! No more killing!" Sarah pleaded, glancing plaintively at Thacka, her eyes welling up with tears. "I'll get my son, but give me your assurance you won't harm anyone?"

"I'm not doing deals here bitch, do it or—"

"Bill!" Parker groaned.

Thacka cast Parker a fleeting glance.

With an ever-so-slight movement of her head and eyes, Parker fixed her stare on the gun under the bed and then added a frown to let Thacka know her meaning. He got the message.

"Get him yourself!" Thackeray yelled as he dived under the bed, collected the pistol and with his free hand pulled the plug on Moloch's life support out of the wall socket. A high-pitched systems failure alarm immediately sounded again, and Moloch started to gag as the ventilator shut down.

Parker was on her knees—she anticipated what was coming next, and she dived forward and hit the deck flat.

Thackeray, on his side under the bed, fired three snap shots, bang! bang! bang! In quick succession, the heads of the Dreamraiders exploded. As they vaporised into stinking sulphurous smoke, the wind suddenly erupted, causing a return of the whirlwind from hell.

Heart racing, Thackeray rolled onto his back beneath the bed, jammed his Glock 22 into the centre of the mattress, and emptied the magazine into Moloch. Each of the bullets tore through the bed into Moloch and left an exit wound the size of a fist in his chest.

The grouping was perfect, the shots had taken out his heart. Thacka rolled out from under the bed and leapt to his feet. The Glock was empty and the slide had locked open. Reflexively, he thumbed the clip release and slammed in a fresh magazine. He stood for a long moment looking thoughtfully at Moloch's corpse... he dropped the slide, then Bang! Bang! Two more rounds, this time into Moloch's head, which blew apart.

The wind suddenly abated, and thin plumes of stinking black Dreamraider residue suspended in the air descended on the three survivors.

Thackeray wiped the black Dreamraider soot from his face with the back of his hand as he turned to Parker and Sarah.

It was over.

Sarah immediately fell into his arms, and Parker joined in as well. They needed a collective hug more than anything in the world, and they all felt they thoroughly deserved it.

"You know what? I'm totally over rotten egg gas!" Thackeray admitted, patting Parker affectionately on the back of her head. "Oops, there goes another shirt!" Parker had smeared blood from her face on it.

The two women were nodding. They could hardly speak; they were far too choked up with emotion, weeping with sheer relief that it was finally over. For them, the ordeal had come to the best possible conclusion: Moloch was dead and had lost out on being reborn—Russell was safe—and the three of them were in one piece, though Thacka's chin needed some repairs and Parker's face and arms looked like she'd gone three rounds with a razor blade.

"Are you guys all right?" Thacka said with both girls in his arms.

"Not really," Parker said with a sniffle, pulling out of the huddle. "It's not all over yet. Steve and the rest of the team will be waiting for us at the station." She wiped blood from her watch face to check the time, "Operation Beltane is due to roll in just over an hour."

"You're kidding me. Tonight?" Sarah said, astounded.

"No choice, honey. We're going to get one crack at shutting this whole catastrophe down in one bust, and it's gotta be tonight."

"Well, come on then," Sarah said, suddenly cheerful. "Let's get you both cleaned up."

"Start on Parker, I've got to make a call," Thacka said as he pulled out his phone and dialled.

Parker picked up her firearm, and they left Moloch in his deathbed and closed the door on him, hoping to never have to look upon his ugly face again.

CHAPTER 19

Spirit of fire come to us
we will kindle the fire
Spirit of fire come to us
we will kindle the fire
We will kindle the fire
dance the magic circle 'round
We will kindle the fire
we will kindle the fire.

"Go into the bathroom, Jess, I'll just check on Russell," Sarah said in the hallway on her way to the main bedroom.

Thackeray was standing outside the bathroom, waiting for the phone to answer when he heard Sarah scream.

"Russell!"

Sarah rushed out of the bedroom and up to Thacka in a panic.

"He's not there!"

With the phone up to his ear, he said calmly, "Settle down, honey. Go and check Russell's bedroom."

The call answered, "Kitty? How you doing, kiddo? You're what? Still at work, do you ever sleep? Those aren't beds; they're autopsy tables! You know, one day, someone will come in and find you asleep on one of them and autopsy you. Ha! I've got another dead-o-deluxe for you... Moloch, no, he's a bit of a mess... Yes, did the job myself and proud of it, self-defence. At Sarah's place, yes, we'll need your expertise and the meat wagon. Yep, he'll look his best in a body bag. I won't be here, but you'll need to take a few things into consideration with the forensics and the death certificate... I shot him because he was possessed. I know there'll be an inquiry, but they won't believe the truth; it's just too supernatural. Okay, we'll talk about it later... no, it's not over for us, we're busting the witches tonight so you can get your DNA samples first thing in the morrow... Okay, see you then... Ciao."

Sarah came out of Russell's bedroom and entered the bathroom guilt-ridden.

Parker looked up from rinsing her face and arms in the sink. "Find him?"

"Yes, I feel stupid, he was in his bedroom sound asleep."

Thackeray strolled into the bathroom, ready to have his chin seen to. "Is Russell okay?"

"Yes, sorry about the panic, he was in his bed."

He kissed her on the forehead, understanding how she felt. "No worries, as long as he's okay."

Sarah cleaned up Parker's lacerations. "There you go. You only look as though the family cat has mauled you now. So now, big fella, bring that chin of yours over here."

"Kitty will be here soon with the meat wagon."

"Did she ask what time she could do the DNA sampling tomorrow?" Parker asked.

"I said I'd let her know. She was more concerned about me shooting Moloch, said there'll be an inquiry."

"It's going to be a tough one to explain."

"Yeah, I told her no-one will believe the truth, what with three demons, a possessed half-dead maniac, and some sort of supernatural typhoon going on."

"Yep, it sounds like the plot of a Wes Craven film. Was she still at the lab?"

"Yeah, she sleeps there. Ouch!" he complained when Sarah

dabbed antiseptic on his cut.

"Don't think for one minute you're leaving me here in this house with that ugly beast in the guest room. He might be blown to bits and dead, but I still don't trust him," Sarah said.

"No, we wouldn't do that to you love, we'll wait for Kitty or the meat wagon, whoever arrives first."

"I better give Professor Klein a call," Parker said, walking out into the hallway.

Seconds later she was back, her face white as a ghost.

"Klein's mobile was answered by a Nurse. He's in the hospital on life support. She said he was assaulted."

Thacka jumped up, "Call the duty Sergeant at HQ, he'll have a report."

Parker immediately dialled and walked off to talk.

After fifteen minutes, there was a knock at the front door. Thackeray answered it and welcomed Kitty's forensics team inside.

Sarah was standing in the doorway of the guestroom, disgusted at the state of it. Moloch's blood and gore was hanging from the walls like stalactites, and blood spatter had painted gruesome murals on the bed and floor. It looked like a Jackson Pollock original. She moved away to let the two forensics officers do their job.

"Think I'll worry about that mess later," Sarah said despondently.

"Forensics will clean up. They do top work... it'll be as good as new once they're done. Take my house keys, you and Russell go there while they do their job. I'll get a cop to drive you."

"No need, we'll stay here."

"Okay, got to go now, love."

As he was giving her a peck on the cheek, she grabbed his hand tightly and looked into his eyes with intensity. "Be careful, DI Thackeray, all right?"

As Parker moved past them in the hallway on her way to the car, Sarah called after her, "And you too Jess. Keep safe, you hear?"

"We'll be right. Geez, it's still scorching hot out here, and it's after ten!" Parker said.

Sarah and Thackeray kissed.

"Keep this shirt clean, will you? It's the third one tonight!" she grinned cheekily.

"See you in a few hours, kiddo," Thacka said with a wink.

In the car, Parker said gravely. "It must have been a Dreamraider that got the professor. He was attacked in the library of the Theosophical Society."

"What's the prognosis?"

"If he regains consciousness tomorrow, he should pull through. They said it's fifty-fifty."

Thackeray and Parker were on time when they met up with Steve, PC Richards, and Detective Connie Lee at the Surry Hills Police HQ.

"We're just waiting for a couple of PORS guys. Oh, here they are," Connie said as the two public order and riot squad officers dressed in riot gear arrived. She made the introductions.

"Sergeants Rees and Connors, DI Thackeray, DS Parker, PC Richards, and Steve Blake."

Thackeray called them into a huddle, "Okay, listen-up guys. I'm not expecting any trouble tonight, nevertheless, we'll be on guard. The objective will be to arrest a number of women who will be ID'd by Steve here. By the way, Connie, what happened to Dorrie Wilson?"

"She decided not to help us."

"I suppose that was to be expected—lucky we have Steve. Any questions?" Thackeray asked before jamming a toothpick between his teeth.

"Yes sir, are we going in hard or soft?" Sergeant Rees asked.

"Soft, we'll surround them. They'll be in a clearing in Melody Park off Beethoven Street in Seven Hills. Connie has the navaid details, and Steve will direct us when we get close."

"How many are you expecting to arrest?" Rees asked.

"Six," Thacka snuck past his toothpick.

Steve piped up, "I've arranged to meet Rebekah there. She'll blindfold me and then lead me into the circle in the bush. You'll have to stay out of sight, then track after us."

"Okay, all go then?" Thacka looked for acknowledgment, got it, and they moved out.

The convoy of two cars and the PORS team's Volkswagen T5 Transporter Police van, in black and white police livery, pulled into Beethoven Street and stopped. Thackeray got out of the VW Beetle to let Steve drive on alone.

After watching the VW drive down Beethoven Street, Thackeray got into Parker's car, with Richards and Connie Lee, and with the headlights off, slowly followed the VW at a safe distance.

Steve pulled up behind three parked cars where he found Rebekah waiting for him alone.

He hopped out of the VW and went to her.

"Merry greet!" Rebekah said, in a traditional Wiccan greeting.

She kissed him passionately. He knew she was high. She handed him a tablet.

"Here's your Molly; it's great stuff. I'm flying."

Steve faked dropping it and palmed it.

Rebekah said blindfolding him. "You said before that you wanted to experience everything; well, tonight will be the night, boy. You're going where angels fear to tread."

She led him onto a bush path.

The police got out of their vehicles, and Thackeray quickly called them into a huddle. "Sergeant Rees and I will now activate our BWV's," Thacka announced.

The body-worn video camera records 1080p Full HD video through an articulated camera at the top of the device, which is clipped onto the stab vest pocket.

"Now, synchronise your watches. It is 23:45," he added, and they set their watches. "Once we see them, we will circle round, get into position, and then go in at exactly 24:05 hours. That'll give them time to get their ceremony underway, so they won't be expecting anything. Okay? Any questions? No questions, good, let's move."

They slipped silently into the bush with Thackeray leading the way.

"Watch out for spiders, Parker; a dirty big one just hit me right on the forehead," Thackeray whispered.

Just as he spoke, she walked into a cobweb strung between bushes, and it freaked her out. She brushed at her clothes madly thinking she had spiders crawling all over her.

Thackeray saw the flickering light from flaming torches up ahead and slowed down. Though the bush they were in was a thicket in the middle of a small park, the clearing in the centre of it was obscured from public view. He gave a hand signal for his team to circle the lights.

Rebekah removed Steve's blindfold. The circle was different than before. Though the edifice was in the centre of the clearing, the circumference was marked with thirteen flaming torches. There were eight witches in white caftans, and three young girls whom Steve guessed were virgins, about sixteen or seventeen years old, dressed in simple white cotton knee-length dresses, barefoot, each with a garland of flowers in her hair—they were all very pretty. There were two guys, one about seventeen or eighteen, while the other appeared to be in his early twenties. They were also barefoot, garbed in white caftans and the youngest was restraining a terrified goat on a leash.

Thackeray and Parker stopped about ten metres from the circle and took cover in the last line of undergrowth to watch the proceedings. Parker was horrified at what she was seeing, but also very wary of spiders.

"We'll wait here," Thacka whispered.

The witching hour had arrived—it was Beltane. The clouds parted as if by magic to reveal a full moon.

Vivian stepped forward, motioned with her right hand and they all removed their clothing. Steve stripped off his t-shirt and trousers self-consciously. A second hand motion from her, and all except Steve, took up a position beside a burning torch.

He was feeling left out of the proceedings, casting his eyes warily about the scene, wondering where Parker and the other cops were.

He noticed the moonlight glint off something on top of the altar—it was a gleaming dagger. The thought stuck him, "Am I the sacrifice?"

Vivian signalled again and this time Nissa and Rebekah stepped forward. They took hold of the youngest virgin, a beautiful blonde girl with a lissome, budding body, and led her over to the altar.

Another signal and the teenager with the goat joined them at the altar, dragging the bleating animal after him. He pulled up on the leash to expose the goat's throat, swept up the dagger and in one flashing motion, sliced its throat open and let the blood gush forth. He lifted the spasming carcass and sprayed hot blood over the supine, body of the girl on the altar.

The witches in the circle began to chant.

"Beloved unknown spirit, we seek your guidance, we ask that you commune with us." Then louder with more intensity, "Beloved unknown spirit, we seek your guidance, we ask that you commune with us!"

The sacrificial girl's pale skin was crimson as she writhed and wildly smeared steaming blood over her body. The boy dumped the carcass of the convulsing goat on the ground and positioned himself at the end of the edifice.

The fervor of the witches' chant had reached hysteria; "Beloved unknown spirit, we seek your guidance, we ask that you commune with us! Beloved unknown spirit, we seek your guidance, we ask that you commune with us!"

Suddenly, it dawned on Steve that the chant was summoning someone or something: a demon perhaps or a spirit. He wondered with horror if they were summoning Moloch!

The witches were now screaming the incantation.

"Beloved unknown spirit, we seek your guidance, we ask that you commune with us!"

Rebekah and Nissa held the girl's legs to allow the young man to gain entry. As he did so, she let out an unearthly scream.

That was the trigger—Thackeray had had enough of the depravity. He checked his watch: it was 24:05. "Go! Go! Go!" he bellowed, stood—apart from the bloodied dagger, there were no weapons visible in the clearing, so he left his pistol holstered and charged.

Steve heard the call, dived for his pants and the iPad concealed inside them, and dressed as fast as he could. The witches were stunned when armed police emerged from the bush and entered the circle. Nissa and Rebekah instantly took flight past the torches and into the woods, while the rest of the coven stood frozen in shock.

Outraged by the intrusion, Vivian seized one of the flaming torches and hurled it into the dry bush, which ignited instantly. Two other witches followed suit, and within seconds, following a week of total fire bans, with the eucalypt foliage a tinderbox, the bush exploded into raging flames.

Thackeray crash-tackled Rebekah, and Parker snatched Nissa from her feet by grabbing a handful of her streaming hair. PC Richards and Connie Lee managed to apprehend the two remaining virgins and walked them back down the path towards the cars. The two PORS officers apprehended the others, only Vivian managed to escape into the bush. Suddenly, there was a horrific shriek! They all froze and stared in the direction where Vivian had run into the bush, and what they saw would remain in their memories forever: Vivian was engulfed in flames, her hair ablaze, her skin blistering, sizzling, and peeling from her flesh, leaving behind a cadaverous creature standing, contorting, waving her burning arms about madly, screaming... until she finally collapsed in a horrible burning heap.

Holding a naked Rebekah by her arms, Thackeray looked up at the smoke rising from the burning witch, and for an instant, he thought he could see Moloch's face laughing, taunting him from within the greasy plume. He glanced at Steve, who was staring at the smoke as well.

"Did you see that?" he called out.

"Moloch. Yes!" Steve said with a look of uncertainty.

In a hurry to get out of the fire's path, Steve slid the iPad back into his pants, pulled on a t-shirt, and went over to the two youngsters beside the altar, both lying next to it in a stunned paralysis, shivering in shock. He tried to get them moving.

"Come on, you two, let's get out of here before we're roasted alive!"

There was a gap in the fire where the pathway had created a narrow firebreak. The police had made a beeline for it, herding their prisoners, disappearing into the temporary corridor of safety.

"This way, don't worry about your clothes, come on, follow them!" Steve commanded the two youths. They shook their heads, rose, and chased after the cops on the double. But before they could catch up, the fire closed the gap and trapped all three of them inside a burgeoning firestorm.

CHAPTER 20

I am a Circle and I am healing you
You are a Circle and you are healing me
Unite us,
Be one unite us,
Be as one

Parker and Nissa were the first to make it out of the inferno to safety. The fire had brought the residents of Beethoven Street out of their houses. With a naked woman handcuffed to her arm, Parker shouted at the householders.

"Someone dial triple zero! We need firefighters and an ambulance here now! Hurry... I'm a police officer..."

She was relieved to see several people with cell phones had stopped taking photographs of the naked people appearing out of the burning bush and had dialled 000 as she'd requested.

Thackeray, along with PC Richards and Connie Lee, brought their prisoners over to the police vehicles, followed by the PORS officers.

"Where's Steve?" Parker asked Thackeray. "I thought he was with you."

"He must be still in there! Let's get everybody into the wagon first."

Sergeant Connors opened the back hatch of the paddy wagon, and Rees ushered the prisoners inside.

Raven, a witch who looked as old as Vivian, with long grey hair that reached down to the back of her knees, scowled at Rees and barked, "What's the charge, copper?"

"Indecent exposure, now get in!" came his curt reply.

"This is persecution, nothing more than an old-fashioned witch-hunt. Bastards!" Raven squealed.

Once they were all locked inside the paddy wagon, the police regrouped.

"Right, we either wait for the Fire Brigade or we go in after Steve," Thackeray proposed.

"I don't think we can risk it," Rees said.

"I can hear sirens," Connie reported.

PC Richards stepped up to Thackeray, "Come on, sir, let's do it."

"Okay, Parker, you direct the Fire Brigade, keep the medics on standby—"

But before he could finish the sentence, two fire engines with flashing red lights and sirens sounding, rounded the corner and screeched to a halt in the middle of the street. Firefighters tumbled out of the huge vehicles and started deploying their equipment.

Thackeray ran over to the first firefighter out of the truck and flashed his ID, "DI Thackeray, we've got three people in there," he pointed. "What can we do?"

"Just stand back, officer, and we'll wet down an escape route for them."

Within seconds, the firefighters were blasting water onto the fire along the line where Thackeray expected Steve and the others to be.

Thackeray went back to Parker.

"Rebekah said it was Vivian we lost," Parker said.

"Yeah, it was terrible, her screams—made me think of witches being burnt at the stake during the Spanish inquisition. Did you notice anything in the smoke coming off her?"

"No. Why did you?"

He put a toothpick between his teeth, hesitated briefly, "I did, so did Steve."

"What was it?"

"Well, I'd put a month's pay on it being Moloch's face, laughing."

Parker shivered, "Now that's spooky… you know they were trying to conjure up a spirit with all that chanting."

"Were they? Don't suppose it worked?"

"Hope not. I've had enough for one night without having to chase a ghost as well."

"Couldn't cope," Thacka admitted.

"Hope Steve's all right."

Sergeant Rees came over and said, "We should head back to HQ, the prisoners are getting rowdy."

"Okay, do that, Sergeant. We'll bring the others, hopefully," Thackeray said with a tired smile.

"Good luck."

"Thanks, Sergeant, well done," Thackeray said, shaking his hand.

PC Richards and Connie Lee were sitting in Parker's car, taking a rest. Thackeray and Parker were sitting on the street gutter, watching the firefighters doing their thing.

The fire was intense. The eucalyptus trees were virtually exploding into fireballs as soon as the flames licked them. The gas and oil omitted from the trees made them extremely volatile. Fanned by the wind, the fire was threatening to jump Beethoven Street to the houses on the other side. Some of the firefighting crew were staunching the small blazes trying to take hold on the dry lawns.

An ambulance arrived, and Parker got up to brief the paramedics.

Thackeray folded his arms and stared at the bushfire. He wondered in retrospect if it had been worth it, and now that he had a family in Sarah and Russell, whether or not he should retire. What he'd been through and, more importantly, what he'd put others through to try and close the case was causing him to question the value of it.

Parker returned, sat beside him, and immediately noticed the downcast look on his tired and beaten face.

"What planet are you on, partner?"

"Uh? Oh, sorry... just adding up the cost, I guess."

"Not thinking of giving up chewing toothpicks are you?"

"I admit the thought crossed my mind."

"Happens when you have dependents."

"Yes, I recall. I stuffed everything up once before, Jess; I don't want to risk it again."

"Mate, you've been a much better bloke and a much better cop since you met Sarah and Russell. If you were to announce you were going to retire, then I'd be the first to shake your hand."

"Don't underestimate your contribution; things improved a lot once I met you. You're the best partner I've ever had, Jess."

"Bullshit, Thacka! I'm the only partner you've had!"

They both laughed.

"Maybe I'll call it a day on my birthday next year."

"When's that?"

"July."

"Aha! A Cancer... Thought so, makes perfect sense—that's why you take everything so personally... you're a sensitive old crab."

"You don't believe in all that zodiac star-sign shit, do you?"

"Astrology, yeah, I guess I do."

"Hmm," he paused. "So do I actually... read mine every morning in the paper, it's like a religious habit, goes well with the morning coffee," Thacka admitted with a sly grin.

"After today, I think I might start reading mine."

"Let me guess, you're an Aries."

"No, I'm a Scorp. What's Sarah?"

"I don't know. That's why I'll wait a little while before I decide to retire."

"What, wait until you know her star sign?"

"No," he chuckled. "I've only known her a week and a half; I think it takes a little bit longer than that to get to know someone properly."

"Geez, has it only been that long?"

"Sure has, you and I have known each other less than a month."

"Yep, and we're still talking."

"That's a good star sign."

Parker's mobile rang, and she answered.

"Parker, oh hi, yes, we got most of them but it was tough. When we went in a couple of the witches started a fire... Yeah, it went up big time... after the total fire ban... yes, most of us got out okay, but we lost one of the witches, and the Firemen are trying to locate three civvies that were trapped... Thacka, he's fine... I'll put him on."

She handed him the phone. He half-hoped it would be Sarah.

"Hello? Sir!" he jumped to his feet not expecting him. 'Thank you, sir, yes, it's been a rough one. Yes, I will. Yes, sir, I'm sorry you got a hard time from the hospital admin. We had to move them quickly... there were circumstances I'll need to explain to you later. Yes, thanks for your support, sir, yes, it ended up the right call. Cheers."

He handed the phone back to Parker.

"Good night, Uncle Dan, thanks."

"Hey, that's a first, having Superintendent Dan Wilks ring to give us a well-done," Thackeray said, surprised.

"That's because it was a job well done, or it will be if we get Blake and those two kids out alive."

A firefighter walked over to them. Thackeray saw by the two pips on his lapel he was a captain. He and Parker stood to meet him.

"DI Bill Thackeray, Captain, and DS Jess Parker."

"Captain Sam Hewitt, we've wet down a channel for your people... the fire is under control but we haven't seen any movement in there. We're going in—do you want to join us? It's as safe as we can make it."

"Fine," Thacka acknowledged.

They followed Captain Hewitt over to another four firefighters still wetting down the pathway that led through the bush to the circle.

"How goes it?" Hewitt asked his men.

"Fine, sir," the senior of them answered.

"Safe enough, Captain?" Thackeray asked.

"Third fire today, this one wasn't as bad as the others though," he explained. "One of them at Pennant Hills burnt out twenty homes and killed six people, four of them from the one family. Terrible."

"Bloody hell!" Thackeray exclaimed.

"Yeah," he sighed. "A young guy had jumped into an old corrugated iron water tank at the back of his house to get away from the fire and boiled to death in it. The fire had been lit by two kids," the Captain said sadly.

"What a tragedy," Thackeray said stunned.

"I think we can go in now. Just stick close," Hewitt said, and then led them into the bush track. The track had been reduced to smouldering stumps dripping with water—it didn't bear much resemblance to what had existed before. The shrubs, bush, and trees lining the track had been left as blackened craggy branches that eerily pointed their withered smouldering claws at the search party, like an accusation of complicity.

Thackeray could see the circle and the altar up ahead but before they got there they came upon a terrible sight. It stopped them dead in their tracks. On the ground in a foetal position hands clawed, a skeletal face with its mouth opened in a silent, agonised scream, was the black, charred body of Vivian.

"Is this one of the three you're looking for?" Captain Hewitt asked.

"No, that's Vivian, she started the fire," Thackeray replied.

Parker averted her eyes from the grotesque remains and in doing so noticed movement behind the altar. She rushed towards it, calling out, "Thacka, quick!"

There, behind the altar, she found Steve, sprawled out on the ground with his clothes smouldering and his hair singed.

His blackened face peered up at her.

Parker reached out a hand to help him up. When he stood, he revealed the two naked youths he had been protecting, huddled together, blistered in places and streaked with soot.

Parker yelled, "Medic! I need a blanket over here!"

Paramedics appeared with blankets and immediately went to work tending to the three of them. The girl was so happy to be alive that she was in tears and shivering.

"Are you all right, Steve?" Parker asked with concern.

"Nothing that a hot shower won't fix!" he joked, looking down at the state he was in.

Thackeray and Hewitt joined them.

"Glad you're all right, Steve, you had us worried," Thackeray said.

"We were right behind you when the track suddenly burst into flames—we had no choice but to double back. Seemed the witches did something right in creating this magic circle because it sure protected us. The fire went right overhead. Bloody hot, an amazing experience, it was like being underneath an umbrella of fire."

Captain Hewitt was taken aback at the mention of magic. He shrugged it off.

"You're lucky to have survived it, son. Most folks panic in those circumstances, run for it, and get burnt alive. You did the right thing covering those two with your body and risking your own life; you saved them, you deserve a commendation for bravery."

"Did everyone else get out safely?" Steve asked.

"Yes," Thackeray said, "but we lost Vivian. The Firemen have done a great job saving all the houses in the street."

A paramedic put a blanket around Steve's shoulders. He was shivering, not from cold but from shock.

Parker took him by the arm and walked him towards Beethoven Street.

"I saw Moloch," Steve admitted to her.

"Thacka said he did as well, in the smoke coming off Vivian's burning body."

"Yeah, it was surreal. As the smoke rose up, it sort of shaped into a face, and it was laughing. You couldn't hear it, but it was laughing, all right. Freaky. They were conjuring up a demon, you know. Did you hear the chant?"

"Yes."

"I think that's what it was about, the sacrifice of the goat, the virgin's blood, and the incantation, all to conjure up Moloch's spirit," Steve supposed.

"But if it hadn't worked, why was Moloch laughing?" Parker queried.

Steve shivered again, but this time from fear.

"I don't know, but it tells me there's a lot more to witchcraft than a girl in red shoes on a yellow brick road!"

"You're not just whistling Kansas."

Richards and Connie Lee walked the two youngsters wrapped in blankets to Parker's car.

A resident shouted out abusively, "Bloody witches, you should've all burnt in hell for starting that bloody fire. You should be fucking locked up!"

Connie gave the heckler a warning, "Sir, keep a civil tongue in your head, please. Go back inside your house; none of us need your abuse. Try thanking the Firemen instead."

"Couldn't have said it better myself," Richards complimented.

Thackeray, Parker, Steve, and Captain Hewitt came out of the park.

"I'll take your car; why don't you take Steve back to your place and get him cleaned up? I'll pick you up in the morning."

"Thanks, Bill. Come on, Steve, give me your keys; I'll drive your car. Nice to meet you, Captain Hewitt," Parker said with a wave.

Thacka shook Hewitt's hand, "Well done, Captain; you guys deserve a commendation."

"No, mate, just like you, we were doing our job."

They watched the medics carrying the body bag containing Vivian out of the smouldering park over to the ambulance.

"Got to catch them. All the best, Sam."

"You too, Thacka."

Thacka ran over to the medics.

"Guys, she goes to the crime lab, Dr Hawke."

"Kitty... No worries, detective," one of the medics said.

Thackeray waved at Parker in the VW Beetle as it chugged past. He got into the front seat of Parker's car next to Connie.

"To the station, Connie, and don't spare the gas."

"Too easy, sir."

Parker opened the door of her apartment and ushered Steve inside.

"Take a shower, Steve, you need it. I need one as well."

She went into her bedroom while Steve opened the iPad to review the video footage he'd taken at the Sabbat. It was horrific. He had filmed Vivian screaming in agony, her body and hair ablaze. Then, to his amazement, he had tilted the camera with the smoke rising from Vivian and caught a face in the smoke. It was vague and lasted only a few seconds, but it was definitely the face of a man, and even though he'd never seen Moloch, he presumed it had to be him. He stopped the video, rewound it frame by frame until he had one clear frame of the face, and then snapped a screenshot. The more he looked at it, the more he wondered if he was seeing things or not, and he decided to get Parker's opinion once she was out of the shower. He put down the iPad and headed off to the guest bathroom to take a shower.

A little later, with a towel draped around his waist, Steve tentatively approached Parker's bedroom door with the iPad and knocked.

It opened to Parker, also wrapped in a towel, with her hair still wet.

"Feeling better?" she asked.

"Yeah, I want to show you something on the iPad."

"Come in."

He followed her into the bedroom, and they both sat on the bed. The still photo he had taken was on the iPad desktop, and he showed it to her.

"What do you see?"

"That's Moloch!" she declared, electrified.

"Now watch this..."

He replayed the section of the video showing Vivian on fire and the tilt up to the smoke, then froze it on the face in the smoke.

"I can't believe what I'm seeing!" Parker said, totally stunned.

"I know I couldn't believe it either."

As she leaned forward for a closer look, her towel fell open and revealed one of her shapely breasts. Embarrassed, she quickly covered up. But Steve had long fancied her and foolishly thought the feeling was mutual. For a moment, he felt the soft, warm firmness in his hand and leaned forward to try to kiss her. His head suddenly exploded with stars as her right elbow caught him flush on the nose. The force of the well-directed blow knocked him backward onto the bed. Parker sprang to her feet. Steve sat up, holding his bleeding nose.

"Get out!" Parker ordered, in no uncertain terms.

And without saying a word, he left the room. There was no way Parker would have anything to do with him.

He stood outside her closed bedroom door, wondering whether he had blown their friendship.

She stood on the other side of the door, knowing he had.

It was 4 AM by the time Thackeray dragged his weary body out of the steaming hot shower, only to fall onto his bed still wringing wet. Almost immediately, his mobile rang. One eye opened, and he peered at the phone. Oh, how he hated that phone. His hand flopped about on the bed like a dying mackerel on the deck of a trawler, and finally, it came up with the phone. He answered, his tiredness evident in his tone, "Thackeray. Oh, Hi Sarah. Yes, I decided to come to my place, I didn't want to wake you guys. Yep, some paperwork at the station, then back here... just had a shower and now I'm ready for a couple of hours kip," he yawned. "Sorry, are you guys all right? Yes, it'll be an early start in the morning. It all went well enough. I'll fill—" he yawned again, "you in later... sorry I'm seriously knackered. Catch you just after lunch. Kiss, kiss. Yes, me too." He closed his phone and dropped off to sleep with it still in his hand.

CHAPTER 21

When the moon has caressed
the soil of ancient ways...
The spirit returns when
the smoke doth rise.
From the chant of life
and deaths crying eyes,
arise entity arise, arise.

gk

Parker had been studiously ignoring Steve, seated near her desk and looking contrite. She was surprised when Thackeray strolled into the office at the stroke of nine.

"Morning boss, I expected you to be late."

"Ah, not this incarnation of William Thackeray! Morning Blake, feeling okay, no burns?"

"I'm fine thanks, detective."

"Steve's got something to show you, Thacka."

Steve held up the iPad and then showed Thacka the still photo of the face in the smoke.

"Jesus! It was Moloch, wasn't it?" Thackeray said, awestruck.

"Yeah, check out the video," Steve said.

He replayed the same sequence he'd shown Parker the night before. As gruesome as Vivian's death was, it was the face in the smoke that left the three of them thunderstruck.

"I couldn't believe I got it," Steve said.

"Gives me goosebumps," Parker admitted.

"I wonder what Sarah would think of it," Thacka mused.

"I'll print you a copy to show her if you like," Steve offered.

"Have you checked my BWV video to see if it's there as well?" Thacka asked.

"First thing I did when I got in, nothing. But it wasn't aimed at the smoke like the iPad had," Parker concluded.

"I suppose so," Thacka agreed, then checked his watch. "I told Kitty she could get her samples at ten; we better get a move on."

"Are you done here, Steve?" Parker asked, her voice tone an indicator that she was still annoyed over Steve's behaviour the previous night.

"Yep, just let me print out the photo for Thacka, and then I'll be on my way. I've got some more writing to do."

"Writing the story?" Thacka inquired.

"Yeah, and it's one hell of a tale."

"Well, you got that part right, that's for sure. Just leave out the demon slayer stuff, okay?" Thacka said with a frown.

Steve handed Thacka the printed photo, and the three of them left.

In the elevator to the interview rooms, Thackeray studied his partner, her face still etched with abrasions. He thought, she still looks like she's been in a fight with a cat.

Parker felt him staring at her and returned the stare. He had a plaster on his chin but looked less beaten up— on the outside at least. They rode in silence.

The elevator doors opened.

"I took the liberty of getting Lee and Richards to take statements from everyone but Rebekah and Nissa. Thought it best for us to do them," Parker told Thacka.

"Good, which witch first?"

"Rebekah. I'll just go get her. They brought her a change of clothes from her house."

"Change? Damn, I was looking forward to interviewing a naked witch," he chuckled.

Thackeray went into the room and stuck a toothpick between his teeth. He flopped into a chair and put his feet up on the desk to wait. After a few minutes, he looked up at Parker entering with Rebekah, and he shivered involuntarily as he felt the uncanny presence of a witch. As she directed Rebekah into the room, all the preternatural aspects of the case rushed back at him.

Rebekah was dressed in the obligatory Goth uniform: a knee-length black waist-fitted dress topped with a black fichu, pointed high-heel ankle-length boots, and her jet-black waist-length hair with those few long white strands at the front.

"Rebekah or should we call you Evelyn?" Thackeray said, gesturing for her to sit.

As she did so, Parker sat down beside Thacka and turned on the recorder to take Rebekah's statement.

"Rebekah please, I don't like Evelyn. Never have."

"You have the right to a lawyer, Rebekah."

"No thanks—can't afford one."

"We can provide a lawyer pro bono."

"I'll let you know."

"Okay, so Rebekah, did you meet Steve Blake aka Kaspar in the Veil chat room?"

"Sure did."

"And then you decided to meet up at the Circle Café in Balmain for a coffee and a chat?"

"Yep."

"How many times?"

"Um, twice I think."

"Were you always alone?"

"Yes... oh, one time Oscar turned up."

"Oscar?"

"Yes, a guy I knew through my coven."

"Is Oscar his real name?"

"No, it's Wolfen... Wolfen Moloch."

"Do you know if Wolfen Moloch had a tattoo of a star on his right forearm?"

"Yes, a pentagram."

Thackeray glanced at Parker. It was confirmation that Moloch had been the attempted kidnapper of the little boy at Eastgardens.

"Do you know Mr Moloch is deceased?"

"Yes, well, so I've heard."

"How well did you know Wolfen Moloch?"

"Very well, he's been doing me since I was about seven or eight."

"What? Um, we'll go into that a little later," Thackeray said, shocked.

"So, did you invite Steve Blake to a meeting of your coven, a Sabbat?"

"Yes, on October twenty-second."

"Can you say what happened at the Sabbat?"

"Yeah, well all the normal stuff, there were six of us, seven with Kaspar, he was the only guy... and then we all got it on, well, Kaspar had did with two others before me. He didn't have sex with the other three because they don't do men, if you know what I mean. While he was fucking... oh, can I say that?"

"Yes, go ahead," Thackeray agreed.

"While he was fucking Vivian—she always liked to go first, Oscar, Moloch, was waiting in the dark for when they'd finished. After Steve had done his thing, well, she went to Moloch so he could take the seed."

"What did Moloch want with the seed?"

"A spell or something, he's a warlock, well was, we didn't need to know what he did with stuff, he often took samples of love juice as he called it... and other stuff."

"Okay, then?"

"Oh, Steve did Nissa and then me... and that was that."

"Did you then take Steve Blake to your home in Newtown?"

"Yes, you know that. He slept there, in the morning he rang her," she said pointing at Parker.

'You mean DS Parker?' Thacka clarified.

'Yeah.'

"Did you call Moloch and tell him Steve Blake had been talking to a cop?"

"No. Moloch called me to ask about Steve. I told him I'd overheard him talking to detective Parker."

"Did he ask for Steve Blake's address?"

"Yes. I texted it to him - that wasn't unusual, he was always asking for stuff, if you didn't give it to him then he'd hurt you."

"When you say he'd hurt you, what do you mean?"

"Like I said, he was a powerful warlock, he had power over us. In the coven we are bound by blood to secrecy, and we all had children to him - if we told anyone about it or anything else, he said he would kill us. We would be the next sacrifice - and he meant it."

"So were there human sacrifices?"

"I've never seen any but we think that's where the children we had ended up... but only if they were boys."

"These are the children he had with you?"

"Yeah. If it was a girl, she would be raised in the coven like me and most of the others. If it was a boy, once he'd turned six, Moloch would take him."

"So you were raised in the coven?"

"Yes, Moloch is my father."

"I see. Wasn't that a problem for the mothers?"

"What him taking the boys? No, the boys were his—we knew we couldn't keep 'em, that's what they was raised for—you know, for him."

"So what happened to them?"

"Some reckon they lived with him to be taught the craft... others say he sacrificed them to build up his powers. You've got to understand Moloch is extremely powerful warlock, he can do things." Her voice trailed off.

"You said he is a powerful warlock... he's dead."

"Yeah well..."

"Okay, how was he given the boys?"

"We delivered them at one of the Sabbats. After the ceremony, he'd take the boy home with him."

"Did the boy go willingly?"

"Yes of course, I told you, that's what he'd been raised for."

"How many boys have there been that you know about?"

"There's been six, one from each of us. Nissa's was the last, before that mine and before that Lilith, Luna and Raven, the first was from the oldest Vivian, years ago."

"So not so many girls were born then?"

"No, he cast a spell to make sure we bore boys. Like I said he's the most powerful necromancer in the country."

"Do you know of any other warlock's practicing like that in Australia?"

"No, he came from England. He was a warlock over there. He told us he was born in Glastonbury in 1933 but once he let slip that his real birth date was 1773."

"What do you mean? I don't get it, 1773? But if he was born in 1933 that would make him... what?"

"Eighty years old!" Parker said.

"Yeah, you wouldn't think so eh? Ha, the body, stamina and mind of a thirty-year old. I told you, he's the best with spells," Rebekah explained.

"And if you take eighty from 1933 you get 1853 and then eighty from that... you get 1773."

"What are you saying Parker?" Thackeray queried.

"Well, it might be that each time he reached 80 years old, he needed to be reborn, so he took a new host," Parker theorised.

"That would mean he was really two hundred and forty when he died!" Thackeray said, astonished.

"Maybe that's the way warlocks have perpetuated since time immemorial," Parker suggested.

"Sounds like a different take on a vampire movie don't it?"

Rebekah smiled.

Thackeray couldn't help but notice her slightly extended canine teeth, then he checked himself, realising he was overreacting.

"Who is your mother?" Parker asked.

"Raven."

"Is Nissa your sister?"

"Half sister, her mother is Vivian."

"Why do you think Moloch would have killed Steve Blake's wife?"

"Because he could... and coz he was probably really only going there to scare Kaspar but it got out of hand or something. He was seriously into sadomasochism, just ask Dorrie. Get her to show you the scars where he'd cut her."

"And how does Jason Little fit in?"

"Santa's little helper, he's a perverted little thing. Always hanging around Moloch for slops, if you know what I mean. Dorrie's jailor."

"So Dorrie was being kept prisoner then?" Parker asked.

"Yes."

"Do you know Richard Riley?"

"Of course, Richard was a regular at our meetings until..."

"Until what?"

"Until he fell for Nissa and Moloch banned him."

"What happened to him?"

"Don't know, he just disappeared."

"So what now Rebekah?"

"I don't know, that's up to you ain't it?"

"If you're lucky you might get off with a warning, we suspect Vivian was Moloch's main accomplice and that you were acting under threat."

"I could have told you that, it was Vivian he came to Australia to be with in the first place. She would have done anything for him. Like, anything."

"Finished?" Parker asked Thackeray.

"Yes, that'll do for now. You'll need to join the others to give a DNA sample. Anything else you'd like to add?"

"No nothing."

"Interview terminated," Parker said as she switched off the recorder. She stood, and as she was leading Rebekah out of the room, Thackeray asked, "Rebekah, just a sec, off the record, is that the last we'll see of Moloch?"

"Huh! I told you he was a powerful warlock."

When the door closed behind them, Thackeray flicked a masticated toothpick into the rubbish bin. Rebekah had confirmed what he feared when he saw Moloch's face in the smoke - maybe this was never going to end.

Parker returned with Nissa and found Thackeray sitting back in his chair, chewing a fresh toothpick. Nissa took a seat, and Parker took up her position beside the recorder.

"Miss Nissa Turner."

"Yes."

"I am DI Thackeray, and this is DS Parker. We're going to ask you some questions. You have the right to a lawyer."

"Don't need one thanks," her demeanor was cool and relaxed.

"Okay. Are you the daughter of Vivian Turner and Wolfen Moloch?"

"Yes."

"Have you had sex with your father?"

"Yes."

"On how many occasions?"

"Since I was a six-year-old—so too many times to remember."

"Did you go to school?"

"No, the coven was my school."

"Did you have children to Wolfen Moloch?"

"Yes, two."

"And they are?'

"Dianne, who was deflowered last night and a boy who disappeared."

"What happened to the boy?"

"On his sixth birthday I gave him to Moloch."

"Why?"

"Because it was ordained."

"And what happened to the boy?"

"Not for me to know."

"Why didn't you ask Moloch?"

"You can't ask a warlock anything. The boy was his. He would've hurt me if I said anything."

"Do you think he sacrificed the boy?"

"Yes."

"What makes you think that?"

"Jason Little said so... he claimed he was there when it happened."

Thackeray noticed a single tear run down her cheek.

"What was his name?"

Her eyes welled up with tears. He knew she couldn't just forget her child, no mother could. He understood that from his own loss— the grief was securely locked away in an emotional cupboard, but it could burst forth without warning. Nissa could see the hurt in Thackeray's eyes.

"You've lost a son... A boy, a six-year-old."

"Yes... and I will never forget him.

There was a pregnant pause while the three of them regathered their emotions.

"Did you and Vivian kidnap Steve Blake?"

"Yes."

"Why?"

"A prank."

"I don't believe that. Why did you do it?"

"I had no choice. Vivian is in charge of Beltane, only she knew what it was about. Look Mr Thackeray, can't you understand that after over thirty years of being in a coven, under the rule of Moloch and Vivian, we have no choice but to do as we are told. If we disobey... then—" she said becoming emotional, "there was hell to pay."

"I understand."

"Do you know Richard Riley?"

Again, a tear rolled down her pallid cheek.

"Yes."

"Where is he?"

"I don't know, he disappeared."

"What do you think happened to him?"

"Moloch probably killed him."

"Why would he do that?"

"I don't know, but he could get jealous."

"Jealous?"

"We are his flock. It was okay to have ritual sex with outsiders but if it got serious, then he got jealous. He's a control freak and a psychopath."

"Okay, thank you, we're done Parker."

"Interview terminated," Parker said and turned the recorder off.

"Will I be going to jail?"

"No Nissa, probably not. If you're lucky you won't."

"I wouldn't mind, it'd be a damn sight safer than the coven."

"Sorry," Parker said as she led her to the door.

"Goodbye detective Thackeray, your new life will be fine with your new family."

"Wait! How do you know that?"

She stopped at the door.

"River, Mr Thackeray, my son's name was River. I'd like to be able to bury what you have of him."

"I will arrange that for you Nissa," he replied sorrowfully.

"Thank you, merry part."

When the door closed, Thackeray stood and stretched. He checked his watch—it was just on ten and that meant Kitty would be outside.

You could set your clock by Kitty; she was as punctual as Big Ben. Standing in the corridor with her medical bag in her hand, she was just greeting Parker when Thackeray came out of the interview room.

"Look out, here's trouble," Kitty said, with her trademark smirk.

"What's that on your chinny chin-chin?"

"No one started an autopsy on you then?"

"No not this time Thacka, but I tell you what. I've got seven different male DNA samples from the blood on Moloch's basement floor and I've matched them all bar one to our six little penises."

"Brilliant, but you said seven."

"Yeah, seems we have one extra."

"Hmm, maybe we missed one. Can we check from the mitochondrial DNA to match the mothers with the samples you're about to get?"

"That's what I was just about to ask her to do," Parker said.

"Sure can," Kitty said with her characteristic crooked smile.

"Well, I'm going upstairs to write up my report and then I'm taking the rest of the day off. I suggest you do the same Parker. I'll see you round Kitty."

"I'll let you know about the seventh victim tomorrow."

"No rush."

"Oh, Thacka, I emailed you Moloch's autopsy report, I have an inkling you might be needing it," Kitty said with a raised eyebrow.

"I'll take your word on that. Catch you later, Kitty.'

"I'll come with you Thacka," Parker said.

They both headed for the elevator.

CHAPTER 22

When the greed of the dream
Eats away at your heart
There's a price to pay
For playing the part.
The selfish win
Then the selfish lose,
Such is the karma
When you choose to abuse.

gk

Parker's mobile rang almost as soon as she entered the office with Thackeray to write up their reports. She answered and put him on speaker.

"Hi Steve, what's up?"

"How did the interview go?" he asked.

"You can read the transcript once we've got them done."

"Did Rebekah set me up? Did she play an intentional role in Niki's murder?"

"No. Moloch had a hold over them, and when he didn't, Vivian did; she was in it with Moloch," she explained. "Mind you, Vivian and Moloch are Rebekah's parents."

"No, you're kidding me! So now we can add incest to the mix. What a story!"

"It's a bit friggin' sick if you ask me!" Thacka said out loud with distaste.

"I don't know, there's something about all this that just doesn't want to go away. I don't know if it's because of seeing Moloch in the smoke or seeing Vivian burnt to a cinder, but it just doesn't feel like it's over," Steve said, clearly worried.

"Yes, I know what you mean," Parker agreed.

"But of course if you want to believe the witches, then maybe it isn't over!" Thacka said.

"What do you mean? A little more info, please," Steve demanded, hungry for facts.

"Well, after interviewing the witches, I got the impression that they believe Moloch dying doesn't necessarily mean he's gone," Thacka said.

"That's like one of your paraprosdokians, Bill!" Parker tried to make light of it.

"What are bloody paraprosdokians?" Steve questioned.

"Google it mate, it's quicker than me explaining," Thacka said offhandedly, as he sat in front of his computer and booted it up.

"Right, peace and quiet now, I need to concentrate. Goodbye Blake."

"Okay, I get the hint, got to find a new gaff, finish my story, submit it and get paid. How's that for a plan? Catch you later. And Jess, I might have to stay one more night at your place if that's all right."

"I don't think she'll cast you out on the street, mate!" Thacka said facetiously.

"Okay, bye," Parker said terminating the call.

Thacka looked up from his computer at Parker with a raised eyebrow.

"Why don't you two get married next week and have children? You seem like a perfect couple."

"Shut up, Thacka, he's staying under sufferance; it was you who ordered it—remember? And by the way, don't forget you owe Kitty and Nulla Nulla dinner."

"One thing you can be sure of, Parker, there is not a chance in the world of them letting me forget that fact."

"You need to clear your conscience," she said with a chuckle.

"Hey, a clear conscience is a sign of a fuzzy memory."

Parker began entering data on her computer and shook her head, "You and your paraprosdokians. Oh, that reminds me, I'm going to visit Professor Klein in the hospital today.'

"Good, give me a ring afterwards to let me know his condition."

After thirty minutes of typing, Thackeray sat back in his chair and jabbed a fresh toothpick between his choppers.

"No-one is ever going to believe this bloody report, Parker."

She held out her hand for a toothpick, "Not if we tell the truth."

Thacka handed her a toothpick.

She stuck it between her teeth and said through it, "Lucky Uncle Dan is sympathetic to the cause. But we'll need to refine Moloch's death certificate to better represent his physical condition at the time of death."

"And we have to make sure CME shit-face Badger isn't the officer issuing the death certificate."

"What do you suggest? Didn't Kitty say she'd sent you something you might need?

Before he could look for whatever Kitty had sent, Badger, as if summoned by the mention of his name, filled to the brim with arrogance, stormed into the office accompanied by another man.

"Badger!" Thacka reacted. "What brings you..."

Badger rudely cut him off.

"This is Assistant Commissioner Waterstreet in charge of special crimes and internal affairs."

Both Thacka and Parker stood in respect of the senior officer and acknowledged with "Sir."

Badger continued with a supercilious attitude,

"I alerted Assistant Commissioner Waterstreet after receiving a preliminary crime scene report from forensics this morning. The report covered the state of the body of Wolfen Molock, a detainee released from the hospital in your care and found shot to death at the residence of Sarah Dixon."

"I can explain, sir," Thacka interrupted.

Assistant Commissioner Waterstreet immediately held up his hand and signalled for Badger to be given the time to finish his statement.

Badger nodded his approval and continued, "Preliminary medical examination confirms that Moloch had been shot to death. After yours and Parker's weapons were surrendered, according to protocol, I have good reason to suspect that once ballistics have finished testing, your weapon Thackeray, will be matched with bullets found in Moloch's body. Do you deny that will be the case?'

"No. I did shoot Moloch… but…"

This time, sporting a smug look on his cadaverous face, Badger signalled Thackeray to be silent. He was confident he had Thacka exactly where he wanted him.

Waterstreet, a tall thin man with an undertaker-like appearance, cleared his throat and then focused his beady eyes on Thacka, "Detective Inspector Thackeray, I'm arresting you for the murder of…"

Before he could finish the statement Superintendent Wilks came in to the office followed by Kitty close behind.

"Ahh! Good morning everyone!" Wilks announced happily. "And to what do we owe the honour of a visit from internal affairs and the chief medical officer?"

"Good morning, Dan," Waterstreet replied. "Badger called me this morning after reading a preliminary medical report from the crime scene of the Moloch case. He alerted me to the fact that Moloch had been shot to death by either Detective Inspector Thackeray or DS Parker. Thackeray has admitted that he shot and killed Moloch, and I'm here to make an arrest."

"Hmm, that would be a little premature don't you think?" Wilks said, shaking his head negatively. "I would have expected medical examiner Badger to follow normal procedure before making such a rash accusation."

"We know DS Parker is your niece, superintendent, and is afforded your personal protection, but this is a murder... Moloch was unarmed, in a hospital bed, on life support, hardly a threat to anyone!"

"There are several presumptions there, Badger, including, for the record, a personal accusation against me!" Wilks reacted angrily.

"Badger was only doing his job, Dan. I'm afraid as CMO, he is entitled to make a call on this."

"Oh, I don't think so, no, no, no... he is totally out of line," Kitty chimed in. "A preliminary report? What is that, Badger? What office issued it, Badger?"

"It was an SFSB site report," Badger replied curtly.

"Strategic forensic support branch, eh, and made by whom?"

"Officer Haddon!" Badger snapped.

"Officer Haddon is a member of the clean-up team... Why, in this case, would you overlook normal procedure?"

"And what is normal procedure, Dr Hawke?" Wilks asked.

"A medical report issued by pathology following a preliminary autopsy or examination," Kitty answered.

"And what office issues such a report?" Wilks requested.

"My office, Superintendent," Kitty said. "In fact, I emailed a note to Detective Inspector Thackeray this morning following my initial examination of Moloch at the crime scene and thereafter at the crime lab."

"So you're going to tell us Moloch wasn't shot to death by Thackeray."

"That's quite correct, CMO Badger," Kitty said cynically. "Let's have Thackeray read us my email to him before you cart him off to prison for doing his job, Assistant Commissioner Waterstreet."

"Go ahead, Thackeray," Waterstreet said begrudgingly.

Thackeray swivelled around in his chair, faced his computer, and opened his email.

"The email says, 'Thacka, I thought you might be interested to know that following my examination of Wolfen Moloch, the cause of death on his death certificate will be respiratory failure, causing heart failure.'"

"That's preposterous! How could you determine that! This is a conspiracy to murder!" Badger erupted, his face flushed red.

"That's a grand accusation, Badger; you seem to be making a habit of doing that!" Kitty snapped back. "Now, who's under the pump?"

"Well then, Dr Hawke, please explain how you arrived at that conclusion," Waterstreet asked calmly.

"Quite simple, Assistant Commissioner, the life support respirator being used to artificially keep Moloch breathing has a diagnostic feature that produces a digital status report, a 24-hour history of the patient if you like, like an aircraft black box. It showed that when Moloch's life support was terminated and he was shot, he had been dead for at least twenty minutes."

"Ha! Are you suggesting Thackeray shot a dead man?" Badger questioned angrily.

"I am, and that is backed up by pathology. The bullet wounds didn't bleed because Moloch was dead when shot."

Badger looked as if he was about to explode with embarrassment and anger.

"Why did you shoot a dead man, Thackeray?" Waterstreet asked, in an effort to understand.

"To make sure he was dead, sir."

"Are we done here?" Wilks asked Waterstreet.

"Yes, Dan. I'm sorry about this," Waterstreet nodded curtly and turned to the CMO.

"We all know why you breached protocol, Badger. Rest assured, I will be submitting a formal complaint about you to internal affairs. Now, get out of here and leave us to get on with real police work," Wilks growled.

Waterstreet led Badger out of the office.

Wilks nodded to Thacka and Parker.

"Thanks, Kitty," Thacka said. "I owe you one."

"One! You've got to be kidding; you owe me your underpants and socks!" Kitty bellowed with a laugh.

Wilks and Kitty left Thacka wiping his brow of perspiration, thoroughly aware the cavalry had just saved him.

"Phew!"

Parker playfully threw her toothpick at him.

"How lucky are you!"

"Oi, don't be wasteful."

Steve entered the offices of True Crime Magazine and approached the receptionist.

"Hi... Steve Blake, I have a meeting with Mr Kingston."

In her early twenties with bleached blonde short-cropped hair and wearing bright red lipstick, the receptionist offered him a toothy smile. He noticed her teeth were streaked red from her lipstick.

"Just a sec. Take a seat Steve," she purred.

She called the editor in chief on the intercom, mumbled something to him, hung up, and then with a big flirtatious ogle said, "You can go in now. You know where to go huh, hun? Oh, and by the way, I'm Tippi."

Steve hadn't sat down; he was too anxious. He acknowledged her with a thumbs up, added her mentally to his list as a future humping prospect, tucked the iPad under his arm, and headed boldly for Kingston's office.

He spotted Kingston across the sea of workstations, and the big man waved him over. This time Kingston was waiting outside his office. Instead of taking him inside, he walked Steve directly into the boardroom.

It was plush. Two-dozen leather back chairs surrounded a long highly polished oblong-shaped mahogany table.

Kingston took the seat at the head of the table, and Steve sat at his right.

Steve was about to speak when Kingston held up his hand.

"Wait."

Steve sat with his mouth shut as half a dozen people filed into the room and found seats.

Kingston tapped the table with his knuckle to get their attention,

"This is Steve Blake. I've agreed to employ him as a reporter provided the story he has written is publishable."

You could hear a pin drop—when Kingston spoke, his staff listened.

"He's done a bullet-point PowerPoint presentation for us with photographs. Trudy."

A nerdy-looking lass in her late twenties with a hip haircut and wearing thick-rimmed fashionable glasses stood.

"Yes, sir."

"Hook up his iPad to the screen, will you? Dave, take care of the blinds and lights."

Kingston seemed to project vast knowledge and the ability to entertain, although both traits weren't always on simultaneous display. Dave, in his late twenties, and looking like a bit of a nerd as well, hopped up and hit a button on the wall that triggered louvers to close over the big windows.

Trudy quickly had the iPad hooked up and ready to go.

"Just hit play," she whispered to Steve with an awkward nervous smile that showed off the braces on her teeth.

Steve fired up his presentation while Dave dimmed the lights. A cinema flat-screen hosted Steve's work.

When it was finished, Dave jumped up and opened the louvers.

Kingston sat back in his chair with his arms folded across his massive belly.

"We'll start with you, Trudy," Kingston announced.

Steve realised a specific process was in operation: everything was being done by consensus.

Trudy stood, "Salient points, an amazing story. The photos are unbelievable, I think we can run it as a feature and easily syndicate it. Hold back a net edition until we've locked down the syndication."

"Dave?" Kingston prompted.

Seriously Gen Y, a classical Millennial, Dave stood and stuttered, "We need to run with it fast because the cops will be all over the networks with it in no time flat. Are the pictures yours or do they belong to homicide?"

"Mine," Steve acknowledged.

"Good. Keep it that way, don't let them have copies until we get the story out; it's the only way of securing our exclusivity. They'll have their own BWV footage that they'll pull stills off. Don't forget that." Dave sat.

"Peter?" Kingston said with a more respectful intonation.

Peter was an older guy and looked to Steve like he was probably the senior writer. Peter eschewed the hip Gen-Y aesthetic for a moth-eaten journalistic idiosyncrasy; untidy hair, unshaven, baggy cargo pants. He had the quick, alert eyes of someone smart and easily unhinged—and certainly looked like he enjoyed an ale after work. He leaned forward in his chair.

"I'll get with Steve and thrash out some copy," he grumbled. "Some of the pics are unsuitable for TC, but they'll be good for syndication to the schlock mags, tabloids like Huffpost, News of the Weird, Crypticmedia, and UFONet—there are stacks of them, you know the drill. Anyhow, good stuff Steve, we haven't had something as hot as this for a while. Welcome on board," he sat back, relaxed.

Steve was well pleased with himself.

Kingston wrapped up the meeting.

"Okay, then let's all get on with it. Leave me with Steve, and you'll each get a brief from Trudy in half an hour."

One by one, each of the six people came over to shake Steve's hand, welcoming him to the staff. The success made him think of his wife. *If Niki could only see me now.* The irony was that if it hadn't been for Niki's murder, there would be no story and no job. Tears welled up in his eyes. Soon he would have to attend to her funeral and deal with the relatives and probably the press. He wondered, *Shit, how are her folks going to handle my story when it comes out? I didn't think of that, did I?*

His thoughts were interrupted by Kingston, "You delivered, son, and I'm keeping my end of the bargain. You can have a desk next to our senior reporter Peter. He's an old dog, been around for thirty years plus, but he can sniff out a winner story better than anyone I know and can really pen it. Work with him—learn from him. Sit with him when we finish talking here and let him come up with hooks for the rags and mags. We'll go with your title for TC, that's True Crime, we call it TC round here—you do have a title, don't you?"

"Yeah, it was on the PowerPoint, Waxing Moon, Mr Kingston."

"Waxing Moon, yeah, fucking love it! What's a Waxing Moon for Christ's sake?"

"It's the time leading up to the moon becoming full."

"Okay, got it, good... have you got clearances from everyone you've mentioned in the story?"

"Clearances, no, why? Do I need them?"

"My oath you do. Ask Peter; he'll give you our standard consent form. You won't need it for anybody formally charged but you will need it for those who aren't... and the cops, of course—in some cases, their boss wants them kept out of the news, so you better check that out smartly."

"Okay, yeah, can't see any real problems there except maybe for Rebekah though her name is a pseudonym."

"Yeah well, if she's critical to the story then you'll still need it. Will that be difficult?"

"No, it should be all right, first I'll have to find out if she's being charged."

"Good, well get on it right away. Just remember people will constantly fail to live up to your expectations of them. So, on to money matters—you'll be on seventy grand a year before tax, effective immediately, with a cash bonus like I promised of two thousand, a car and a piss-poor expense account, standard holidays, flexible hours—a reporter's gig is 24/7 anyway. If you keep coming up with top stuff, you could be earning double that in a year. What do you say?"

"I want a piece of the syndication of my stories, call it an incentive."

"That's what I like to hear, a feller who knows what he wants. No."

"Okay, then I'll go elsewhere."

"Five percent."

"Done."

They shook hands.

"I hope this is the start of a long and happy relationship, son. Just remember what I say goes. Peter will give you a list of our publication policies and conventions. We have our own particular style that you'll have to write to. Other than that, mate, don't bludge on us, and you'll always be on our side. Welcome to True Crime."

The big man pried himself out of the chair and then walked Steve out of the boardroom.

"Peter's over there," he stretched out a flabby arm and pointed the way.

When Steve got to Peter's desk, he found a vacant computer terminal and chair opposite.

Peter looked up from typing and said with a two-pack-of-cigarettes-a-day voice, "That's your spot, Stevo, now sit down, and we'll go through some stuff. First, transfer me all you have on the story. It's a Wi-Fi office."

Steve sat, opened the iPad, logged on with the password Peter gave him, and dropped the files into Peter's Dropbox.

"Mr Kingston said I'll need consent forms."

"Beefy, we call him Beefy, he doesn't mind. Consent forms— yeah, well, getting clearances can be tricky, especially if one of your stars in the story has the shits or gets a whiff of a quick buck."

"Damn, never thought of that!"

"You might have to lick a bit of arse to get what you want, but at the end of the day, it'll be well worth it."

"I'd better strike while the iron's hot then."

Peter was speed-reading Steve's story on his computer while he talked, "Yep, I would... You'll need these homicide cops Parker and Thackeray to sign off pretty quickly before their Super shuts 'em down... and this chick Rebekah, she's integral to the plot, so she should be your priority. Look, why don't you leave the story with me? I'll knock it into shape and come up with some by-lines, you go get the important consents like right-a-way. Got wheels?"

"Yeah."

"Cool. Did Beefy promise you a new car?"

"Yes."

"Then keep on his back; it took three years to get the one he promised me, he can be a bit sketchy."

"I'll send him an email to put his offer in writing."

"Good thinking."

Steve stood up. Peter handed him a business card, "Here's my cell and email. Tell Trudy on your way out to get you some business cards made up. She's your production point person, anything like that or booking meetings, blah, blah, it's Trudy, definitely not Tippi."

"Thanks, Pete."

Peter viewed the world as an endless string of immutable factoids, wound up like a ball of twine. For Steve, that was refreshing. He bounded out of the offices full of enthusiasm.

Once out in the street, he stood kerbside and hurriedly dialled Parker on his cell.

"Hey Jess, listen, will you and Thackeray sign consent forms so I can use your names in my story? Aha, I see, can you run it past Wilks as soon as possible? Pretty please... Thanks. Are you guys charging Rebekah and Nissa with anything? You're not... okay... only Moloch, Vivian, Jason Little and not Dorrie or the others. Call me back okay? Thanks, bye."

CHAPTER 23

I, was your sacrifice
And innocent victim
Of your deadly bite
Spellbound by your hellcat charm
You swore you and your witchcraft
Meant no harm.

gk

Steve hopped into the VW Beetle and opened the iPad to check whether the office's Wi-Fi reached the street. Fortunately, it did, and he had managed to find a parking spot right in front of the building. Now it was a matter of convincing Rebekah, he thought to himself, logging on to the chat room at The Veil website. He was in luck; Rebekah was online and chatting. "What an ace day I'm having," he mumbled as he signed in.

Kaspar: Merry meet!

Rebekah: Well, if it isn't the whistleblower.

Kaspar: Hey, don't blame me... If Vivian and Nissa hadn't kidnapped me, there wouldn't have been a bust.

Rebekah: Tell me another one—you've been working with the cops all along. I know because they told me.

Kaspar: Well, you were working with Moloch.

Rebekah: A bit different, sonny boy; Moloch was my father.

Kapsar: Well, we won't go into that.

He didn't want to get her offside, or she might not sign the consent. He could tell by her attitude that it wasn't going to be easy.

Kaspar: Hey, I miss you.

Rebekah: Yeah, well, get used to it.

Kaspar: Ah, come on Bek, there's no need for that.

Rebekah: You reckon?

Kaspar: Let's just start again. What do you say?

He got no reply.

Kaspar: Bek?

Still nothing.

Kaspar: Ah, come on, Bek, don't be like that. You're not getting charged with anything—it was my wife that was murdered.

Still nothing. Without Rebekah, his story would have no legs, and he was becoming anxious. He couldn't imagine losing everything he'd just gained: a career, money, self-esteem. He was just about to sign off when she came back.

Rebekah: Sorry, I was talking to Raven.

Kaspar: How is she?

Rebekah: As well as can be expected.

Kaspar: Can I see you?

Rebekah: When?

Kaspar: This afternoon.

Rebekah: Maybe. Where?

Kaspar: I don't mind, but I'd prefer your place if you know what I mean.

Rebekah: Okay, three o'clock. You know where it is. See you then.

Kaspar: Merry part.

Rebekah: Yeah, merry part.

He logged off, kicked back in the seat and let out a big sigh of relief. Again he was feeling pretty good about himself, and not at all conscious that he was mercilessly using her for his own gain.

Thackeray finished his report, sat back in his chair, a toothpick between his teeth, and grinned through it at Parker. "Done."

"Geez, you're quick, I've still got heaps to do."

"I'll send you mine; it might help."

"Thanks."

Steve walked in just as the phone rang. Parker answered it.

"Homicide, DS Parker... Hi Kitty. Yes, thanks to you; otherwise, it could have been us in remand. Yeah, the look on Badger's face when you nailed him was priceless. You have? Okay, I'll check it out. Thanks. Yeah, get some rest. Bye now." She put the phone down and said, "Hi Steve."

"Hey Jess," he said as he plonked into the spare chair.

"That was Kitty Thacka; she's emailed us some info."

"I got the job," Steve said excitedly. "Plus a car, plus a syndication percentage and expenses—I'm officially on staff at True Crime Magazine."

"Well, good for you," Thacka said offhandedly.

"Yeah, well done, Steve," Parker smiled.

Thacka and Parker opened their email browsers. Thackeray sat back in his chair and read out loud.

"So, Vivian is the mother of Nissa, Lilith, and Raven... I thought Raven was an old hag... anyhow, and Raven is the mother of Rebekah and Luna... each of them matched with the DNA from one of the boys' penises, and Vivian matched with the extra DNA fingerprint Kitty found in Moloch's basement, presumably from the seventh victim, the one we must have missed. The three virgins: Celeste sixteen, her mother is Lilith, Indigo sixteen, her mother is Luna, and Diana, seventeen and now deflowered, is the daughter of Nissa. Moloch was the father of all of them, even Vivian? Now isn't that amazing. And the two boys at the Sabbat were not related to any of them, just ringers. So there you have it, the whole family tree."

"Unbelievable! So, Nissa, Lilith, and Raven lost both parents. And what about Vivian being his daughter as well, how is that possible?" Parker said.

"With Raven now the oldest, it probably explains why she was so angry, after watching her mother burn," Thacka added.

"Vivian must have been under fifteen when she had Raven because she was sixty-seven when she died, and Raven is fifty-two."

"Did you hear from Superintendent Wilks?" Steve interrupted.

"Yes, he agreed to the releases but wants approval of the final copy for local print," Parker said, a little coldly put off by the impolite manner of his question.

"That should be fine. Here are the consent forms—all you have to do is sign," he had filled them out before coming to the station. Parker and Thacka exchanged glances. Both read slowly and then signed, Thackeray amending his signature "Subject to approval of copy for local media." Steve stood ready to leave—he had what he wanted.

"Okay, so now you've got to get the witches to sign consent forms, I presume?" Parker said with more than a touch of cynicism.

"Not if they're charged," he replied.

"We're only charging Jason Little, so it might be an uphill battle," Thackeray said.

"Do you think Sarah would sign a form?"

"Certainly not—and neither her name nor her son's will appear anywhere on our public police report. Even the surviving witches seem to know nothing about her—so we'll be keeping it that way, do I make myself perfectly clear, Steve?" Thacka glared at Blake.

"I hear you," Steve said, his elation deflated.

"Best leave out that part of the story anyway, Steve; it's bizarre enough without it. And nothing more on the Professor; he is, after all, in the hospital fighting for his life because of you!" Parker said, with an edge to her tone.

Thackeray turned his computer off, stood, and while stretching announced, "Well, that's it for him. He's taking the rest of the day off."

"Him being Thackeray," Parker pointed out for Steve's benefit.

"Steve, you need to know that knowledge is knowing that a tomato is a fruit—wisdom is not putting it in a fruit salad."

"Thank you so much for that pearl of wisdom, Thacka. I presume that was one of those paraprosdokians you've been telling me about, Jess? I still haven't Googled it because I'm not sure how to spell it."

"A word of advice, Steve, if attacked by a mob of clowns, go for the juggler," said Thackeray tipping his non-existent hat with his forefinger to Parker as he left.

Parker swivelled her chair to face Steve, who was shaking his head.

"That bloke's got the weirdest sense of humour."

"Not really. So, how are you going to get Rebekah to sign?" she asked coolly.

"Do I detect a note of jealousy in your tone, detective?" he said, attempting to flirt with her.

"Not bloody likely!" she rolled her eyes.

"I'm meeting her this afternoon. Want to come with me?"

"What for? No, I've had my fill of witches forever, thought you might have too. So, I'll leave you to that. But no distress calls if you get kidnapped, okay?"

"Under control," he said.

"That'll be the day!"

"I'll see you around seven for a celebration drink."

"Yeah, I'll be celebrating that I'm at last getting my apartment back!" She said with a wry smile.

"Awe, have I been a bad boarder?"

"Put it this way, if I'd had any choice in the matter, it would have been to let you fend for yourself!"

"Ah, come on Jess, without my cooperation, you wouldn't have closed the case."

"Without you, we wouldn't have had the case! By the way, your Beamer is out of forensics; you should collect it."

"I'll miss the old Beetle."

"Oh, and we heard from Niki's parents; they're arriving from Perth tomorrow to view the body and make the funerary arrangements. I don't suppose you've spoken to them yet?"

His face had drained of colour at the news. "Oh... um, no. I'll catch you tonight."

He was trying to avoid any discussion about Niki's parents. Parker noticed but put it down to apprehension and guilt over Niki's murder. She watched him leave, then continued compiling her report.

Steve got into the VW and immediately rang Peter at True Crime.

"Pete, hey, it's Steve. Yeah, got the consents from the detectives; I'll drop them off at the office for you. Take Sarah and her son out of the story. Yeah, I had to do a trade-off to get the consents. No, I don't think her being out will make much difference. No, I'm on my way to Rebekah's place to get hers now. They're only charging Moloch posthumously with eight counts of murder, Vivian as an accessory, and Jason Little the dwarf for accessory to murder on one count; none of the others are being charged. But I did get some extra info from the cops on Oedipal love that's sure to sex up the story. Yes, for one, Vivian was Moloch's daughter as well as the mother or grandmother of all the witches in the coven, yeah, sixty-five years old. Yeah, I know it's hard to believe, isn't it? Moloch fathered them all. I'll fill you in on the rest later. Ciao."

He terminated the call, then carefully tapped the phone against his bottom lip. What if Rebekah won't sign the consent? He shrugged off the thought as not worth contemplating and drove off, bound for Newtown.

Parker stepped out of her car in the police vehicle section of the car park near the entrance to the Prince of Wales Hospital in Randwick. She had phoned earlier, just after Steve had left the office, to check on Professor Klein and had been given good news—Klein was conscious and out of danger. It was a sunny day, and not nearly as hot as it had been the day before. The sun on her face and the smell of the ocean in the air from nearby Coogee Beach made her feel happy to be alive. She crossed over Easy Street and entered the hospital, bound for the elevator.

When she exited the elevator at the intensive care ward, joy at feeling alive became even more meaningful when she saw the suffering faces of the sick, injured, and infirm. Even the people in the waiting room wore sad, sullen expressions. Parker knew the room number and was proceeding along the corridor looking for it when a nurse stopped her.

"It's not public visiting time, miss; you'll need to stay in the waiting area."

Since the last ordeal with the nurse at St. Vincent's, Parker was in no mood to be tolerant and was just about to give her a blast when the nurse added courteously, "Unless, of course, you are with the police."

"Detective Sergeant Parker," she flashed her ID. "I arranged to see Professor Klein."

"No worries, Detective. Sorry about the procedure, but you more than anyone would know how trying it can be dealing with the public at times. He is in room 707."

"Yes, I understand. Do you know anything about his condition?"

"I've just come from changing his dressings. He's taken a beating—several broken ribs; one came close to puncturing his lung. We had him on LS overnight because he'd taken a serious bump to the head, and it's best to take all precaution."

"For sure! Will he be all right?"

The nurse broadened her smile, "Yes, he's a tough old bugger, that one. A couple of days here, and he can go home. Could do with a little TLC from a relative or someone for a week or two."

"I'll see to it; thank you," she glanced at the nurse's name badge. "Myrabelle," she added courteously.

Klein was in a room on his own and connected to several medical devices. He appeared to be asleep when Parker entered, but one blackened eye immediately opened when he sensed a presence.

"Police always arrive too late," he croaked.

Parker smiled, amused and impressed by his sense of humour in the face of the ordeal he'd been through. She sat on the edge of the bed and took his hand, careful of the IV needle inserted there.

"I don't know what to say, Professor, only that I'm glad you're alive."

"I wouldn't be if it hadn't been for my old security guard mate, Walter. Seventy years young, and he still managed to chase that bloody monster out the window!"

"So it was Gaap then?"

"You bet it was, and before he decided to kill me, we had a good chat."

"What, it spoke to you?"

"No, Moloch had a spell on him to stop communication, but he understood everything I was saying."

"How do you know?"

"He acknowledged me."

"I'll be damned!"

A nurse poked her head in the door. "Everything all right Al?"

"Yes thank you, Deni."

She ducked back out. Parker smiled, "Al huh? Mr Popularity."

"You haven't seen nurse Blee yet, now she's a real sort."

Back on track, Parker had never considered Gaap might have been intelligent enough to be reasoned with.

The Professor continued. "I believe it had been summoned from hell or some other alternative reality, to put it simply... to do Moloch's bidding and kill at his command."

"Well, you weren't at all wrong in assuming that, Professor, but it seems to be over."

He smiled and relaxed somewhat, "So how did you get on with Moloch?"

Parker dug in her pocket and produced a piece of paper.

"Thacka got Moloch transferred to Sarah's house with all the life support equipment."

"How?"

"Connections. You know, pulling favours—comes with the badge. Sarah and her son Russell were in Moloch's mind, so they were stuck—a pair of zombies at the hospital—Thacka had to get them moved or they would have had doctors all over them—we didn't have time to tell the quacks why they looked like they were in a coma. We had found the murdered boy's body buried under the 7th stone of a replica Stonehenge theatre setup in Centennial Park, and when we found the body, we managed to stop them terminating Moloch. The CME agreed because we had evidence of a murder, but it was really so we could give Sarah and Russell the time to get back out of his mind into this world."

"Go on!" Professor Klein sat up, clearly fascinated. "I've got to meet this Sarah!"

"Sarah and Russell made it back, and Thacka, she and I were in the spare room at her house with Moloch when he somehow managed to possess his almost dead body. He summoned three demons, including the one that attacked you, Gaap, and he threatened that if Sarah didn't give him Russell, he'd have Gaap kill me!"

"He's incredibly strong, that Gaap; he could have easily done it! Is that where you got—"

"The scratches, yes!" she paused, reflecting on her near-death at the hands of a creature that shouldn't exist. "Then Moloch went all weird and started speaking in a foreign language—I wrote it down afterward, here." She handed Klein the piece of paper.

"Hand me my glasses from the side table, will you please, dear?"

He put them on and read the note out loud.

"Zirdo... Iadnamad... Elila... Micalzodo... Sannir... Madriaax—Finis... Blaziziras... Iada... Lo... Kia. Very interesting and well done in writing it down."

"What language is it, Latin or Greek?"

"Neither, it's Enochian, an occult or angelic language discovered by John Dee and Edward Kelley in the 16th Century, England. Kelley was a medium, and Dee a magical investigator. They believed the language was revealed to them by angels."

"Angels? What does it mean?"

"It translates thus: I am the undefiled knowledge of the first ether—let's see here... mighty in the parts of the heavens... executing the judgment of the master."

"I don't understand."

"He's declaring that he acts for his master and that he has been given the power of knowledge to do so."

"Who is his master then?"

"I'd say Choronzon—the guardian of the Abyss—a very powerful demon. I don't know if you have heard of Aleister Crowley, but as an occultist and conjuror early last century, he spent a large part of his life trying to summon Choronzon. But look, the important thing here is we must stop Moloch. He can't be permitted to seek a new host."

"I don't understand—Moloch is dead!"

"What!" he struggled to sit up—the adrenalin surge from hearing Moloch was dead triggered an alarm.

"Settle down, professor—" Parker said with panic in her voice, agitated by the constant buzzing from the heart rate monitor. "Calm down, professor... Yes, he's dead, Thackeray shot him... and the three demons... in fact, the forensic pathologist reported that Moloch had died from heart failure well before Thacka shot him... so Thacka didn't kill him."

"So, let me get this right... Moloch was possessed and animate, even though he was physically dead?"

"Yes, according to the digital diagnostic from the life support respirator."

Klein had gotten over his panic but he was far from relaxed. He spoke with a grim determination.

"Then it's far from over, Parker. Though he might be dead in this life, he's very much alive in another—that means his spirit will wait to find a new host at the next opportunity."

"Are you saying he will come back somehow at Beltane next year?"

"Precisely. In the meantime, he will have occupied a sub-host."

"Who?"

"It could be anyone, one of the witches... anyone he has come in contact with really—they wouldn't even be aware of it until his psychic powers start to manifest."

"You're kidding me?" she thought briefly. "That would explain the face in the smoke!"

"What face? What smoke?"

Parker swallowed her fear at the memory.

"When we raided the witches' coven last night, one of the witches, Vivian, accidentally set herself on fire and in the smoke that rose from her burning body, Thackeray and Steve Blake saw Moloch's face, laughing in the smoke. It wasn't an illusion, Steve filmed it on an iPad."

Klein removed his glasses, closed his eyes and pinched the bridge of his nose in mindful consternation.

"Professor…?"

"Just pondering, Parker… I found the book containing the means to stop Moloch. We need to get it from the Theosophical Society library, so I can use it to stop this demon."

"I will get the book if you arrange it. What's it called?"

"The Corpus Hermeticum. But listen to me—what is most important is that we will require Moloch's corpse for the calling to succeed. Do you understand? Should his body be destroyed by fire— as in cremated, we will not be able to perform the exorcism."

"An exorcism! But isn't that a Catholic ritual?"

"Yes, but there is also an occult exorcism."

"But he's dead! Why would you need a dead body?"

"Because even after death, a bond continues between his physical body and his spirit… as a spectre, he will only be totally free when that bond is broken. You see, that's what he wants. He wants us to cremate his body—that is why he was laughing at you: he thinks he has won!"

"So presumably, if we don't cremate him and then don't carry out the ritual, and because we have no way of knowing the identity of the sub-host, we won't be able to stop him resurrecting when the time comes."

"Correct. Somehow Moloch learned I was a threat and sent Gaap to prevent me from using the exorcism rite from the Corpus Hermeticum. Perhaps one of his witches saw the newspaper article."

"No, I suspect he was eavesdropping on police talk from his deathbed."

Nurse Myrabelle entered and interrupted the conversation.

"That's enough chatting for now, Professor."

Parker got the hint.

"I'll go directly to collect the book; then I'll visit you this afternoon."

"Good, just remember, there's no time to lose."

"What time can I come back, Nurse?"

"Three o'clock will be fine, Detective."

Parker let go of Klein's hand, stood, took a deep breath, and let out a sigh. "And I thought this was over!" she said dispiritedly.

"Still a ways to go, I'm afraid; perhaps you should rally the troops... there's an outside chance things might get ugly again."

She nodded dolefully, her face showing the signs of a lack of rest over the last weeks.

Steve knocked on the front door of Rebekah's Newtown, terraced house and Rebekah's voice resounded from inside.

"That you Steve?"

"Yep sure is!" he acknowledged.

"Come on in its open… I'm upstairs!"

He entered and started up the staircase to the second floor praying silently with every step for the power of persuasion to convince her to sign the consent form. When he entered her boudoir, he found her sitting on the bed clad in a flimsy black satin robe, her knees drawn up painting her toenails.

She glanced at him with an alluring smile and said, "Merry greet Steve."

Encouraged by the affable reception, he sat down beside her on the edge of the bed and reciprocated her Wiccan greeting,

"Merry greet. Nice shade of black."

"I like my toenails black. What do you want to talk about Steve? I don't think you came here to check my toenails."

Steve had his pants off in a flash, slipped onto the bed and mounted her from behind.

"Oh Steve, that feels so good," Rebekah groaned.

He heard something rustle behind him, looked over his shoulder and saw Raven with a knife.

Before he could react, she knelt on the bed behind him, grasped his testicles and held the blade to them.

"Raven no!" Steve yelled terrified.

"Sweetbreads for dinner mum?" Rebekah purred.

"Oh, I think so dear—one of the Coven favourites."

Steve's scream was so loud it could have raised the dead. His great day had just turned to crap.

Sitting in her car in the hospital car park, Parker decided to phone Kitty to check on Moloch.

"Hello Dr Hawke..."

"Hi Kitty, it's Parker..."

"You're seriously not going to hound me for DNA results, are you?"

"No... no, not at all... I—"

"Have you finished your report?"

"Yes, it reads like an episode of the Twilight Zone."

"I wouldn't doubt it, so what can I do you for?" Kitty said.

"I need to know the process with Moloch's body..."

"Oh, it went off about an hour ago."

"What? Where?" she exclaimed, surprised.

"It was released to the Coroner's office."

"But why?"

"Just normal procedure..." Kitty said nonchalantly. "It's treated as a death in custody. Once we've completed the post-mortem, we hand it over... and in this case, there wasn't a lot to hand over."

"What do you mean?"

"He was already a mess from the bike accident, and then Thacka made more of a mess of him... so, by the time we'd finished, there wasn't much left at all."

"What happens to the remains?"

"If there's no inquest and the Coroner's office is satisfied with the post-mortem results, the CMO will order the body cremated, that is unless there's a burial caveat in a will, or a special request from a senior member of the family of the deceased. Otherwise, once Badger has signed off on the cadaver, because Moloch was essentially being held in remand, either it will be cremated at the State's expense or released to the family."

"So it's in the morgue, and the person in charge is Badger!"

"Yes, our cadaverous friend."

"Okay, thanks Kitty, I'll give him a call."

"Why love, what's the problem?"

"Oh, I'll explain later. Bye for now."

She hung up and nervously chewing her knuckle dialled Badger's office.

"Hello, this is DS Parker, can I speak with CMO Badger please? When will he be back? Tomorrow? Then can I have his mobile number? Yes, maybe you can, I'm one of the arresting officers on the Wolfen Moloch case, I was informed by Chief forensic pathologist Dr Hawke that your office has claimed the body... yes, I need to know the status of it. Yes, whether it will be either released to the family or— okay, can you check now or do you want to call me back? Good, thanks, I wait on."

Holding on the phone for details was a tiresome reality of detective work, especially when having to deal with government red tape. When Badger's PA came back, Parker's face suddenly drained of colour.

"What do you mean the body has already been released to the family? Who signed for it? Yes, I'll wait... Hello, yes, who? His daughter Ms N Turner... yes, but why was it released so soon after the post-mortem? Oh, approved by CMO Badger, I see. Thanks, no, that will be all." She terminated the call and sank back into the car seat, angry as a cut snake. "Bloody Badger! So what now?"

Thackeray pulled his car into the driveway of the Dixon residence in Randwick. When he got out of the car, he noticed Russell, dressed as a cowboy, playing with Reece, a boy from next door about the same age.

Russell spotted Thackeray and called out excitedly. "Hey Bill!"

Thacka walked over to the two boys playing at the side of the house.

"What are you young rascals up to?"

"Russell just shot me, but I'm not dead," Reece said defiantly.

"He is so dead, he just won't admit it that's all!" Russell complained.

With his coat draped over his shoulder, his navy-blue necktie loosened, and the top button of his white dress shirt undone, Thacka looked relaxed. He beamed the boys a big smile.

"I can relate to that, fellas. Where's that mum of yours, partner?"

"She's in the kitchen making chocolate cake for us," Reece answered for Russell.

"We're going to have a war over the swings out the back now," Russell said.

"Okay, boys, go for it. See you later."

"Last one to the swings is a rotten egg!" Russell yelled, and the two boys scurried off.

Shaking his head from the memory of the smell of rotten eggs, Thacka sauntered over to the front door and entered the house to find Sarah.

The mix-master was making a thunderous roar, and Sarah didn't hear Thacka come into the kitchen. He leaned on the architrave of the kitchen door, full of love and admiration, watching her busily mixing a cake. She turned the mixer off.

"I hope it's chocolate!" he said.

She jumped with fright.

"Ahhh!" she put her hand on her heart and giggled at her stupidity. "You spooked me. Yes, it's chocolate all right, worse than that, it's double chocolate."

He strolled over and took her in his arms.

"Good enough to eat."

"Me or the cake?" her eyebrows managed to rise higher.

"I don't know, a double chocolate cake is a pretty serious competitor."

Her eyebrows finally came back to a normal level as she grinned, "Did you see Russ on the way in?"

"Yes, he's playing with what-zis-face from next door out the back."

"Reece. Hey, I've got something to show you," Sarah said excitedly.

"Okay."

She let him go and pulled on a pair of green rubber dishwashing gloves.

"Are you ready?" she asked.

"Yep."

She slowly reached out two fingers, closed her eyes, and then touched Thacka on the forehead—and—nothing happened.

"See, the gloves work. No flash, I'm not inside your head."

"Oh, you're in there all right, but not physically. Does that mean you'll be wearing the green washing up gloves from now on? Lovely, might start a new fashion craze."

"What, don't you like the colour?" she giggled, showing off the gloves like a hand model. "Sit down, give me a sec while I bung the cake in the oven, and then tell me all the latest about the case."

Thacka sat at the kitchen table while Sarah finished preparing the cake for baking.

"Well, I'll start from last night. When we went in on the Sabbat, they were all naked..."

"Oooo! How many of them?"

"Six witches, three young girls, sacrificial virgins, two teenage boys, Steve Blake and a goat."

She looked back from putting the cake tin in the oven.

"A goat?"

"Yes. We were all in position ready to go in when the boy with the goat cut its throat and sprayed it's blood all over one of the girls the witches had held down on a stone altar."

"Hmm, sounds familiar."

"Makes me wonder how they could have held these naked orgies for so long without the locals calling the cops."

"Maybe the witches cloaked the circle in a magic shroud."

"A magic shroud? I don't have a lot of experience with those."

"And then what?"

"Next minute the young boy started screwing the girl."

"Nice, get any pictures?" she said, covering her distaste with a joke. Thacka ignored the jibe.

"So, we went in to arrest them. Oh, I missed a bit, all the witches were chanting some sort of mantra over and over. Anyhow, as officers grabbed a couple of the old witches, their leader, Vivian, grabbed a burning torch and threw it into the bush. Well, after the heat wave, the bush was like a tinderbox and just ignited. Two of the other witches followed suit and quicker than you would believe possible, we were in the middle of a blazing inferno."

Aghast, Sarah closed the oven door and sat down at the kitchen table opposite Thacka, horrified but eager to hear more.

"Hell! What happened next!"

"Vivian pulled away from Sergeant Rees and ran into the blazing bush—then we watched her burn. It was awful. She burst into flames screaming, I'll never forget it. Steve had put his clothes back on and was standing near me, we both looked up and saw this—"

He produced a folded A4 sheet of paper from his inside coat pocket, unfolded it, and laid it on the table for her to see.

"Moloch! The smoke... it's Moloch's face but how? Is this for real?"

"Nothing fake here, it's real all right, I couldn't believe it myself. Steve had an iPad and took the shot."

Sarah sat back in the chair stunned. Thacka continued the grisly tale. "Apparently the incantation the witches were chanting, with the blood sacrifice and the gift of virgin blood was all intended to conjure up Moloch."

"And it did!" she said, staring at him, her face pale.

He picked up the paper, folded it, and put it back in his pocket. "What do you mean?"

"He was in the smoke, Bill, he hasn't gone anywhere, spiritually, I mean."

"A ghost, is that what you're saying?"

"That's one way of referring to a spirit, go on."

"Anyhow, moving right along. The fire brigade who were with us put out the bushfire, no-one else was hurt and no houses were lost. So then, it became a case of interviewing all of the witches this morning. As it turned out, after the DNA tests were matched, Vivian, the oldest at sixty-five, is the mother of three of the witches, and Raven in her fifties, the mother of two. Moloch fathered them all, including the three girls, who were his grandchildren, and get this; Vivian was his daughter as well. The murdered boys were all sons of the witches. They were all given to Moloch on their sixth birthday because he is their father and the warlock—therefore—as far as the mothers were concerned—he could do whatever he pleased with them. And we now know what he did."

"Wait a minute, that doesn't add up. How old was Moloch?"

"The jury is out on that one, love. By normal standards about eighty odd years."

"What, no way?"

"Yes, without a doubt at least that! But according to the witches, he was actually born in England in... get this... 1773."

"You're kidding! That would make him, let's see... hmm, two hundred and sixty years old! Come on, how is that possible?" she said, sceptical.

"Because he reincarnated every eighty years into a young boy as a new host," Thacka said.

"Unbelievable. So, what is their fate? The witches?"

"Nothing, we're charging Jason Little, who lived with Moloch, with accessory to murder, and Moloch gets eight counts, and Vivian one. That doesn't really matter because they are both dead. But you know what's the most frightening?"

"Don't tell me there's more?"

"After I finished interviewing two of the witches, I asked them each a personal question. First was Rebekah, the girl who originally took Steve to the Sabbat and gave Moloch his address, which led to his wife being murdered."

"Okay."

"I asked her if that was the last we'll see of Moloch?"

"Why did you ask that?"

"Because of the photo and that these witches seemed to be trying to raise him from the dead or something."

"Fair enough. What did she say?"

"She said, 'I told you he was a powerful warlock.'"

"Meaning, he might be gone for now but not forever?"

"I think they believe that. Maybe it's so," he agreed.

"What did the other one say?"

"That was Nissa; it was her son who was buried under the seventh stone, killed by his father. The boy's name was River. Nissa is different from the others; she seemed to resent Moloch over it, so cared for her boy... As she was leaving the interview, she said, and I quote, 'Goodbye, Detective Thackeray, your new life will be fine with your new family.'"

"What?"

"I know, she knew nothing about my personal life, none of them did, only Moloch."

"Do you suppose he told them?"

"God knows. But you'd think not."

"You think that it's witchcraft?"

"I think that's what we've been dealing with all along and that it might never go away."

She reached across the table, took his hand, and focused her eyes intensely on his.

"Bill, I don't want to have to worry about demon Dreamraiders and the likes of Moloch ever again."

"I don't know what to say, Sarah," he wrinkled up his nose.

"Moloch once told me there's no place for me to hide. He said, 'even in your dreams you are vulnerable.'"

"What a terrifying thought."

"I'll do some research on the subject. I've been studying Spiritual Hypnotherapy online at the IMU—the International Metaphysical University, learning how to better understand my psychic gift. Maybe I can find a way to reverse all this black magic."

"I don't know, Sarah, isn't that a bit risky?"

"I don't think we have much choice now, Bill, especially knowing that Russell is psychic... and from what I can make of all of this, a wound has been opened that now needs to be healed."

Thacka's mobile rang, he checked the ID. "It's Parker," he said to Sarah with an apologetic wince. Sarah nodded for him to take it. "Hi, Parker."

Parker explained that she had seen Professor Klein and what he'd told her, emphasising the urgency of performing an exorcism. When she told him that the family had legally taken the body from the morgue and that Badger had approved it, Thacka flopped into a chair shocked.

"What should we do?" Parker asked plaintively. "Should we act on Professor Klein's advice? Should I get the book?"

Thacka stared into Sarah's concerned eyes. She could tell instinctively there was trouble brewing. She took his hand.

"Yes, yes, get the book, Parker," Thacka said. "It can't do any harm, I guess. Let me think on this overnight. No, I'm just not yet convinced there is anything to worry about as far as we're concerned. I know, I know... I thought it was over as well—it still might be. I'll catch you at the office first thing. No, you did good calling me. Okay, bye." He slipped the phone into his pocket, stood, and began pacing the kitchen floor thinking out loud.

"Professor Klein says Moloch's spirit won't rest until it's exorcised in a pagan ritual from his remains. But his body has already been claimed by his family."

"What? How could they have done that so soon?" Sarah questioned.

"Bloody Badger!"

They locked eyes. Tears welled up in Sarah's eyes. "I just want it over, Bill!"

"Let's not jump to conclusions, huh? I told Parker I'd sleep on it, so let's just put it out of our minds and enjoy our time together."

He took her in his arms and whispered in her ear, "Whatever happens, I will protect you," they kissed passionately. "You know I could easily get used to this."

"What do you mean, taking the afternoon off work or embracing me?" she said amorously.

"I think both have their merits. How about we go upstairs and discuss it in depth?"

The kitchen was warming up, and not just from the cake baking in the oven. Suddenly, the romantic moment was shattered by a loud, frantic scream from Reece in the backyard.

"No, Russell! Don't!"

"That's Reece!" Sarah said, concerned.

She jumped out of Thackeray's embrace and went to the kitchen window to see what was causing the ruckus.

"What's Russell up to now? Bill, look!" she yelped with dread.

Bill hurried over to the window to look.

Armed with a toy pistol, Russell had Reece, a smaller boy, on his knees with the gun up to his head.

"Don't worry, love, boys will be boys," Bill said, making light of it.

But their smiles quickly turned sour when Russell raised the gun and pistol-whipped Reece hard across the side of the head.

"Argh!" Sarah shrieked.

Reece collapsed on the lawn, out cold.

Russell reached down, extended two fingers, and touched the unconscious boy on the forehead.

A blinding astral light flashed in Russell's mind's eye.

The fire in Moloch's basement incinerator raged, and the human remains within sizzled and crackled. Two mysterious figures, cloaked in black hooded caftans, stood before it, bathed in the flickering, consuming pyre's light. One of them held open a weathered tome. Long, delicate fingers, adorned with beautifully red-painted, manicured nails, gently closed the book. Its front cover bore the title 'Corpus Hermeticum.'

Both figures removed their hoods, and facing the dying flames, they spoke in unison, "Merry part, Wolfen Moloch! Merry part!"

Nissa had found redemption for her son, River, and for the years of her father's abuse. Dorrie had achieved atonement for the torment and humiliation she'd endured, under the maleficent warlock's oppressive grip.

ABOUT THE AUTHOR

G.L Keady, a native of Sydney, New South Wales, embarked on a multifaceted journey through life. After graduating from Sydney Grammar School, he managed his family's opal mining and merchandising business. In the 1970s, he transitioned into a career as a composer, musician, and record producer, later delving into music videos and cinema in the 1980s. Subsequently, he ventured into writing and directing motion pictures, animation, and television series. With a Master of Arts in Writing from Swinburne University, Melbourne, he eventually became a full-time author.

Today, G.L Keady calls the South Coast of New South Wales, Australia, home. He shares his life with his daughter, his loyal dog Floyd, and a vibrant community of blue tongue lizards, all of whom inspire his creative journey. His diverse background in business, travel, music, film, and literature has shaped him into a captivating storyteller, transporting readers to enchanting worlds both real and imagined.

VISIT

www.bigislandpublishing.au